I0831388

The Linden's Red Plague

Also by Ann Chamberlin

Historical Novels

The Sword and the Well Trilogy:
The Woman at the Well
The Sword of God
The Sword and the Well (2013)

The Joan of Arc Tapestries:
The Merlin of St. Gilles' Well
The Merlin of the Oakwood
Das Erbe der Ermiten (available only in German)
Gloria: The Merlin and the Saint

The Reign of the Favored Women Trilogy:
Sofia
The Sultan's Daughter
The Reign of the Favored Women

Snakesleeper (originally titled *Tamar*)
The Virgin and the Tower
Leaving Eden

The Valkyries:
Choosers of the Slain

Mystery

The Book of Wizzy

Nonfiction

A History of Women's Seclusion in the Middle East:
The Veil in the Looking Glass
Clogs and Shawls: Mormons, Moorlands and the Search for Zion

Scratch-and-Sniff Picture Books

The Fair Maid and the Pirates
The Witch's Cottage

THE LINDEN'S RED PLAGUE

The Valkyries
BOOK II

Ann Chamberlin

Epigraph Books
Rhinebeck, New York

Paperback ISBN 978-1-951937-88-1
Hardcover ISBN 978-1-951937-89-8
eBook ISBN 978-1-951937-90-4

Library of Congress Control Number 2020925183

Book and cover design by Colin Rolfe
Cover art by Arthur Rackham (1910), photographed by Plum Leaves

Epigraph Books
22 East Market Street, Suite 304
Rhinebeck, New York 12572
(845) 876-4861
epigraphps.com

Für Ute
Leider ist meine Geschichte Mythos

author acknowledgment

This book is dedicated to my sister-in-law Ute in thanks for her help and support over many years, especially with my bookshop.

Thanks again to Ute and her husband, my wonderful brother Ralph, and their three sons—who are willing to store more books in their garage than anybody ought to.

As usual, scores of teachers, family members, friends, librarians, and publishing people have helped. Here is a list of the most outstanding: Linda Cook, Jeri Smith, Francesca Koomen, all the women of the Wasatch Mountain Fiction Writers; Teddi Kachi, Karen Porcher, Curt Setzer, my mother, my sons (the one who helps with the computer and the one who speaks German and attends operas with me), Gilles, Rod Daynes, Giles and Ann Florence, John Keahey, Connie Disney, members of Xenobia writers' group, Natalia Aponte, Christine Cohen, Vaughne Hansen, Virginia Kidd of blessed memory. Paul Cohen, Colin Rolfe, Dory Mayo, and the folks at Epigraph. The Salt Lake Folkdancers, especially Ann Wright. Miguel, Don Juan, and all my friends at the Arizona Renaissance Festival. Reinhard Hermann who assured me when I asked what a German would have for breakfast before they had potatoes, "No. First the potato was invented, then the German." I hope his memory is not offended that I gave my characters no potatoes. All of the wonderful people I've met over many years in Germany. *Viel Spaß beim Lesen.*

Those people I may have overlooked know who they are and know that I couldn't have done it without them. Thanks to one and all.

In stories of our fathers, high marvels we are told
Of champions well approved in perils manifold,
Of feast and merry meetings, of weeping and of wail,
And splendid deeds of gallant daring I'll tell you in my tale.

—First verse of *The Nibelungenlied*

Siegfried's Song

I'm called Fafnirsbane, the hero fatherless.
I'm orphaned motherwise as well, save Alberich,
A dark dwarf, dottering in his dotage.
They say the friendless are foes to fear.

I'm the eldest bairn of a broken blade.
The blood-road Balmung was the thing that bore me.
And I forged it when Alberich failed,
By the whispered word of a one-eyed wanderer.

So with such a sword slung by my side,
It was off I fared to find my fortune.
The first that I drew out was a dragon from his den.
With the bucket Balmung I drew a bath of blood.

Within the grotto glittered a brood of gold.
Of this nested cache I became the cuckoo.
I'm called the heir of a dragon's heart,
And of a vestment that renders invisibility.

Then, in a small-sailed ship I set to sea,
By the whispered word of a one-eyed wanderer.
This place I found, far and fierce,
And no soul save one, sleeping on a stone.

In golden brynie, bassinet and bearskin,
Here was a partner for my exploits.
With Balmung's lance I loosed the lacings—
A golden tree, a woman in men's trappings…

PART 1

Brynhild's Awakening

chapter 1

I OPENED MY EYES ON a world that could only be the product of the chilling-fevered imagination of the one-eyed God. It was either twilight or predawn, an unreal half-light. I was lying on a boat-shaped block of red-black rock thrown from the earth in a fit as of nausea at a meal that did not agree with its otherwise solid insides. The block thrust high above the surrounding landscape and echoed metallically with the slightest movement of the iron plates of my brynie. The rock sheltered under an overhang of sorts, but still lay basically out-of-doors, and the snow-shawls of a blizzard whirled around me as if they had no knowledge of which way was up and which was down.

This confusion controlled me for a moment or two. I was surprised to find that very few of the flakes reached me, though in the sky there seemed to be less than the width of my finger between any two. Those that did reach me were no more than a drop or two of the lightest rain—and warm. The simplest explanation for this wonder seemed to be a great cloud of steam that bottomless cracks breathed from the earth below as body heat. The steam surrounded me, swirling and writhing like a thing alive, and had a thick sulfurous smell that seemed to have turned my lungs to stone.

As it kept off the snow, so the steam had no doubt been capable of keeping off the sun as well for the duration of the curse, however long it had been since I first felt the jab of the sleep thorn in my side. What had Odin said? *'Til sons were sires.* A generation at least. But it couldn't have been that long, surely.

My lungs were not the only thing that seemed to have turned to stone. Every limb felt the weight of centuries upon it, and my joints, stupid with lack of use, ground like pestle on a new quern. It seemed to take forever to bring myself to sit upright with my legs dangling over the edge of the rock, not too far above a floor littered with other rocks, rusty with lichens, lying like chips of whitewash off a weathered wall. And when I was upright, my head swam in the unfamiliar attitude as if wafted away on the steam itself.

The spell is broken, I thought. *I have overcome Odin by the strength of my body alone.* But that was not true. Feeling for my brynie's stays, I discovered they had been cut by some sharp blade. As for the wielder of that blade, however, I saw none. Only steam and blizzard above, steam and lichened rocks below. Who could have parted my brynie, the metal-clad hauberk that inspired my parents to name me Brynhild—that shielded me, yet concealed the barb that had consigned me to sleep?

I fumbled more within the cut stays of my brynie and found the accursed thorn. It was no more than a simple hawthorn. Whatever magic Odin had rubbed it with had long since worn away. I tossed it from me with a movement that set my head to reeling, but I was gratified to see I still had the force to send the thing beyond the screen of steam, out of my world of concern—forever.

My next concern was for my bladder. I took care of that in a hurry, not bothering to take too many staggering steps for the purpose.

And then the stomach. I had never been so hungry and thirsty—no, not even in my worst hungry days in the lean early springs of my childhood. I was faint with hunger. If I did not eat almost instantly, I felt I would collapse into a sleep more permanent than the last.

As Fate would have it, I had not gone more than two steps before I stumbled over a knapsack. I opened it up and discovered that it contained a lump of smoked meat of some kind and a bottle of water. I satisfied my needs at once. Great as they were, it didn't take much to fill them—a pair of good-sized strips sliced off the meat and four or five swigs off the bottle, and my stomach, unused to any activity and shrunken to the size of a housewife's needle case, ached with satisfaction.

It was only then that I stopped, with an ache in my heart as well, to consider that undoubtedly it was not Fate at all that such foodstuffs were the first thing I stumbled across upon awakening. These were not *Fate's* will but Odin's. Now what spell had he cast on me in my weakness? I looked at the goods more closely. The knapsack, of deerskin, was of common form. It told me nothing. The meat was smoked beyond recognition, although if forced to guess from taste alone, I would have said "heart." It was too big to be the heart of any animal I knew of, however, even with my portion gone.

The water bottle told me a little more. It was a long-necked redware vessel, its sides twined with a pattern of vines that turned to heads and claws and wings, then twisted back into vines again. Such a disregard for barriers of form and species was a hallmark of magic—or of Celts in general.

At last I looked at the implement I'd used reflexively to cut off my strips of meat. It was a sword. Not just any sword, however. I'd only had it in my hands once before, and then only for a moment, but it was not the sort of blade one can ever forget—the dancing sheen, the perfect weight, the foreboding runes. I had certainly never thought to see it again, for I had seen that blade shattered out of Sigmund Volsungsson's hands by the spear of Odin. It was Gram, the Volsungs' sword, what Sigmund called Balmung, the sword of deep contention. It was shiny and fresh, as if but newly drawn from the forger's fire, tempered in worm's blood.

I sat down good and hard on more volcanic rubble, cradling the sword in my lap, considering with all my effort what this might mean and what I should do about it. The steam growing thicker all around me didn't help clear my brain any. Before I'd come to even the first glimmer of a conclusion, I heard footsteps approaching, loud and scuffling on the metallic gravel below.

That settled it. There was only one thing to do. I got to my feet—*oh, but it felt like a generation since they'd taken weight!*—and hefted the sword—*oh, but it was a crushing weight!* Lifting the sword in a defensive position in front of me, I decided that come what may—magic-sending or troll or giant—I wouldn't let it take me without a fight.

The mist clung to the figure like broken reeds to something rising from a bog. But soon enough it revealed the being—a man well-built and powerful as any I had ever seen. He didn't seem to be a sending, not at first. But one could never tell for sure.

"Stay back!" I shouted.

My voice cracked with disuse, but served its purpose. The creature stopped in his tracks and stared.

"I warn you," I said, more firmly this time, though it did occur to me that he might not understand the human tongue. "I may appear to be but a maid, but I warn you, I am a maid of Odin. I know how to use this thing. And you, I see, are unarmed save for that small dagger at your side."

The creature bowed his head and replied, "Certainly, divine *dís*, it shall be as you command." There was no problem with his understanding, although his speech was thick with the mystical tones of Celtic that had not rubbed off when he learned our speech. "That sword you have is mine; it was my father's before me, but it brought him nothing but ill. It was a gift of the One-Eyed Wanderer, and whenever Odin sees fit to reclaim it, the Volsungs are more than ready to let him have it. Please, lady, allow me only to retrieve my beggarly possessions here, and I will be off."

He gestured toward the knapsack. So amazed was I by his humility, that all I could do was nod consent. He crept up to claim the sack, appearing puzzled by the bottle being outside, and puzzled still more when he picked the deerskin up and found it emptier than he obviously had hoped. He said nothing, however, but hurriedly stuffed the bottle back in its place and moved off, carefully stepping backwards down the slippery slide of rock.

The moment he turned his back on me, I sat down hard on what had been my bed. My whirling head craved to lie down again for a moment, but I saw the creature pause again at the edge of sight. As he looked back, I straightened my posture.

He turned away and looked through the mist again, then back at me. Then he sat down on a boulder as if there were no place else in the world for him to go.

The wind blew the steam here and there, and when it blew away from me I could see him clearly. Where he sat, he was not as protected from the storm as I was, and a dusting of snow settled on his head and shoulders. I could sometimes see him so clearly that I could watch the frustration building in his shoulders under that snow. He began to try to shake the mounting frustration from him by casting stones pointlessly off into the world beyond the mist where I couldn't see. And when this did nothing to stem the tide, he turned to me, plucked up his courage, and approached again.

"Look here," he said. "I've got to have that sword. Just for half a day, perhaps, no more."

I responded to his speech as implacably as I could, answering neither with word nor with movement. I certainly did not loosen my grip on the sword.

"Look," he began again. "It wasn't my idea to come to this place. I saw the old One-Eyed Wanderer on a rock at the water's edge, and I called out to him, asking where I might find friends and habitation. He pointed in this direction. *This* direction! That God—if he is a God, which I doubt—is a liar and not to be trusted. For I set off rowing in this direction, and this is where Aegir's winds and waves brought me. Dumped me. Stove my boat in on these rocks in a land that, so far as I've been able to tell, hasn't a single tree growing on it for repairs. Repair hasn't been the uppermost thing in my mind, however—rather, what to eat. There are no trees, nothing grows here. There are a few birds and things, but I have no bow and arrows, no snares, and have yet to find suitable fiber for such things. I have some fishing line, but with my boat beached I've only been able to fish off the skerries and, truth to tell, I haven't caught a thing in the two days I've been here. Then I find you, cut off your brynie, and as if in answer to a prayer, I look out and see that a great fish has been washed up into a shallow pool down at the beach. He was the biggest thing I'd ever seen and would do a man all winter. At least long enough to get his boat fixed.

But when I went down to investigate, I left the sword here, which was a mistake, because this creature has a hide like a dragon. The thrusts of my dagger have made no impression. He still lives, even, and unless I dispatch him in a hurry and carry at least some of the meat up off the strand, the next tide will sweep him off again to swim happily in the deep from whence he came.

"Now, I've no desire to thwart your Odin's will, be he God or no, but I've also no desire to die here slowly, helplessly, of starvation. I've no knowledge of runes to conjure you by, divine *dís*, but I'm also not afraid of death so long as I don't go slowly to the realm of Hel. So," he drew his dagger, "I'll fight you for that blade Balmung if so it must be."

Now my head had cleared somewhat, at least enough to realize the sense of his words. He had seen this place beyond the steam, as I had not. What had I expected—that there would be fields in a place Odin said was beyond the reach of ordinary mortals? Fields as far as the eye could see, and in every field a shock of grain left for Odin? And that All-Father would let me glean off his portion? The only food and water I knew of were now in this stranger's hands. If I wanted more, which I was already beginning to, I would have to fight him for it. Either that, or we would have to come to some sort of understanding.

Compromise was not the way I was used to doing things as a Valkyrie, and it was clearly not this creature's way of doing things either. But somebody had to give something, or one of us would shortly be dead. The dead one would probably be me, my head feeling the way it was and with the creature fearless of the Gods as he seemed to be. Warriors' fear of had once been my surest defense.

Still, I knew I must be on my guard and not give in too much, or even appear to give in at all. "I'll keep the sword," I said. Before he quite lunged for me, I stopped him by continuing, "But I will go with you and see this beast that the waves have washed ashore. And it may be that I will cut off some portion of meat to keep you."

The fight went out of the stranger with a deep sigh. He shoved the dagger back in its sheath and showed me his open hands. "This way," he said with a toss of his head.

chapter 2

I HAD NO SHEATH. MY scabbard and buckler, as far as I knew, were still lying at the feet of the pike holding my horse Faxi's lifeless head somewhere on the shores of the Great North Sea. So I flung Gram up to my shoulder and carried it so. Gram was such a blade that it could cut by glance alone, so I had to be careful. Still, this was the best way to carry it, always at the ready.

The stranger led me down a tumble of rocks and quickly out of the steam. Snow was still falling, but the wind that brought it had finished its task and was gone, leaving the flakes to fall evenly and lightly. Once out of the steam, I could hear the ocean, and very shortly the snow had let up enough that I could also see the ocean spreading endlessly at my feet. On all other sides, the land spread endlessly as well, as humped and barren as if it were ocean petrified. Certainly, given my first impression, the stranger's assessment of the lifeless nature of the place seemed honest. Nonetheless, I kept him before me, even when the terrain flattened out towards the sea and we could have walked side by side. It seemed the most prudent thing to do.

The edge of the waves didn't stop him, and I didn't let it stop me, though my skirts soon became weighted and my legs numb with the frozen water. We made our way out to what I took at first to be a small island of smooth, purplish stone—heavily barnacled. But this was an island with an eye, a large baleful eye wrinkled with wisdom, that blinked at me from the level of my waist. And somewhere, far above my head, a blowhole breathed in and out with deep mournful sighs.

"It's not a fish," I said. "It hasn't got gills. It's breathing air, much as you or I."

"But it hasn't any legs," observed the stranger, "just these fins, and way off here under the water—a fishy tail. Which is fortunate, else it would have run off by now. Or lunged at us and crushed us while we sit here chatting. Look, the tide's already past the ebb. Are you going to use that sword, or am I?" His hand played again on the hilt of his dagger.

I was hesitating. If this man was just a man, not some evil sent to me by Odin, then perhaps this fishy creature was the sending, waiting just for me to strike the first blow and release the evil upon us. Indeed, I could tell it was a male creature. Its sex was wider than my thigh and longer, and drifted here and there to the throb of the waves in a grotesque yet very threatening manner. The man seemed content to ignore this pink horror, even stepping on it causally as he paced back and forth before the spectacle of a mountain of food. It was the sword he was not going to let either one of us forget.

I was not about to give up the sword—that thing that made a man of me—so I moved out of view of that sad, yellowish-gray eye the size of my palm and out of view of the threat of the sex, and I thrust. A fountain of blood poured past me and onto my companion. It was warm blood like ours, not the cold ice water of other fishes. My companion seemed unimpressed, even to have it all over him. He merely wiped the blood from his eyes with bloody hands and watched anxiously for the next blow.

This fish monster was not like any other thing I'd ever killed before. Other fish only required dragging them into the air and very shortly their flapping would still. Men, deer, boar, even birds have bodies enough like my own that even without training in throwing spears at straw manikins, I had a pretty good idea where to strike—just by feeling the throb of life in the neck, the ebb and flow of air, and the drub of the heart beneath the ribs. This thing had no neck, no ribs that I could see. So my thrusts were haphazard and for some time merely tortured the beast. I had cut off two great swaths of hide and flesh before the quick gasping breaths finally ended in a long, wailing sigh and my panic could also ease.

Swath after swath I cut, as tall as a man and as thick as the blade was long. When I had hacked the swath free on the side of the fish's body, I flipped it over onto my companion's back, and he would wade off through the water and up the shore out of reach of the tide.

He also helped where he could with the dagger, but it was clear just how little use it would have been without the sword. The creature was fat to the depth of the sword and beyond. Under that was flesh, dark and coarsely grained. Steam rose from the life-warm carcass into the snowy air. The foam of the waves was a deep pink broth at my feet, and it seemed the most natural thing in the world to use the cuts I'd made as a stair to climb to the second story of the creature's back and begin to cut there.

Eventually I worked my way down to ribs as big as oars. I lifted a pair of these out and down to my companion, for such wonders might have their uses. Then I began to work on the innards until I found myself in the hollow of a fair-sized cave.

"This must be the creature's heart," I called to my companion as I took all my strength to heave the deep red muscle up to him where he stood on the rim. "Who could imagine a heart of such a size?"

"Dragons' hearts are at least as big," the man said, as if dragons' hearts were something people came across every day. "If not bigger."

I rested a moment from my labors, leaning against the hilt of the sword, and stared up at him trying to ascertain by throwing him a wry smile whether or not he was telling a tale. It seemed he had no wry smile of his own to return. He only stared back with a face full of bland and childlike innocence for a moment before disappearing from sight down the side of our kill and pulling the heart off after him.

I puzzled at this for a moment, but when I could make no immediate sense of his words, I turned back to the wall of my grisly cave, trying to determine what to turn the sword on next. Even as I stood considering, there was a sudden rush as of a mighty wind, and before

I could place it I was over my head in icy salt water that hit me from above with the force of falling rock.

I fought my way to the surface and hardly had time to sputter the water out of my lungs before I was hit by another icy rock wall of water. When this receded, I felt an iron grip on my left arm; the man pulled me from the carcass.

“I should have warned you,” he said as I choked and sputtered. “The tide’s coming in. I think this is about all we can do. Go on. Get to shore. Here comes another.”

I slid shoreward over the beast’s nose as fast as the limited air in my lungs would allow. As I slipped into the chest-deep water, I had to brace myself on the creature against the undertow. My heart gave way as I felt another rush of water lift the carcass up and take it back a foot or two before it settled into the sand again, lighter and less permanently moored since our day’s work on it. In my momentary panic, I looked back for my companion’s strong arms again, but he was nowhere to be seen. I wanted to call his name, but as far as I knew, he didn’t have one.

“Man!” It had a foolish sound to it, but embarrassment would have to wait for another time. “Man!”

His head popped suddenly out of the pit I’d dug in the carcass, and in his hand was the sword Gram, which I had carelessly dropped when I felt myself drowning.

Four good whacks at the carcass had him another brick of the beast. He rode the carcass through another wave that tugged it out four or five more ells, and then he, too, abandoned ship and came up to where I stood—nearly frozen physically and mentally, with movements made clumsy by deep water.

“Come on,” he barked hoarsely, blue at the lips. “Don’t you know how quickly a man can perish in water this cold?”

He thrust the hilt of the sword into my fingers, so numb that they could barely accept it. He readjusted the brick of butchered fish up on his shoulder, caught me firmly under the elbow, and dragged me along as well.

“Come on!” he repeated, annoyance in his voice now but totally oblivious to the fact that, just moments before, nothing at all had stood in the way of his ridding himself of that annoyance forever. "Come on."

"Where … where are we … we to go?" My teeth were chattering so violently that speech was almost useless.

"Why, to your place, of course." He was still fairly dragging me along. "What do you call it? It hasn't any walls to speak of. One can hardly give it the name of "house." Still, there's no doubt that it's much more hospitable there in the steam than in this wind and snow on the beach. And, what with night coming on …"

Even as he finished his speech, the first of the steam hit us like a blast from a furnace, or so it seemed, rising up from cracks in the rocks. It blinded us at first, and I wondered how on earth this man had ever found the courage to penetrate into such a supernatural realm in the first place. Was it true then, as Odin had said? Was this indeed a man who knew no fear?

We reached the little room-sized space in the midst of the steam where my rock was. It was the rock I'd been sleeping on, no doubt, but this man was more at home with it than I was. He dumped his brick of flesh our day's labors had created down on the mound, and it filled more than half the space allotted us. Then, with his dagger he quickly cut himself a manageable slice and ate it raw.

"How can … you be sure this thing is edible?" I asked. My teeth were still chattering, but perhaps not quite as much as before. I stood numb and stupid in my soaking clothes, stiff and frozen solid in places.

My companion shrugged. "Easy. I've been snacking at it all day as we worked. Here. Try some. The fat is particularly nourishing." He handed me the next little mouth-sized cube he cut. When I didn't immediately take it from him, he said, "Go on, try it," and pressed his hand against my mouth until I opened to accept it. My throat immediately rose up to meet this morsel that was somewhat salty but, more to the point, somewhat rotten in flavor. The texture, too, was at first objectionable, meeting the teeth like cheese but also like a gelatinous mud that refused to disintegrate. Two more chews, however, and the savory saltiness and creaminess prevailed with the help of my ravenous hunger. I began to chew more vigorously.

And then I stopped mid-chew again. "What are you doing?" I blubbered around the brick of fat.

For there stood my companion before me, having doffed both cloak and grey woolen tunic, as naked as the day he was born—only much, much more masculine. How used I was to life among the Twelve, where brynies and tunics were tossed aside casually to reveal a uniform nakedness of women! The swing from breast to hip to pubic pelt seemed to us the most natural, indeed the only, form in the world. This form of firmly sliced angles seemed an aberration in comparison. Perhaps I had even come to assume that under the tunics of the men alongside whom we fought must be the same curves as we had. As one day differed from another in length and outward show, but in a common curve of sun across the sky, all must be fundamentally the same. But then, not all Valkyries must have been as unconcerned as I. I remembered Thora—how she must have been attracted to something under the dark Frank's tunic that piqued her curiosity more, even, than divine maidenhood.

I could not share Thora's curiosity in the presence of this man. His body seemed unnatural to me, as if the sun one morning had decided to rise in the north and, instead of arcing, come barreling across the landscape at horizon height to set in the south. Like that of a new-hatched chick was the yellow down collected on the platter of his flat chest. It funneled downward across the flat of navel and belly like an arrow or a pointing finger in a blatant cry for attention to the part that hung below. That part had the power, if Odin spoke the truth, of sundering me forever from the strength and exhilaration of battle, that occupation which was the only life I knew or, I thought, could ever find purpose in.

My thawing hands worked on the hilt of Gram. I should disarm him of that weapon right now, now that his weakness—and mine—were so openly exposed to my mind and hands. But I did not.

And perhaps that was the greatest mistake of my life. Or the wisest choice.

"I'm going to bathe," my companion said nonchalantly. "Unless you want to go first?"

There was such a tone in his voice that told me, for all forms of politeness, he had his heart set on this bath and might well fight me for the privilege if it came to that. As I had no idea what he had in mind and found my head stupefied with other thoughts, I didn't bother to counter him. If he would kindly remove his obscenity from my sight, I would be sufficiently grateful.

My companion walked over to one of the largest vents out of which steam was pouring and kicked thoughtfully at the water welling up within. He seemed to find it decidedly to his liking, for he quickly sat down at its edge and then eased himself into the water. He went completely under, vanishing from view for a moment until, for all my considerations of unmanning him, I felt a wave of panic as I had when he had vanished into the cavity of the great fish when the surf rolled in. He rose to the surface soon enough, however, with a great sigh of satisfaction. He flipped his soaking hair out of his eyes in a great arc that sent droplets splashing and steaming in all directions. So absorbed was he in the pleasures of his body and warm water, that he never opened his eyes but turned his back on me and scrubbed at beard, neck and underarms with continued grunts of delight.

I swallowed my morsel of food and went to cut another. While I chewed, I sought something else to set my mind to work on. It was a very tight little world the steam confined my sight to, and I happened to notice what seemed to be a curious birthmark on my companion's back. He was scrubbing the dried blood off it with handfuls of sand. Precisely in the center was a heart-shaped patch of smooth white surrounded by a redder, rougher skin in all places else. It looked, in fact, like nothing so much as a linden leaf.

"Ah. You see it." My companion's voice startled me. "I wondered if it could only be felt—or if it could be seen as well."

"Your … your birthmark?" I stammered.

"Hmm. Only I wasn't born with it. Shall I tell you its history?"

I shrugged with feigned carelessness. "Only if you want to. And if it's a tale worth hearing."

"When I killed the dragon. See, I killed him by digging a pit and hiding in the pit so I could hit him in the soft underbelly as he crawled over me to his lair. Well, there was so much blood that the pit was soon full, and I was very close to drowning. When I worked my way out of that drenching, however, and when I had eaten some of the dragon's heart, it came to me in the song of birds that if I didn't wash the blood off me for three days, it would have the power to make my skin impervious to any arrow or sword-thrust. So I didn't wash. When I finally did, I found my skin covered all over with this permanent thick red scale. I also discovered that a little linden leaf had been in the pit with me, and that it had stuck to my back right there while I dozed and waited for my prey. This leaf prevented the magic blood from reaching me. That is the only spot on my body where I am vulnerable." End of story. He dove back under the water.

Now I realized a number of things, one of which was that it was totally uncharacteristic of him to divulge so much at once. This was the longest speech I was likely to get from the fellow unless he was sorely tempted, and I credited his sudden loquaciousness to the warming, softening effects of the water.

Another realization was that this was the second time he had mentioned close contact with a dragon, a beast I myself had never seen, nor had anyone else I'd ever known. Indeed, I highly doubted their existence. My companion, however, clearly did not.

And, finally, was the fact that if his skin was as he claimed it was, I had no chance against him at all. My considered attempt to fight him for the sword or to unman him would have ended in serious embarrassment, if not my death. He must certainly credit me with outstanding powers if he had hesitated to try that skin out against them. However, his tale could just be lies, as those of a man who, when the odds seem too great, claims to have ten brothers just over the hill for whom he must only whistle. Yes, it could be mere tale-telling and bluff. But then I thought I should bluff about my prowess as well. I knew to tread cautiously here and test every move I made, like a man heading out on thin ice.

"So why do you wash after killing this beast today?" I asked when next his head appeared, and the ears were shaken free of water. It had also occurred to me how like his tale of the dragon pit were the actions of the day, when both of us had vanished into the carcass of our kill, boiling as it was with surf and blood. It just might be that here was a man who liked to take the events of the day and weave them into a yarn at night. Geirönul had been such a one among the Twelve, but we all expected that of her and looked forward to recognizing our own exploits among unseen wonders at the end of a campaign.

"This was no dragon," my companion said confidently, and vanished into the steamy water once more.

Somehow, I got the feeling that this was not a man who made tales.

chapter 3

"HERE'D YOU LEARN TO DO this?"

My companion's mind seemed to have been wandering a bit, relaxing, perhaps. My voice called him to himself. He set his mouth in the tight half-smile he'd taken to wearing whenever he was forced to confront my existence. He shrugged, looked at the work as if anybody should be able to do it, and shrugged again. He was using his dagger to cut thin, even strips of the breathing-fish flesh and hanging them up to dry in the sun that had fought its way out of the storm but still seemed weak, like an invalid who needed to be fed on thin broth.

"It's the only way to keep it," he'd answered to my earlier prodding as to the why of his actions. There'd been another ironic smile, as if I were a half-wit.

We had found a bit of driftwood, unsuitable for building but serving well enough for small fires to help the drying process along. It could not be used for drying racks, so my companion had propped the beast's rib bones between stones and was using them for that purpose instead. I was trying to help, but a sword, even Gram, was not the tool for this work. As thin as he cut the pieces, they would dry quickly, even in this weak sun, and without rot. It was clear he had done this sort of work before, as I never had. We ate dried meat and dried fish when I was a Valkyrie, but somebody else always did the

drying. From childhood, which was one lifetime—no, two—away now (my life as a Valkyrie and now this new one that had no name yet) I only remembered the hunger gruel and, on special days, soured milk. Never any meat to be handled.

"My name's Brynhild," I'd offered earlier. This was the night before, when he'd come out of his bath and rolled himself up in my bearskin—*my* bearskin—to sleep. I certainly wanted to join him in a clean forgetfulness, but we needed names at least first, or so it seemed to my propriety. The only response he'd given me was an ironic smile. That was the first time I'd noticed this expression of his, or at least the first time it annoyed me. But he didn't give me fair exchange until I prodded, not without a note of irritation, "Well, what's yours?"

Another empty, ironic pause.

Yet more annoyance in my voice: "Haven't you a name?"

"Siegfried."

His voice was muffled by the fur, but I knew there was no mistake. I'd heard him right. A Volsung name. Volsungs were supposed to be extinct—if Odin's will meant anything anymore in this new world. But the man offered no more and pretended to fall asleep instantly.

So I entered the spring and found it even more delightful than I could have imagined. I hadn't washed in … well, I still didn't know how long it had been, but the blood-warm water made me know it had been long indeed. The warmth seemed to come up through the water in tangible ribbons from a thin crevice in the rocks at the bottom. I had to squat to get my hair wet. The strands of my braids seemed petrified together; it was like crumbling sandstone to work them apart. When I finally worked the water into my scalp, I was enlivened as with a powerful tonic.

I washed out my dress as well. The linen was no longer white. The day in the beast's belly had stained it a pink, which would quickly dry a dingy brown. What a pity! Nothing was as striking as the pure white of a Valkyrie. But then I wasn't a Valkyrie any longer, was I? I hadn't been one in an expanse of months—or maybe it was even years—for I noticed that, even where there were no bloodstains, the linen was yellow as if with age. A large piece of it broke off in my hands from sheer brittleness. Then I remembered something odd about my brynie when I'd been taking it off as well, something old and odd. I reached out of the pool and tried it again. Bits of the once-shiny iron came off in my hand, rusted quite away. The leather was cracked and powdery as well. Perhaps it wasn't a matter of years, but more like a matter of decades. *No! Impossible!*

I sent a scowl off towards the silent bearskin. There was certainly no one here I needed to impress with a Valkyrie's dress garb. But no one I could ask to untangle the riddle of age for me, either. Even if he had been communicative, I couldn't show him any more ignorance than I could help. I needed every bit of strength, feigned and otherwise, that I could muster.

"Siegfried," I called out of the pool.

My dress was spread out to dry, but this presented a new difficulty—what to cover my nakedness? At home with the Valkyries, I wouldn't have given nakedness a second thought. But I knew I had to stop considering Valhalla my home.

Yes, I got the name right. And he was not asleep, only pretending. He sat up when I spoke, as if conjured by runes. I could see, for it was still quite light—maybe this new world didn't even know nighttime—how his hair was drying in plump ringlets in such a delightful way that they invited touch.

I spoke with more annoyance than the situation warranted. "Siegfried, that's my bearskin you're using."

Siegfried said nothing, but got up and, in four quick movements, cut my skin—my beautiful hard-won totem skin—in two with his dagger.

It wasn't that half a skin of that size wouldn't serve almost as well. Indeed, a whole skin is so heavy as to be almost unmanageable unless one is a berserk. It's what it symbolized for me that caused the grief. If I hadn't felt totally removed from my life as a Valkyrie before, I did now. I didn't like this new world of sharing.

I stayed awake under my half-bearskin for as long as I could because thoughts of the imposition of sharing reminded me just how dangerous this man could be. We never thought of rape as Valkyries.

Now I did, and it was not pleasant. I hardly dared to sleep and let my guard down. I kept my hand on the sword. I had been asleep for a long, long time, but sleep is not like gold coins which you can hoard for a time when you need to be alert. The hard, cold work to which my body was unaccustomed, and then the warm bath, all conspired against me. Soon enough I did sleep, deeply and unmolested, and woke with a start to this dogged and intimidating situation—meat drying, ironic smiles, and an almost religiously kept silence. Several days went by in this manner.

Siegfried had brought his water to this place—wherever it was—in some earthenware pots of Celtic make. As some of the springs nearby produced a fresh, clear water, he was able to empty the pots. We found that when lowered into the hottest of our hot water pools with a bit of fishing twine, they served very well to render the beast's fat. It smelled fiercely foul, but now it would keep. Strips of flesh could be threaded on the same twine and lowered into the same pool and come out boiled, though without the benefit of any gravy it was a bit dry and craved the fat to go along with it. Meat from the great fish tasted good enough even raw, but the liver was inedible.

At the end of three or four days, the rest of our hoard—save that which we, but mostly Siegfried, had industriously dried and rendered—began to go off. I certainly wished now I'd been a better hand at drying. Siegfried refused to believe it altogether. He said he'd never known meat to rot so soon and insisted on breakfasting on the stomach-turning stuff. It didn't take long for him to become violently ill, so I hauled the rest of our hard-won carcass back down the hill to the shore for the tide to wash away while he lay under his bearskin and tried to keep his moans to a minimum.

That's what comes of not being afraid of anything, I thought. I knew it was no use even bothering to speak my thoughts aloud. It was a lonely, smelly job, and I had to retch about it once or twice myself without having even tasted the stuff.

By the time most of the rotting mess was down on the shore, however, I saw that it was attracting birds, birds who were not harmed by either the odor or the eating. There were feisty skuas with their hooked beaks, guillemots with their brilliant orange feet contrasting with the plumage gone from white to black for the summer, gulls, and terns in clouds. I could come right up to them with another load, and they didn't start. It was as if they'd never seen a person before.

On my last trip, I stayed away longer than usual, and Siegfried started up when I reappeared. Had he actually missed me?

I held up a brace of birds for his fevered inspection. "They were tamer than barnyard chickens," I explained. "See, I fashioned this little net out of some of your twine."

But all he greeted my success with was another ironic smile, as if to say, *Well, finally! You're carrying some of your own weight around here.*

He didn't say anything. He didn't have to. I hung up my birds to season on the space the drying meat left us on the rib bone and didn't say any more. I hated this sharing. I didn't have to share everything, and words were certainly something I could do without if he could.

The sickness left him sooner than it would many a man. To my mind, he still looked a little green in the face, but that didn't stop him taking my net—our shared net, I guess, made from his twine and my labor—and going down to try his own hand at it.

So I went off on my own as well. While sitting quietly, waiting for the birds to land in my trap, I'd taken careful note of the cliff that blocked off the rest of the coast from our view to the west. On its dark grey face, I'd noticed white scars as on a man who'd suffered the pox in his youth. Or as if from centuries of skua guano. Closer inspection taught me that indeed it was guano. And the storm that had been blowing when I first awakened had quickly melted away, sharing this feature with many late spring storms—it came at the season when the skua and a dozen other species had their nests on that cliff. I hitched up my skirt into my belt, lined the bottom with a soft nest of moss and, braving the sheer wall and the wings and beaks of the angry parents, I sought out and found the most convenient toe holds. The cliff face was a world sketched on a bit of hide and then turned on its side. Tufts of nesting material, new on top of ancient, were plastered to the cliff with lime like whitewashed wattle and daub. I quickly gathered a skirtful of eggs.

Actually, I gathered two skirtfuls. The first one was lost. The brittle linen tore again and sent them tumbling in a mass to the rocks on the shore. The birds came and cannibalistically feasted on them as I sat and cried over the mishap for a while, cried over my rotting dress that now exposed my knees in places, cried over the half-formed birds inside some of the eggs which reminded me of my half-formed brother and sister bears from my former life, which reminded me of my sundered bearskin. Presently, however, I came to see that this accident was good. I got the refreshment of a long weep, which had been building up in me and was a clear sign that I'd left the Valkyries far behind. But I managed to have it away from Siegfried, so I got the benefit without the loss of face.

After that, I was ready for a second foray, and the varied harvest I collected cheered me as a basket of dyed eggs to celebrate the advent of spring might, at the festival of the goddess Eastre. There were the plovers' cream-colored eggs sharply pointed on one end and heavily speckled with brown on the other, the greenish eggs of the eider duck, the brown egg of the tern thickly spotted with brown and lavender—and the largest of all—the gull's eggs, greenish-brown and spotted. I also saw burrows in the cliff top where the puffins would nest. They weren't about it yet, but the males had the colorful growths on their bills that indicated they were breeding. Puffins in their burrows, puffins flying low with frantic, choppy, clumsy strokes. Puffin eggs and puffin chicks—these would add yet another dimension to our diet, the flesh of the adults being dark and rich.

Siegfried had only caught one bird himself, for the bait was vanishing rapidly and the birds were learning to be wary. He was also perhaps not fully recovered yet. Still, he had no more than his infuriating smile with which to greet my skirtful of eggs. All right, so my ragged skirt was up to my thighs, and in the climb down the cliff face one of my brooches had ripped through the linen, leaving one shoulder bare. I hadn't wanted to set down the eggs in order to repair it.

The eggs themselves boiled up very nicely in the steaming water, each species with its slightly different flavor, stronger or more sulfurous. Some of them even had the start of chicks in them, whose tiny bones, boiled, gave a satisfying texture to the meal. Then I tossed the empty shells out on what was becoming our midden, attracting yet another gull who allowed himself to be caught. Yes, the net had grown under Siegfried's care with a hidden cache of twine, but my skills had not suffered either. Indeed, I could congratulate myself, even if this impossible man could not.

The next day, he took the net again, this time to the cliff—*my* cliff. I let him have it. Meanwhile, infuriated at being left without the net again, I went for a walk along the shore in the opposite direction. The tide was out, and my prints left little puddles in the saturated sand. The first thing of interest I came to was Siegfried's boat. It was a little thing, less than a quarter the size, say, of Helgi's war boats, with only one pair of oars and oarlocks, and a pair to spare. Perhaps the real world wasn't too far off if Siegfried had come from there in such a simple craft.

I wasn't at all sure, however, that he had come from any *real* world. There was certainly the air of dwarves about him, perhaps giants and trolls as well. He wasn't going anywhere soon, at any rate. Beached on high ground as it was, the dimensions of the hole in the boat's bow were only too clear. The hull, even under the benches, held nothing of promise. Knapsack, twine, dagger, sword, and jugs—he'd already brought it all to our house of fire.

Further on down the shore, however, I had the good fortune to find a colony of mussels in a tidal pool. I pried them off their rocks with Gram, but there weren't many. Tiny bubbling holes in the sand declared the presence of clams, but I'd need something to dig with. Hands alone, I proved twice or thrice, just weren't fast enough. A length of driftwood presented itself and did the trick.

Then I found a great tangle of seaweed. The shore here was made of sea-smoothed stones as black as night on which the ribbons of orange weed lay in brilliant contrast. It was like the colors of an oak wood in the days before winter's first storm when the changing leaves stand out against the trees' dark trunks. But here the scene had been condensed into fewer dimensions and the weed ran narrowly clinging low to the ground as if with only tenuous life. My fellow warmaid Eir had come

from a place near the shore and told us that her people sometimes ate the weed. I tried a little. It was salty and chewy and seemed nourishing enough when it had sat in my empty belly for a while. I filled the rest of my skirt with the weed.

chapter 4

I WOKE UP EARLY THE next morning when I could still hear the deep, even breaths of Siegfried's sleep beside me. Only another half-smile had greeted yesterday's new discoveries. What was the use of trying with this fellow? I turned away from him either to mull this problem over or, preferably, to fall back to sleep, although there was daylight. There was always daylight in this place. That didn't mean anything.

But then I realized what it was that had awakened me. I was bleeding; my woman's time had come. Quick calculation told me that it was right on schedule, as if my time of sleep, however long that had been, had been but a single night. I was relieved I was still a woman, still full of potential. Of course, if Odin's curse were to be fulfilled, I would have to be. Perhaps this was part of the curse. At any rate, I had not become a grey old hag during the time of the sleep thorn, although Siegfried's reaction to me and the state of my brynie and dress told me perhaps I ought to have become one. That was some consolation.

But suddenly there was the greater concern, how to absorb this flow and keep my state from this man. There were no rags to spare in this bare-bones existence we were enduring. Perhaps some feathers from our plucked birds? Too messy. And I could never conceal those at such close quarters. No, the best thing to do would be just to leave for the duration. I had never been ashamed like this before. Was I ashamed? Not exactly. But this man had taught me some sort of modesty I'd never felt in Valhalla before.

Quickly but quietly I took four good handfuls of dried meat, two leftover boiled eggs, and a plucked and roasted bird. I stuffed these into a sack made of my half of the bearskin and went off, leaving the deep-sleeping breaths of manhood behind me.

I went off in a direction neither of us had ever been before, away from the shore, up from the hot springs and inland. The rocks here would not betray my footprints as going along the sand certainly would have, particularly since there had been a damp drizzle during the night.

It was only when I felt the wetness of the rocks as I used my hand to help me climb and saw the little puddles collected in the round hollows of this curiously light and friable stone that I realized it had drizzled and considered that shelter might be a problem. Once I got out of the stream and away from the shore, past the rocks, the summits of the distant hills that ringed the horizon of this land were covered with eternal snow. I even came upon drifts of snow closer at hand in sheltered spots. But this did not turn me from my resolve. I would find something. And anyway, I had been out alone in snow before.

The way up was covered in scree. Where plants had a foothold, they were more advanced due to the heat of the hot springs, I would learn, than they were elsewhere in that land. Some spots were yellow with buttercups or carpeted with thyme in full bloom. Still, there was the scree between them where nothing could hold, least of all my footsteps. My footsteps sent the loose materials flying in a series of small landslides, a thing that seemed never to have touched the face of this land before. Even so, I managed shortly to come up out of the steam and out of the fog that had accompanied the drizzle at the seashore.

Then it seemed that I entered a different world, although one no less eerie and even more empty than the one I'd left. I discovered my head was aching with the silence, being away from the rhythmic roar of surf for the first time in—well, however long it had been. The clouds were snow drifts blowing across the ice-blue of the sky with the same silencing effect. There continued to be multitudes of birds. My heart stopped when I even saw a raven, and these called to one another from time to time, but they had no word for me.

No word for Odin, either, I hoped.

Of other creatures there were none at all. No bear, no squirrel, no rabbit, no deer, no cow, certainly no human—not even their spoor, though I searched the ground where it was damp earth and not unyielding rock. Between the snow-capped summits were fields divided by vitrified cliffs whose high, sharp points seemed to vie with each other to deprive me of the sight of what little grass managed to spring up among them. Rivers and fresh lakes abounded in the landscape; the lakes well-supplied with fish, the rivers much obstructed by rocks and shallows.

I breakfasted on dried meat. Soon I found a stream to wash it down with and to follow. It would lead me back to the shore when my time was over. I walked most generally north as well, when I could. There was no forest to get lost in. I didn't mean to go far, but there wasn't anything else to do but walk, and the landscape had a bizarre allurement to its strangeness.

It is true that I'd had little enough conversation with that man who'd pretended to keep me company for five days. It was also true that I'd eaten many unaccustomed things in that time. But now, as I walked it was the first taste, that dried lump in Siegfried's bag, that came back to me, rising in my throat and unable to be washed away by any quantity of the bitingly cold and clear water in the stream. It occurred to me now that Siegfried had never mentioned it. Of course, he hadn't mentioned much of anything, but he also hadn't even offered it in his sullen, silent way as an addition to our already curious hodge-podge fare. I still had no idea what it was I'd eaten. Perhaps it wasn't meant to be ingested. But I had eaten it and, five days later, it still had no ill effects.

On the other hand, with no constant male distractions around me anymore, I had to admit that it was still with me, a lingering aftertaste and … and something more. The taste went up my nasal cavity and entered my brain until I thought—no, indeed it was true—that this unpeopled landscape itself began to speak to me. And answer when I dared to speak to it.

I saw a plain, paved with smooth-sided rocks, six sides to a stone. "You are in the courtyard of giants," this plain said, "set in mosaic."

I came upon mounds of black cinders. "We are the giants' fire pit gone cold," they announced. Under the ash in places were preserved banks of snow, *under* the dusting of ash. "The fire is more recent here than snow."

In places, the rock was weathered like honeycomb. "Here, the giants' bees have been at work."

In dozens of places waterfalls shot out off cliffs. "We are the silver-white hair of the Norns." The colors of the rainbow played on their spray like a Gods' bridge over their ravines. Their innumerable tendrils of streams pulsated across the meadows like so many veins with blood. In the morning they were low enough to wade across, but by evening—if evening indeed it was—they were too heavy. "Just like the blood of your flow."

Elsewhere, rocks swirled with dull red markings. "Mother Earth's blood, which she has stanched with lichens."

At one point there was a great field of eider ducks, with a nest hidden behind every hummock, and the tufts of their feathers sacrificed for the new generation, blowing like snowdrifts in the wind. At first, I thought to gather the eggs, but the season was so far advanced that only rotten ones were left. The first two I touched exploded, so I left them alone. But this was easier said than done. There were so many of them, and they were so well concealed in down and burrows, it became a game to see how far I could get without loosing that gorge-wrenching smell and clouds of black with my heel. "Ha! Thought you'd get me with that one, did you?" I asked the birds. "One point for me."

"But another two points for us," the birds replied as the explosion from one egg made me jump onto another. "We win!"

There were many bogs that appeared quite solid until one foot or the other plunged in up to the knee, and I had to flounder desperately to get out, to reach the blocks of twisted and contorted black and porous stone that were strewn through the bogs and so onto solid ground. I didn't dare listen very closely to what the bogs said. I sensed the quality of dwarfish spells luring me to my doom.

Over all was the sky, seeming to proclaim, "I am the inside of the giant Ymir's skull, set here by Thor when he created the world from me." Ymir's thoughts scudded by on the clouds.

And then I came to a place through which a stream as red as blood did flow. I bent to touch it, but found it congealed to stone, although its reds and oranges were as bright and fresh as if the blood-letting had happened just moments before.

I crossed the blood, dropping my own blood fresh upon it. On the other side, moss was growing. "Sit on me. Rest," it coaxed. I didn't need much coaxing. It was moss of a color I'd never seen before, light green, but of an intensity of hue that blinded. When I got up, my blood on it in contrast was also brilliant. Surely there had never existed such colors before, except perhaps very rarely for an hour or two in midspring, and then only in the imagination of man.

I realize now that the voices I was hearing have a name. At the time, however, it came to me as such a new thing that I failed to realize that others to whom the same gift had come had long ago named it "poetry." Poetry and, in certain cases even more rare, the gift of prophecy, which always comes in verse. Seiðr, too, I would name it when the memory of the priestess in my childhood came to me. Now it seemed a sort of possession—frightening, but at the same time a thing I trusted implicitly. If it had told me to cast myself down from the height of that high block of stone like that waterfall, I would have done so. Poetry is Odin's realm, and I feared he possessed me. But then I touched my neck, free of his torc, and knew it was not so. After all, he stole that gift, didn't he, from the Vanir and the dwarves? As he wanted to control everything, so he wanted the verses and runes to conjure by. But this I felt came straight from the earth. This was the Vanir gift, pure and simple. Something I'd sought all my life to escape. I'd been indeed quite rude to the Vanir before. And still they welcomed me with open arms.

Before my time was over, the pulse of poetry had acquired the dimension of saga within me. It had the power to turn the idlest passing thought into magic runes that I recited aloud to myself and to this magical world over and over.

A little walk further, and the stone blood rose above the plain, making an archway as smooth and even as if formed by the most skilled of craftsmen. "I'll be your roof," it said. "You can stay under me for shelter."

And so I did. I found the whole roof and walls of the arch, which was almost a cave, were covered with beautiful, tiny ferns with solitary mountain flowers nodding here and there among them. The arch's mouth was closed with the thick branches of shrubs, and behind these I found enough dryness, my bearskin enough warmth, for my needs during this time. It also provided shelter for a floor of soft mounds of moss. I scraped this off its rocks and set it to dry. Before my time was quite over, but when it was growing lighter, I found that this moss was absorbent enough that the thought of returning to the man began to sound pleasant again. I slept alone once more, but set off the next morning carrying a supply of the moss with me. I retraced my steps, greeting all the features of the landscape as old friends, hearing their friendly greetings in return.

Then, as I was crossing a boggy heath, I heard it say in its sloppy voice, "Let me introduce you to someone new." I looked where it gestured broadly and saw white and purple heather, and low mounded pinks in bloom.

"A pleasure," the flowers sang, returning my delight as I knelt to them.

"Take us with you," the pinks begged later, when I told them I really must be on my way.

"Yes, please do," chimed in the numerous, tiny voices of all the little blooms that make up heather. There was a sort of poppy, too, in the most barren spots, a poppy in many but very fragile colors instead of the unabashed but monotonous red we were used to at home. These pinks and yellows were the colors of blooms frozen in ice, the colors life might have if we viewed it always through the carbonation of a mineral spring. "We won't be any trouble," said these shy little colors. "We'll ride with you in your hair. We'll be a crown for you."

And so I made a wreath of them, tucking up my braids and weaving them in with pleasure.

And I came back to the house of steam.

Chapter 5

THE HOUSE WAS DESERTED. IT was still early afternoon. Of course, I couldn't expect Siegfried to be lounging about while there was still energy to spare and things to do. But most disquieting was the absence of any of his—*our*—stores. His—*my*—bearskin was gone, his jug, his dagger—all.

I hurried down to the shore, following his footsteps in the sand to the deep depression where the boat had lain. The boat was gone. Drag marks scarred the beach until they were healed by the waves. *He was gone.*

A storm was brewing. The clouds, like great black giants' fists, clenched the horizon as a man clenches his skull when he has bad visions. Salt spray sprang into my eyes, and I met it with blinding tears, tears as hot as the spray was cold. Now indeed I was abandoned.

I'm not sure how long I stood there on the shore, heedless of the coming storm that was already blowing up a gale, heedless of the waves. I had been standing well above them, but now they reached my knees and dragged my immobile feet down into the sand to mid-calf. Then I thought the loneliness had really turned my mind because, as I looked out into the storm and the sleet that was beginning to drive into my face along with the spray, I thought I saw a small boat floundering out beyond the surf.

I turned to get out of the storm. I would at least demonstrate I had my wits about me. But with my last look at the lonely sea, I saw that my eyes did not deceive me. Another swell lifted the little boat up into my view, and I saw it clearly. It was a boat, it was Siegfried's boat, and most importantly of all, it was Siegfried in it with his back to me, rowing with all the strength he could muster. Then I saw clearly, too, that he was not having an easy time of it. The wind-swept water was up to the gunwales, sometimes over them, and the boat was floundering badly.

The whoosh and hiss of waves spoke to my mind the words of a song, a song full of the coughing break of "k-k" and the sibilation of "s-sh." What precisely the words of the song were, I could not recall once they were up and out—but they were magic words, drawing words, pulling words, helping words of the tugging rune.

Siegfried, still rowing, entered the surf, his efforts helped by the waves and by my song. Then he stopped rowing. Another wave pulled him sharply down and away from shore, and it was clear he had to abandon the boat or be pulled under water with it. He quickly secured the oars and slid into the freezing brine over his head.

He came up gasping. He refused to desert the sinking craft, however. Sometimes he could stand where he was, more often he could not. He knotted the rope of the boat around his upper arm and—half walking, half swimming—began trying to haul the thing in. I sang to his efforts.

And then, in a movement, I was out in the surf too, battling attack of wave and wind to reach his side. He was standing more than he was swimming by the time I neared him, but the boat seemed just moments from going straight to the bottom without him. And he was at the end of his power.

He heard my splashing and singing as different and above the storm and surf. He looked up, and such a look of salvation crossed his face as I have never seen before. "Brynhild!" he cried. It was the first time he'd said my name. Indeed, I'd assumed he'd forgotten I'd ever said it for him. And for a moment he seemed so transported, so focused on me that he quite forgot the boat.

"Don't let go of the rope!" I called to him. There was that half-smile again, but for the moment I didn't care. We quickly put our minds to more important things.

The water was midway up my brynie and sometimes higher, ice-cold. But I worked my way alongside the boat and helped pull. It was almost immovable with floundering. If it hadn't been for the help of the waves, which I coaxed with my song, all would have been lost. Soon enough, working together, the bottom dragged. Then we could turn it over, get rid of most of the water, and drag it the rest of the way up to shore, out of all danger of the storm. In the process, I noticed that it was the scraped hide of our great sea beast with which he'd tried to mend the craft, but which in the end had failed and hung loosely now from many corners.

That work done, my song died as I was overcome by shivering and panting all at once. We both stood up and looked at each other over the prow as if at some hidden signal. And then—and do not think that I was too much affected by the singers of romances—I felt the earth move beneath our feet. It was a slow but definite jerking roll, as if the ground had little more substance than the waves we'd just been battling. And we moved with it.

Siegfried looked away from me quickly and smiled his smile. Then the motion and the moment that preceded it were over.

"Come on," I said, growing angry all over again. I hoisted one of the oil pots out of the hull and waved him to the other. "Let's get out of this storm before you catch your death."

Siegfried said nothing but followed me up into the steam. Horses are more conversant. He reached the shelter in silence, where both of us put down our burdens and stood staring longingly at the wonderful warmth of the bathing pool.

"Are you going in first, or am I?" I finally asked.

Siegfried said nothing, but sat down blue and pinch-lipped, which was an acquiescence I was too cold to quibble with.

"Why don't you get under the bear rug," I said. "I won't be long."

He did so, actually muffling his head away from me as I stripped. My first dive under the blessed water loosened the flowers in my hair, and I tossed them from me, feeling their foolishness and no longer able to hear their enticing little songs.

When I had laid my dress out to dry and was ready to come out, the problems increased, for he had taken his half of the bearskin along with him in the boat, and it had been lost at sea. The raging storm had settled a sort of gloom like twilight over our house through which the steam wandered like clots of buttermilk. I couldn't see my companion very well in this light. I could barely hear him over the gale when he slipped into the pool.

I couldn't see him, but conjured before my eyes was the vision I'd had of him as we'd studied each other over the bow of his wrecked boat. I saw the frenzy into which the wet drove his curls, the ice blue of his eyes, his beard as thin and lanky as he was, hardly concealing the few blemishes that sprouted here and there amongst it and declared him to be so much younger and more vulnerable than he usually seemed. Under his arms, the hair was downy like eider nests. There were his legs, sturdy like timbers we so lacked in this place, rough with the sandy redness he had all over, soft with the blond moss of his hair, further roughened yet made vulnerable by the goose bumps of his battle with the sea. His woolen tunic clung to the slab of his chest, the pectorals holding it still up off his stomach, and they heaved with the heavy panting of his exertions.

I shook the vision from me. There was great danger here, a danger of magic that required magic to counteract. I filled a finger with the end of my month's blood and drew a rune of protection on the blade of Gram. Then I sang:

"And now the fifth rede:
As fair as you see
Brides on the bench abiding.
Let not love's silver
Rule over your sleeping;
Draw no woman to kind kissing.

"The eight rede that I give you:
Unto all ill look you,

And hold your heart from all beguiling;
Draw to you no maiden,
No man's wife bewray you,
Urge them not unto unmet pleasure."

I laid the sword beside me under the bearskin. After a long, long while, I heard Siegfried get out of the water. He seemed to have put it off as long as he could, perhaps until he thought I was asleep. It didn't take long, however, for the corners of the wind that broke in on us to bite the warmth of his soaking, and I could hear the violence of his shivers.

"Come on," I spoke into the gloom, giving him, I think, a start. "My half of the rug is still large enough to give some cover to the both of us. I have put a spell on the sword Gram, and it will lie as surety thus between us."

Siegfried said nothing, but entered gratefully. It was quite some time before the jerks of his chill subsided, though I willed the warmth of my body in his direction. When the chill did subside, I felt another wave of danger from him I didn't know whether my magic was strong enough to ward off or not. I fought it the best way I knew.

"Why did you take your bearskin just for a little fishing trip?" I asked, my voice rough with anger.

"I went for no little fishing trip." The gloom seemed to have power to loosen his tongue a little. "I meant to leave this land of ice forever."

"You would leave without me?" I blurted it without considering what weaknesses this might show in my carefully constructed defenses.

He said, "You left without me."

And I realized that he was right. There was no defense to this reproach, and I couldn't explain my reason for going off so suddenly. So I said nothing.

Presently Siegfried broke the silence. The slowness of his speech betrayed a great labor in the words as if he were a craftsman and they were a filigree over which he had worked long hours. "I figured," he said, "that a great <u>dís</u> like you, a great divine woman—I figured that you were present in my life just long enough to save me, to teach me how to live in this place on skua eggs and seaweed and hot springs, and that once I had learned these things, I was on my own again. I figured that you had gone back to Aesgard or Valhalla or wherever it was you came from. I assumed I was free to go if my poor mortal skills could figure out how to accomplish it. I see I have disturbed you again and had to be saved by divine intervention once more. I hope this is the last time. I'm not the hero I thought I was, I guess."

He fell into a clumsy silence. It was a very long silence during which each of us listened for the other's breath and tried to keep our own deep and even, keep it from betraying too much about us.

At last Siegfried slept. I realized I myself could not sleep until I took Gram between my legs and released myself. The rub of rough red rock on my bare skin was painful, but the release was delicious. I climaxed three times and could easily have done it three times more, but then it seemed by the breathing next to me that Siegfried was not asleep. He seemed to be awake, listening, thinking—Odin knew what. Quietly I replaced the blade between us, turned my back on both of them, and eventually went to sleep.

chapter 6

OME MORNING AND THE GALE'S death, we could better assess our situation. The gale had washed the water-logged bearskin up on shore. It was impossible to get it to revive its former softness, and no amount of beating and rinsing in clear water would rid it of all the sand and salt. But it was warm and serviceable, and would prevent the close discomforts of another night such as the one we'd just been through.

With the rest of the stores, we were not so fortunate. All the dried meat was gone, back to the sea from whence it had come. The two jugs of rendered oil alone had not washed overboard, but in preparation for his journey, Siegfried had dumped the emptier of the two out and refilled it with fresh water. I could tell he was cursing himself silently for this move, so I didn't bother to heap more curses on him. Certainly, it had been the most reasonable thing to do when he had thought the repairs would hold and escape was possible.

There were still the skuas, guillemots and their nests on the cliffs. The eggs were hatching now, and the little chicks, when they had plumped out a bit, would be easy enough to catch—and sometimes the adults could be caught in the net stretched across their nests when they returned from fishing. The puffins were nesting and, even as adults, flew clumsily. At low tide there were sometimes shellfish and always seaweed. I found that the moss that overran the place was edible, and patches of tall angelica, or wild celery, could be found shooting over it. The purple stalks, the tender leaves, the crunchy, piquant seeds—all were edible. Most nourishing of all were the roots, bolder and earthier than the leaves, eaten fresh in slices dipped in a little of the great fish's oil, or boiled and mashed with the same and a sprinkling of the seeds on top.

Then I took Siegfried inland to the river I'd encountered on my wander. It was teeming with great fat silver salmon, trout, and red-bellied char, which he had no difficulty catching with some line unraveled from the net and a hook spared from the shipwreck baited with young skua flesh. The salmon was not as flavorful as it might have been, which made me judge, although I had no setting sun to go by, that the season must be getting on into summer. It boiled up nice enough in our cooking spring and dried well on the giant fish's rib bones. Sometimes, when we were lucky and found some driftwood, we even roasted some fresh, eking out the wood with a little heath. There was never any wood suitable for repairing a boat, however.

It seemed that both Siegfried and I were more loath to let each other out of sight than we were before—before when I, at least, had daily wished he would just pack up that leaky boat of his and be gone. I spent lots of time sitting beside him on the banks of the salmon stream, sometimes with a hook of my own, sometimes with no excuse at all. He was no more communicative than before. And when I was near him, the countryside fell silent for me as well. Sometimes I would wander off on my own for half an afternoon or more just to hear something speak, even if it was only runes conjured by a wind across the boulder-strewn meadow in my mind.

One day I came back and pointed out to Siegfried the tall cone mountain in the distance that had been at the center of my solitary conversations. The cloud of smoke on its crest seemed larger than usual. "A giant must live in that mountain," I mused. "He is fuming with some sort of hidden anger."

Siegfried looked where I pointed but didn't seem inclined to argue with me or to agree. That was all of our speech together for that day.

Nearly three weeks passed. We began to see sunrises and sunsets, and I knew summer was going. We had followed the salmon far up the stream, ever closer to the smoking giant in his mountain, as far as we could reasonably go and still return to our shelter before it was dark. The fish were thinning out now, and we hadn't dried as much as we should have. I hoped they might return after spawning far inland, but I couldn't be sure. How were we to pass winter in this land where even summer had been difficult and not free of ice?

And a more immediate question loomed. Soon would come my moon time again, and then how would I handle it without losing my companion?

Then came the day when Siegfried and I were sitting on the bank of the stream, side by side. The surrounding countryside was a gentle tapestry of broad valleys and boggy upland moors, breeding land for the purple loosestrife and the white-blooming grass called Baldur's Brow, named for that God's beauty spread like sheets to bleach in the sun. And, of course, innumerable bothersome midges. Siegfried scowled silently into the water where his line vanished, but I got the impression it was a studied concentration.

I had just about determined that the first fish he took I would volunteer to carry back to the racks and cut up for drying immediately. I could tell my time was going to begin any moment, and that seemed as good an excuse for temporary escape as any. Only Siegfried hadn't caught a single fish yet. I would have dropped a line of my own if I thought it would help, but we hadn't even seen a sign of one.

Then, all of a sudden, the earth shook itself beneath us. It was more violent, if possible, than the previous time, and certainly lasted longer. It seemed an eternity that the rocks bucked and rolled beneath us, more than the most spirited horse I'd ever tamed in the corrals of Valhalla. There was time for me to turn to Siegfried and cling to him compulsively. He returned the embrace. Although it meant that he lost line and hook, at the moment it seemed that the world would end, and things like fish line and hooks were needless vanities. Great boulders shook themselves out of the stream bank and thundered into the stream. The earth itself thundered and billowed, as insubstantial yet as menacing as clouds before a gale.

Finally, the motion subsided. I extracted myself from Siegfried's arms and tried to recover some composure, if not dignity. But I could not help exclaiming when I had recovered my voice: "What in the name of all the Gods was that?"

"I thought you knew," said Siegfried. "I assumed you knew."

"How should I know about such a horrible thing as that?"

"Well, it's happened before, here in this land of yours."

"Yes. I remember. When we had just pulled your floundering boat from the waves."

"You didn't say anything so I assumed—"

"You didn't say anything, either. You never say anything." I stopped accusing and added, "Assumed what?"

"That you knew what it was. Indeed, that you had called it up, whatever it was, because I had dared to stare at you too long. I couldn't help it. I mean, here you had come, divinely, just when I needed you most to save the boat. And you sang it to you with the power of your voice, and you stood there with your white dress all clingy wet to you and this crown of poppies and heather all tangled in your braids, and I couldn't—I couldn't look away until you reprimanded my presumption with a good, divine shaking."

I had taken away my hands, but Siegfried had not taken away his. The memories he conjured, indeed, drew them up into my hair to touch where the flowers had been. I got up and moved quickly away, although my knees were still shaking so much that I could hardly walk, and my shoulders and head where he had touched them burned as if scalded.

"Yes, yes, I remember that," I said sharply, angry at having to make the next confession, "but I had nothing to do with that."

"You didn't? What about the other time?"

"What other time?"

"The first time. When I first braved the steam and discovered you lying there under the bearskin asleep on the rock. With your helmet and brynie on."

"I . . . I don't remember any of that." Another maddening confession.

"Well, I thought you were a man. I thought, 'My prayers are

answered.' I'd been so alone, you see, since … since Alberich betrayed me. All my life, actually, for he was never much company. I'd been so alone, you see, and praying—only I even felt abandoned by the Gods, Alberich's Celtic Gods being as dark and inhospitable as he was, and me a stranger to the gods of my own race. So perhaps it couldn't be called praying, but just holding a thought in my heart so dearly that every waking action was colored by its urge. I was praying for a hero to come and be my companion, someone who was my equal and worthy to join me in my exploits, in my life.

"'Here he is,' I thought when I saw you. 'Kept under some evil spell which I must only learn to break. So I pulled back the bearskin, cut the laces of your brynie when the leather was too brittle to untie, and took off your helmet. And there all this lovely red-golden hair fell out, and beneath the brynie I saw … saw that you were a woman, not a man. And then the earth moved, and I knew I must not presume any more. I guess I dropped my sword there, where I was, and as soon as the ground had regained its stability, I retraced my steps down to the shore. There it was that I saw the great breathing fish. 'Thrown up from the sea by the rumbling earth,' I decided, and I understood that you were my salvation, but not—not the companion I had hoped for. For what companionship can there be with the mortal and the divine?"

I thought furiously about this long speech of his in silence for a while. But I did not dare to look at him looking at me as I did so.

"It is Odin who shakes the earth," I finally declared, "Odin who is divine. He has set Thor to battle the giants of the underground with his mighty hammer at just these times in order to keep us from …"

I didn't complete the sentence, but walked off further, walking quickly to bring forth some thoughts up in a hurry and trample down others. I walked and walked, back and forth, still in confusion and not a little afraid.

Suddenly I heard Siegfried's footsteps behind me. I turned to him with part joy, part anticipation, part apprehension. But I quickly saw that what had been consuming my thoughts had been the furthest from his, shaken from him by the acts of a God.

"Look! Look!" he shouted, his gaze not on me where I had hoped for it, but firmly fixed above and beyond. "The giant in the mountain," he exclaimed. "The giant! His hall is on fire! Thor has driven him back and torched his hall!"

And so indeed it was. The cloud above the mountain had suddenly become orange-red. And as we watched, lightning ignited in that cloud as from a thunderstorm. The mountain coughed once, twice, then I lost track of the number of times. With each cough, like a man in the final throes of the coughing sickness, he coughed up blood-red clots of rock and flame. But rather than growing weaker with the loss as a dying man does, the mountain seemed to gain strength instead.

And then, even as we watched, the earth shook beneath our feet once more with a horrible shudder, and one whole side of the mountain split from foot to crown. Out of this wound—such a wound as only the greatest heroes of sagas are credited with—a great torrent of blood burst forth and thundered straight down towards us.

Siegfried caught my hand and pulled me back to him. But the earth shook again, and we stumbled down together in a heap. We stayed where we fell, too struck with fear or with wonder at the spectacle to move. Eventually we did move, only to be knocked off our feet again.

We never did make it back to our "house" that day, perhaps because we realized we would be no safer there with our backs to the mountain than where we were facing it head on. The fury to which we were witnesses occupied the whole island in any case, perhaps the whole mid-earth and Aesgard as well, as far as we could tell. So, there we sat for a day and a night and a day.

There was a time when the stream of mountain-giant blood crossed our salmon river, and the river bubbled at our feet and poached the salmon for us. I remember nightfall, the sunset in the west being nothing to the sun that continued to burn there in the north. Even in the darkest point of the night, it cast Siegfried's face in a coppery glow which I dared to touch, afraid it might be melting. He clasped the hand there and leaned the hair of his cheek into it, but he did not return my gaze. I tried to say something, but there was too much noise, so I thought it better not to try. We didn't talk, we didn't sleep.

We sat and watched and merely turned our heads when we could watch no more. Even when we looked away, the heat and the roars as of all of Hel's hounds told us that there was no relief.

And then the river of burning mountain blood could be seen rolling down on us, and it was time to move. The blood river was moving faster than a man can run, as fast as a good horse. The heat from it was scorching, blackening everything it touched and sending little puffs of fire into the meadow grass wherever it passed. But we managed to keep to the high ground, and it followed the low, humping and rolling over itself like some live creature. I wanted to ask Siegfried if this was anything like his dragon, but we were not speaking. The earth itself was doing all the talking that could be done.

Then all at once, I scurried one way to high ground, Siegfried another, and a branch of the blood river unrolled itself quickly between us.

"Brynhild!" I heard Siegfried shout over the creature's roar.

He approached the thing without fear—much as he may have done the dragon, I imagine—and plunged in his dagger. The creature was black and smoking on the outside, inside red as blood, the same as had been the breathing fish we had found. But the dagger had even less effect here. Siegfried pulled his hand away only slowly.

I could feel the heat from where I was and gave a little shout of warning. His hand should have been instantly full of angry burn blisters, but he seemed to react only to my reaction, not to pain. The dagger stuck in the beast's flesh and was carried on and away with no stopping it.

Only then did Siegfried back away from the air that oppressed the lungs.

"Never mind!" I tried to console him, but consoling works better when it doesn't have to be shouted. I don't think he caught every word over the earth's roar, but gestures served. "Let's keep in sight and follow this to the sea."

So we did. And when we did, great was the battle raging between fire and water. Lumps of fire dropped off the rocks into the sea like honey into brewing mead, and the ocean hissed and roared in anger and in pain. The mountain blood cooled and formed more stones, along which more blood curled, farther and farther out to sea. There was a bank of steam at their collision point at the furthest edge of sight.

We discovered the hilt of his dagger, permanently embedded in the hardening flow carried almost to the sea. But the blade itself had vanished, melted in a twinkling in what was hotter than the hottest forge.

And then I slept. Clouds from the mountain had turned day to night, so it was difficult to tell how much time had passed. I could not have slept until the fury was over, so I assume I slept as soon as it was over, but neither point do I remember. When I awoke, it was to Siegfried's voice on the unaccustomed calm. I found myself covered all over with a fine grey dust that got in the eyes and crunched between the teeth. Siegfried was likewise brushing the dust from himself and calling across the still-smoking blood. "Brynhild? Are you all right?"

"I'm fine. And you?"

He said he was fine. He did not favor his hand, as I thought surely he must.

"I think it's over," he said.

"Yes, it seems to be."

"And the blood seems to be cooling a little, to a hard, black stone."

"In places."

"I'm going to try and cross it and come to you."

"No, don't."

"The boat's on that side too."

"The steam house is on yours."

"The boat looks unharmed, from what I can tell, although the waves got pretty high, what with the thrashing of the ground and all. Yes, I think I'll try here."

"No, Siegfried, please don't try it. The blood is still smoking in too many places, and the rocky parts of it seem too weak to hold."

"I'm not afraid to try."

"Well, then take some of my fear for you."

"You, Brynhild, fear?"

"Call it second sight if you will. Wait another day at least," I said and began to clamber up away from the beach.

"But where are you going?" Siegfried jogged parallel and easily kept up with me. If I turned my back to him, I could have run faster, but I wanted to avoid that at all cost. "I'll be back."

"Don't go away again."

"You, Siegfried, afraid?" I said slyly. "Don't be. It will be no longer than last time. And I will return, I promise. Wait for me, please."

"Where are you going? To the mountain? If you're going to fight the giant now while he sleeps, now while he is wounded, I must go too. I will not have you fight him alone."

"If there is such heroism to be done, believe me, I would want you along. But now you must not come. It is … it is magic, not heroism."

I turned my back on him.

"Brynhild, you are hurt. I see blood there on your skirt."

"Believe me, it is nothing. It is only part of the magic, love."

That stopped him dead in his tracks, whether it was the mention of magic—or the other word. "I see," he said. "You bleed as the mountain bled—and will tame it so. I see … my love."

I was only too glad to get out of his sight. But it was more than the coming of my womanhood, an event that left a telltale trail across the countryside that once had been so many colors but was now only a feeble, choking grey. On my side of the mountain's flow, where Siegfried himself could not see and which now would be cinders like everything else, I had caught a glimpse of what looked to have been the unhewn trunk of a tree. The bark could still be seen on it in some places. Though fire-blackened, it was not wave-battered. Where there was one trunk, there might be more. I had only to follow the cooling flow inland during my quiet time alone.

chapter 7

N THE SECOND DAY, IN a little pocket where the warm sea breezes were caught and cuddled, I found them. A stand of scraggly white-barked birches, scragglier now that the stream of fire had burned a swath through them, entombing a good third of their area in impervious black stone and scorching another good swath to either side. The black on white made a skeletal contrast. Most of the trees were mere bushes only, coming to my shoulder, if there. But interspersed among them was the lower growth of wild geranium in purple bloom. And some of the trunks remaining after the holocaust were tall enough to deserve the name "tree."

I set Gram to the two biggest trunks that were left. Indeed, they were not very big, but they were straight, and I couldn't carry more than two.

It took much longer to drag the trees back than it did to find them. Most of the leaves and branches wore off as I carried just the heavy trunks, one under each arm. But on the sixth day, I stopped to rinse out my dress in the fire-altered course of our river and put it on wet, as any rock I set it on to dry would leave it grimy with ash. I hoped to find more flowers, but there were none. They were likewise buried under ash. Now I approached our very familiar territory.

I saw that Siegfried, too, had counted the days. He was watching inland and saw me coming from afar. He waved and began to lope towards me, the stream of fire-blood now just one vein of congealed rock among so many others. Then he saw what I was dragging and began to run.

When he reached me, he caught the timber from me—caressed it, embraced it, exclaimed and wondered over it. When I attempted by a word or two to gain a little of the same for me, I got none of it, only that same little half-smile and that glance away.

Siegfried carried both logs the rest of the way at a pace with which I was hard-pressed to keep up. He took no thought to join me for rest or refreshment at the shelter but brought the logs straight to his boat. There he paused briefly to rub his hand. I knew he wasn't hurt, just missing his dagger.

"Use the sword," I said, pulling it out of the belt I had improvised of long grass and handing it to him.

He took it and looked away, half smiling. Then he rubbed his hand again, as if performing an act of magic. There must be truth in his tale of dragon blood on the skin, for anyone else coming so close to such heat would have lost the hand. Was I a fool not to sense Odin nearby?

And that was the last pause Siegfried took. I went about our old round of tasks—hauling seaweed, setting traps, fishing, preparing food, soaking in the bath—but I did them alone. I even slept in the shelter alone, so loathe was Siegfried to leave his task as long as there was any light to work by. He slept by the boat if he slept at all, and I carried food down to him where he would stain his new wood with fingerprints of fish oil rather than set it down even to eat.

Sometimes, when I ran out of things to do or could do some of them sitting down, I would sit beside the boat and watch. I could see she was of blonde oak with a keel plank. She was a good little boat in spite of the damage she had sustained—five planks on a side in her pristine condition, the planks clinker-built and fastened together with iron nails. She had a gunwale, was propelled by oars, and steered by means of a larger oar suspended as a rudder from the stern. The row-locks, affixed to the gunwale, were reversible, handy for quick changes of direction in an impetuous sea.

I watched how Siegfried split long, smooth planks from the birch trunks, how he cut them to size, planed them with Gram's edge, and forced them, dampened between rocks, to take on the curve he wanted. I watched him groove the planks so that each overlapped its neighbor with water-tightness, how he fashioned wooden pins from the scraps of wood and burned holes for them with a smoky fire made on a few of the shavings and a firm twig. He used tendons from the great fish for the binding, which would swell when wet to prove a waterproof seal. It would also give some of the beast's sea worthiness to the craft, although I noticed Siegfried used no runes or other magic over the work. Then I watched as he used the last of the breathing-fish oil to pitch her.

Siegfried was silent in his concentration. The only sound of life was his hammering and scraping and the birdcalls like laughter. I turned my face into the tear-smarting wind and heard that wild laughter. If one were to be here alone, I thought, with nothing but that sound for company, she would very shortly go mad.

In all of two days, he was done. The birch stood out on the better oak like a sore thumb on Siegfried's hand—if he'd been capable of having such an injury—but the work seemed solid, and Siegfried was pleased. The next day he took her out for her maiden run. He was gone most of the day and returned with the hull full of deep-sea cod, which he expected me to gut and clean all by myself with my restored but clumsy-as-ever Gram while he rested from the effort. I found myself a sliver of razor-sharp obsidian and used that instead, hanging the fish splayed and flat from the rib bones like so many white bats. I was unable to keep myself from thinking all the while, *He could have done as much himself.*

The next day it rained, sheets of sleet on my drying cod.

The next day, it cleared, but Siegfried puttered. At least, that's what it seemed like to me. They were just little tasks that occupied him: filling the jugs with water and setting them in the hull, going over every inch of his work again as if the first time had been clobbered together by a child, giving each sliver the attention of a mighty oak.

That evening—and night was falling ever earlier these days—he sat winding and rewinding his fishing twine. He meant to take that along with him as well. There'd be no fishing and no trapping without that twine.

"It should be clear again tomorrow," he said.

His voice startled me. I don't think he'd said two words together since I'd returned with the wood. I'd been getting used to the idea of him rowing off without a word, without a backwards glance and only an infuriating half-smile.

"Yes," I said, not bothering to justify that self-evident comment with more.

"I should be going."

"Yes."

"I mean, the season's getting late. Any later, and the danger of storms will grow too great."

"Yes."

The sky certainly seemed clear enough. I looked up to it rather than to the shadowy bulk of the man sitting on what had become "his" rock across from me. The sky seemed more fathomable. The stars were brilliant. The frosty bright toe of Orvandel, the giant eyes of Thaissi, Freya's shimmering necklace, and the Small Bear—sacred to those of us who claim a bear totem. But there was no sign of the big one. This confirmed Siegfried's observation of how far the summer was advanced. And the North Star was there, too, the axle through which the entire mill of the universe turned, grinding out Fate. It was so high in the sky that I could see it even as we sat facing the pounding ocean to the south, reconfirming just how far north I was, how harsh the winter was likely to be here, how far I was from anything I knew—how lonely.

"Brynhild?" The sound of his voice in the darkness made me feel the loneliness already.

"Yes?"

"What are ...?"

"What?"

"What are those scars on your back?"

For all the dark, I could feel his eyes on me as if he could see both through the dark and my dress as well. How often had they been so, when I was in the warm bath, when my back was turned, when he had feigned indifference. His eyes burned, more painful than when the bear's claws had first sunk into that flesh.

"It is nothing."

"Tell me."

"It was a long time ago."

He didn't say anything, but the silence seemed to plead again, *Tell me. Just before I go.*

"A bear," I said. "That's all."

"A *bear*," he repeated in wonder and disbelief. "Was that the skin I cut?"

"Yes."

"You shared with me?"

"Never mind."

"I'm sorry. I will leave both pieces with you. I'm—"

"Never mind. It was a long time ago. In a different life."

We fell silent again, as silent as the night between us. There was no sign of a storm, and the sun had set as blushingly pink as one could hope. Still there was something in the air full of anticipation, very like the charge before a storm when, on a hot summer's day, tinder-dry grass could burst into flame of its own accord if Thor the Thunderer but glanced at it.

And suddenly, there burst a great streak of green across half the velvety sky. Had it been lightning, it would have vanished just as quickly, leaving a smell of sulfur in the air. But this light lingered, lingered, lingered, then grew like the blooming of a bud. It waved through the sky like a hero's banner, like the skirt of a dancing girl. And as if that skirt were made of diaphanous silk of the rarest sort, colors shot up and down it as she danced in torchlight. Mostly the light it caught was green, every shade of green from the pale yellow of young leaves to the deepest forest moss. But also, near the top, there danced reds and purples and every flashing, flickering mixture of those colors in between.

Only half knowing what I did, I slipped my hand over Siegfried's where it rested on his knee. This was a wonder made all the more wonderful because it was shared, because his presence and equally silent awe assured me that I was not going mad. No one I could ever describe this sight to would believe me, having never seen it themselves. Or, if they did, they could not begin to imagine it in all its almost oppressive wonder. I touched because my hand ached to touch. I only resented that at some place long distant in time and space I might not touch that hand in that same way again or whisper but a brief, "Do you remember …?" and recall the whole thing to our minds and so give it reality again.

But suddenly, I had more to regret than that. For first, I felt Siegfried's knuckles grow tense beneath mine. Then they jerked away as if I had burned him like more mountain blood. I tried to turn my attention to the sky's glorious display, but though my eyes were open and staring, I could not. Neither, it seemed, could Siegfried. After a moment, he gave up all pretense and bowed his head. In another, he shuddered as if I were still too close for comfort. I was debating whether or not it would be better if I got up and moved away when he beat me to it. He walked clear down until the ocean licked his ankles and watched—or didn't watch—the sky until the lights faded, and only the unchanging stars remained, winking down impassively.

With a heavy heart, I went up into the shelter. Sometime later, Siegfried joined me there. I think he must have thought me already asleep, for as he shuffled under his half of the bearskin, he murmured, as if hoping only he would hear, "This is indeed a place of wonders. What must the hero be like who may be granted the privilege to enjoy such things forever?"

There was a gruffness in his voice that made me think he had been crying. I tried to match his murmur when I mused, "And what must the heroine be like who can ever win release from such a place of lonely banishment?"

"Brynhild?" I heard him sit up.

"What?"

"Why … why do you send me away?"

"I don't send you away."

"You are willing to battle a giant to win logs from him to send me on my way. You provide me with logs, lend me the sword, dry fish for provisions, everything I need to leave."

"You want to leave. I find you what you want. It is my consuming concern—and unfathomable."

"You don't need me to protect you. Like no other woman I've ever met. You can kill a bear and think nothing of it. You don't need me. If only I could tell what would make you happy."

"It would make me happy … if I could please you. But that seems impossible. You, as I, seem condemned by the Gods never to be happy."

There was a pause. Then he said, "It would please me to stay here forever."

"While I think only to leave."

"Leave *me*," he interpreted with a sigh.

"Break the spell," I insisted.

There was another pause. "If you please, if it doesn't distress you too much to be with me, I would like to stay."

"And be likewise under Odin's curse? I think it would be better if we both tried to leave and so break it."

"Then shall we attempt it tomorrow?" he said in disbelief, "You and me together?"

"Siegfried," I said, impatience snapping in my words, "Siegfried, why do you persist in thinking I don't want to be with you?"

"Because the earth quakes. Mountains blow up. The sky dances with light."

"That is Odin, not me."

"You are of Odin—or something even more divine."

"I was. Are you afraid?"

"Not—not of Odin.

"If you are to help me fly from this place, you must defy Odin."

"I don't fear Odin, I assure you. Alberich used to curse me because he said I fear nothing."

Alberich. The name was familiar. But wasn't that the name of all dwarfish Celts?

Heedless, Siegfried went on. "I didn't fear his Gods because they supported so small and petty a man as he. But he taught me that Odin was no more than he, so I never learned to respect Odin either."

"Then you fear nothing, indeed. You are the one he said would come—"

"But it seems I do fear."

"If you don't fear Odin, you fear nothing and can break the spell."

"But I do fear. I fear *you*."

I laughed out loud. "*Me?* I am nothing to fear. I am a woman, a woman under a curse."

"I have not known any women. Alberich taught me that all women have magic that would weaken me. He taught me how my own mother abandoned me."

"Did your mother abandon you?"

"She died when I was born. Alberich said it was because she preferred death to mothering me. When he was having difficulty mothering me. Since then, that is all my life—my experience with the women I have met has been that either they are too fragile, so that I fear they may break if I come close—or they are too simpering, so that it grates on my nerves and offends my heroic spirit when I do so. Or they have laughed at me for, truth to tell, my manners are those of a dwarf, and I have never learned any others."

"You fear I will break?"

"No, not at all. I have seen plainly that you will not. You are like no woman I have ever known. Always, before, it was easy to leave them, and now it seems to me that I fear only one thing, and that is that I must go out into the world again—without you."

"Some people would call that fear 'love.'"

"Would they so?"

"Indeed."

"Is it?"

"Oh, I'm not the one to ask about that. Ask the Goddess Freya. Or better yet, ask your own heart."

"You're laughing at me." As he said this, I could almost see the sideways turn of his head and the ironic half-smile that had so annoyed me. And certainly, for all the dark I saw it clearly for what it was, a defense against the only thing on earth he did fear, and that was the laughter of the strange creatures he knew so little about and which he called women.

"No, Siegfried. If I laugh, it is at myself. Because I have begun to ask myself that same question about my feelings for you."

"Have you? Brynhild, *have you?*"

I had to laugh at his earnestness. "Yes."

"Brynhild, just then, when you touched my hand, on the beach with the lights—"

"Yes," I said, tears suddenly flushing my eyes, for I knew now that my wish to always have that spectacle to share had a chance of being answered. Sharing was not all a giving thing.

"Then, I wanted so much to … It was like something I've been yearning for all my life. Like something my mother left without telling me. Something …"

I could tell he was fumbling in the dark towards me. So I began to reach for him as well.

We both touched Gram at the same moment. I felt as much as heard him suddenly withdraw before the sword.

"But there is your rune," he said. "I know it is of great power. I respect it."

"Well, it is easy enough to do away with …," I began to say.

Then I, too, stopped with a sudden *respect*, shall I call it? Certainly, I had this serious consideration: was it Siegfried's very guilessness and innocence that might be my undoing? Where he could not win me by force, is this how Odin meant to accomplish his curse on me? Once I lost my maidenhead, there would be no strength left in me for anything save the simpering fragility of the rest of the women of this world that had so disgusted Siegfried. Then I should be abandoned on this island for certain. No. Much as my heart, nay, all my body in a way I had never thought possible before, yearned for this man—I knew I must get out of banishment first. Then? Well, then it would be as my Fate was written.

"There is nothing I would rather, Siegfried, than to remove this rune for you. But now, now I think—if we are to set off on this great journey in the morning—I think now we both must sleep."

"Yes," Siegfried agreed.

But we didn't sleep. At first light, we thought it best to abandon the pretense, so we packed up the last of our belongings and stepped out of the shelter of steam for the last time. Thus, we left that world of wonders for someone else to discover, wild and uninhabited as it was, and shoved the little boat off into the endless ocean. The rising sun seemed to form a bridge of dappled light across the waves that we could travel on eastward without even getting our feet wet.

chapter 8

"HE SETTLED LANDS ARE TO the east, about ten days over open sea," Siegfried told me.

"Open sea?" I repeated. "You mean, there is no sign of land for all that time?"

"None," he said. "There is a current that will help."

His nonchalance did much to impress me with his personal heroism to have come so far to find me, but it did little to give me confidence in myself for the return trip as the last of our strange little home sank below the horizon. Now there was nothing but a few thin slats of wood between us and the deep, a few thin slats through which I could feel the hungry smack of every wave.

Siegfried seemed fearless enough. "It will help to row as much as we can, however."

At this word, I set to rowing with the spare oars with the best of frenzied wills.

"The open ocean requires a different technique," he told me as our oars almost instantly collided.

"It is not my stroke that is at fault," I sulked, "but the oarlocks that are too close together."

"Not at all. It is necessary to keep both our weight and the weight of all our cargo as close amidships as possible. You could come closer still. It gives greater stability. Now the stroke, short but powerful." I tested it, and he said, "No, shorter still."

"But there is no pull from the follow-through with such a stroke."

"Gliding as one does on a river or lake loses its usefulness, particularly in the confused seas caused when the waves resound off skerries and reefs. Many short, strong pulls—say, three or four to every one an inland rower makes—that's the best way to deal with things out here. There, yes! Only more, quicker!"

Sheepishly, I discovered he was right. Then I lost all sheepishness as I pulled to his call, and we went faster, faster, until it seemed we were fairly skimming over the face of the ocean. The gunwales rose by half a board above the wave.

"Yes, faster!" Siegfried cried, laughing with exhilaration.

A full board rose above the water line. The lighter prow met each wave high with a bend and crack and easy, quick return. It seemed we were flying over the water. Suddenly a horrible sound came from under the hull as if we had dragged on a pebbly beach.

"No, no," Siegfried called as my stroke floundered. "Keep it up. That noise is nothing. It just means there is now air mixed with the water under us. It makes us skim even faster, almost as fast as birds through air. You'll know when we start going too fast. The gunwales will shake. There is no danger until then."

I worked to get the stroke right again, and then we pulled—up past the skimming, up until the gunwales did indeed begin to shake.

"Terrific!" Siegfried cried, and I bloomed in his praise. "I only managed to reach that once or twice on the way out here by myself. Drop her down just a bit, and we can keep her just below that point all the way."

We rowed, sometimes three, sometimes four hours at a stretch, over a sea as calm and flat as a girl-child's chest. Then we spelled each other, one pulling while the other tended fishing lines. But mostly we talked.

First, I had to explain how it came about that I won Odin's ill favor and the curse of the sleep thorn. And when I came to tell about how I had taken the queen of the Goths off and hidden her with the dwarves when her husband died, Siegfried stopped me.

"Alberich did you say the Celt's name was?"

"Something like that."

"But that was the name of the dwarf who raised me. Was the name of the woman Signy?"

"It was. Signy Volsungsdaughter."

"She was my mother. I never knew she was a queen. Then you are the one who saved her life, who allowed me to be born."

"I don't see how that's possible."

"It was a maid of Odin who brought my mother to the place."

"But was it such a place, a forge in a dark hollow?"

"Exactly."

"There must be some mistake."

"I know the place like the back of my hand. I grew up there." And he proceeded to relate so many details about the hovel and the twisted old man we found living there that, though I had no memory of three quarters of them, it did indeed seem to be the very same place, the very same stunted little man.

"So tell me, please, about my mother."

"I don't remember much about Signy Volsungsdaughter, to tell the truth."

"Tell me what you know."

"She was tall, fair. Very brave, although bravery seemed not something that came naturally to her, but something she had had to learn. And very determined to have her own way."

Siegfried was taking a rest from rowing now because with me he could. He sat to face me, smiled his little half-smile again, but met my eyes when he did so. "Something like you, I should say."

I didn't like the idea that I should be so much older than he, that I could have been his midwife—or his mother. I certainly didn't feel that we were anything but within a very few years of each other. Siegfried, for his part, gave this idea not a second thought. If anything, this connection seemed to make me, in his mind, something that had been missing in his life, the mother he had never known but longed for so desperately. But because I was not really so, and only a surrogate, the one desire could feed another.

He let me take another pull on the oars, then smiled his little half-smile and said, "That is a powerful sleep thorn Odin has, isn't it?" That seemed to be his comment on the unbelievability of it all, and I took it as a compliment.

Then it was time for Siegfried to tell me his tale, how he had been raised by the hunched, dark dwarf whose language was his native tongue, but who made no secret of the fact that he hated anything tall and blond with a passion. Alberich had become all the more abusive, verbally when he could no longer dominate physically as Siegfried grew every day taller and blonder.

"I do believe he would have run me through with this very Balmung while I was yet in my cradle had he been able to reforge it. But he tried repeatedly and failed as many times. It became clear to him that there was a spell on the metal, and that mine were the only hands into which Fate had given the ability. He would have to nurture me until strength was mine, and then teach me his dark craft."

"So then you reforged Gram—or Balmung, as you say?"

"Yes."

"It should not have been possible."

Siegfried picked up the blade from where it lay gleaming bright on the dark of my bearskin and handled its keen, even weight.

"With my own eyes," I continued, "I saw Odin split it with his spear. What a God has sundered should not be able to be forged again."

"Actually, it was a one-eyed old man who taught me the trick."

"A one-eyed man?" My heart began to beat faster.

"Yes. Alberich had taught me all he knew, and it still wouldn't forge. And then, one day when the dwarf was out burning wood for charcoal, this stranger happened by and showed me just the way to twist the metal together under very high heat until it was as good as new. I could show you how I did it if we were at the forge now. Really, quite a neat little trick—"

"Did this stranger wear blue?"

"Yes, he did. Just the color of the sky. And he pumped those bellows while I worked, pumped them something fierce, as if there were some divinity in the wind of them."

"Divinity. Indeed, there was divinity. That was no stranger. That was the God."

"He was just an old man. Strong for a graybeard, but an old man just the same."

"So he seems to all but those who know him—those who know him all too well."

"He was gone before Alberich returned."

"Alberich knew Odin. Of course, he would be gone."

"Alberich would have recognized the Wanderer from my description and told me. Ah, but he hates Odin. It was Odin who conquered his people and drove them to the furthest corners of the earth. To Alberich he is no God. No God at all."

He looked at me expectantly. "Brynhild, why do you stop rowing? Are you tired? Of course, let me take a turn."

But I stopped Siegfried's hands from going to the oars. I suddenly found the simple rolling up one wave and down the next, helpless, doing nothing to try to change where the elements carried us, to be the most honest of existences. For a moment, any other was unthinkable.

Siegfried twisted his wrists around to catch my hands and held them fervently. But I pulled from him and turned away, longing for the embrace of the unrelieved expanse of deep instead.

"Brynhild, why do you turn away? What have I said or done?"

"I begin to dislike this business," I said, and a chill ran down my back.

"What? What business?"

"This. *This*, that I have let myself be drawn away by you."

"Brynhild?"

"You should have died, Siegfried. Odin wanted your uncles to be the last descendants of Volsung. He put a most dreadful curse on them. A great battle was fought—I participated in it before you were born—to wipe your family and its memory from the earth. I was condemned for disobeying orders at that battle. When I saved your mother, it should not have been done. It went against Odin's will."

"The will of a grouchy old man—"

"Gram was your undoing—supposed to be your undoing. Odin

named it that—"Angry"—and forged it in the first place just for that purpose. He cracked it and laid the curse on it. I begin to fear …"

"Brynhild, don't fear. As long as I am with you—"

"I begin to fear that Odin means to destroy me by the very means that I defied him. Somehow Gram found its way to *you*."

"Alberich always said my mother brought it with her, hidden in her bosom."

"I should have known about that."

"Not if she didn't trust you, as a servant of Odin."

"Not only have you reforged it, but Odin helped you do it. He knows you're alive but doesn't attempt to kill you."

"Just let the old fellow try it!"

"Siegfried, please!" I exclaimed as an extra high wave swept over the gunwale and left us ankle-deep in water I had to bend and bail. It was suddenly very important to me that I do so. The expanse of sea was suddenly terrifying. "Please don't tempt him. Not here, not now."

"I tell you, that old man doesn't scare me a bit. He may be clever, he may be cunning, he may even be something of a magician, but he is no God. Not what I look for when I look for a God. I'd sooner call myself a God."

"Siegfried," I pleaded.

"The old man can't hear us here."

"No? Look, there's a pair of his messenger ravens following in our wake."

"They are nothing, just birds."

"They watch us wherever we go. They overhear us and report back to him. They lead us to our doom."

"Perhaps we are only nearer to land than I imagined."

"Siegfried!"

"Very well, if it will put you more at ease, I'll keep such thoughts to myself."

"Please."

"But it can't keep me from thinking them."

"Still, don't you find it odd that he has conspired your demise, yet now allows you to live? Not only that, but helps you along your way?

Didn't you even tell me it was a one-eyed man in a wide-brimmed hat who pointed you in the direction of my sleeping rock?"

"You mean that was the same fellow who helped with the forging?"

"I'm sure of it."

"I suppose it might have been the same fellow, and now that I think about it, yes. But it hardly seems possible that such an old codger could be in such widely separate places—"

"He is the Wanderer, I tell you. He is a God. Who should know better than I?"

"So? And does this make you think twice about your choice to leave the island with me?"

"Yes. Yes, it does. Although Odin knows I had no choice. It wouldn't have taken me long to die all alone there in the natural Vanir course of things."

"Does it make you think twice about *me*, then?"

There was such potential for pain in his voice that I couldn't tell him the truth. "No. No, not at all," I said.

Perhaps he was able to sense the doubt that had grown in my voice, and this was the reason for his actions. At any rate, he dropped the oars at that moment and, with his hand that should have burned, fingered a gold ring he wore on his left hand. Perhaps he was deciding whether or not to toss it overboard and send it to the bottom of Aegir's realm, a snake-offering to the World Serpent whose thrashings under the deep gave rise to waves. I was strongly impressed that this golden image of a snake holding its tail would invoke that serpent's peace throughout our passing. But that seemed not to be his thoughts.

"This ring is part of the hoard," he said. "The only part I bothered to bring along."

Then he proceeded to tell me again how he had killed a dragon, bathed in its blood and left his booty—the dragon's hoard, in the care of certain friends of his, the princes of the Burgundians—while he went off in search of more heroism.

This detail of the Burgundians was new to me. "Is that young Giuki then?" I asked. "I fought a battle with him once—to my further grief."

"Giuki was the father of these princes," Siegfried said.

"So all my generation has moved on. What you say of the sleep thorn is true."

"Upon my life, it is," Siegfried said. "Giuki died in his bed of a fever. He was ashamed to do so and not in battle. He drew his sword with his last strength and tried to kill himself—*risting*, it is called. Rather that than to die like a woman."

So, did the strange threads of our former lives come to entangle us like so much seaweed as we rowed towards them.

chapter 9

"OOK!" I CRIED. "LAND!"

"We are three days still from possible landfall," Siegfried told me, yet he took up his oars to urge the boat at its skimming pace towards the thing we saw, whose great whiteness pierced the sea's even roll.

"It is a mountain," I said. "A mountain of ice."

"Ah, yes. There were many more such on my journey out in the spring. Little ones and some much, much bigger than this. I saw big ones birthing the little ones with a great plunging roar, like great cows calving."

"Shall we not go closer still?"

"It is no solid landing place, for all its looks," Siegfried said, beginning to backrow. "See how it moves along with the current, almost as fast as we can go. It could crush us to kindling in a moment."

"Gulls have found a happy home there."

"You and I are not gulls."

"Now I see others around it, little ones. Little sea hummocks. Like a great sheep with her lambs."

"Yes. Well, I think we should keep clear of such an enchanted, barren land."

We saw one or two floating mountains after that, but kept clear.

We also saw a number of the great beasts such as we had killed for meat that first day together on our island. Their broad, black backs would heave out of the water like nothing so much as yet other floating islands. And then water would spout from them as though each island was provided with a clear fountain of its own.

Our water began to go low, with two of us drinking what had served only one before.

"It would be nice if one of these beasts would stay on the surface for a while," I mused. "Let us cast ashore and test their streams for freshness."

Indeed, sometimes they did seem to stay above—following along in our wake for a space, eyeing us with the curiosity of children. "But can you imagine the destructiveness of a toddler of that size?" I commented.

Siegfried didn't know what a toddler was, and I had to explain. There were indeed some aspects of life about which he was wonderfully ignorant.

"But perhaps they have come seeking revenge for the one of their clan we killed," I said then. "Perhaps they can smell his fat on our planks."

"Perhaps," Siegfried said. "But I think you were right the first time. They are only curious. You see how they all leave us eventually and continue on to the south."

"Do they all go south?"

"Yes. Watch! See?"

"Do you suppose they are migrating to warmer waters for the winter, as birds do?"

"So they might."

We wondered at that marvel for a while, birds of such a size. The thought made us lay to our strokes all the more, for if such great beasts fled the coming onslaught of winter in this region, all the more should we. We continued to see the south-swimming beasts from time to time. We even gave them a name. We would say to each other, "There goes another wheel," commenting on the great rolling movement the creatures made as they surfaced. It gave some comfort to imagine them as swift-moving wheels carrying us in a cart over solid ground. "*Whal* is our word for 'wheel,'" I told him.

I remember another time when Siegfried had decided to settle himself down in the hull for a nap.

"What a luxury to do this," he said. He still attempted to keep his weight centered in the boat, even when he stretched out, which meant nestling his head against my knee and propping his long legs up in the stern. It was a good thing both of us never tried to sleep at once; there would hardly have been space. "Before, when I was alone," Siegfried continued. "I didn't attempt to sleep at all. Sometimes I would doze in spite of myself, but it was dangerous. It is nice to share such duties as keeping watch."

I bent over his head there on my knees and saw how the skin on his nose and cheeks was peeling from the glare of sun on sea and revealing the tender pink beneath. I knew my face was the same. I could feel the tight glow across the bridge of my nose and could see that my arms were peeling too. That peeling vulnerability on him made him seem so dear. I buried my head in his curls, reveling in how the salt spray released the masculine scent of his scalp. I was wonderfully happy, more than I had ever hoped to be again.

On the seventh day, a storm blew. It was not a bad one, thank Aegir, that watery God. Mostly what we got was a good and constant drizzle that obscured the horizon, followed by a wind that lifted white caps, but little more.

Come light the next day, the storm had settled into a dense fog. It was so thick that looking through it over the gunwale toward the end of the fishing line seemed as if peering through fragments of grey cheesecloth to the equally damp, grey sea. The fog was thick in the lungs and condensed around the nose and mouth in little droplets.

"It is best not to row when it gets like this," Siegfried said. "We have to be able to tell which direction we're going in, or we might row far off course. It is best to trust to the current."

I understood the reasoning for this, but it was maddening to be in such straits and to be able to do nothing for one's own salvation. Then I felt the dragon's heart rise in my throat, up to my brain, and it became a rune. Into the gunwale of the boat I cut the magic signs, marveling how suited they were to formation in such a pass, even by so clumsy a blade as Gram was in close quarters. And I sang,

I know a ninth rune: when need I have
To shelter my ship on the flood.
The wind it calms, the waves it smooths
And puts the sea to sleep.

When I could sing no more—and I dared not tax my throat too much, for there wasn't much water left in the bottom of the second jug to whet it on—I dozed. I awoke and dozed and woke again in a state that was as dense and without definition as the fog cloaking us on every side and giving us no sight at all to give us life. It was difficult to keep one's mind from drifting, from mixing real with unreal, night with day.

On what seemed to have been the second day, however, the last of the water trickled down our throats, Siegfried stirred me out of my stupor.

"What is it?" I asked, still groggy.

"Listen," he whispered.

I listened. My ears seemed full of fog.

"Listen," he repeated. "Surf."

He swung round, grabbed his oars, and began rowing towards the sound with all his might. Then I heard it, too. Beneath our boards, the rhythmic lurch and creak of the sea had become much more erratic, as if coming at us from three sides at once. And over the groan of gunwale against oars, oars against sea, came another rhythm, the steady crash and pull back of sea against shore.

I shook off the bearskin into which I'd huddled and took up my oars besides. Very soon, waves were chasing us, but in the midst of this, Siegfried suddenly lurched, whipped the left oar out of the water and began to work the right one like mad. "Swing her around starboard, quickly!" he yelled, and I tried to copy his movements before I understood the reason. "Those are cliffs up ahead there. Most of the shore on this west side is cliffs. We must go around the south coast until we find a softer rise."

Now I really came to appreciate the purpose of the short, tight strokes as we were dragged by confused seas close enough to the sheer, two-hundred-foot cliff to see it was layered like an egg cake with cream and strawberry colors appearing suddenly out of the fog. The waves throwing themselves—and us—against it had the force of the whole ocean behind them, and the sound thundering off the cold, wet rock deafened me.

Against all of this, both of us rowing furiously, we managed to turn the boat from the cliff. We skirted a menacing stack that stood out from the shore like a demon and came round quickly to more sheltered, even water where we could ease our way between the skerries. Then we heard the serious, welcome grinding of shore along the hull.

"We're beached," Siegfried exclaimed redundantly, though he, too, could hear better than see that this was so. He tossed his oars aside and leapt overboard into the water. I followed and helped him drag the boat the rest of the way up the shingle. Solid ground hit my wavering knees like a wall of stone.

"These first islands are uninhabited," Siegfried told me.

But there was fresh water and green, rocky hills in case any herdsmen and their flocks ever dared to come so far. We rested for three days, turning the boat as a shelter against the wind, until that wind and another drizzle had cleared the fog away, at least enough so that we could see another, larger island asleep on the sea less than half a league away. We rowed to it quickly, working our way around its high cliffs with the winds howling straight off them to the southeast until we could see another island, and we rowed to it. The currents were sometimes insidious and treacherous here, but after any great battle there was always promise of rest. So we worked our way south and a little east over half a dozen islands more until there was nothing but grey open sea before us again.

"This is about a three days' stretch," Siegfried told me as we filled our water bottles again on the last island. "Not so bad as last time."

We waited a few more days for the clearest weather we were likely

to find in this part of the world, which meant that the sun was no more than a tear-filled eye overhead. Then we pushed off. On the third day, just as a very dangerous-looking storm was brewing, we floundered to shore once more.

chapter 10

HIS ISLAND WAS INHABITED. A widower and his daughter lived in a single, small room half-buried and sodded with moss. Siegfried had stayed with them on his outward journey for almost a year. It was the old man who'd helped him build his boat and taught him the skills to sail it. Siegfried was therefore already on terms of easy camaraderie with them. This was enhanced by the fact that they spoke a dialect of his native tongue. Of my language they knew not a word. This people, I learned, had fled to this outpost of the inhabited world when the Romans overran their homes in Gaul.

Siegfried seemed a different person altogether as the trilling sounds of Celtic speech tripped freely and casually over his tongue. I didn't understand what was said, of course, but every other pronouncement of Siegfried's seemed to be a jest that set our hosts to chortling. They obviously found him a very congenial and entertaining man, and those were certainly the last two words I'd ever thought described him.

"It's just the language," Siegfried told me. "Our language itself has power to charm."

I didn't believe that. I've known plenty of people to be witty and charming enough in Germanic. I'd even been considered so myself, though these people clearly thought me little better than a bump on a log.

Our host was a tall man for his people, which is to say he came about mid-chest on me. But even more than tall, he was broad. A great, thick, swarthy, black-haired bear of a man wearing no more than a stiff sheep-skin kilt belted about his waist. When he first strode down the shingle to greet us, he seemed very dirty to me. Closer inspection taught me that this wasn't dirt, but drawing in a sort of blue-black pigment that covered, as far as I could see, every inch of his body save for the palms of his hands and the soles of his feet. A wade into the sea to help pull the boat ashore did nothing to disturb the designs.

I must have been staring like an idiot, for Siegfried scolded me for my rudeness. "Yes, it's permanent," he said. "It's a dye made from wood ash and the blue juice of the woad plant. It is pricked under the skin with bone needles in the designs you see. It is a painful process, so the more drawing he sports, the greater and braver a man is considered to be. That is why this branch of the Celts call themselves the Priteni or Picts, the men of designs, that is, the men who are so brave they can have pictures pricked all over them. They also use a compound of woad as a styptic for battle wounds and as a war paint for those who haven't been brave enough to make it permanent. All of Aed's pictures, however, are his everyday peace wear. He is a brave man."

Siegfried turned now to his host to explain our conversation, and the man grinned and nodded with pride at what he took to be my admiring gaze. His smile pushed the pair of intricate swirls and rosettes which rode, one on each cheek, up into the twinkle of his black eyes.

It was not much later that we sat, crowded around a fire of many peat bricks for the honor of guests, but far too many for the small space of the house. Even stronger than the smell of peat—which, since childhood, had given me an uneasy feeling because of my Uncle Erik's surreptitious theft from the Bog—was the smell of wet sod. Having been outside now for a generation, I found a roof claustrophobic. This roof in particular gave concern, for it was corbelled of very large unhewn stones mortared only with dirt—dirt which, I could tell, was scraped out by the inhabitants in a desperate search for nourishment during the winter hunger, making the construction all the more insecure.

The peaks of half a dozen little sleeping-alcoves, which also served as seats around the fire during the day, met under the top stones at a height Siegfried told me our host was proud of, but it did not allow me to ever stand up straight. Had there not been such a roaring fire, I might have been able to stand there in the center and, on tiptoes, peer out of the smoke hole like some sort of weasel. This hovel had all the light and air of a burial mound, and if this was all the fallen heroes had to look forward to, it's a wonder Odin ever managed to get anyone to fight his battles.

The daughter was serving oat cakes with butter, which made a nice change from the fish that had been most of our fare for months. However, she was not a very good cook, and the butter was a bit off. The fresh she had started to churn when she saw guests arriving had yet to come. Heavy on the ewe milk, it would be white and sweet when it came, full of the peaty flavor such grazing gives its product. If pressed of all moisture, it could keep indefinitely: useful, I thought, for a sea voyage, though this didn't seem to be a priority in anybody else's mind. There was an old saying I remembered from my childhood that if the butter failed to come, the churner must be in love. The blushes of the girl and the chortles of the men as she worked made me think the Celts might have a similar saying.

In this atmosphere, I watched Siegfried bloom into a creature I didn't know. I realized that we had known each other up until then in the most unusual circumstances. Our relationship was tugged neither this way nor that by any other relationship, with no other tie in the world having claim of priority, somewhat altered personality, or present politeness. *Who is this stranger sitting next to me?* I asked myself. *Who, so congenial to this man of such wild appearance, and who even speaks the same tongue with all the little nuances and private jokes as if they'd lived together all their life.*

And then Siegfried laughed out loud, a thing I'd never heard him do before. His laugh threw him backwards against the stone of his bedstead wall with such force that I feared for the stability of our corbelled roof. He—yes, Siegfried—slapped his thighs with laughter and then had to wipe a tear or two off the peeling skin of his cheeks, which made him laugh all the more.

"What was that all about?" I demanded when I thought he had breath to answer.

"Well …" Siegfried began, but had to stop for more laughter, in which the bear-like man with deep growls and even the daughter with a happy blush and a twitter joined. Each one's laughter nourished the other's for a while and so, I expect, did my continued ignorance.

"Well?" I demanded presently.

"Well …" Siegfried eventually found breath to try again, gasping still and wiping his eyes. "I've told old Aed here that you are my sister."

"Why on earth did you do that?"

"Oh, I don't know. It just seemed to be the most logical explanation I could think of on the spur of the moment when I was making introductions as to how we came to be traveling together. I mean, we're not man and wife, nor are we master and slave. I didn't want them trying to put us up in the same bed."

"You didn't?"

"Did you?"

"No."

"Well, anyway, that's what he thinks."

"Very well. But that doesn't seem to be much of a joke to me."

"There's more."

"Well?"

"It seems that after I left them early this spring, these good folk found they missed my company."

"You're flattered, I'm sure."

"It's more than just flattery. Aed's just made me an offer of marriage."

"What?"

"I mean …" And now I could see him struggling with the Germanic tongue as if just these few hours had made him forget all he had ever learned of it. "I mean, an offer for you. He wants to do bridal exchange. I take his daughter and give him you, my sister, in exchange."

I was speechless.

"It's really a great honor."

"What—what if I'm already spoken for?"

Siegfried looked at me hard for a moment, as if determining whether I was serious or not. Then he remembered his fearlessness and said, "That's no problem. Among these people, a woman may marry as many men as she wishes. Indeed, the more matches she has made, the more attractive she is, for a man thereby wins many more allies."

My suitor interrupted now with a question of some kind that included a gesture towards me. Siegfried hastened to reply, something that pleased our host and set him laughing all over again. The daughter, too, chirped into the conversation, then rose to fetch more butter with a swish of her skirt that sent the white peat ash swirling skyward in the midst of the flames. She had a thick head of curly dark hair, which in the firelight caught streaks of red. She was as angular as her father was round, with the shoulders under her brooches as knobby as those of a raptor. They were hunched, perhaps because, never having been a Valkyrie, she never learned to be proud of her height, which like her father's, was uncommon among her people, though she was shorter by nearly a head than I. Or perhaps it was having to live all the time in this cave that hunched her. Nonetheless, she had a merry, open face as freckled as a strawberry and speech like a song. Even if I couldn't understand her, the tones were intoxicating and, in this case at least, I caught the basic idea. Her father made her some teasing remark, then swatted her behind in appreciation. And everybody laughed again.

Without a word, I rolled over into the stone-slabbed and ridged bedstead where my bear rug and allotment of borrowed, lice-infested rugs and bolsters had been put. This brought another loud guffaw from the three with whom I was condemned to share these quarters. With my back to the fire and the party, I worked down among the softness, seeking the coolness of the honest stone. The stone had come too strongly under the influence of that monstrous fire and, though it was rough, it was also warm, and would hold the heat undoubtedly long after the fire had died and been banked. I tried to capture sleep, but my hunting it made it skittish. I certainly had no success in trapping it after I had seen the daughter take up the more comfortable seat on the bench next to Siegfried. She sat, I noticed, with her bottom very close to his, so he was obliged to slip one arm around her and press the other up against the curving stone roof of his bedstead. In my tossing and turning, I found only Gram pressing next to me. Gram, which accidentally nicked my finger when I reached for it in the dark. With the blood, I refreshed the power of the rune on it and then added another, formulating a new verse in my mind as I did so, a verse like an oath which spoke of undying devotion. To nothing but a sword would I ever make such a vow. Gram, fitted to my hand, my only trust in the world forever to the end of my days.

I had not felt so lonely since Faxi's blood had spattered Odin's arm.

chapter 11

OME MORNING, AED HAD PRESENTED Siegfried with a fine new dagger, and there was a bundle of new woolen cloth at the foot of my bed.

"Aed's daughter gave this to you," Siegfried explained.

"I wish she hadn't."

"She gave it to you as a sister."

"It's rough stuff. Spun by a girl who wasn't paying any attention to what she was doing."

"Well, I don't see that you have anything better to give her in return. And I'd like to see you try your hand at the spindle or the loom."

Siegfried went off in a huff to find Aed's daughter, whose mother's good dyeing kettle had sprung a leak, to see if he couldn't tinker it solid again for her.

And I put on the rough dress after all because of the looks Aed was giving me in my falling-apart linen. That, one of the last vestiges of my Valkyriehood, I would keep only to bleed my womanhood into.

Aed's daughter said something cheerful when I was dressed, and Siegfried translated. "She says she thinks it becomes you very well."

"And what about you?" I snapped. "What do you think?"

I tried on my brynie. It didn't feel comfortable with all the roughness of the wool pressed beneath it and would probably chafe if there was any work to be done at all, dressed like that. But there were impressions to be made here. Then I strapped on Gram and crept out of that burrow.

I had no idea of where I was going. I only knew that I wanted to escape. Unfortunately, this island was not very large. Just over the first hummock, I walked directly into the small herd of five ewes, two nannies, and a cow which Aed was busy milking. He kept them in a movable fold so a different patch of grass could be fertilized every few days. The sheep had short tails and soft, fine, many-colored fleeces that could be plucked off by hand. Their carcasses would be small but sweet. Aed's technique for milking the ewes was to straddle them facing backwards, reach under and squirt the milk forward into his little earthenware jug. I suppose it kept them quiet during the process, but the ewe seemed to lose a lot more dignity this way. It was nothing short of obscene.

To turn around now and go in another direction would indicate some cowardice or want of purpose, and that was the last thing I wanted to show this man. I kept going, dodging fresh manure—taking long, brisk strides.

I suppose Aed began with some sort of greeting. I kept my head down and did not respond. Then there was an offer of a sip of frothy new milk from the jug he had slung to his hip. I refused. I had not breakfasted, I was indeed getting thirstier every minute of my walk, but I firmly refused until he abandoned his jug to the morning flies or a clumsy hoof, and came without it.

There was more talk, of herds I suppose. I didn't like the way he fondled the cows' udders in passing, trilled some word, and then pointed towards my brynie with the broad smile of self-congratulations for having made some sort of terrific witticism.

I told him a firm, no.

This island and the ones beyond it were as convoluted as cast-off rugs. Through the shroud of morning mist, one could see the other side of the bay, stepping steeply skyward in cliffs. The sky was always more or less low and overcast, and it didn't take much for earth and sky to meet as fog. The close-cropped grass was slick with dew. My strides grew more cautious and, all at once, there was Aed himself beside me, matching step for step. The man was used to this terrain, but I was not. With an easy, effortless gait, he kept apace of what was a scrambled concentration for me. He had time and breath in the process for a great deal more lilting talk.

Now Aed flung back his cloak to capture a hazy bit of sun on his bare flesh. He pointed this way and that along our route at boundary stones, local sites, something that had a running commentary to it. Having taken one unguarded look at the thrust of his pointing arm, I couldn't help but follow a pair of serpents that twined up it in the strange blue dye under his skin. He noticed my attention, and that changed the subject. We began a guided tour of the points of interest on that landscape. Aed slapped his chest whereon hung a permanent triangular medallion, snugly fitted in every part with intricate swirls. It was pierced by a broken arrow, the point of which ended at one nipple, the butt on the other. What looked like greaves were permanently fixed to each shin, the face of a file-toothed giant glaring off each kneecap. Across his abdomen paraded four fantastic beasts with long legs and necks intertwining, each reaching to bite the flank of the next but one. And on each hairy thigh bristled a fearsome boar. The pumping of his walk set those tuskers at one another with a charging to and fro with all the vitality of a real duel. As far as I could see—and the man wore only the most cursory of sheepskin kilts—the clash of these beasts met with all its fearsome force in his groin.

I really hadn't regained my breath after the climb, but I set off again across the highlands. This wasn't much of an island, as I'd already noticed. I could see the far side of it from this vantage point already. I did not have too long a leash to run on.

And then I had an even shorter one: Aed had taken hold of my hand. I turned to him with my guard up, ready for a fight. I tugged at the hand, the blue bird talons on its knuckles testing his weight against mine. His was the greater by about twofold, but I was certain I could throw him easily. A Valkyrie never barred holds. I would go for the face—yes, the eyes or the beard, they were always vulnerable. Taking a good look at his face confused me, however. For all his endurance of pinpricks, Aed had the same face of open innocence as his daughter. And as I stood contemplating violence to that innocence, an astounding thing happened. Aed opened that openness even more, opened his mouth and began to sing.

I had never heard such a song. I didn't understand the words, of course, and I'd never heard a man who wasn't a bard sing anything that wasn't either a war song or a song of victory when he was in his cups. Had it been a woman singing, I might have called it a lullaby, it was so sweet and gentle an air in a voice high for a man, but strong and resonant. I wanted to laugh, but I couldn't. I smiled instead. Now, smiles lifted Aed's tone until it could sting the eyes, as sweet as the sharp breeze blowing across the pink bloom of heather and the call of gulls to their mates. Or as the piercing blue of his eyes in the midst of all that black hair and macabre tattooing.

I was indeed almost prepared to declare myself dangerously charmed by the whole thing when suddenly a different note sounded in the melody. I looked up and saw a raven, one of Odin's own, such as I hadn't seen since we'd set sail from the Land of Ice. My heart grew sick with panic, and I knew this Pict was putting me under a spell in order to make a slave of me like any other woman is a slave. It very nearly worked, for even as I thought the thought, the song ended and, as a housewife winds yarn off a skein and knots it to her work, I felt myself wound into this man's arms and a firm hand on my buttocks pressing me to him. And now my advantage of training was gone. At such range, his weight stood an excellent chance of overcoming me.

I did what I could with a quick knee to the groin and felt the bear-like arms give remarkably easily.

"Wicked tool of Odin!" I shouted at him.

His reply was measured and calming, as one speaks to a skittish colt. But as I backed away, he kept coming, showing those deceptively open hands. It didn't take long for him to back me up to the edge of an escarpment. It could be climbed down, but it would take my undivided attention, and this man demanded that right now. His shout and gesture were perhaps of caution about the cliff, but I couldn't take the chance of reading good will in them. He was still stepping cautiously towards me with those open hands.

I drew Gram out of its sheath. Even that didn't stop him. Perhaps his was not a religion that armed its women, for all this talk about many husbands to one wife.

"I know how to use this," I warned. "I am a Valkyrie."

Aed reached for me, as one reaches to harness a horse, but Gram touched him first in its anger as if it had a life of its own and, once drawn, must strike before being resheathed. Aed gave a little cry of surprise as if wounded more in the soul than in that painted body of his, then fell. I didn't stop to see how bad the hurt was. I saw my way open and I didn't waste a moment to take it.

chapter 12

I RAN WITHOUT STOPPING DOWN to the little burrow of a house, leaping over boulders and slipping on dew-wet grass all the way. Once inside, I didn't waste a moment waiting for my eyes to adjust but gathered my things together—the bearskin and my linen rags—by touch alone. The daughter's gentle questioning voice I ignored, but not the proffered oat cakes and new butter, finally come, love or no. These I swept out of her hands along with a fine-looking cheese from the hearth side.

Siegfried's "Brynhild, what's the matter?" I likewise ignored.

He wasn't far behind me when I hit the shingle. By the time I'd cast off the boat and climbed in, I was certain he'd be upon me. But taking up the oars was the first chance I allowed myself to look back, and I hadn't been stopped yet. Then I saw that my pursuer had taken the time to go up the hillside a bit, and the look on his face told me things were not well for Aed—or, therefore, for me. Siegfried was not to be turned aside again. He was up to his knees in the waves already, and I was amazed at how difficult it was to fight an incoming tide with one pair of arms alone.

He was swimming now, and I still had surf to pass. Such mighty strokes of the arms, I couldn't help but be in awe of them. I almost forgot to row. Another hasty oar stroke, and I saw one set of knuckles on the gunwale. I stopped rowing and used one of the oars to give those knuckles a blow that should have broken them all. But this hand was not to be broken. Another blow, and there were now two pairs of knuckles looking over the rail at me. I instantly gave up all thought of rowing further and threw my full weight to starboard, for off portside that most powerful of humans was trying to capsize me.

The boat gave a great lurch from side to side and took on water, as if serving as prey for a sea monster. I clung to the rail with all I had and fought to steady it again as soon as I could—not attempting anything, not even another whack at those hands, lest I lose grip and balance altogether and forever. Siegfried's hands had not let go either, although the water must be far over his head by now, and there was nothing for him to brace himself against. I saw the knuckles grow white as they prepared for the strain of another effort. This time, they hoisted his whole body up into play. The fierce blue of his eyes met mine over the object of our pitching battle. I braced myself for the lurch, but the eyes released me and disappeared below the gunwale. No doubt he was merely swinging down for a better grip. This time would do it, there would be no slip.

The eyes heaved up over the gunwale again, and I read in their icicle blueness that he meant to kill me. A son-in-law has an unquestioned right to claim *wergild*, or revenge for his wife's father, even if the man was killed before he ever met the girl. Indeed, he is considered a coward if he does not do so. And not only did Siegfried mean to kill me, but he was one of the few men on earth who could overcome me in an honest fight. Aed, though heavier and full of singing magic, had been no real challenge to my skills. I had known of Siegfried's superior capabilities from the first. He would not have been able to overcome all of Odin's hurdles to find me if it had been otherwise. But always before, I had weighed us together somehow—we two against all the violence of the world, as well as Odin's malevolence. This trial had reckoned out in our favor. Now, for the first time, I measured his strength against mine instead—he in one pan of the merchant's scale, I in the other. The lurching boat was the scale, but the verdict was no less certain. This was a very dangerous, life-threatening man. He could have conquered me from the first and now probably eventually would. My task was to put that day off as long as possible even if, as it now seemed, it could be only a matter of minutes.

That great, fair, square body heaved up over the side. But instead of coming down hard on the gunwale as I was bracing for, he slipped himself quickly and easily into the boat itself, a feat very few could have done indeed without capsizing it. I had to make some quick adjustments in my own distribution to help maintain the equilibrium. In the same set of movements, I drew out Gram. I took up a stance on one bench—sitting being more stable than standing—and faced the seat into which Siegfried had flopped like the day's catch. He sat there now, hunched, panting, dripping, and scowling into the hands clasped between his legs. Our knees almost touched in the cramped quarters on the boat. I kept Gram rigidly on him, much as I had not an hour earlier on Aed himself.

"You used *that* to kill him, too, didn't you?" Siegfried spoke at last, glancing up only to toss his head at Gram to indicate what he meant by "that."

"He is dead, then."

"The milk in his pitcher was warmer."

There was a pause in which Siegfried expected me to say something. Finally, I managed, "He wanted to shove me off a cliff."

"He wanted no such thing. Perhaps he meant to save you from a cliff and you misunderstood. That seems more likely. I do know for certain he wanted nothing more than to take you for a wife. That was an honor, Brynhild."

"I do not feel honored to be offered a place in that fellow's cow herd."

"He meant no insult, I'm sure, but you took it. He knows how valuable a good strong woman can be, having been a widower for so long, having to do his own milking."

"I am to be flattered to be asked to be a milkmaid?"

"It is good to have a place—any place that is truly your own—work to occupy your skills, product that you can take pride in, warm company at night."

I didn't mention at this juncture that dairying was not one of my skills. Much as I might disparage it, at that moment Siegfried was ready to make me believe that knowing nothing of this craft would be an admission of sorry weakness.

"You had no objection to his daughter."

"She's nice enough."

"Nice enough. I saw you sitting together on your bed last night."

"I'd marry her, certainly. For her father's sake, not her own. He was such a good man, Brynhild, like a father to me. Such a gift of the gab. He could keep us laughing all night every night 'til Ragnarök."

"I didn't find it so."

"You could learn to understand. Or did you consider him an animal and therefore free game, simply because you couldn't understand him?"

It occurred to me that it might have been Aed's quick wit, which had kept everyone in stitches around the fire, that had made of Siegfried a sociable person. The laughter had not been at my expense at all.

"And such a voice!" Siegfried continued. "I wish you had heard him sing, just once, and you would have thought of him differently."

"Actually, I did hear him sing."

"You did?"

"A little." Then I had to confess, "It was nice. It seemed nice."

"A love song, perhaps. He told me he had one in mind, just for you."

"A love song? What does that mean? I didn't know there were such things."

"I certainly don't know any," Siegfried said and looked up and off to the next island with a wistful sigh. "Poor Aed!"

"Poor Aed!" I echoed. "He was a tool of Odin to unempower me."

"He was no tool of Odin. He didn't even know that fellow's name. He had very different Gods, very different."

"Odin can work through anything on earth."

"Not with someone who'd refuse to recognize him."

"Like you? Like your foster father Alberich?"

Siegfried ignored this insistence. "Poor Aed," he repeated. "He who'd never met a soul—neither man, woman, nor child—in his life he couldn't charm with his tongue and voice, had the misfortune to try and court you—you to whom his gifts meant nothing."

With another great sigh, Siegfried swung around on his bench, put his back to me, found a pair of oars, and thrust them into the sea. "See how well they pull, these oars he carved for us?"

I looked on amazed.

"Better start rowing for all you're worth," he said. "Hear that?" And I did hear something, now that he mentioned it—a high, long wail coming on the wind off the island. "That's the daughter. She'll have found her father now. Her keening will bring all his kinsmen from the neighboring islands."

Gram went limp in my hands. I wouldn't attack a man from the rear, even this man I probably couldn't defeat any other way, even though I only half believed his tale about the dragon's blood and the linden leaf on his back. Still, I was wary. "Why are you doing this?" I asked.

"Because if they get half a dozen or so men in a long boat, they might overtake us."

"Because you told them I was your sister, and they can take a sister's blood out of her brother. In fact, they prefer it that way."

"You know I'm no coward. I'd fight twelve of them if I had to. I just don't want to. No more killing of these people, these people who should have been mine, but I was condemned …"

I put down Gram and picked up the other set of oars.

"You and I are condemned, Brynhild," Siegfried said with the rolling rhythm of his strokes.

"Condemned to be brother and sister?"

"In a way. Condemned to do violence just when we should most hope for peaceful acceptance. Condemned, perhaps, to be wanderers forever."

PART II

Wanderer's Curse

chapter 13

"OU SAY WE ARE CONDEMNED to be wanderers?" I said and pulled at the oars. "Wanderers like Odin?" Another pull. "Wandering makes us divine?"

"Odin again." Siegfried pulled. "Is Odin the measure …" *pull*, "… of all things for you?" *Pull.* "Your feud with him …" *pull*, "… means more than the life …" *pull*, "… of a good man like Aed." *Pull.* "You refuse good men …" *pull*, "… who love you …" *pull*, "… for the sake of one …" *pull*, "… who has condemned you." *Pull.* "Perhaps it's Odin you love." *Pull.*

"Nonsense." *Pull.* "I'd do anything to escape him." *Pull.* "But you may be right." *Pull.* "This wandering is my condemnation." *Pull.* "That doesn't mean …" *pull*, "… that you must join me."

There were a pair of pulls now before Siegfried spoke. "I killed Alberich, you know."

"Your foster father?"

"Yes. The only kin I ever really had. It was—a misunderstanding of sorts. Like you with Aed just now."

"That was no misunderstanding."

"Well, perhaps too much understanding, then. You see, after I'd killed the dragon, Alberich told me to smoke the heart so he could eat a bit of it. A bit of dragon's heart, he told me, gives you understanding."

"What sort of understanding?"

"It depends. One person is taught to see the future, another to know the speech of animals." He leaned to the oars, then spoke again, in rhythm. "In my case, I learned to know the speech of birds."

"You ate some, too?"

"I didn't mean to. I simply scorched my thumb a bit while turning the meat with it and put the thumb in my mouth. Some of the juices, I suppose, were on my thumb, for suddenly I knew what the sparrows were chattering about in the tree overhead."

"What did they say?"

"One said, 'These humans have killed for gold again.' Another said, 'They're always doing that, aren't they? If we sit and wait here long enough, I bet the little dark one kills the great fair one over it before the day is done.'"

I looked at him, puzzling over his tale as he continued. "'You may wait around if you want,' said the one I now know was female. 'I have more important things to do.' With that, they both flew off."

Siegfried rowed. The boat was skimming now, high on the water and making the pebbly sound of air and water mixed.

"Well?" I asked on the forward row.

"Well, that planted the seed. When Alberich came back from wood gathering, it did seem that he was acting suspiciously. He had the ax still in his hands and always seemed to be trying to get behind me, where the linden mark is. Or so it seemed to me."

"And?"

"And? I picked up Balmung and killed him. I thought at the time it was so I could sit in peace. Now I am more convinced there must be some curse to that blade, that it was rightly named Gram and not the optimistic Balmung. I think it kills not where I will but where …"

"Where Odin wills. He is a god who thrives on conflict, who induces it at every chance, for it is conflict that turns men to him in devotion."

"You may say that if you will. Such images do seem suited to this case. Or the notion I heard a Christian spout once, that if you live by the sword, it will also be your undoing."

"I know no other life."

"Nor do I."

"It is as if I must blame Odin for having robbed me of any other life."

"Still, I regret." His face soured. "My own father, or the closest thing I'm to have to a father, to any kin at all, in this life. If I'm not to marry Aed's daughter …"

"You could marry someone else. The world is wide."

"Not so wide that I don't know how it would be. It is my fate. Any place I may go, I will always find myself an outlaw."

"Like me. So you could—be with me."

"But you don't need a man. Not like Aed's daughter. Listen to the keening!" He held the oars still for a beat. "A woman like that cannot live without a man to take up the other half. What's to become of her now?"

"I don't need a man. Why do you say that?"

"Because you don't."

"Odin says I do. In this new world."

"Odin says—Odin says. I don't care what Odin says. I've got eyes. I've seen for myself. I've seen what you did with one blow to Aed."

"He was not a man for me."

"That's not the way to tell him. I don't want to be told that way."

"I wouldn't tell you that," I said.

"You already did tell me that."

"When did I …?"

"You told me out in mid-ocean that I was only the means Odin used to lure you off the island to his grim vengeance."

"That may be true, but I'm coming to accept my fate. At least, I'm coming to resent any other possibility but the fate of you and me—" I think the wind caught my words and carried them away, for Siegfried didn't answer or make any sign that he had even heard.

I tried again when the wind had settled a bit behind a low cliff on the next island. "Perhaps I don't need you as another woman needs a man …"

"Or a man needs a woman."

"To fight my battles."

"Or to cook his food. It works both ways."

"For others."

"Yes. For others. But not for us."

"Perhaps I don't need a man. But I can want one. A certain one. When he is not just any pair of helping hands."

"When he has a boat to get you where you're going."

"Many men have boats, Siegfried."

"When he gets you to wherever it is your promised one waits." This was said on a stroke that was too strong, and we lost the beat.

"I have no promised one."

"You told me to tell Aed you did."

"I didn't."

"You did. I must say, that came as a … as a shock to me."

"So did the fact that I was supposed to be your sister. I had thought that you and I …"

"I told him you were promised."

"And still he came on."

"I told you. A woman can take many men in his culture, the opposite of yours. He definitely thought it was worth a try."

"But if you are promised to Aed's daughter, I may not still try."

"I am not promised. Or only promised to vengeance if I return among the Picts."

We rowed.

"You said there was treasure in the dragon's hoard," I pursued presently. "Was there much?"

"Mountains," Siegfried said, as if it were no more than mountains of sand of which he spoke.

"And this treasure, you left it for safekeeping among the Burgundians?"

"Yes."

"Then you will want to be heading towards the Oder River."

"Burgundy isn't on the Oder."

"It was when they fought the Goths."

"It hasn't been there since I was a child. I only remember Alberich speaking of it—how Agnar had been killed and Giuki had fled before the onslaught of the Huns, to whom the Goths are now allied. The sons of Giuki now rule a small kingdom on the Rhine. That's where the treasure is."

"I see."

"This is part of it. As I told you before, the only part I kept."

Letting his stroke go lax, Siegfried handed something to me. We had been rowing hard for some time now, but I was not sure we could afford to take a rest yet. Nevertheless, I let up on the oars too and looked at what he handed me. It was the gold ring I had noticed before, the serpent with ruby eyes biting its own tail. Now as I held it in the little cup of my hand, I could tell that it might qualify as "treasure" on its own. There was the thought now that I had it, I could throw it overboard as a snake-offering to the World Serpent. But there was the urging intensity of Siegfried's eyes on me and the warmth of his finger still on the cold metal.

The boat was bobbing idly near a fjord in which a colony of sea lions had come to birth their young. We could hear the females singing their hauntingly human nursery songs, which the males, just the two of them there, supported from time to time with their deep bellows.

"Sometimes the dragon's heart juice teaches me the words of animals as well," he mused, watching the creatures thoughtfully.

"So, what are the sea lions saying?"

"They are happy to be together, happy to have wives and young ones, happy to see that their good life will continue on the rocks they call their own. What a mystery it is to me, the ways of a man and wife. I … I mean, one can hardly keep from being close, even if death lies in the way, close without ending. What end can there be? And yet—"

He censored himself, floundering, I thought, on a sea of naïveté. To rescue him, I changed the subject. "Tell me, Siegfried, whatever became of the dragon's heart if Alberich didn't eat it?"

"It's there," he said, kicking idly at his knapsack on the floor of the boat.

"Then I have eaten dragon's heart too!" I exclaimed and told him how in my great hunger on awakening from the sleep thorn, I'd eaten the first thing I came upon, never asking what it might be.

"And?"

"Well, I suppose I may have gained some power to make runes," I replied. "I don't remember having that before. We learned a little of the skill in Valhalla, but no more than the basic letters. Odin kept all that skill to himself. And sometimes it seems as if I hear the earth herself talking to me."

"That'll be it, then," Siegfried nodded. "Take that gift seriously. If it comes from the dragon, it must be very powerful."

I nodded.

"We two are the only ones on earth who have eaten dragon. We will be lonely and misjudged by the rest of those who have not, no matter where we go."

"But you wanted to stay among the Picts."

"Because, as I said, there was a home ready there, a nice home. If I was the source of your destruction, as you said, at least we could be together there as brother and sister. Being in-laws would also give us cause—"

"I see. Now I am not so angry that you called me your sister. And angrier at myself for Aed's death. But there is the treasure. We can build a home of our own with that."

"I guess. But I know that treasure, as you do not. I can't help but think that any home built on that will be sterile and pretentious."

"I will make runes that it may not be." I looked up then, blinking into a hazy sun as I watched a pair of ravens circling one another overhead and cawing.

"What are the ravens saying?" I asked Siegfried, remembering how one of the old retired Valkyries had known their language in Valhalla. Had she eaten dragon's heart? I wondered. Perhaps it was not such a fantastic commodity after all.

"They speak of Aed," he said. "The one meant to feed on him, but found him carefully guarded by a weeping daughter. He is disappointed and tells his mate it is not worth the trip."

I blinked back up at the birds. Yes, indeed, that did seem a possible meaning to their cant. I wondered how it must be to have birdsong resonating as words in your head all the time. Very disconcerting, I should think, especially when you were trying to hunt one. Perhaps I did not want to hear what the earth said. It had been a comfort—alone in that strange, icy land. But how would it be when we got to shore—the words and wills of folk conflicting with the words and will of the land under them, to which they gave no second thought? Perhaps it was a mystery confined to that land, my ability to hear such things. I heard nothing from the sea, at any rate. And nothing when I was with Siegfried, although Siegfried's ability with the birds was not hindered when he was with me. And could he speak to them in turn—send them on errands, perhaps, as did Odin? Not just ravens, but hawks and gulls? What power that would mean. To be joined to that power …

"Here's your ring back," I said as I saw Siegfried turn from eavesdropping on the seals and spit on his hands to get rowing again.

"I meant it for Aed's daughter," he said, without turning around. "You keep it."

"I certainly don't want it then," I said. "A promise ring for a girl whose father I've killed."

I thought to toss it overboard. It might have been better if I had, given its future. But I didn't.

"Keep it for yourself. As a promise ring for you. Unless you'd rather remain unpromised."

"I'll keep it," I said. And I couldn't pick up the oars again without touching Siegfried's hair, drying in its delicious ringlets. I left my hand there for a pull and a lift, a pull and a lift, matching the rhythm of his rhythm.

"Thanks," I said, returning to the oars.

"Thank you …" I heard him say, but his voice was muffled, and I imagined he'd said, "Thank you for taking it."

"But no more talk of brother and sister, then," I said warningly.

"No more brother and sister."

I slipped the ring on. It fit nicely on the third finger of my right hand, just as if it had been made for it. It hadn't seemed such a good fit at first, when he'd first handed it to me, before we'd talked about a gift of runes. A rune had come to me actually, after that, a rune of power to whisper over a promise ring. And now—it fit!

chapter 14

E WERE NEVER OUT OF sight of land now for more than an hour or two at a time, and often that was the fault of fog rather than of distance. We could skip-hop from isle to isle at whim and at the whim of the weather, and we made good time. We were, in fact, in view of the mainland—the last thing I'd seen before the sleep thorn overcame me—when the first serious storm of the year broke upon us. We rode it out for a night and a day, fearing we would go under the whole while, yet unable to do much more than bail and consider the awesome will of the gods, as we couldn't decide which ones to pray to. Heaven had plenty of case against each of us, anyway. All the while the sea was like a blacksmith's file on our hull.

Sometimes, as he would jostle past me going from one end to the other, wherever the emergency was, Siegfried would stop, crouching low in the middle of the boat. This was not just in the interest of centering the weight; he would stop here suddenly, press my face between his hands and say: "This … this … by my life, this is what I most fear to lose. The sight of you. Has Fate finally taught me to fear?"

But then, lest his fear prove true, he would fling himself into the battle against the elements again with all the more fury.

That night the storm finally blew itself out and we both sank into an exhausted heap, not rousing until light. Come the light, I realized

I was sleeping with my head on Siegfried's chest, my arms clinging to him, his to me, and our legs all entwined. I didn't dare to move, hardly dared to breathe, but I couldn't keep my heart from drumming wildly at the proximity. Perhaps that was the noise that awakened Siegfried, for very shortly, he stirred. He moved with stiff, slow movements as he extracted himself from the tangle while trying not to waken me. I continued to pretend to sleep. I heard him make water over the gunwale, wash his face with a handful of brisk sea water and gnaw on half of the last bit of dried cod. Then the oarlocks were slammed full of oars and the boat lurched forward. That was what I allowed to stir me. The rest of the journey, we were both very conscious of the closeness we'd allowed—painfully conscious, yet totally silent—and gingerly avoided any more.

We were much relieved to find land still in sight. As we rowed nearer, however, it declared itself to be other land, not what we'd hoped for.

It turned out to be the island of the Danes.

Helgi was, as ever, their king. In the manner of many hard people—like stone, he did not seem to have aged much since I'd last seen him, victorious over Thora and her people in Saxony. It may even have been the same red ribbons I had seen before, tangled up in his bleached blond beard. The same storm had brought him home as well, home from his annual summer full of raids. He was effusive and brimming with generosity as only a man can be whose boats ride nearly to the gunwales in the water, so loaded with booty, and who sees long months of enforced idleness before him. Siegfried and I were led into his hall, which had the name of Heorot, meaning "hart," standing above all other halls as the hart above other animals of the forestland. Heorot had been founded already by the Dane's first king and namesake, Dan—but it was his descendant Hroar who first set to sea, a Viking, and first appointed the hall with great treasures. It was Hroar who also founded the town of Roskilde near Leire, at the head of the Isefirth. As Helgi welcomed us as guests from the high seat, whose tradition he carried on in rough but effusive style, it was

difficult to imagine how it was that I could possibly have lost more than a season or two in sleep.

For my part, however, I was not recognized. Certainly, I was in a heavy, somber, woolen dress of Pictish weave, with none of my warrior trappings on display, and in the tow of a man. Even in the tow of such a man as Siegfried, this left me a far cry from the Valkyrie who had once toppled Helgi's boat in the surf and had been a cause of his rout. Perhaps I was a little more tongue-tied and seemingly submissive to Siegfried than was becoming, but this was for the very good reason that I had no desire whatsoever to be recognized here and now.

Now, Siegfried soon made himself at home amongst the fourscore warriors settling themselves down to winter pastimes in Helgi's hall with the ease of men who know they will not know hunger or cold or sobriety at all during the coming months. There are perhaps men left on this world who'd feel uncomfortable in such a raucous, theft-based society. But Helgi's men had murdered all of those in the neighborhood and taken their women for their own, so such men of conscience were a vanishing breed. If Siegfried were uncomfortable, he tried as hard not to show it as I tried not to be recognized. And if he were slow to add stories or songs of his own to the rowdy recitation of theirs, no one noticed that. At this time of year, the stories were all new and fresh, one coming fast upon another's heels, and the only complaint being when one man started before another declared himself finished. Charges of causing death by boredom with the recitation of thread-bare stuff were many months off.

At the other major pastime, that of tests of physical prowess, Siegfried had won himself pride of place within the first three days of our stay. It was clear no one could beat him. Helgi had given him the bench next to his own high seat, and challenges basically stopped. Oh, there were some, those made mighty in their cups, who forgot themselves and challenged. Or there were two who thought they'd take on his one, never mind calls of "Foul!" Or there were some whose ingenuity set them to devising new handicaps for the new hero of the hall. Siegfried graciously accepted even such challenges as these and still won every bout.

In spite of my desire to lie low, the desire to take on some of his battles for him began to grow greater. I remembered how pleasantly the evenings would pass in Valhalla as we maids worked to keep up our skills, and I was certain I could beat at least half of these Danes handily, perhaps everyone in the hall, in fact. Everyone but Siegfried. I certainly ached to try. But he'd introduced me as his woman, so it was out of the question. I'd asked him to do that, hadn't I, when my heart leaped at the recognition of the figure in the high seat? How could I ask for more? And yet I did.

I began to ask Siegfried in whispers: "Couldn't you let me take on this one? He's drunk, Siegfried."

"But he's a man, Brynhild."

"I've taken on men before. Why, as a bear for Odin, I took on whole halls of them."

"Spare me the fairy tales of Odin."

"It's the truth."

"Besides, even drunk, this one has a mean back hold. Trust me, I've faced it."

"You faced it and won in three seconds flat. I only want to try." I hated sounding like a whining child, but that's what I was reduced to.

"Brynhild, it's out of the question."

"To make you proud of me." I was learning women's wiles, wasn't I? In fact, I was the one who craved the pride.

"This will not make me proud. Quite the contrary."

"Please."

Finally, he gave in to a chuck on the chin that made my flesh creep with the personal debasement of it. But then I learned that my debasement had only just begun.

"Helgi, my host," Siegfried said, draining half his flagon just to wet his tongue for such a speech. "My woman here wants to fight."

"Does she, indeed!" Helgi roared with laughter. "What have you got, a Valkyrie?"

"Perhaps," Siegfried replied. "We must test her mettle, mustn't we?"

"I've tangled with Valkyries before," said Helgi, "both in their feathers and defrocked. I tell you—they're greatly overrated."

The cruelty in his voice made me long to make him my first victim. But, alas, it was not to be.

"Bring on the best of your women, Helgi. Here's my dagger, and this feathered helm—" *my* feathered helm, he was wagering, "—says my woman can beat any one of yours."

And so she came out of the shadows, a tall woman with rust-colored hair and, before I could speak a word in protest, I found myself in the midst of a "girl fight." The indignity of it almost put me out, as the men roared and cheered and laughed us on, betting as they might on their horses at the Odin games, giving no credit for a skillful throw except when my opponent from mere fear got a good hold on the dreadful clumsiness of my woolen dress and ripped the shoulder out, exposing one of my breasts. I'd quickly had enough and, most unsportsmanly, heaved the other woman up and dumped her into the keg of mead beside the door, putting an end to it in the most dignified way I could.

When I fastened up my shoulder and strode back across the hall to join Siegfried on his bench, it was him they were congratulating. And he, for his part, was chortling with the best of them and gathering up his winnings as if he'd been the one to win the bout. That was the last time I sought to fight.

Eventually, as the hall found other entertainments and humiliation cleared out of my head a bit, I began to see, for the first time in my life, with the vision of women. We were strangers here in a hall like this, I realized. Yet strangers of a most intimate kind, who understood all too well every reference, every nuance, and then more besides. For all that it was our native language, none of its common hall phrases expressed *our* meaning. We were observers and, although observation didn't make for either disinterest or dispassion, not being an immediate actor did lend our minds a certain objectivity. It rapidly became clear just how much unworthy, childish, indeed downright foolish action men, as the actors, must take as holy dogma and perform as sacred rite. Alas that we could never speak our perspective—except, perhaps, to each other.

I began at last to do what a normal woman would have done at once, and that is to seek out others of my kind, if for nothing but confirmation of my view of things. Unfortunately, I'd begun badly by fighting and beating the best of them, trying to win an in with the tactics of men—tactics it was a woman's initiation, mystery, and most honored rite to disparage.

The main food of that season was the black sour soup made from the blood drained off the animals slaughtered for winter. It appeared on the table day after day in the hall of the Danes, and its smell permeated the place. Sometimes there were dumplings in it, but when there were, the men got them first. Mead became the staple instead.

As Helgi's women made their silent circuit from benches to keg with empty horns and back again with full, I began to try to catch an eye, to smile, to be friendly. But even as she pressed a flagon on me, I could make no woman meet my eye.

Presently, Helgi called one of the women to join him in the high seat, and I thought, *here is my chance.* But it turned out to be my opponent in the wrestling match whom he singled out for this honor. She had changed her dress, but her hair was still wet and reeking of mead. I felt shame to see her like that—as much as she felt to be seen.

And one could hardly call it an honor that she was selected. For he set her on his knee, not the seat beside him, and almost at once his manhood was roused. Immediately, with no more preliminaries but a great roar, Helgi threw her across the table in front of him and proceeded to use her right there before us all as other men dared use the serving maids only in the darkest corners, or outside.

Such an antagonism there was to their struggles, and antagonism the company followed with interest and even bet on. How many times their brave leader had the strength to make her come before he himself gave out? Such performances were often considered to be a form of worship to the god Frey, he who is the boar of fertility. They counted the screams of her orgasms in chorus: "One! Two! Three-ee-ee!" And when Helgi held her hands back above her head and rode her hard, they chimed in with his growls of "Fight for it! Come on, girl. Fight for it!"

At last, Helgi himself was spent. He rolled back to his high seat, trusting his tunic to make him modest of its own weight, laughing with satisfaction and reaching for his drinking horn. The attention and accolades of the hall remained with him, but my eyes followed his mate as she, too, rolled off, clutching her half-removed garments about her as best she could, and hobbled off to answer the "Mama! Mama!" cries of a little wide-eyed boy with an embrace. A mere toddler—referred to as such by Siegfried later, as proud as any toddler of his new word—was this eldest son of Helgi. And suffering, so I saw, from a flat, over-large head and bowed legs that made him teeter like a sailor just home from the sea when he walked. Rickets. Both of his parents were as fair as could be, and the hair of the child was white rather than blond, so my mother must have been wrong when she attributed the disease to dark complexions. Then I remembered Thora, and how she said the disease was due to immorality in the child's home. For all the distaste of their congress, Helgi and this woman were man and wife. Was there other immorality present?

Of course, Helgi's wife, the toddler's mother, was not very old herself. Though big and well-grown, she couldn't have been more than twenty. It was in this last glimpse of her, shame-faced and flushed, seeking escape from the glare of the light in her son's embrace, that I got the jolt of my life. For in that light, at that moment, I felt sure I recognized her, those pinched features, that rusty hair. I also knew why I had found the weight of her hips so familiar when we had fought together. I was certain I had wrestled her before.

I dared not follow her at once. I gave time for the cries of the child to subside, time for her to lullaby him to sleep, some quiet time for herself. I would have liked to have given her more time, perhaps, but Siegfried reached for his flagon then and found it empty. He was in the habit of refilling his own, but this time I took it from him before he could get to his feet. "Let me get that," I said, and made my way back to the cask at the door, just like any common serving maid.

Other girls were there, dawdling as long as they could around the barrel with secrets not meant for me, but the one I sought was not among them. I went out into the biting chill of the night to empty my bladder. I found my insides still strangely confused by the sight I'd witnessed there at the high seat, not two ells from my face. But this did not find the girl for me.

I wandered about the strange, dark yard for a while, mostly stumbling on scenes of lust the master's example had driven his men to. But then, presently, I saw the dance of a rush lamp and heard the clink of keys dangling from a belt. I crossed the yard in their direction, watched those keys open a storehouse door guided by that light, and then followed them all inside.

"Oh! You startled me."

"I'm sorry," I said to the figure against whose broad hips the keys dangled, on whose red hair the lamplight gleamed. "I didn't mean to. I … I only came to apologize. I'm sorry I dunked you in the mead cask."

"That's alright. I know your man set you up to it."

"What men make us do, eh? I mean—I'm sorry." I didn't apologize for leaving her with the false impression that Siegfried was responsible for my feistiness. From the way she turned her head and the light away from me when I said this told me that my words referred in her mind to the scene in the high seat, and I felt it necessary to apologize again.

"That's all right," she forgave me still again, when she had overcome her shame. "You are very strong." She retreated to the safer, original subject. "You might almost have been born a man."

"So it seems," I said, laughing self-consciously. "It would have been better for us had we all been."

"Oh, I don't know," the woman said, thoughtfully running her light up and down the shelves that lined the walls of the storeroom.

"This is a wonderful storeroom," I had to admit, and it was. The light caught just the outer surfaces of what hinted at being even greater hoards: gold, silver, brass, jewels worked into armor and weapons, jewelry, cauldrons, decanters, flasks, and bowls of all descriptions stacked to the ceiling. The plundered wealth of anywhere in northern Germania where Helgi's longships could reach.

The woman set down her lamp and helped herself to a handful of rings, put a new necklace about her throat, and caught up her meady hair with a pair of emerald-studded combs that set off the copper of her hair most prettily. She admired the whole effect then in a beautifully etched mirror.

"I come here to comfort myself," she explained. "It comforts me to know that I wear the keys to such a place about my waist. Helgi can force them from me whenever he likes, of course. But as his head wife and the mother of his heir, they are mine. It is a comfort to know that any time I want, I have access to the accumulated result of the power of such a man. Any time I want, I can take what I want and buy what I want. I can buy fealty, devotion—perhaps even assassination. Who knows? Any price I could meet. Not bad for a girl of a poor family abducted as a mere child."

"Helgi stole you, too, then? Just like all the other things here."

"I was only thirteen winters old. But then, what else is a woman's fate?"

"You are from Saxony, aren't you?"

"Yes. How did you know? I'd thought I'd lost the accent by now."

"No accent."

"From a little sod house by the sea where my family kept a few cows. Not my real family. They always said I was but a foster child, given to them by a maid of Odin in answer to their prayers. But I never felt a stranger there. I suppose … I suppose I'll never see the place again now."

I let her struggle with her emotions in silence for a while before I asked what I knew I must ask next. "What is your name?"

"Yrsa," she replied. "It's a strange name, I know. My mother—my foster mother—always said it was Latin, though she knew no Latin herself."

"It means she-bear."

"Yes, I know."

"You know Latin?" she asked in surprise.

"No," I replied. My head was almost reeling from the oppression of the curse that this revelation meant, as if the air in the storeroom had suddenly grown more than dank—deadly. "But now I know the worst that womanhood can bring."

chapter 15

I TOLD YRSA AS BRIEFLY and as painlessly, but as irrefutably as I could, that I was that Valkyrie who had carried her but a few hours old and given her into the hands of her foster family. I told her of her mother Thora, how she had ridden with me and been my best friend, although I couldn't say where she might be now. I told her under what straitened circumstances her mother had given her up—but not, however, with what hatred. Then I came to her father. There was no softening that blow, though the evil of it was almost unspeakable.

"Your father raped my friend, your mother, on that same day he killed her own beloved husband, the man she gave away everything for. Your father was on a Viking raid, as he had undertaken every summer before and, I suspect, since. Your father's name is Helgi Halfdansson, that same man who abducted you from Saxony as a child, who fathered your son, and tonight lay with you on the table before the high seat in the view of all his men."

Yrsa denied, then believed, then wept and mourned. "That is why my son is so ill." Then she said, "You must go and tell this to my husband—my father—I mean Helgi—at once."

"I?" I was taken aback. "The man is practically a berserk without the aid of Odin."

"Yes, but he will believe you much more readily than me. Me, he would only accuse of lying, and he would beat me. You are a Valkyrie. He will believe you and, should he grow violent, you are strong enough to resist him."

"I haven't the power to proclaim right and justice that I once had."

"Then perhaps you shouldn't have proclaimed it so freely to me. Now that you have, you must. You must walk into the hall at once and declare One-Eyed's curse upon the mating—upon its fruit, my poor little son—upon this whole hall and even all of Denmark because of this evil."

I came to believe the justice of her claim as she had come to believe me. But where I had been prepared to tackle any man in that hall physically, the skills she asked for now I felt seriously lacking in. I told her I would try and left her in the storeroom among the hard, cold purchase-power of Helgi's booty. I returned alone to the hall, remembering to fill Siegfried's flagon only because I had to pass the cask at the door where men too impatient to wait to be served sank their horns in deeply and brought them up, arm and all dripping to the elbow.

So I presented Siegfried with his drink. It was rather belated, and the other men were already teasing him about it. But what disturbed me more was the look with which Siegfried met my eyes. It was not so much a look of impatience as it was of sudden possession, as if my one gesture of servitude, for all its ulterior motives, suddenly gave him the right. Before I'd had time to sit long beside him, certainly not long enough to get the echo of the men's teasing out of my head and form some words of dire prophecy against their master, the look took on substance.

It began with an arm about my shoulders, but quickly advanced to a general fondling of everything, breast, thigh, and above with a sudden and voracious discovery. At first, I tried to press his hands away, but this was impossible under the scrutiny of a hall that took Helgi as example. So next I tried to escape to bed, but this was also of little use, for, having declared ourselves not brother and sister, Helgi had assumed the opposite of a man and woman traveling together and assigned us together the honor of one of the few guests' sleeping closets. Thither Siegfried and his demanding body pursued me, closing the closet door behind him against the knowing grins of Helgi's hall.

I realize now I was like the man who, finding his back on fire, runs and so is consumed. I should have dropped right where I was and rolled in it. Had I stood up in the hall then as Yrsa counseled and pronounced the dreadful curse of incest upon the lord of that hall, I would have broken the web of the spell on me. But I mistrusted the runic powers I'd been given by a taste of dragon heart, clung to the physical solutions of my old life, and so came under the curse as well.

What he had witnessed in the high seat that night, whether incest or no, had given Siegfried power. Having been raised by the least demonstrative of old bachelors, he had never learned how it was that men and women dealt with one another. He had had desires before, very strong desires, perhaps for Aed's daughter and for me, I was certain. But always before he had smiled in irony at himself for his ignorance, turned his head, removed his hand as from a fire. He'd never understood his feelings to be appropriate. But now he'd seen a demonstration of the entire gamut given sanction in the high seat. I'd given him further sanction by filling his flagon for him, as other women did for their lords. The floods of his desire, given that chink, could hardly be contained. Alas that it was the sight of such evil as Helgi's that was teacher to such desire!

With superhuman force, I pushed Gram between us that night, but after such a night spent with each of us struggling alone against our opposite closet walls, I knew I must flee much further than a common bed if I were to save myself.

"You're running away again?" Siegfried stammered, relentlessly pursuing whatever abrupt turn I made in my hasty preparations so that there was always an arm, a shoulder, or a leg in my way. "I hope you haven't killed anyone. Helgi is a much more difficult opponent than Aed."

"I killed no one."

"Then we must stay. Helgi has extended winter hospitality to us."

"There are a hundred halls to extend the same."

"It would be rude, however, to leave before spring, now that we've been accepted here."

"You may stay if you wish." In fact, I wanted to pray to—to whatever gods I had left that listen to me—that he did stay. But I didn't say that out loud. I guessed that demonstrated what my prayers really were. How determined I was to run, though all my back was on fire, and the front as well.

"I won't … I can't … without you. You wear my ring."

"You may have the ring back if you wish."

"Brynhild, I'd rather die."

"Then you must join me in rudeness. Because if I stay, there will be greater rudeness still. Worse than mere rudeness. Somebody will die." *It might very well be me*, I added to myself.

So in spite of all entreaties, both of Siegfried and, what was more powerful, of Yrsa's pleading eyes, we rowed off from Denmark before the sun was quite up that morning. *If I must lose my Valkyrie powers*, I consoled myself, *at least it won't be under the gaze of a berserk like Helgi.* But maybe even out of his sight, the shadow of his curse had power to pursue. It was not just his but Odin's curse, after all. It certainly seemed like we were pursued, if only by the desire that at every stroke sought to pull our hands off their oars and send them to one another.

On the second day, we came to shore where, so long ago, Odin had first set his curse on me. A pair of bull walruses was fighting for territory on the rocks again but, as there was no sign of Odin, I assumed this time they were only walruses. Unless, dread thought, I had lost the ability to see the god as well. It was further disconcerting to see with what interest Siegfried watched the winner return to the caresses of his harem. I kept my eyes trained on the moral lesson of a horse's skull and forelegs stuck upon a cursing pole at the final edge of land.

If meeting Signy's full-grown son, Thora's full-grown daughter and young grandson had not convinced me of how much time had passed, these remains of dear Faxi certainly did. Though it seemed like only months since I'd left them with the blood still reeking on them, the bones were picked completely clean and bleached, dry and white. The lower jaw had vanished altogether, but the upper jaw remained, now pathetic until almost comical with the buck-thrust of its teeth uneased by gracing flesh. The cannon bones—how fragile and thin they looked! It was impossible to imagine how they ever could have carried me so swiftly, so strongly, so faithfully. And then the hooves—the front nails weathered and split and pulling away from the great bone behind until a touch would have separated them.

I began to say a few words to Siegfried to try to explain what it was that had happened in this place. I think he understood the sobriety, but more of an understanding I gave up as impossible to transmit. We went on.

chapter 16

WE ROWED OUR WAY INTO the low fjord called the Schlei, which cut deeply into the mainland. At its mouth, the inlet was already so shallow that there were pools of swans swimming amongst the gulls and eider and mallard ducks, and herons were taking our wake upon their knees as they went about their business on the flooded sand banks. Otherwise there was nothing on this bar of dune, which ran down to the waves of the Amber Sea on its outer side and trailed off into brackish marsh on the inner.

A league and a half within the inlet, the banks closed in, wooded in spots and very beautiful. The Schlei curved away to our left like an inland river, though the water remained salty. Here and there was more settlement, fishing villages whose most substantial building projects seemed to be the maze of paling fence winding throughout the water's shallows, as if an elaborate trap for evil spirits. They were, in fact, traps for herring. The fishermen's hovels, cringing among boulders that seemed to have been flung from one shore to the other in a battle of giants, were much less remarkable. The smell of woodsmoke at work on the late autumn's catch of older fish deciding to make for sea again after the warm weather's spawning was a cushion to the smell of brine.

We rowed our way up to the very most inland tip of the Schlei, where all the legends of my youth told me the Angles' first king, Skeaf (or sheaf), drifted to shore as an infant, untended in a pilotless, rudderless boat, his head resting on the god-gift of grain that gave him his name. His son was Skild (or shield), whose body when he died was set adrift in the same rudderless boat his father came in—and disappeared who knows where towards the wind-swept Codan, the Amber Sea. Skild's son was Beowulf, the hero who slew monsters. But I have heard other folk claim these ancestors as well.

Here we stopped to rest in the early afternoon, after a day and a half of steady rowing, hoping the sharp but sunny weather would last through the morrow when we planned to begin the seven-league portage to the Treene River. This route would cut across the narrow neck of the Jutland and spare us several weeks' rowing around the peninsula in open seas which, at this time of year, could quickly blow into death before safe harbor was found.

For all that this passage was well-known to merchants and tradesmen, there was no more settlement at this staging point to receive them than there had been all the length of the Schlei. A single, foul-smelling inn Siegfried and I decided it was better to avoid in favor of the less vermin- and thief-congested out-of-doors.

What could be called the beach proper quickly gave way to farmland, yellow or brown, and autumn-bedded. Here and there among them stood an Odin sheaf eaten, so far as I could see, only by sparrows. Away to the northwest ran a spine of thinly forested hills whose naked beeches became one with the grey sky. I found something unsettling about those hills and so, having gone up behind a mortarless stone wall to relieve myself, I continued on and up towards them to investigate.

The farmlands were dotted with bogs, ponds, quicksand, and little lakes—as if, even this far up the fjord, the sea was loath to give up territory. I circled around these low places, right to the foot of the hills. Then suddenly it hit me so strongly that I had to say it out loud to the hopping, grazing sparrows and quail. "Why, these are the Little Bears, the hills that bounded my view when I was a child. Only I'm seeing them now from the south instead of the north, and that's why I felt so uneasy, like the world was somehow turned around. Just over that hill is the valley where I was born."

As the rise of the hills began, cultivated land gave way to the scrubby heath that was so familiar, the heather in its last dry and deep purple bloom. My legs bruised a red-berried juniper, and the smell was so strong and evoking that I had to turn and run. I startled the sheep grazing nearby so they bolted on incongruously spindly legs under wool growing long for winter, and ran in the other direction. In my mouth was the very taste of the fragrant lamb that had fed on such juniper and heather. It was like no other taste in the world. It was as vivid to me as the tufts of red wool knotted in each floppy right ear. That was, I remembered so well, how Uddrun's clan marked their herds.

When did you ever eat meat as a child? a more rational part of myself demanded. *I must have*, the rest of me sang, *at Yule, perhaps, or spring. Some time so rare and wonderful that the taste did not escape.* This song was as if giving harmony to the song of the rest of the earth beneath my feet. *I must have eaten it, to remember it so well. In any case, the feed flavors their milk as well. How I remember that!*

Such a torrent of singing words filled my mind, a word for every beat of a foot upon the ground as I raced back to the boat. With these words I hoped to win Siegfried to the sudden passion that consumed me. "We should go over that hill, Siegfried, Siegfried and my heart. We should settle there among my kinsfolk as man and wife. The shame of being a returned Valkyrie is suddenly nothing to me. I have such a yearning. Is this madness—to be sitting around the buckets of blood with all the women, bundled up to our chins against the hours of hands in cold liquid, making blood sausages? The smell of thyme and sage on our hands. And that mutton—even raw, you can smell the flavor.

"You see this?" My flow of words plummeted onward, even though my running stopped for a moment to allow me to bend and pick a fistful of late-blooming chamomile. I ran on, pressing the distinctive scent to my face. "You see this? You may think this is only used to nurse the sick, those with headache, toothache. Excitable children. It is bitter. But it is also nourishing and sustaining. If the winter hunger gets too fierce. It is famine food. Trust me, I know such things."

Then I found that in my mind these words were not meant for the convincing of Siegfried. I was imagining myself teaching this to a pair of little girls, a new generation who took my words to heart with a sober wonder at the wisdom of their elders, which it seemed experience and years could not be enough to gain. Some of it, in their wide eyes, must have come straight from the mouth of a god. That seemed the best audience.

And then, for a long, awful moment, it seemed I would not even get to try my words of wisdom out on Siegfried's stony skepticism. He was no longer waiting for me by the boat, or anywhere in sight.

I called his name. I walked a dozen paces down to the shore and called again. At first, I was angry, angry that a mere man should make me feel this way. Just before a wrenching sense of abandonment overran that anger and the other, opposite feeling I'd been nursing of finally having found a home, I saw him. Yet another hundred paces further on, the farmland gave way to a patch of wildness that ran straight from hills to fjord. Siegfried was at the edge of this land, his back to me. I walked deliberately towards him, the anger returning and growing, making my walk noisy and putting a sharp edge on my voice as I called his name again.

"Hush! Get down," was his reply in an anger only his wish for silence kept from equaling mine.

I tried to control my temper and did as he bade me, crouching behind a knot of hazels at the edge of the wild land. The last of the nuts clustered in the almost-bare limbs, and at first, I thought that was what he wanted me to notice. I had a sudden, beautiful and vivid memory of just such a day as a child competing with squirrels for such nuts, and I thought—hoped—this is what he was inviting me to—a carefree day of childhood. My anger dissipated.

But it was not the nuts that had attracted his attention. He was looking through the bare branches to the wild heath beyond. A stallion of holy white stood on a hillock there, mane in the wind, keeping watch over a herd of half a dozen mares grazing with their offspring.

"They are very handsome," I agreed in a whisper, forcibly forgetting the sweet tang of hazelnuts.

"It would suit us very well, don't you think, Brynhild, to be horsed? Instead of always wearing out our arms on the oars."

"If one could catch and tame such a wild mount …"

"Of course you and I could do it."

"I hesitate, though, Siegfried."

"You are afraid, Brynhild? Of a horse?"

"Their sire is white—a holy horse."

"It's the white stallion I mean to have."

"Siegfried, you must not. He's a son of Odin's Sleipnir."

"All the better to have a good bloodline."

"Siegfried, you will attract attention and draw down the god's wrath at every turn."

"What? You mean to sink into obscurity? You, Brynhild? Into the bog of average, everyday folk? I do not. I would rather die. If this is your plan, you cannot be the companion for me I thought you were. That horse is my companion."

I looked at him in disbelief, almost horror, but he did not meet my eye. He had eyes only for the horse who tossed his mane to the wind and whinnied a challenge to all comers. That refusal to exchange glances suddenly flooded me with such terror as I had never known. Never had I flinched so at the thought of any bodily harm, any frontal attack of man or beast. Only this threat of abandonment in obscurity could induce such a panic, the thought that Siegfried might prefer to share his life with a dumb animal rather than me—that threat not to attack, but to simply, easily turn his back and never feel a tug upon his innards to match the tug on mine.

"Besides," Siegfried added presently at just the instant, or so I thought, before my heart should have burst, leaving him no ears to hear his words but the horses', if he cared to speak up. "Besides, he said I could have him."

"He said? Who said?"

"An old one-eyed wanderer who was just here, gathering driftwood along the beach. Just here before you came."

I looked frantically all around at the empty beach and hillsides but saw no one, not even the telltale flight of a raven in the sky above.

"He's gone now."

"That was no beggar-man," I said, "of this you may be certain. It was Odin."

"So the horses are mine for the taking. You say they are Odin's. This man certainly spoke in possessive tones. He said I could have one. He has only given what is his, as any open, generous man might do."

"No gift from Odin is an open, generous gift. Trust me, Siegfried, not him. Trust me, he means our doom with this gift. Or my doom, at least."

Again, I was frightened by the casual manner in which Siegfried met my fears.

"It was not quite a free gift, after all. The old man said I must drive the herd into the Schlei, and the horse that feared not, but came out on the other side, swimming, that was the horse for me. How I wish old Helgi were here now, so I could set another wager with him. I'd wager anything it's the stallion and the stallion alone who has the mettle for such a feat."

Helgi now. Even Helgi Hundingsbane was a more tantalizing companion.

"Well," said Siegfried, standing now, not because I had agreed to anything, but because the wind had turned suddenly towards us as if by magic, sending the smell of horse strongly into our nostrils instead of our scent to theirs. The stallion markedly, as if at a signal, lost much of his watchful tension and even bent a graceful neck down to crop a bit of lunch for himself. "I mean to go get a little fire going. A fire," Siegfried repeated as if I were half-witted, "for the drive. Do I have your help or not?"

That wasn't a question. It wasn't even a challenge, as one man to another, as he might throw down to Helgi. It was an outright threat.

And so, before I had time to form any other words, either protest or defense, there I was, nursing the first few sparks of a heather and driftwood fire on the beach. Meanwhile, Siegfried grew smaller in the distance, rowing across the Schlei to be ready to claim whichever horse Odin should bring out upon that shore for him.

Soon I had a smoky, slow-burning bundle of heath in each hand. With them I approached the herd, swinging wide inland past the hazels. The stallion already knew something was afoot. His head was up again, mane blowing across his wide, intelligent face, his nostrils flaring at the smell of smoke.

I gave a yell, the good old riding yell of the Valkyries. My first attempt at it failed, strangled in my throat at the blasphemy. But the thought of Siegfried's look if I should fail him quickly loosed my vocal cords again. I yelled, and the mares and their young were off with clouds of seagulls.

The stallion did not run, however, but stood his ground. He turned to face me, tossing his broad, hard head threateningly. He charged a trotting step or two towards me, then reared, hooves flying like deadly maces in a battle.

I flinched a little but didn't run, feeling Siegfried's eyes on me from clear across the Schlei. I waved my torches at him, and a sudden drop in the breeze caused the smoke to sink back down about me thickly, thickly enough that it gave the stallion pause. The wind dropped the mane into his eyes to further unnerve him. He set his tail to me and began to work up a run towards the Schlei.

It is possible that diversion was his motive. I had seen brave stallions do such before, and certainly this is what I assumed was his purpose as it was happening. The rest of the herd had turned when they reached the sudden drop of land before the Schlei, so steep that no herbage could gain a foothold on the soggy mud that dropped to a foot or two's worth of beach at low tide. One skittish chestnut colt, much like his father perhaps, had not turned quickly enough, and he was floundering there to my left, mud and water up to his barrel while his mother squealed with worry and encouragement. I ignored them and went single-mindedly after the stallion as, if he were diverting and I had no wits, I should indeed have done. Nonetheless, foremost in my mind was not what the horse wanted, not what I wanted, but what Siegfried wanted. That might well be called witless. I, personally, could have done very well with that mare. Even the colt would be no small catch, a year of taming care giving me all the horseflesh I could desire and no Odin-claim upon his coat. But Siegfried, I knew, had his heart set on that white stallion.

The stallion took the bank in a single, effortless leap and was now in the Schlei. I wish I'd thought about it then. If I'd stopped to think about it, it would have been clear that diversion cannot have been the motive behind that grey forelock. I was not going to follow him into that icy water; he was abandoning his charges on firm ground where I moved with more ease. If I'd thought about it then, as I do now, I would have gone after the mare. I would have at least toyed with the idea that the stallion must have been trained to do as he did. Indeed, it did seem that the very wind tugging at his mane and pressing his flanks taught him where to go. There was no reason for him, any more than his mares, to enter that water, and once in, not to have swum around and come back on the near shore. I had only my smoking twigs, after all, and no clear cul-de-sac to force him through. He kept on swimming, however, raising foam on the glass-smooth surface of the Schlei. He swam straight to Siegfried as if led by a bridle and, once the horse had clambered up on shore and shook himself dry, Siegfried claimed him as if that bridle had merely been passed into his hands.

I sat by the little fire we had made but allowed it to go out for want of fuel. I sat with my knees curled up to my chest, hugging them and resting my chin on them. I sat and watched Siegfried race his prize up and down the far bank as if they'd been made for one another. Even the boat, I realized, with all our stores and the bearskin, was over on that other bank.

chapter 17

EVENTUALLY, THE TIRED BUT EXHILARATED man and horse rode around the tip of the Schlei to where I sat, still hugging my knees. They came at a perfect tölt so that Siegfried's blond curls did not wave an inch up or down against the horizon. When they were upon me, Siegfried pulled his mount up and slid off the bare back.

He stretched luxuriously, seeming to embrace the sky, and trumpeted his joy. "He's wonderful!"

"So I gathered," I said to my knees.

"His name is Grani." As if the horse himself had told him so. "Would you like a ride, Brynhild?"

"What, you haven't tired him out?"

"Never! This horse cannot be tired. He will go through fire if you ask him."

I watched the man currying his mount with a handful of stiff dried grass. I listened to the words with which he curried the animal's ears, "Here, boy. Good boy." Nonsense, like so much nickering. Or like the words men say to each other when they think they are alone. I remembered that the last time I had ridden, it had also been a white horse, Faxi. The last time I had ridden, it had been as a Valkyrie. It had been not so much as horse and rider, but as a force of nature. My heart caught in my throat at the thought that this could never be again.

I watched how Siegfried gently picked up one hoof after another—the hooves were shod—and took such care of heel and the slight depressions in the hock. I got to my feet then, remembering the first lesson the riding mistress had taught us at Valhalla: *If you fall off, get back on instantly.*

"I'll take a ride," I said.

"Great," said Siegfried.

He held Grani's head to quiet him while I went round the left side. I pushed his hands away: "I don't need help."

The moment the horse felt my weight upon his back, it would not have mattered how Siegfried held him. The horse broke away with a scream of protest and leapt into the air with fury. I'll confess I was taken quite by surprise. One jarring crash of hooves upon the ground, and I lost all hold. The next leap left me with only ground below. And hard ground it was, too.

By the time I recovered my composure somewhat, Siegfried had recovered his horse and had him standing calm and stately as if nothing had happened.

"There, boy. Good boy." They were talking male talk to each other again.

"He's not really broken yet," was all the concern Siegfried bothered to show me.

Now, I knew that wasn't true. The horse was shod. I had been watching the whole time and never saw Grani flinch once from the moment Siegfried approached him. It was not that he was unbroken, but well-trained. Too well-trained indeed.

Get back on instantly, I heard Hilda's voice in my head.

"Let me try again," I told Siegfried, brushing off Aed's daughter's dress and hitching it up into the belt to be a little less clumsy.

"Are you sure?" Siegfried asked.

"Certain."

I met Grani in the eye. It was only his left eye I could see and, because of this, he seemed one-eyed. It seemed I could see Odin's very soul in that eye, hoping to crush me with a look. I refused to flinch from that look but hoisted myself up, my leg up and over.

Both Siegfried and I were better prepared this time. He hung on and I hung on, but the muzzle had soon yanked itself free of those large, strong hands, and they could do nothing more for me. The great barrel of horse rolled itself between my thighs like on a storm at sea, but with yanks and fiendish twists old foam-bearded Aegir never thought of in his frothing brew.

The horse was determined, but so was I, determined as I'd rarely been before. I hung on much longer than anyone could have hoped for. Even the horse seemed surprised, or at least wearied, and began to take his jumps easier.

Too late I realized this was but another ruse. The back was out from under me again.

Still, I congratulated myself that my fall took place much further away from Siegfried than last time. I felt I'd proven something to someone, even if to no one but Odin and myself. The soil I landed on this time was much softer too. I didn't feel half bad as I struggled to get up, determined to try once more. But as I brought my arms up beside my hips to lift myself off the ground, I found them buried to the elbows with just the easy pressure I had put on them.

This was no ordinary sand Grani had carried me to before dumping me. Each separate grain was so suspended in water seeped to shore from the Schlei, that in appearance alone was it like sand. In all other ways, it behaved more like water, a water in which one could neither swim nor find bottom, where neither humans could walk nor fish could swim. It was quicksand.

When first I'd fallen and lain still, there had been no problem. Flat on my back, the morass was able to hold me as well as water would while I floated. But now—once I'd tried to get up, failed, and lost balance—I panicked. Foremost in my mind was a panic not to appear helpless or foolish before this man and his god-gift of a horse, and this aggravated my struggles more. Every drag of my nails across the deceptively dry crust of sand on top only served to sweep more sand out from under me, and I sank deeper. The quickness of the sand was so like a mouth, sucking at every limb, that I had no difficulty believing it to be a thing alive. And then I had no thought for appearances, only the perfect sense that this unstable land of my birth would claim me, one way or another.

The sand was up to my brynie, to my shoulders. I swallowed a mouthful of gritty, salty water—or perhaps I only tossed it into my own mouth with my flailing. Soon enough I found a sturdy length of driftwood in my hand. It had seemed like a lifetime, but it was soon enough. At the other end of the branch were Siegfried's good strong hands—at the end of his cautiously extended leg, a rope, and the other end of the rope was firmly knotted around the white stallion's neck. Cautiously, deliberately, with no sign of deadly panic, Siegfried and his horse pulled me to safety. The sand closed behind me with an angry smack of unsatisfied lips.

Then, beneath me was solid ground. And over me, Siegfried's face, searching anxiously for signs of hurt in me. With undisguised relief, his hands found out the familiar features of my face by gently brushing away clumps of sticky sand and stringy strands of hair. Then his mouth found mine, sucked the sand from it, breathed sweet, life-giving air in. I could not have been in very bad shape, for I groaned for the sheer, tantalizing, impossible pleasure of his touch.

Siegfried misunderstood the desire in that groan. "Come," he said. "Let's get you some warm shelter and dry clothes."

He helped me up and led me by the hand to Grani. A look of firm disciplines passed from man to horse, Siegfried mounted, then helped me up before him. Grani plodded in the direction Siegfried's knees pressed him as easily as an old work-worn gelding to his stable at the end of the day.

Knowing what I know of Fate now, I suppose, had we tried to stay in the boggy narrows of Anglia, something would have happened to make us outlaws again. Perhaps it would have been Siegfried's turn to kill my kin in a moment of misunderstanding. Our only goal now seemed to be the treasure in Burgundy. The homeless can seek the sterile shelter of base metal; for them there is no other.

There was no doubt that Grani made the portage much faster than it would have been without him. And there were many places where a horse could be made to tow a boat. This became particularly true when, a week or so later, we entered one of the many mouths of the Rhine where the World Mill under the sea had churned up great dunes of grist, the ground flesh of world-forming giants. Riverside ranks of stiff poplars gave way to hills frothing with beech and spruce forests. But I would not abandon the boat as Siegfried wanted me to, now that the ocean was all behind us. I would not leave myself totally dependent on that horse. I rowed the boat myself alone for long stretches where the horse couldn't tow, rather than leave myself at his mercy.

Oh, certainly Siegfried made a fine figure on that white stallion, as fine a figure as could be found even if one had to rake dreams for it. He certainly turned heads, and it was more with unabashed envy than with awe. A god horse, that was clear to everyone who saw Grani. But it was also clear that this was a god man, and so had a perfect right to the perch. Of course, I couldn't see what sort of figure we cut when Siegfried pulled me up to ride before him with Gram at my side during long stretches while Grani dragged the boat. Perhaps it was not quite so fine. But still I knew with a thrill that ran up my thighs to the back of my neck that I could be proud to be part of such a picture. In fact, a great terror of mine—so great that on more than one occasion I came very close to allowing the boat to be abandoned in order to avoid it—became the fear that I might be denied that part. I grew willing for long plodding passages of thrilling closeness through scenery that seemed so inglorious in comparison. I grew willing to do anything to stay in that picture.

Yes, it was hard to resist when I was actually on the horse with Siegfried's arms around me. For every good intention, it never took more than half a league— in fact, I convinced myself that horse knew just the rocking gait to accomplish this—before I could feel Siegfried growing hard against my tail bone. His great, strong hands would find my thighs as we rode and move higher. And I would lead him as he led the horse, with a press of leg and a gentle hand.

But there was little escape in the boat, either. The sight of that glorious man and horse trotting easily along the shore—watching, waving, yearning towards me—let nothing else into my imagination on which to ruminate. When a halt was called for the night, and Siegfried would come to help me drag the boat ashore, my arms would eagerly seek out the strong support of his waist, jelly as they were from long hours of repetitive, lonely rowing.

I could blame it on Helgi Halfdansson, the example he set in front of all his hall that taught Siegfried in direct and simple terms what a man might expect of a woman. But the Dane is not the only one to blame. There is that horse. Sometimes I would see Grani fix me with one or the other of his eyes, Odin's eye, and I knew. With such knowledge, I managed to keep up the power of the runes much longer than perhaps even the god had imagined.

But such knowledge was also part of my downfall. Siegfried even said it, one evening when he saw the horse and me shooting daggers at each other.

"Don't be angry with Grani," he said, "because he won't let you ride without me. He won't let anyone else ride but me. Some horses are just like that. Don't be angry. Be glad. Because if he had never thrown you into that quicksand, I never would have learned."

"Learned what?" I snapped, more at the horse than at him.

"Learned that you can need rescuing, like any other woman. That there are some things you need me for."

Siegfried had no idea of the full impact of what he was saying. Indeed, I'm not sure I realized it all then, either.

As the moon began to wax again, I could not deny that the power of Gram and my runes on it was weakening, and there was nothing I could do to strengthen it. Practice had given Siegfried's hands wonderful skill. Each night, in a matter of minutes, he could go from beginning to where I'd stopped him the night before, and my own desire would meet his and carry us further, before even I was aware of how or what had happened.

And so it was on the first night of snow. It wasn't much of a storm, just enough to crust the emptied fields on the north side of the furrows like shadows, only white instead of black. But it was enough to give us that much less space to walk off the effects of being together, enough to drive us all that much closer in upon ourselves. Before I could say what had happened, Siegfried had rolled upon me, then brought me back on top of him. And in a desperate, groping fury, I realized it was his thigh so firm and right between my legs where always before I'd used the hilt of a dagger. I couldn't have stopped riding it if Hel herself had stood in my path. It was only with the grateful shout of release that I realized I was riding on the ooze of Siegfried's similar satisfaction and that, whether he felt it or no, he had been lying all the time with his back on a useless Gram.

"You must go on to Burgundy alone," I told him in the iron chill of the morning.

I remembered a crumbling wall of grey stone and the uneven stairs behind him. I memorized the sound of his boots on those stairs, the shadows on the stones' faces, every dent in the intervening mortar. But I didn't dare to let my eyes meet his, so afraid was I of their power. And when he gripped me hard from behind in protest, just when he knew I could least resist it, I had to fairly scream with pain, "You must! Please," I said, with effort and more calm than I felt. "Please. Go on to Burgundy, get the treasure, and return to me with it here."

"You will marry me? If I bring the treasure here?"

"Perhaps marry is not the word, for I don't know that witnesses will make any difference, and I don't know that we can conjure any witnesses, two outcasts as we are. But if … if I can feel myself the mistress of … of something, if I can wear the key to such a hoard about my waist, a solid treasure against the vicissitude of humanity and their prodding by Odin, then yes, yes, Siegfried, I will give myself to you, take you to me, and let the curse of Odin fall where it may."

"I will go," Siegfried said, although he made no move to do so, and only grew firmer, more demanding against the small of my back. "I will go at once and return. A week … ten days at most. It shouldn't take me more than that. Then I'll return, by my life I swear it."

"Then go," I said with rising impatience and tone.

And he was gone. He hadn't the strength to turn and wave goodbye. And I only dared to look up and see the fading figure once I heard Grani's hooves a long way off. What I saw was a lone man, still dark in morning's shadows, glorious in his aloneness, riding with determination against the powerful flow of the Rhine.

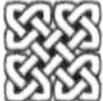

PART III

Shamaness

chapter 18

IT WASN'T UNTIL I'D GONE to ride Gram alone—a rather unsatisfactory exercise, I must confess—that my head cleared enough to look about me and appraise my situation for the next week, ten days at most. That wasn't a long time, but I knew I must do something to make the time pass quickly, and improving my surroundings, especially when I could expect at least one other storm during that time, seemed like the best thing to do.

Now, the place where we had taken shelter for the night was an old abandoned defense tower—whether Roman, Celtic, or even older, I couldn't say for certain. It had once been two stories high, but the roof to the upper story had collapsed, leaving only the barest minimum of stonework to stand on and overlook the battlements. Even the lower roof, with all the rubble to reinforce it, leaked heavily in places. I took care of these holes first. The walls, though mortarless and only dirt-set, were solid and suffered no drafts. It didn't take much of a fire to keep the place cozy. I quickly came to look on the tower as any maiden might on her bridal chamber, and set about to furnish it accordingly, as best I could with the resources at hand.

It must have been the Romans who'd built up the time-gnawed stone of the tower, I eventually decided. For, nearby, in neglected terraces bounding steeply down to the Rhine, I found overgrown vines of the grape, such as only Romans are known to grow; indeed, such as they cannot live without. There was a little lichen-covered statue of the Roman style set in the midst of the hillside. A plump little boy, seeming as proud of his naked manhood as he was of the bunch of grapes he dangled above his head, he was probably a tutelary god of the place. He continued to act, though no one had brought him offerings in a number of years. For all his charm, I found such gods too insipid and placid for my taste.

Frost had blasted the grape leaves red so they crunched smartly underfoot, but clusters of fruit still clung to the vines. They were small and shriveled, but I found them chewy and sweeter than any bilberry or dried sloe. So I stripped the entire vineyard on a day of sharp, clear weather. The overgrown vines made rough but handy baskets and, at the end of my labors, I had a dozen of them stored along one dry wall of the tower. I sang runes of flowing brooks and birdsong as I worked, to banish gnawing thoughts.

Now if only I had a bit of wheaten flour to make a wedding cake, I thought. *If only I knew how to bake!*

My mind was cleared when I was away from Siegfried. Once away from the arrow-thin focus of life with him, there grew space in my mind for a myriad of other things. The landscape, for instance, began to talk to me again.

Young feathers of yarrow chirped out from under the straw of their spent parents. *Find us, pick us, thin us out!* I boiled them up into a green mass like spinach but with a sweeter anise flavor. *Find us, take us!* called a hoard of nuts in a hollow log. *The squirrel who gathered us was hunted by a fox. Take us.*

Then I found deer tracks, the tracks of a doe and her fawn, half-grown, with the shadow of white spots still on his back. I shut my ears to what they might have said when I stalked them, but was nonetheless much relieved when a five-pronged buck, gored in a battle with a wild boar, jumped between us, his large, moist eyes pleading for me to put him out of his misery.

And then I would push the little boat out into the Rhine's great stream to fish and bob there, hours on end. River traffic was remarkably slow, most travelers having bedded down for the winter. Those that did pass were in too much of a rush to beat the next storm to waste time with me. So there was nothing to do but watch the arm of Father Rhine, vibrant under a sheet of grey armor, caress the breasts of Mother Earth, and listen to the quiet murmur of their lovers' talk.

It happened one evening, the weather being warmer and I having rowed further upstream than usual, that I witnessed a very strange phenomenon. I found myself in a particularly rugged section of the river gorge. A blanket of clouds lay above the left bank. It was sucked aloft in scarf-swirls, as if about to reveal hidden, dancing mist-wraiths, leading to the effect that the sun had already set.

In fact, the sun had not, and it burst out of that cover just at the last moment. Then, pressed as it was like a red berry between the grey quern of hills and the clouds, now a granite grinding stone, its rays burst out with intensity. The slap with which they hit the high grey cliff opposite, on the east bank of the river, was as audible as if a handful of gold was tossed onto a table. And there the gold was, glittering on the mountain peak. Then, even as I watched, the cliff face, slapped awake, began to hum. Now, I was becoming, if not inured, then at least accustomed to hearing life from unpeopled countryside. And I decided that, even as a jug of cold water may crack when set to a fire, so was the natural explanation of warm sun on the cold rock face. But the song that I heard as the result was no less wonderful and hauntingly beautiful for all of that. I found myself totally under its spell, and it was only by merest luck that the setting sun broke the spell, and I was freed in time to save myself from the pull of a very fierce current up against the treacherous rocks at the foot of the cliff.

The river narrowed sharply at this point, its full volume having to jostle through a space a third its normal width, and it took a very sharp turn around this rock at the same time. Had the sun set but a moment later, had my boat been but a knuckle's width more drag, had I pulled against the current but one pull less, I am certain I would have been lost and dragged under by a current so strong that no mortal could hope to fight against it.

In spite of its dangers and my narrow escape, the magical lure of the phenomenon was so great that I knew I had to visit it again.

The next evening, there was a bone-chilling rain, and I stayed by the fire. But the clouds had separated somewhat by the next afternoon, like the unraveling of a loose weave, and I returned to the spot. I approached it by land this time. It seemed safer. After conquering the tangled net of bare, scrubby trees that battled me wherever there was foothold on the cliff face, I reached the flat smooth rock at the very pinnacle, thrusting out unsupported by rock below over empty air—and the river a hundred ells or more down. Looking across all that shimmering, moist air, I saw that the clouds were just right again; indeed, such was the form of the atmospherics, that it must happen often. I had hardly stopped panting from my climb when the sun's rays struck again, hitting me full in the face and sending the deep vibrations through the rock until I was panting again from the thrill.

It wasn't until the sun dropped the world into a sobering chill that I looked down and saw disaster. A merchant and his handful of slaves in a little boat not much larger than mine—careless, perhaps, in their haste for winter shelter—had been lured into the trap. With a sound that rent the heart, the boat was already cracking up on the rocks. But even as it happened, the crew failed to lean all their strength to their own rescue. Arms continued to point up in my direction. I am certain there was only wonder in their pointing, for I knew what the spell was like, witnessed from below. But I couldn't help but think there was accusation as well. Accusation of me for being part of the spell and luring them to their fates.

I scrambled down the cliffside as well as I could in the diminishing light, often at risk of my own neck. But by the time I reached the water's edge and clambered about there, clinging to the wave-wet rocks, it was too late. I only found two slave's bodies and, by the violent blows to their heads and arms—once-solid bone draped over rock with no more skeleton than wet rags—it seemed they died as their boat had done, more from skulls crashed on the rocks than from water in the lungs. I buried these men close to where I found them, as deep as the bones of Earth would grant me access. These places remained unmarked and nameless.

It was, however, a strange quirk of Fate that much of the merchant's wares came ashore unscathed. I rescued three great chests full of rich goods that the water had hardly touched at all, plus a number of fine furs and bolts of cloth that only wanted drying out by the fire. Now, when I hung the tower with these against the drafts, laid out a brass carafe and goblet service embossed with hunting scenes, stuck a new ivory-handled dagger in my belt, and wrapped the new belt around a new dress of smooth red silk, I felt very comfortable indeed, wanting only Siegfried to come and share it with me.

It had been ten days. I expected him every hour and wasted a lot of time gazing off from the top of the tower towards the south, the direction from which I expected him. But then a glance stolen towards the west told me that conditions in the sky were right again. It would be another magical sunset. Convincing myself that this would be my last chance to experience it, certainly alone, and that tragedy could not possibly repeat itself, I hurried off to the rock, leaving the fire going so Siegfried, if he came while I was gone, would understand that he was expected.

The climb was, if anything, more difficult, for the easiest handholds were on the north face, and the light snow that had fallen in the meantime lingered there and made the way treacherous. However, the sight and the deep rumbling were, if anything, more entrancing with the bite of cold to them. Unfortunately, what I had thought impossible happened again: another little merchant craft was caught up on its lure. It was almost as if the river knew when a boat was coming, whispered to the cliffs to gather the seductive silk of clouds about them, and so spring the trap, seemingly on purpose. It was almost as if I, too, were part of the trap lured by the magic, to be an extra bit of bait—a tall, blond woman sitting up on the rock where the lonely, homesick travelers never expected a woman alone to be.

Well, I mustn't do this again, I thought, though my body was still throbbing from the rock's song, and I knew such temptation would be hard to resist. *It will be easier when Siegfried's here*, I told myself, *when I don't have to seek out rocks and sunlight as balm for my loneliness.* But before escaping off to the tower to wait for him, I knew I had to see if there was anything to be done for the victims of this wreck.

One solitary blob of black was still managing to keep afloat by the time I reached the water. So it was possible, if luck was with a powerful swimmer, to elude the curse. The man was already much closer to the far shore than to where I stood. On the far shore, the slope of the bank was easier and the current less treacherous. I helped him as best I could with will alone and the recitation of some help rune that came into my head. When at last I saw him safe, safe but chilled to the bone and naked among the shadows of the river-seeking trees stripped of their leaves on the far side, I waved to him cheer and congratulations and held up such of his goods as I had so far managed to salvage. His reaction was understandable, I suppose, but still disheartening. As far as I could tell, although I couldn't hear the actual words over the distance and the roar of the river, he was calling the wrath of heaven down on me in a fearsome curse.

I brought his goods back to the tower so the water wouldn't damage them any more during the night. I didn't even look into the chests, expecting the survivor soon to come and claim them. And then we could sort out the misunderstanding. By first light, I decided it best not to wait for him, but loaded all the goods up in my boat and rowed to the left side of the river. I found no sight of the man, either dead or alive, though I searched and called the better part of the morning. It disquieted me somewhat to think that he must have gone off somewhere to report the *theft* (he would call it) and murder to someone, doubtless some local lord. It also disquieted me that he might think he needed more than himself to come and claim his goods. Would an armed troop be called up against me? My loneliness would be disturbed in any case, even if Fate allowed that the entire countryside was not called out in hew and cry against me.

I certainly wanted to do all I could to demonstrate my good intentions. But simply to leave the goods unguarded in a neat heap on the left bank was to court further disaster. Anyone might come along and claim them, and then how would I demonstrate my innocence when they found me? Surely, they would have no choice but to believe I'd buried the goods somewhere to keep for myself. No, the best plan was

to keep them safe until the merchant came for them himself, and then to prove my innocence by quickly and helpfully handing them over.

Better still would be if Siegfried came and took me away to my new life, and I could just leave the goods anonymously in the tower. Yes, certainly, that would be best. But that plan was contingent upon Siegfried. It was now the eleventh day, and a storm was brewing. I had to cross back across the river and seek shelter for myself and the goods in my little tower alone.

Chapter 19

HE STORM BLEW FOR THE better part of two days, during which time I had great opportunity to consider what I should do. I made a careful inventory of the salvage from this second wreck, and it was rich indeed. There was even a pair of pouches full of precious gems. This was not something somebody was likely to forget about as long as he was alive. Then I spent a great deal of time considering what lord it might be with whom I would have to deal. To the best of my recollection, this was Frankish land. At least, it had been when I rode with the Valkyries, a little blob of eastward thrust the Franks had made across the Rhine with the alliance of Rome. The deserted vineyard told me, however, that perhaps things were not quite as they had been.

Considering all this, I didn't know what to expect if I couldn't expect Siegfried to return. *Perish the thought!* I had no choice but to expect Siegfried.

The howl of the storm blew off, and the first sound I heard in the beaten silence it left behind was that of horse hooves. *Siegfried!* I thought at once, and jumped up to see. But almost as quickly, I realized there was not one horse, but four, five. I bolted the door and climbed up to the second story of the tower to peak through the crumbling battlements to see.

It was indeed five horses. Ponies, really, all of them dark, shaggy

and brown, and all a good two hands shorter than Grani, if not more. I knew such ponies. I'd ridden against them half the world away in Gothia. Hunnish ponies. Waves of fear came over me. These feelings seemed the most natural thing in the world at the time, but soon I decided it was Odin's fear I felt in washing waves. I had felt that same fear in Gothia and had failed to recognize it there too as Odin's fear of what he felt to be an unnatural evil. The discomfiture of a god was nothing to sniff at, unless I considered this was a god whose curse I was trying to escape, and the world was full of gods. But it was difficult to escape old habits, especially in the face of danger and the unfamiliar.

The riders rode Hunnish style too. Short of stature, they inclined forward, their lower leg held by tight stirrups in a sharp angle with the thigh. This allowed the horse to move with lengthened neck and outstretched head at one end, tail at the other. I would have found the attitude awkward and comical if I hadn't seen the deadly grace of its swiftness at their battle with the Goths. This was all attained without the use of spurs too. Each Hun did carry a whip, cocked up under his arm and decorated with feathers or strips of cloth, which made me think they were more for show than speed, because I hardly ever saw them used.

As the ponies raced closer, I could see that, indeed, the riders were the small, dark, fearsome creatures called the Huns—man as if but an extension of the beast. As I watched with fascination, one of the riders bent his legs even tighter under him until he got his boots planted on either side of the saddle, onto which he brought himself to standing as steadily as if he were on the ground, even while the pony continued to walk forward. From this vantage point the Hun peered keenly about the countryside around him, even more keenly towards my tower. He pointed it out. The Huns urged their ponies on to me. *This is black magic*, I thought.

They were now close enough that I could see that the face of one of the riders did seem to be not quite so flat, wild, and brown as the rest. He rode differently, too, his legs nearly dragging on the ground on either side of his pony's belly, with marked awkwardness compared to the others. Still, his clothes were without doubt the felt trousers and fur cap of the Huns. At this incongruity I decided even Huns must have their chances of nature.

What could Huns possibly have to do here in Frankish territory? No good, certainly. They were spies, worse—freaks, a blight, dust on a table. Digging into the armaments among my booty, I grabbed a nearby bow and arrows and swept the bothersome Huns off with a quick stroke of the hand. I hardly stopped to be conscious of it.

Before they realized the first of their companions had been hit, I'd taken out two more with a single arrow each. One more I got, but the last one swerved and galloped out of range before I could redraw my bow. Just before he vanished from sight, he swung 'round in the saddle and got off a parting shot of great accuracy—any greater accuracy, and it would have been the end of me. It missed my head by an inch, but that inch was enough, so I let him go. *It's two hundred leagues he has to ride before he'll find others of his kind*, I thought. *Why, a man may die of old age before he covers that distance, even on the fastest pony.*

Presently, I crept out to look over my booty. There was a virtual armory of fine weapons—some, the likes of which I'd never seen before. The bows were a wonder of construction, made of part wood and part what I decided must be animal horn. Such artificial fabrication was bound to disintegrate after any hard use, I thought, as was the double curve of the thing, which could only be described as foppish. Yet when I took a trial shot, I couldn't believe the strength and distance I got—a nearly twice my usual best, so the shot went wildly off. I thought at first this must be a freakish accident, until I tried it again with the same result, only with slightly better aim as I compensated somewhat for the extra power. This was no accident at all. These bows were powerful, made so on purpose, by magic. Almost, I might say, the work of evil spirits. The arrows and the swords, though their blades were curved like half-moons, were also fine.

Two ponies escaped, but another two I captured. Their manes were hogged, which I found ugly, but a handy tuft was left at the neck for the rider to vault up into the saddle, should the need arise. And short manes had the advantage of not getting tangled in the bow string while riding and shooting at once. The ponies were almost too small to consider riding, but their trappings were fine indeed. The saddles were constructed of leather and a strange warpless sort of wool. They were comprised of the two leather pads I'd already seen one of the Huns use as an outlook platform. The pads lay side by side over a blanket of that same strange wool, avoiding the pony's spine and distributing the weight to his muscles instead, giving him greater ease of movement. The pads were joined together by birchwood arches at front and rear, and kept in place by girths, breast-bands, and a form of breeching passing 'round the quarters above the hocks. No wonder a man could stand on this as stably as on the ground, even as the horse moved.

The stirrups were of fine carved wood, more serviceable than ever we Valkyries had. I could pick up two men off the field at once with these, I thought. One of the ponies even wore armor, leather sewn with little iron rosettes.

I went to bury the dead, but found as I did that one was not quite ready to go. It was the tallest, lightest-faced one. He was, as he had barely breath to tell me, the survivor of the merchant's ship. He was a Roman by birth, but spoke good German from his years in trade up and down the Rhine. It was indeed a Hunnish lord to whom he'd taken the tale of his plight. Hunnish clothes they'd given him to wear, and a Hunnish party they'd sent with him to right the evil he'd suffered. I had not killed all of his protectors, he informed me—those who would come to revenge his death and that of his companions—I could not begin to. The Huns were a people as numerous as the stars in the heavens, and the realm they called their own reached from one end of the world to the other after lightning conquests under their kings Bleda and Attila.

Then his lungs could bring forth nothing but a bubble of blood, and he died.

chapter 20

IEGFRIED DID NOT COME, UNLIKE the happy ending in an old wives' tale. The Huns came instead. The snowy, bare-twigged forests on all sides of the tower were dark with them. And they were all too real.

It was me against fifty, maybe a hundred, Huns—I never could count them all. I assumed my time could be numbered by hours, if not less. And yet, when a day and a night and another day had passed, and I was still alive—and ten, maybe twelve, Huns lay dead, inviting Odin's birds to feed, I could kindle a glimmer of hope. It was clear that these strange, bowlegged men, though unbeatable on horses, were not much when it came to the tactics of siege, for I certainly would have been overcome if they had been.

They demonstrated no idea of what to do when the terrain was anything but pancake flat, and showed no patience to learn. I couldn't be sure, of course, but it seemed to me that after two days, a good number of the troops got bored, tired of being wet and cold and picked off like crabapples from a tree the moment they carelessly got in range. They rode off. Of course, they might have gone for reinforcements, but the commanders left behind didn't seem too encouraged by the prospect. There also seemed to be an uneasy sense among them—not surprising, considering what they must know of me so far—that they were dealing with something more than a mere woman here. Magic

was involved, I read on their otherwise hard-to-read brown faces and in their otherwise unintelligible gibberish that sounded nothing so much as like the croaking of frogs. Magic that was greater than they were.

I further noticed how clumsy they were on their feet, as if every step on their bandy legs gave them pain. I was certain that horseless, I could outrun any of them, even in full armor and heavily armed.

These last two notions gave me the seeds of a plan. At first, I thought I wouldn't have to put it into effect until my food supplies ran low—a week or two at least. But then one of the more enterprising Huns organized a raid to try and burn my door down. They made themselves into a sort of turtle, all their little round shields forming a shell over their heads. In this guise, they threw a jug of oil and oil-soaked faggots against the door, then thrust a torch into it before I managed to drive them off with arrows and stones prized out of the crumbling walls. Then I finished off the flames with a well-aimed water-soaked rug and a fizzle.

The door was left blackened but no thinner. I had been forced to use such a quantity of arrows to drive back the attack, however, that I found my supplies seriously depleted. Arrows were the best, indeed the only, way to deal with these Huns from the tower walls. I determined to use lances more frequently, whenever the range was close enough. Axes and swords were only useful in hand-to-hand combat, and if all thirty of them, or even half that number, got close enough for hand-to-hand combat, all the swords in the world could not save me. The simple fact of the matter was that I'd kept them at bay with my arrows, and I had only enough arrows to fend off one more assault like that—and no supplies with which to make more.

There was also the problem of exhaustion, for one cannot watch as thirty can and still have strength to fight when the watching and waiting ended.

After the attempted fire, there were two days of storm during which the Huns made no move—or, if they did, I couldn't see them through the whiteout. I tried to keep warm, conserve my strength, and keep watch all at the same time. It was during this period that a bit of magic came into my head, a rune to sing and carve into my lance handle, a toss of green wood into my fire to make a choking smoke that could waft out and fill the forest. Then I took out my bearskin and swung it over my head, chanting,

> "Let there be fog
> And let there be phantoms,
> Weird marvels
> To baffle my hunters."

I also sang over a length of the sturdy wool I knotted together. I put a piece of oak inside each knot, spitting and singing on it to make the knots as strong as a ladder rung. I wasn't certain that this would work, unskilled in the art as I was, but it was worth a try. Singing helped to concentrate my mind on what my unmagic mind had determined to do.

It was the dark just before dawn. The sky was moonless, but it was already lighter than it had been, for the stars had come out of the storm and were like chips of ice in the bitter cold. I could not put off the enactment of my plan for another moment.

I thrust the point of a lance into a scrap of wood left on the tower's second story. The deep runes I had carved into its ash wood I colored with blood cut from the inside of my thigh. What was left of my old bearskin I set on this pole, poor battered head upright and peering over the battlements like a good soldier. I set another lance butt-first into some rubble nearby and draped a corner of the skin over it to arm my retainer. I took one last trip downstairs to fetch the bottom of a broken jug and to give the pair of ponies I had stabled with me a hurried mound of hay. As I did, I paused with a pang to look around at the red silk dress spread across my bed of furs, and the silks draping the walls as a bridal chamber. But there wasn't time for sorrow. Taking only the weapons I could carry without being weighted down, those that could prove most useful, plus a good woolen cloak and a bit of dried venison and the last of the raisins in a pouch, I left the protection of the inner tower for the last time.

Back up on the battlements in the bitter predawn once more, I kicked over the fire, which I'd moved up there to help with the watch, after having rescued just the broken shard full of coals. I set the coals on the shard within the bear's mouth. They glowed satisfactorily through the skull's empty eye sockets and outlined the teeth. I murmured one rune of replacement over that glowing head, then I tossed the length of knotted worsted over the battlement. I swung myself after it and climbed hand over hand to the ground.

I was wearing Aed's daughter's woolen dress for warmth. Even tucked up into my belt, it made climbing difficult. But the knots in my ladder proved as firm as any wooden rungs, and I reached the ground, sinking over my boot ankles in the fresh snow with but a hint of rope-burn warmth in my hands.

This sinking was not good. A step or two from the tower, however, the snow firmed up with a solid crust. I draped the cloak from my shoulder to drag behind me so it might look as if only the wind had passed by. I took one glance backwards to see the bear winking at me from behind the darker dark that was the parapet. Then I crept forward, mouthing the words to my hiding rune as I went.

Perhaps the rune worked. Or perhaps it was just Fate. Dawn called a fog out of the surrounding forest. I stepped into that cover quickly and gratefully, and determined to keep the rune on my lips.

Almost before I knew it, I was upon the first of the Huns' low-burning fires. With wonderful good fortune, the Huns tending it had set no watch, or if they had, he had gone off momentarily to relieve himself. There were four brown cocoons cuddled about the fire within a low ridge of snow they had built as a sort of fort for themselves. Once I'd determined which end of these amorphous blobs was the head, with Gram it was a simple matter to detach that part from the rest, despite folks having always declared Huns to be neckless. Only the third one gave me any trouble. He stirred before he died, giving an unintelligible grunt with a clear note of question, which was just enough to awaken his only companion still asleep. Number four I had to run a couple times through the chest as he rose in amazement, not nearly so neat a job. Still, it was done, and I wasted no time in stepping out of the low snow wall once more and beyond to where five horses were hobbled.

I chose the tallest one, still an uncomfortably small beast. Before I mounted her, I cut the hobbles on the rest of them to add confusion to my tracks. When I whacked the flanks to give the first one the idea, however, he whinnied as if calling his dead master to witness the indignity. I didn't dare hit the rest.

It was easy enough to mount the low pony I'd picked as mine without a saddle or bridle, a little more difficult to control her. She was obviously very attached to her master and didn't take kindly to orders from anyone else. Still, I hadn't ridden with the Valkyries to no purpose. Even with my weight, which must have been more than she was used to, she knew how to take a good gallop and, before I heard the cries of alarm from the Hunnish siege line, we were far enough away that, if I hadn't been expecting them, I wouldn't have known them for what they were.

I sang my rune of concealment louder now. The fog grew correspondingly denser.

My plan was to ride north to the closest village I knew of, a squalid place of only five houses that Siegfried and I—or, as I was coming to say to myself more and more frequently now—I alone had passed on my way upriver. I couldn't beg there for asylum. Even in normal times, a young woman traveling by herself with no claim of kin on any villager would be highly suspect. Surely, she had brought the curse of adultery upon those who did know her and would bring the same to any new town.

Or she was a witch.

In these unnatural times when, if what the dead merchant had said was true—the Huns had broken the bounds of the earth and ruled everything—a German girl riding into their village on what could only be a stolen Hunnish pony would be even more cause for alarm.

Still, I ought to be able to sit down by a goose herd somewhere or, if the storm kept even webbed feet close to the yard, at least be seen straggling here or there with a bundle of faggots. Come dark, I could sleep in a byre warmed by beasts' breath and, in the morning—let

come what may. If I took off the helmet and brynie, in Aed's daughter's wool, to Hunnish eyes—eyes which had only seen me, if at all, in warrior's garb—here I would be part of the scenery. It was German eyes I would have to avoid more carefully.

chapter 21

HE SQUALOR OF THE VILLAGE did not improve when I looked down on it from the edge of the woods with the consideration that it might be my new home for a while. Even the hex signs marking the plaster walls of the huts with the protection of Thor's hammer seemed colorless and dead in the winter light. The barest wisps of smoke floated up to join the evaporating fog from only the main houses. The baking house was cold and dark and seemed likely to stay that way, the weather blowing heedless through the door left ajar. This spoke of fuel used very sparingly. And no one had been to these woods to gather more to make the frugality less, at least not since the storm. This was unfortunate, as I could not mingle my footprints with theirs. I could not even see where they had much food stored and figured the Huns must have taken it. Most people will set out a little bit every evening "for them"—*them* being elves, or maybe just the poor in a community, the wayfarer, like me. I had thought to help myself to that at least. But if they were hungry, as it appeared, they might not even set out a token. I would be hungry too.

Still, there were substantial manure piles before every farmstead, the first thing to greet a visitor. I remembered from my childhood how proud people were of their piles. Large piles meaning many cows, fertile fields. It was remarkable, and a little incongruous, that these people should have such large piles at this time between the early winter dunging of the fields and the spring cleaning of the stalls, and yet have no observable granaries or root huts, no stores of winter fodder. Perhaps they were workers of magic.

Overcoming this hesitation, I broke a dead branch off a nearby tree. *Get rid of the horse*, I told myself, *and bring a gift of kindling.* I was about to give my little Hunnish pony a whisk on the flanks and send her off running when I saw some movement in the village. It was easy to notice, for at this time of year nothing moved unless it had to. Men in particular would never stir from their bench by the fire.

When I enter this village, I thought, *dressed in grey wool like this, this is the sort of life I'm stepping into. Waiting on oafs like that.* Was that option truly better than death at the hands of the Huns?

The movement that caught my eye was indeed a woman, bundled up in grey and bent towards the cold so she seemed old, but she could have been any age. Younger women usually served their elders, and unattached women such as I would be, served most of all. This woman moved through the yards about the steadings where the snow was almost pristine. Cows shared the same roof as the folk and could be milked without discomfort on the coldest day. If there were milking ewes or goats, they would be brought under the same roof as well, three or four to a cow's stall. Most of the other livestock would have been butchered and salted down as winter came on, and would therefore be under the same roof as well, or in some storehouse I couldn't see. There were perhaps one or two byres with live animals in them in the entire village. The villagers had seen the storm coming and given these beasts extra food. Nothing moved in the village but the pallid smoke, until this woman who moved like smoke along the ground. This was enough to draw attention to her.

I was surprised to see that she fit her footprints into the only other prints to be seen in the yard, and even more surprised to see that they headed, not to any byre or possible storeroom, but to the closest manure pile. The jug she carried was not full of kitchen scraps, which in any case would go to some animal for processing first before they reached the midden. Her movements seemed furtive, more than just against the cold. She looked up and around when she reached the pile, like a doe sniffing the air. I stepped behind a tree and out of her sight.

Then she began to dig with a spading fork into the midden. The upper crust of the hill under the snow was frozen solid, but she soon broke that away in blocks and reached the part that was soft and easy to handle. Yes, I remember how those piles had a life of their own. This one gave off warm steam to the frigid air as she stirred the inner core.

And suddenly, there in her hand was a whole cabbage, the loose leaves of the head flapping off the dirt, as good and fresh as if she'd just cut its stalk in the field. Here some turnips, a bunch of carrots. Her basket full, she moved to the next pile and soon had her jug full of wheat.

So that was it! The Huns must have pressed hard, but these wise folk had hidden their winter stores where no Hun would think to look for them, in fresh earth kept from freezing under their middens. As a child, I had heard people say, when a raid from the Saxons was expected, that this would be a thing to do, but I never actually saw people store in anything but the usual mounds of plain, sandy earth or little lean-to storehouses. Or perhaps, remembering the hunger of my childhood, perhaps we never had enough to bother storing.

These were clever folk, and not so beaten down by the presence of the Huns that they might not take me in if I presented myself as a fugitive, say. My plan was good and taking better shape all the time. I suppose I could get used to being the one sent on dirty errands to the midden while the men sat. Eventually.

I raised my branch to send the pony on its way again, but then I saw the woman, just covering her work on the manure pile so it wouldn't look disturbed, suddenly start. She turned instantly and ran for her house, disregarding the cleverly won carrots that tumbled from her skirt on the way.

I heard them first, a crunch like the breaking of an arm on the silence of the snow. Then I saw them as she had seen them, riding on the village—a hoard of Huns in their fur caps and winter cloaks, like so many bears on horseback. These were not Huns from the siege of my tower; they were coming from the east, and even Huns could not have made a circuit quite so fast. This was a party of about twenty more, but if they could appear in random, unannounced bunches like this, anywhere at any time, the old world was indeed a different place, and overrun with them.

The Huns—as one body to one shout—pressed their ponies' flanks and shot from an amble to a gallop. The woman had reached the safety of her home by now, and her menfolk were clustering at the door. But she was not what they were after. In my attempt to keep hidden from her, I had exposed myself on the east. And now, seeing her own kind, my pony whinnied at them joyfully. It was me they had seen. Me—a tall, blond woman, and one of *their* ponies.

Now I whisked my pony's flank, but only after I'd straddled her once more. She flew like the wind. It took me too damnably long to realize much of her eagerness must have been due to the fact that we were retracing the morning's steps, riding home to her master in her mind and, in my mind, straight into another band of Huns, these with revenge on their minds.

I turned her west, towards the river. She obeyed, but only with reservation. Her gallop seemed to have an *Are you sure? Are you sure?* limp to it.

"I'm sure! I'm sure!" my branch whip kept trying to tell her. "Sure as death!" But the Huns don't raise stupid, dull-spirited animals. Whipping couldn't teach her much.

I managed to keep well enough ahead of my pursuers, riding along the riverbank, once I reached it, for an hour or so. Sometimes I couldn't see or hear them, but they always knew where I was. There was no time to think that I might erase my tracks in this fresh snow, damp and impressionable with the day's relative warmth. Sometimes I was able to concentrate enough to sing a snatch of rune and, just so much, a snatch of fog would drift around and be my friend. But it never lasted very long. The Vanir willed it fair today.

And every time I caught a glimpse of Huns, they were just that much closer. There were many more of them now. The first band must have joined with those from the tower, and now all were thirsty for blood. And they were good horsemen, such good horsemen. If I hadn't been so afraid of what it meant for me, it would have thrilled my heart to see them ride. I had ridden with the Valkyries, and these men were excellent, every one of them.

It became difficult to stick to the riverbank. It was growing uneven and rocky, building up to the great thrust of the singing rock. My pony, used to the steppes, didn't like this at all. Then again, neither did their ponies. Still, the temptation was great for me to turn inland, in spite of the fact that it would give them the same advantage it would give me. But then, around the skirts of the cliff, I spied an unnaturally moving mass of brown against the snow. It was a second group of Huns, mustered by some magic, to cut off my path ahead.

I turned back to the rocks again, but my pony had had enough. And so, I suddenly realized, had I. *Enough!*

I pulled up and dismounted, careful to do it on stone from which the sun had melted the snow, so I would leave no trace. I touched the pony's flanks one more time and let her ride off into the snow alone. She wouldn't make nearly the tracks she'd made before with me burdening her, but it might make my pursuers stop and think for a moment at least. In any case, I'd had enough of bouncing on her small back.

I labored up the cliffside, having to stop frequently to warm my hands which grew too numb to tell whether it was stone I grasped or thin air. I was only halfway to the top when the Huns appeared at the base. At that distance, I was out of arrow shot. Out of the reach of their arrows, but not out of the reach of mine, for mine had the pull of the earth on their side. Whenever I got to a firm ledge, I turned and got off a few telling shots, enough to allow me to climb to the next ledge with respected impunity.

The Huns had to abandon their ponies now, as I had done, and I saw that Fate had not quite abandoned me yet. As I had already remarked—for all their grace on horseback—dismounted, they waddled on their bowed legs like so many toddlers. The cliff's face clearly daunted them, as if it were a place infested by spirits, indeed.

I reached the top. The Rhine flowed, deep and sluggish with cold so far below. On every other side now were Huns, fear and clumsiness their bane. I could pick them off with ease, but they were not stupid animals unable to learn from others' mistakes. Their climbing improved.

Then, my bow string snapped. I didn't have a spare. I did as we Valkyries always talked of doing but had never been forced to attempt. Indeed, it was the part of our hairstyle that I still kept, to braid up our hair in two main plaits but to set out a third, thinner braid above the other on the left side. As quickly as I could, I tore this hank of hair out of my head and fastened it to my bow. Its spring was superb. But even with what might prove to be the best string I ever had, and even without wasting a single shot, my arrows were not going to last forever.

I didn't look much at the Rhine to my back, nor to its distant shore. I hadn't time. But presently, the light began to change. The sun was setting. I knew it would hit the cliff, and that the cliff would sing. The knowledge made me smile. I felt a little glow in my heart, the good feeling of exhaustion at the end of a job well-done. I couldn't enjoy the feeling long, however, for there was another Hun, close enough for me to see the whites around the black of his squinty little eyes.

I reached for an arrow. It was my last. I took that Hun out, right through the white of his eye, but he was quickly replaced by another. That was in front, and on the other sides he was joined by two of his brothers.

I threw my empty quiver at one, my bow—gold with my hair—at another, a loose rock at the third. Rock climbing was so strange to them that they all three lost their grips and fell—one to his death, taking the fellow behind with him. Another would need a good bone setter, but the third was only scraped and with a savage yell kept coming.

They were on all sides now, swarming like so many brown ants to a drop of honey. I threw all my spears and more rocks, which then were gone. I took a deep breath, closed my eyes for a weary moment, and then drew Gram.

And then—then, the rock beneath me began to hum.

I don't think it had ever resonated with such a deep, rich tone. The vibrations came up the solid rock and through my legs. It was thrilling.

And then I saw that what had stopped me with its thrill had turned the Huns to stone with terror. There was silence for many deep, long breaths of good, chill air. And then the Huns began to scramble away, backwards, down across their companions, even to pitch forward to their deaths—anything to get away from the sound and the wondrous light. Their screeches were deafening, but even when I could no longer hear the hum over them, I could still feel it, close and strong and deep.

The cliff sides cleared as the rock continued to hum. And then the sun set, and there was silence. I stood on the top of the rock in the silence, above everything, alone.

The world lost its color in the gathering gloom. My legs lost their strength, and I sat. The sweat stopped and began to freeze on my skin. I let my head sink to my knees, but lifted it up almost instantly. There was something down there in the dark below. I looked hard into the darkness and saw nothing. I looked again, and there were at least three of them, giant, sending, or Hun—it was hard to tell in that light—creeping up with the stealth of cats after a mouse.

I got to my feet, but they felt stupid beneath me. Now there were ten of these dark things on all sides, all sides now but the one with the open air and the Rhine below.

Gram tried to go rigid in my hand, but my legs and arms weren't behind it. And then I put up my blade. I turned my back on the clambering sendings, walked to the edge of the rock, and called out, "Very well, Father Wanderer! You win!"

Then I stepped off into thin air.

chapter 22

IT WAS A LONG WAY down. I hit the water with a force that seemed to split my face from my nose inward and sent cold blackness with it. Had the water been stone, it didn't seem it could have been harder. But my brain shook itself from the blackness I'd longed to overwhelm. A sense of bitter wet cold took over, and my response to that, at first unwilling but soon inescapable, was to fight.

I fought my way to the surface and breathed. The current dragged at me, gnawing like a beast at its prey. I fought it. *It can be fought*, came to my mind. *You've seen it done.*

The current threw my knee against a rock I couldn't see. The shore was close, then. The other side was safer, but I was cold and exhausted. I fought the cold. I fought the exhaustion. A wave surged over me, but I fought it off.

Another rock, this one above the water. I clung to it. The current tore me off. I fought my way to another rock. This one was more substantial. I fought to cling to it, then to pull myself up and out of the water.

This was solid rock, but there wasn't much of it. Panting there, I saw the other rocks that marked land, but they were separated from me by a torrent. I couldn't stay where I was. Icy water rushed over my rock in rhythmic surges, and the evening air, with a stiff, northwest breeze to it, was colder still. I fought to regain my breath, and when I had but barely—for the cold was likely to keep it from me until it left me altogether—I slipped off the rock and into the torrent again.

I fought and infinitely later gained the shore. There I lay, gasping for air and jerking with cold like a landed fish.

Until this point, my battle had been a reflex to survive. Now what? I was on shore, but to my knowledge there were Huns everywhere on that shore. I should have swum to the other side, after all. I thought perhaps I should then—but, no, I was too exhausted. Worse than exhaustion, I felt the dangerous cold sleep moving though my limbs, wringing the jerking from them, but leaving them with what I knew would be death. In another minute, I would lie down where I was and cease to care.

But at the moment, I still did care. I struggled to stand on feet I could no longer feel and turned towards the only warmth I could think of. It didn't matter what stood in the way.

I stumbled over land I knew fairly well but was too cold to negotiate carefully. I stumbled on, and then suddenly it occurred to me that, by all rights, I should have run into a Hun by now. Weren't they all over the place, their ponies and their arrows?

Here, indeed, was snow churned to slush and mixed with mud and horse droppings. Here, surely, many horses and their men had stood and milled and argued in their strange, clipped tongue. But they were gone. The churned-up snow was turning quickly back to ice beneath my frozen feet, now that the sun had set. There were no Huns.

I struggled on, I knew not how long, no more cautiously, but no less relieved either.

And then, there was the tower, a great, silent bulk against the rising first slip of a moon, its great friendly stones catching my staggering arms. The door, amazingly, was still locked from the inside. The Huns had not battered it down when they discovered me gone. Why, I hadn't even been looted. But I had to go in the way I'd come out, the hard way.

I found the cord down which I'd climbed. I was thankful I hadn't taken the time to tear the thing down at my escape, as I had thought

to do. The knots were still as rune-sturdy as rungs. The question was whether my senseless hands could climb it. I slipped enough in the first few feet to warm them well, and then there I was, over the parapet at the top, cracking the frozen folds of my skirt as I went.

In a daze of cold and disbelief, I turned towards the stairs—and my heart stopped cold. There before me was a fearsome figure with glowing eyes.

Of course! My bearskin, with the coals still somehow glowing inside the skull. Now I actually chortled with relief. I scooped the shard up and threw the rug over my shoulders. With the coals and the banked embers of that morning's early fire, I soon had a good-sized log on and, before I was even certain it would catch, I had fallen into a deep and exhausted sleep.

I was up in the morning as soon as I could shake the previous day's damage. All the damage was not gone, of course. There was a fierce aching in my left little toe. It was an unnatural white; I was probably going to lose it. Like Orvandel the great archer of myth, I thought, whose frost-bitten toe was tossed by Thor up into the sky to become the North Star.

I made myself a cup of warm broth by boiling strips of venison, but my biggest concern was that the smoke from my fire would draw the Hun's attention to this spot once more. I served the broth up in a goblet from one of the merchant's chests—bronze, so it carried the heat—and I soon had to wrap the stem up in the edge of my shawl. Then I took it up to the parapet to have a look around.

There were no Huns. The perimeter of my view was entirely abandoned to nature—all but one spot. I returned to that spot and looked again. Off towards the east, at the edge of a birch copse, rose a woolen thread of a fire as from a spindle. At first, I thought it could only be a natural phenomenon, the start of a forest fire, perhaps. But in this wet and cold, that was impossible.

Then I saw the figure tending the fire. I couldn't see it clearly, not even so much as to tell whether it was male or female. But there was no horse, and that made me feel quite certain it wasn't Hunnish. I stood on the parapet, quietly drinking my broth. I saw how the smoke from our fires swayed off and then back with each breath of wind, as if speaking to one another in a silent, wood-scented language. I drank my broth and wondered what this strange fire at the edge of the birches might mean.

For three days, we and our fires watched each other. Sometimes, especially at night, I thought I could hear a weird, high singing coming from the birches, then a drumming. In the morning, all was silent but watchful again.

The third day was warmer than it had been for some time. The figure stretched to the warmth, as I did, and shook itself of some of its bundling wraps. It stepped away from the birches a little as if to get a better look at me. Then I saw clearly. It was a woman.

A woman? A woman! All this time I'd been so watchful, imagining—imagining who knows what sort of giant or ogre, and here it was, only a woman!

It didn't take me long to decide on and then to carry out a plan of action. I left the battlements, climbed down into the tower and threw off the double bars holding the door. I walked across the pristine snow towards the birches and the dark figure that stood out against their icy white. The woman had something steely grey in her hands. Could it be a sword? Could this be a Valkyrie? I walked with my left hand swinging on the hilt of Gram. There was no honor in running a mere woman through, but I could certainly do such a thing if it was called for.

"I thought it might be you," the figure said to me in greeting.

"Indeed?"

"Yes."

"Well, I never expected … What is your name again? I'm sorry, it's been a long while. I've forgotten yours."

"Rüdeger," the figure said. "There is no reason why you should remember me."

It was not a woman after all. It put a good spin on what was a whorl, not a sword, in its hands and let it drop. It was the priest dressed as a woman from the Yggdrasil shrine in the mountains south of Gothland.

"And what might you be doing here, so far from the cave of the Norns?" I asked.

The boulders of the face cracked with a little smile. "It is a long story."

"I should imagine. But what are you doing precisely *here*, sitting in the snow in front of my tower?"

"I've been sent after you."

His birch fire had produced some fine coals, and its aroma was attractive. I did not let myself succumb to the attraction, however.

"Who sent you?" I put my right hand on Gram. "Odin? The Norns?"

"No. The Huns."

Now my heart felt a supernatural twinge, and Gram came a palm's breadth out of its sheath.

"It is not what you may think," Rüdeger said. "Be calm."

"The Huns are not what I think?"

"Oh, certainly, if *they* were to come and get you, you should draw your sword. But they have given up and sent me instead."

"You are their … their sending, nonetheless. You obey their orders?"

"You have no need to fear from me—Brynhild, isn't it?"

"Yes."

"Please, sit down by the fire, and I'll tell you all."

"If we're going to be friendly," I said quickly, before I could think better of it, "why don't you come into the tower? Put a roof over your head for a change."

"Thank you," Rüdeger's smile cracked like ice on a frozen pond through the three-days' growth of his beard. "I should like that."

All my wariness couldn't resist the relief that suddenly flooded me to see that smile in a familiar face.

Inside the tower, I set the bear rug for Rüdeger to sit on. Then, pressing a brass goblet full of steaming broth into his great, cold, male hands, I said, "If you're going to tell me all, you'll have to start a long way back. I've been away for … for quite a long time."

"Yes, I know about Odin's sleep thorn."

"I must say, you for one don't seem to have aged a day."

The face under the white coif smiled. He took a sip of broth, then brought the stub of candle from out of his skirt pocket. "I still have this, you see. Though there were times during the past years I've wanted to burn it out. Several times during the past three nights, in fact, I almost tossed the whole thing into the heart of the fire."

This was the candle that Verðandi, the Norn of present action, had given to his mother at his birth. He would live as long as the stub of a taper did not burn down. He returned the candle to his pocket, took another sip of broth, and looked around the warmth and coziness of my room appreciatively.

"You say the Huns sent you?" I asked, wary of his appraisal.

"You've made quite an impression on them, Brynhild."

"And they've made an impression on me. I'm going to lose this toe to frostbite, thanks to them."

I yanked off my boot and wagged the evidence at the coif. The coif nodded, as if confirming, *Yes, it looks like you'll probably lose it.*

"A great sorceress lives in this tower—" Rüdeger began.

"A sorceress!"

"That's all the word among the Huns. She sits on top of an impossible crag, calling boatmen to their deaths and stealing their treasures."

"It's the rock that sings," I said. "I go to hear it, and the river is treacherous there."

"Yes. The local folk have long known of that rock and call it the Lorelei—'she that lures.' But now a woman has been seen with that rock, and that makes it … well, more personal, more malicious, shall we say?"

"I tried to help those poor men. And I saved their goods for them."

"Put them to good use, I see," he commented with a toss of his head to my furnishings.

"I'll be happy to return them whenever they come."

"Of course. But one man did come, and you killed him."

"He came with Huns. I didn't realize, until it was too late."

"You killed him and three of the Huns' top guard. You kept a whole battalion at bay for a week."

"It wasn't more than four days. Then I ran out of arrows."

"Then you flew out of the tower, over their heads by magic, and kept it guarded by a bear spirit that couldn't die."

"Because it's been dead a long, long time," I said, pointing to the rug he sat on and telling him how it was done.

Rüdeger nodded and smiled, and then proceeded to describe the rest of my exploits, concluding with how I had walked up sheer rock to the Lorelei's perch, drawn my sword to make an earthquake, and then called on my father, who rose up from the Rhine and carried me away with him on a foaming white steed.

"So now they've sent *you* against me?" I asked incredulously.

"Defeat magic with magic."

"Magic."

"Men who dress as women are, among the Huns, the most powerful of magicians. 'Shamans,' they call them. As are women who dress as men." He nodded towards my brynie and helmet.

"I see. But you're no Hun."

"No, I'm not. And I've seen some of the Hunnish magicians do some really incredible things. But they decided to send me instead, I guess because you're a Germanic phenomenon, and no shaman I've ever met can be bothered to learn German. They spend too much time speaking in tongues that no one can understand, I guess."

"And are you a great magician?" I smiled.

Rüdeger smiled back. "I need to keep them thinking I am."

"How long have you been with them?"

"Nearly fifteen years."

"You must be some kind of magician, to have stayed with those monsters so long."

"I'm no more a magician than you are. I am only different from what they know and expect, and that is magic."

"Fifteen years you say you've been with them?" I looked at Rüdeger now with more wonder than originally spurred by the incongruity of his person.

"Yes. Ever since they overran Gothland and all the area around the Yggdrasil shrine."

"The Huns have overrun the shrine? Does this mean they've felled the sacred ash, the World Tree? Have they burnt it?" *How can the world still exist?* was the question I heard in my voice but didn't speak. *But then, this world of the Huns is not much like the old world I left, is it?*

"No, thank the Vanir and the will of the good Norns for that. You see, it was I who met the Huns on their horses at our gate, as I used to meet everyone. It was only me. You're right; I couldn't have stopped them. It was a hot day towards the end of summer when the ash keys lay already drying on the ground. And they had torches in their hands. One thrust of those torches into those keys or into the turning leaves, and the whole shrine would have gone up, Yggdrasil and all. But they stopped when they saw me and jabbered away in their strange tongue for a while. And the upstart of the conversation was, so I learned when they bothered to send for a translator, that they would spare the shrine and all the treasure they knew must be within if I would consent to go with them and work my magic in their favor. So, for the sake of Yggdrasil, I did."

"So, for your sake, Yggdrasil still stands."

"I assume it does. At least, the world hasn't come to an end in the meantime."

I didn't tell him how unlike the world I'd left was this new one.

"That's pretty much the same deal they're asking you to cut," Rüdeger said. "Or rather, asking me to magic you into accepting. To come and work your powerful magic for them."

"And then they'll let me be?"

"Pretty much."

"Even if I can't work magic?"

"Until they have a job like this for you to perform."

"Which, Rüdeger, I'm pleased to announce, you seem to have carried off with flying colors."

"So it would seem."

Our eyes met in a communion of firelight, and then I said, "I suppose I shall have to go and meet the head Hun."

"His name is Bleda."

"King of all the Huns?"

"He is king of this neck of the woods, in any case. Yes, it would be good form for you to meet."

"And then I guess I should change into something a little more … say, like the remnants of my battlemaid costume."

"That would be appropriate."

"With a lot of red silk to make up for what age has gnawed out of leather and brass."

"Good."

"So you will excuse me while I change?"

"Of course."

I undressed before him with as little regard as if he had indeed been a woman.

Some time later, we rode toward the Hunnish town on two Hunnish ponies, the two I'd captured from the first foray and kept with me in the tower. I was in full Valkyrie regalia and more besides, although it must have been almost too much for the little creature under me; Rüdeger rode primly side-saddle on my left.

We came in sight of the Hunnish settlement, and it was so expansive—covering two hills that I could see and more beyond—that I had to speak with sudden cheeriness to my companion to keep my courage up. Besides, my toe inside its boot was working itself up to falling off, and that was a constant reminder of the last time I'd been face to face with Huns.

"I heard you drumming and singing, Rüdeger, I think," I said. "At night while you sat outside the tower."

"It's true," he admitted and actually blushed. "Well, that is how the Hunnish shamans work, and I thought…"

"You thought it might work magic?"

"I thought at least it would keep my candle in my pocket, my courage up, don't you see?"

"Your courage, Rüdeger? You were afraid of me?"

"Afraid of bears or wolves or whatever might be out there in the woods. Afraid it might be a real sorceress I couldn't handle."

"Instead of me, whom you can."

"Yes, that's it."

"Ah, Rüdeger," I cajoled, laughing. "Maybe you are some great and powerful magician. Maybe you are indeed."

chapter 23

WAS QUITE CERTAIN THAT the rolling valley half-a-day's journey from the Rhine had been unpopulated, a good place for meadowing horses, when I last knew it. It was now home to tens and even hundreds of thousands—throngs of people for which I knew no numbers high enough. What seemed to me to be the rapid appearance of this settlement that could only be called a city, a metropolis, could also just as rapidly become a disappearance. For all the dwellings, I soon understood, were tents. Only they weren't tents such as we northern folk were used to: angular, striped, woolen awnings on poles. They were a patchwork of skins stretched on low, collapsible frames. The frames, round in base and rounded on top, appeared like so many weathered haystacks, winter fodder for a herd of celestial cows.

Between the tents, compounds were made for the ponies to the south and west of the humans' dwellings, to be out of the wind. Each corral had a good supply of hay, the scraps of which fell like basketry into the mud and froze there. When the ponies stepped on it, it crunched like basketry breaking. Ponies' breath must have been a main source of heat in the city—that and ponies' dung. The smell of it burning for fuel permeated the air. There were other animals too: fat-tailed sheep, a few goats, and scrawny, miserable chickens with wet, bedraggled feathers. None of these warranted a modicum of the care showered upon the horseflesh, and the rest of the beasts struggled for a living without human aid off the horse's leavings as best they could.

It surprised me a little that the Huns, having succeeded in camouflaging their own city as a dung heap, should have failed to see through the disguise of their conquered people's victuals. But maybe they could afford to turn a blind eye.

As soon as we approached the outskirts, a cry ran like wildfire through the tents. People thronged to see us, children first. They were little round, brown children, nearly naked from the neck down in spite of the cold, but all their heads were carefully covered with the tight bands that would permanently deform them by the time they were four or five. They tumbled out of the cow-pat tents to stop and stare. And though they resembled a mass of squirming maggots, scattered liberally over them was the plunder of two continents. The nakedest infant in his mother's arms nonetheless sported a torc about his fat double chins worth a prince's ransom.

Then came the men, fearsome grimaces on every face, scarred and hairless as they were, though many sported moustaches, thin and dangling to their waists. Their eyes were almost nonexistent. Even in the tight passages between houses— such passages could hardly be dignified by calling them streets—few men deigned to dismount but twisted backwards and forwards in the saddle as interest warranted. They could even lie on their moving mounts as other men might lie on their couches at home.

There were the women. Their eyes, too, seemed to vanish behind high, flat cheekbones. I noticed many of them had pleasant figures—short and bundled in shapeless winter furs though they were.

But the children, the children drew back my attention again. They were as open and intelligent-seeming as ever one could hope to see, for all the crippling bands about their heads, with bright black eyes and quick smiles. *Such qualities may perhaps still be present in the adults,* I told myself, though boys as young as eight, as soon as they had had their bands removed, knew only too well how to put on the mask of fierce ugliness.

With such observers, our progress soon became more of a procession, squirming and worming its way through the haphazard layout of tents. There was some order here, the mold of some symbolic system, for over every door hung an emblem of some kind, a horse's or a sheep's head, a bunch of colored ribbons, a stylized moon fashioned of silver. Family crests, I guessed. And on one, a quiver—making me work out that it was the dwelling of a bow-maker—and a miniature anvil on the dwelling of the smith, confirmed by an outdoor forge.

And such order continued into their throng's behavior, for never did the press of wonder at our foreignness crumble into hostility. Indeed, young boys whose rowdiness threatened to poke and prod us in a rough curiosity were sharply reprimanded by their elders and cringed back into place. All in all, the impression was of awe and, though shouts continued, they began to take on a rhythm, and then I thought I could hear recognizable syllables in them.

I looked back at Rüdeger. He nodded and almost smiled. Yes, his face told me. What I heard was his name Rüdeger, strangely twirled and with consonants served by mere glides.

Our ponies picked their way carefully, but with snorts of happy familiarity at the head of this procession for about half the distance through the valley. And then we approached the King's tent. I could tell because we began to take a slight rise, and the women and children became scarcer and then vanished altogether. The swell of procession on either side of us was now composed entirely of men, men such as I had slain perhaps two score of, men toughened by war until they were like walnuts and not given to the frippery of gold worn by their dependents.

The tents gained somewhat in size and dignity as we went towards the center, as much as any dung hill could be said to gain in dignity. And then someone caught the bridles of my pony and Rüdeger's, and Rüdeger gestured for me to join him in dismounting. Then I knew we must have arrived at King Bleda's doorstep. Only a few storm-soggy banners atop a pair of wooden spires on the mounded roof marked the fact. I followed Rüdeger and a great press of curious, finally dismounted men into the twilight within.

We passed through an entryway of sorts and then through a proper door frame set in the skin walls of the tent. The wooden door itself would do any permanent fortress proud, perhaps not in size but certainly in workmanship. It was intricately carved with a pattern of diamonds and lozenges and inlaid with mother of pearl. It hung on rope hinges. Every other door we had passed had been simply made of skins. Rüdeger gestured to me that it was considered impolite to step on the threshold.

Inside, I was amazed at the feeling of great space given by the circular walls and upward-sloping roof. The circular smoke hole at the crown of the roof was doing a brisk business with the massive log burning in the round hearth below it. The acrid smoke had blackened the roof skins all about the hole and, when the smoke was successful in reaching the sky, it flowed through an intricate pattern of crisscrossed willow wands which served to hold up the entire structure. This hole and the fire provided the only light. But it was by this light that I understood that most of the stuff covering the inner walls was not fur at all. Or, if it was, it was from some rare, strange beast. Neither was it the product of a loom, for I could detect no warp, woof, or selvage. I recognized it as the same stuff the ponies' saddle blankets had been made of, but now in such quantities. It seemed to be regular sheep's wool, but worked upon, and so it was. Rüdeger told me later that it was wetted, beaten, and fused together without a loom at all, and was called felt.

Inside this principal tent, or "yurt" as the Huns called them, the felted walls were beautifully dyed in reds, browns, and whites—and appliqued with sharply contrasting colors in intricate designs. Opposite the door, on the northern wall of the tent, bundles of rugs and furs raised a platform only a few inches above the floor. Through the dimness and the smoke I couldn't clearly see the man who sat there, but I knew I must be in the presence of the King. Rüdeger gestured that I should walk around the fire into this presence to the left-hand side, the western side, while he went around to the right. There was a deep murmur of wonder at this from the spectators who filled the tent. This, Rüdeger later explained to me, was because we had shown ourselves to be powerful shamans by flaunting usual custom:

the western half of the yurt is usually reserved for men, and no woman would dare to trespass while men were present for fear of the evil said to accompany such action. I came through unscathed.

"This is Bleda Khan," Rüdeger murmured, showing me how I should bow to him, deeply, from the waist with both hands pressed in front of me. The King was a conqueror, of course, used to receiving the homage of people who didn't know his customs. But it helped confirm my power to demonstrate that I knew my manners. I couldn't have told Bleda from any of the other Huns I'd killed. He was perhaps a little plumper, but no more extravagant in dress. Not even the fleece hat was different. Like all the others, I could almost see the moths swirling in mating frenzy above it.

Bleda made a gesture, and Rüdeger translated. We were to sit. I sat as gracefully as I could on the floor. Such a seat was not made for the long limbs of northerners. All the assembly sat at the signal too. At least a hundred men had managed to squeeze in and, though they found the operation much easier than I, one hundred men armed to the teeth couldn't all sink to the floor without a great deal of clinking of metal on metal. This served to remind me that surely some of the men I had killed must have brothers, fathers, or sons now present. I knew I must put great faith in Rüdeger's magic myself if I ever thought to get out of this tent alive in any way but by floating with the smoke that curled directly at my back towards the open hole.

Now Rüdeger and Bleda exchanged some words. Rüdeger nodded and turned to me to translate their sense. "Bleda Khan says, 'So, Rüdeger. You prove yourself a fine magician. You've captured this sorceress.'"

"And what did you say?"

Rüdeger blushed. "I said, 'Thank you, my lord.'" He continued, "Bleda Khan would now like to ask you some questions."

I looked the khan straight in his squinty eyes amid the deep brown creases and scars of his face below his moth-eaten hat and nodded. I had no choice now but to undergo this test. I might as well put the best face on it.

Bleda spoke, and Rüdeger translated: "You are the sorceress who has destroyed so many of my men?"

"Well, actually—" I began, but a look from Rüdeger told me to sit up straight, look this fellow right in the eyes again, and answer with a proud and simple, "Yes."

There followed a quick survey of my deeds with the Huns, all of which I claimed with that same yes.

"He wants to know by what spirit you do these things," Rüdeger said, hard-pressed to come up with a better translation than this.

"What does he mean?"

"Shall I answer by the god Odin?" Rüdeger suggested.

"No. No," I answered firmly. "I do this by myself."

Rüdeger ventured a syllable or two of this, at which Bleda began to frown at oncc, dangerously.

Then I broke in, "And with the help of my spirit, my totem, the she-bear."

This, when translated, brought a serious nod from Bleda and a similar murmur among the congregation. One retainer close to Bleda's side bent and whispered in his lord's ear. Bleda repeated it aloud, then Rüdeger translated it again for me. "Bleda Khan says it was the bear spirit you conjured to sit watch in the tower while you flew away. His men saw it."

"That's right," I said.

"Do you work spells?"

"Yes."

"Do you cast out evil spirits?"

"Yes."

"Do you cure the sick?"

"Yes."

"Do you read the future?"

"Yes." It was getting so easy to lie like this, with a translator in between, that I hardly thought of the consequences of being caught in these lies.

"By what spirit do you prophesy?"

Bear spirit obviously wouldn't do here, or he wouldn't have asked

again. I felt a burning dryness in my throat and, for some reason, it brought up a familiar taste. I told them of the dragon's heart. This impressed very well.

Bleda made several quick sounds to a retainer and, from somewhere in the depths of the yurt, a black object was presented to me with great solemnity. It looked like nothing more than a broad shoulder bone of a sheep that had been blackened and cracked by being left in the fire.

This, Rüdeger explained, was exactly what it was, "The bone of a sacrificed ram." He cleared his voice with growing discomfort and translated further: "This is how their best shamans prophesy. They read what is written in the cracks of a burned sacrificial bone. This particular bone has posed a problem. None of the shamans in Bleda's entourage has been able to read it. The Khan wants to know if your powers can tell you what it says." Rüdeger added hastily, "Never mind if you can't. Just do as I do, and tell them blade bones are not what you read."

The notion of being able to read anything in the object that was getting my hands all sooty was fascinating. "And tell them what?" I asked him, never taking my eyes off the blade. "That I read the rune sticks such as our seiðrs toss or what? I can't even do that."

"Indeed," Rüdeger said, a little nervous that he may have led me wrong, with possible discovery of both our frauds. "I thought it better to confess to them I did nothing but spin. I'd better tell them bones are not for you."

"No, wait," I said. The burning of dragon's heart was growing in my throat. And suddenly I saw in just the way I twisted the bone at that moment what reminded me of the map of the world we Valkyries had studied during our training.

"The Huns control the world," I declared, in my best reading voice.

Rüdeger translated. The swelling of feeling in the tent at my back told me that was good, if the soundlessness did not.

I looked at the blackened bone with a single deep fissure snaking across it. I ran my finger through the fissure. *A map of the world.*

"Bleda has a brother?" I asked, recalling the dying words of the Roman in the company of the first group of Huns who'd tried to dispatch me.

"No need to ask him," Rüdeger said in tones hushed with awe of his own. "The whole world knows that he does. The whole world—but you."

Bleda said something for which I hardly needed a translation. It could only have been the question, "What does she say?"

Rüdeger translated into Hunnish, not without hesitation.

"Attila," Bleda breathed. I needed no translation for that, knowing it was his brother's name, recalling it too from the words of the dying Roman. Bleda and Attila, the two Hunnish kings.

"Attila is the name of Bleda's brother," Rüdeger explained in a whisper. "His younger brother by another wife."

"Do they share the throne, or ...?"

"The vast empire their uncle Rua left to them, they divide between them."

"Attila! Attila!" The name rang in my head, and I sang it out as a rune.

"Attila, the scourge of heaven,
Beware the scourge of heaven,
Bleda, Bleda, beware.
Beware Attila, Attila."

Rüdeger had grown as pale as death. He didn't begin to translate, but my rune hardly needed translation. There was an angry and growing murmur through the crowd. Who dared to speak against their khan's own brother? I even heard a blade or two yanked from its sheath.

But suddenly Bleda calmed them all with the uplift of a hand. "Attila," I heard him repeat. Then he got to his feet and made a long pronouncement that Rüdeger translated.

"Now it is clear to me why none of my shamans could read this bone," he began. "It's not that they couldn't, but that they wouldn't. They didn't dare say anything against Attila because he is son of my dead lamented father. But of what use to me are cowards, either on the battlefield or in the shamans' tent? Only she, only this

woman-who-is-a-man, only she came here, knowing nothing of our ways, and had the courage to speak the truth of what heaven has written here: 'Beware Attila.' Well, now I am warned. Believe me, I shall not, in future, turn my back on him. I have suspected as much for some time. No, almost since we were children together, I have mistrusted Attila. He has a dark and violent temper, though even I, Bleda Khan, was afraid to speak it. Now she gives me the courage. And now, let everyone within the sound of my voice accept the verdict, and let riders carry it beyond, wherever the Huns and their ponies ride. This is indeed a powerful sorceress. I cannot hope to control her. But let it be known that I feel it an honor to declare her my sister. Any who have suffered at her hand, come to me for compensation. I pray then that she will deign to look favorably on me and mine and work her magic in our behalf."

How odd are the ways of the world that we turn to strangers to see us with the clearest eyes! Not only did I, by some magic, help Bleda to see his brother more clearly, but he in return helped me to admit that there really was some power to my dragon's heart runes. I had scoffed at the idea, or thought of it as useless confusion in my brain until that point. Now, not only did I see the gift, but I was given the means to improve upon it. By Bleda's grace, I was granted my little tower to hold as an independent sovereign. Huns from all over, as well as their subject peoples, carried my fame abroad. It wouldn't be long before I would be kept as busy as I could be, and far from want by the gifts they brought when they came seeking my wisdom. I was also granted right to the booty shipwrecked on Lorelei's cliffs. With me or without me, the rocks would continue to sing, and the wrecks continue to happen in those treacherous narrows. Anything else I lacked, I had but to ask Bleda for, and it would be given, though I would often risk offending him because I didn't—couldn't—ask for more. Clearly, with such arrangements I would have no needs at all.

It was to pursue this life that I would be set free from the Hunnish settlement. But first, Bleda insisted that I spend three nights on his hospitality, blessing him with my presence. And it was during this time that he gave me in return perhaps the greatest boon of all, the confirmation of my powers by their juncture with those of all the other holy shamans, prophets, and priests Bleda had swept to him like booty from every corner of Europe and of Asia.

chapter 24

WE COULD HEAR THE DRUMMING long before we reached the shamans' tent. It was drumming such as I had heard Rüdeger do alone in the cold at night, before he spirited me away from my tower. Only now it was much louder and with many more intricacies of rhythm weaving in and out of the icicled air. Inside the yurt, the sound was almost painful. There were perhaps a dozen shamans, each with his drum, some surrounded by drums. Some blew into squealing shawms. Some had set a bow onto their drums so that when the string was plucked, the sound reverberated into the skin with such intensity that even my vocal cords began to vibrate until I felt close to being strangled. I certainly couldn't fill my throat with sounds of my own in competition. Every drum was hung with miniature metal figures—a horse, a star, a bow and arrow—that rattled with each thump, and each drumstick had symbolic rattles too.

And the costumes of the shamans jangled with thirty pounds of metal or more. Some wore mirrors to catch the good spirits and frighten off those that meant us harm with the image of their own visages. Some wore iron replicas of bones, as if their skin had been turned inside out. To all this racket, singing was added, each song seeming different and in a different key. There was even a trio of men in somber robes of Roman drapery who muttered what seemed to be Latin in an undertone.

"Christian priests," Rüdeger said when I commented on their outstanding appearance, outstanding because of its stark plainness compared with the wild menagerie of other costumes present.

When I expressed surprise and said that I had never seen such people, although I'd heard of them among the Romans and their allies, Rüdeger replied, "They've actually won more and more converts among the Germans in the last few years. But so much for heavenly victories. See, they, too, have been swept along with the Huns like everything else. Bleda wants their magic around him as well."

Those three did look distinctly out of place, and their chanting seemed more a call on their God to preserve them from their surroundings than a joining in with the otherwise prevalent mood.

The first matter of business, for which the drums had to fall reluctantly silent for a while, was to consecrate me for the position of shaman to the Huns. The "Father Shaman" and his nine attendants, also called his "sons," had gone earlier in the day to fetch water from three clear streams. Libations of soured mare's milk had been made at each spring and, on the way home, wild thyme, juniper, and pine bark had been gathered from the frigid forest. When they returned, these things were set to boil in the spring water over the hearth, and now a he-goat was brought in, smell and all. A few hairs were clipped from his right ear and added to the pot. Then his throat was cut, and a few drops of blood allowed to enter the pot as well. The meat was passed out of the tent for the unseen women to prepare, which didn't take long because the Huns like their meat nearly raw, still red and jiggly. Rüdeger declared a rumor that the Huns' favorite way to prepare it was to place the steaks under their saddles in the morning, ride hard all day, and by evening the flesh would be warmed just to their liking. He smiled as he said it, and I took it to not be true. He also added that under the saddle was the handiest place to keep their long journey rations, dried jerky, which did there acquire a softness and a horse-saltiness that they preferred. I thought to take up that trick myself, but there wasn't time for that sort of preparation that night. Platters were presented, and we partook.

There was prophesying from the goat's shoulder blade, which took the longest to cook and seemed, at least in Rüdeger's translation, to suffer no hitch on this occasion. The omens were very graciously in my favor.

Then the water in the pot was declared purified, and I was told to take off my boots and strip to the waist. With my boot, my blackened toe came off. This caused a great sensation. The Father Shaman claimed it, took it into his drum, chanted over it and, after due ceremony, tossed it into the fire. I tried to stop this, feeling emotionally if not physically some attachment to the thing still. But Rüdeger counseled against interrupting the process and, when it was done, a new star was declared to have appeared in the sky as the toe ascended heavenward through the smoke hole. The congregation all trooped out to see and, in fact, there did seem to be a new star up there, one that I had not been familiar with before, in any case, shining most brightly that night. I winked at it, and it winked back.

We all trooped back into the tent, significantly refreshed and duly impressed, and now it was time to pick up where we'd left off. I stripped to the waist. This caused another sensation. There had been bets laid as to what indeed would be found on that chest beneath my brynie. There were some heavy losses taken in that tent full of only men. And my breasts, no less startled by the bright light than the viewers were startled by them, took a number of reverential strokes from the closest participants as I breathed deeply and told my own body not to be shy.

I knelt in the center of the tent, facing the fire, and there the Father Shaman dipped a whisk of birch leaves into the pot of purified water and daubed me on each naked shoulder, murmuring advice as he did so, which Rüdeger translated. "Think of the poor, help them and pray always to protect them from evil spirits. If a rich man and a poor man summon you at the same time, go to the poor man first and, afterward, if you have time, to the rich man."

I wondered whether the Christian priests had undergone the same initiation, without the lost toe to show for it. If so, what had they thought of the process? They seemed none too pleased with me as I tossed the switches of my braids to my back, refastened the clasps of my dress, and put my brynie back on.

Then the drums began in earnest again, and there was eating, drinking, and dancing. There were braziers full of a sweet-smelling smoke set throughout the room. The smoke soon made me quite light-headed. I had no drum of my own, but Rüdeger let me join him on his, and I soon determined to make one of my own. I loved the feeling I got that all the stray pieces of my being were gathered up and concentrated in the palm of my hand. I even saw in a sort of trance the place in the forest by the Lorelei's rock where I should find the best-sounding wood to take for the task. Rüdeger said his was from a scion of Yggdrasil itself. The drumming numbed and mesmerized me almost immediately, but, though this might have seemed a contradiction, I felt my powers of concentration were at the same time greatly magnified. Of course, the sweet-smelling smoke might have had something to do with that as well.

And there was the drink.

"What is it?" I asked Rüdeger. I'd taken a sip of it first and felt bubbles of fermentation at the back of my throat as well as a powerful sting on the tongue.

"Fermented mare's milk," he replied. "It's fierce stuff. I can't take much of it."

But I found it to my liking and drank a lot, as well as taking a few swigs from a drink they made with mushrooms and herbs that Rüdeger wouldn't even touch. I felt it working from the back of my throat, mingling with the dragon's heart, rising up into my brain. I put on my bearskin and danced with the other shamans, some of whom were birds, some stags with horns, that I stalked. Then I grew thirsty and drank some more.

I don't know how many hours or even days later, Rüdeger exclaimed to me, "This *is* an honor!"

"What is that?"

"Father Shaman is going to attempt an ascent."

"What is that?" I asked, having some difficulty forming the words.

"He will ascend through the seven heavens. And try to bring the rest of us with him."

"How will he do that?" It took an effort to say those words as well.

"Watch and see."

A great tree was brought into the tent now. It had been dug up, roots and all, and was placed with roots near the hearth, bare limbs through the smoke hole.

"In their native lands, the Huns choose birch trees for this ritual," Rüdeger said. "But birches are not common in the woods around here, and the few we had were quickly used up when they first arrived. It was I who suggested to them that our sacred ash might serve just as well." Rüdeger seemed quite proud at this influence on Hunnish practice.

Two other ash trees were set up outside the tent, their roots actually sunk into the ground. A cord was strung from the left-hand tree outside to the one in the center of the tent. On this cord were strung strips of cloth the colors of the rainbow. The stripped bones of the he-goat were stuffed into a sack with some straw and hung in the third tree. "So the goat can regenerate himself," Rüdeger indicated. Then a long rope made of horsehair with many small animal pelts—squirrel, mouse, ferret, hare—dangling from it every few feet was bound round the tent three times, binding us all within.

Now Father Shaman re-entered the yurt, threw green birch branches on the fire—somewhere there was enough birch for that, it seemed—and began to fumigate his drum. The drumhead grew taut and released into the warm, yellow heat the smell of the goat from which it had been taken. In the light, the many bizarre, magical pictures painted on it in black danced as if alive. Father Shaman began to pant with his effort.

Father Shaman's animal was the brown owl. His cap had the actual beak of such a bird peaking over his brown face, the wings feathered back from his brow. His cloak had a collar of ruffled brown owl feathers and many bronze mirrors on the body that caught the firelight and flashed it in our faces like lightning. Black marten pelts alternated with white ermine in the coat, and there were many snakes of stuffed felt weaving in among them, some with real fangs, sometimes three heads to a body, sometimes three bodies to a head.

"He is calling his spirits to him," Rüdeger said, explaining the low, deep chanting the shaman had begun. It continued for a quarter of an hour or more with little change, while everyone sat and waited and watched.

And then suddenly, there was a different voice in the tent. I was certain I had seen the shaman's lips move, but that they could go out of their deep chant to this high, fluty sound so suddenly was hard to believe. Then there was a third voice, chopped and chirpy.

"Those are the spirits responding," Rüdeger whispered. "'I am here, lord,' they say."

The shaman moved his drum as if catching something within it, and the drum seemed to grow heavier and heavier with each catch. Provided now with three unseen associates, the shaman began to drum again, a slow thunk-a-thunk, and proceeded to circle the ash tree.

His drumming and circumambulation grew faster and faster and wilder and wilder over the course of a quarter of an hour or more until suddenly, with a great shout, he leapt up to the lowest of seven notches that had been cut in the tree trunk.

"He's reached the first heaven," Rüdeger said, after he'd cleared his throat by joining in the shout of triumph that greeted this feat. "His song says he can see the earth below him, all in splinters." And the brown-owl-faced man shielded his eyes and looked about from his perch in all directions. He could turn his head, it seemed, almost as the owl can, from front to back without turning its body, and it was as if his horizon were not the felt panels at the back of the yurt at all, but the furthest end of the steppe.

Now, I was already impressed that a man as old as Father Shaman seemed to be, wrinkled as a rain-ruined plum, could undertake the physical exertion he'd already done that evening. He could still leap higher and longer than his younger assistants. But by no stretch of the imagination could I say that that little notch barely an ell above the hearth's flames could be anywhere near the first heaven, and I told Rüdeger so.

"Watch," he said, and offered me another pull of the mushroom-herb drink.

And then, suddenly, I seemed to be drawn up to the post with Father Shaman. And I, too, looked out—and could see past a yellow desert and beyond a brown one, to the edge of the world. Father Shaman flapped his wings to carry us higher. I felt the strength of those wiry shoulders, and I felt the rise. But as we rose I saw there, at the edge of the world, the mouth of a cavern that seemed to call me to it with a song I could hardly ignore. I wriggled with the allure of that place and would have thought nothing of dropping the hundred or more ells we seemed to be soaring above it now.

But Father Shaman carried us on, up to the second heaven where he somehow managed to bring forth all the bombinations of thunder from a puffing of his cheeks, the flashes of lighting from the folds of his cloak. Even the smell of sulfur was there as lightning struck, or seemed to strike, in various spots around the tent with billows of acrid smoke.

In the third heaven, Father Shaman found his drum-spirit horse wearied and let it take a rest while he read of future plagues and poor harvests that threatened the Huns and what sacrifices should be made to prevent them. There was the distinct sound of his horse drinking from heavenly waters, and then we proceeded.

In the fourth heaven, he bowed to the sun, the moon, and the fixed stars.

In the fifth, all the spirits of animals were found, and the entire tent joined in cacophony here, yelping and growling and scratching and biting. Even the Christians hummed their "Te Deums" and "seculorums" like a hive of bees.

In the sixth heaven, there was the diversion of a hare hunt through the clouds while Father Shaman scampered and danced hare, hound, and hunter all at once—quivering as a hare, sleek as a hound, and poised as a hunter—as much as any could ever hope to see.

In the seventh heaven, we entered the abode of the Great One, which turned out to be the very yurt in which we sat. I found in the magic of the moment that I could understand these words which Father Shaman addressed to the Great One.

> "Blue slope that has appeared,
> Blue sky that shows itself!
> Blue cloud, drifting away,
> Blue sky unattainable,
> White sky unattainable,
> Watering place a year away!"

I heard the voice of the Great One himself answering, commanding Father Shaman to pick live coals from the hearth and eat them. He did, and blew rings of smoke. The Great One granted words of blessing, great booming words coming out of the tiny frame of a man who had eaten fire. Father Shaman was swinging on a branch at the very top of the smoke hole, making the rainbow of ribbons sway. It was a branch so small that one thought a real brown owl might have broken it. When the voice of Great One died away in words that defy translation either into Germanic or even into Hunnish of the everyday plane, he dropped from that height to the felt on the floor and collapsed as one dead.

One of the shaman sons went to pick up the Father's drum and drumsticks and put them dutifully away. Then the celebration slowly got to its feet again, cautiously, staggering at first like one stunned, and stepped gingerly around Father Shaman. An hour or two later he came to, rubbed his eyes, drank a great quantity of mare's milk, and greeted those around him as if he had just returned from the ends of the earth.

"What did you think?" Rüdeger asked.

"Very good. Very interesting. Very …"

"Magical," he supplied.

"Yes, magical. That lightning, that eating the coals. I mean, the whole thing. A terrific show, a terrific experience. But I have one question."

"What is that?"

"What was that cave I saw at the beginning?"

"What cave?"

"The cave I saw from the first heaven. It beckoned me …"

Rüdeger grew thoughtful, then stepped away for a moment to speak a few words to the closest son shaman. The son shaman looked up at me sharply, but it was impossible to read his yellow, fire-lit face.

Rüdeger returned. "Red Stag tells me it was the entrance to the netherworld that you saw."

"What? To the realm of Hel?"

"Some call it that. It is a very powerful shaman who can even see the entrance to the place. Red Stag himself has never seen it. And to descend there as Father Shaman has just made this ascent, well, that is something beyond the ability of any man living. Old shamans in times past, they say, made the journey. But that means being able to follow the trail of the dead and bring them back alive."

I looked up and met Red Stag's eyes. I thought it might be deep reverence I read there now.

"So how does one get there?"

"I don't know. Even Father Shaman doesn't know."

I took another swallow of mare's milk to clear my head and think about what I'd seen but found it only made me very, very sleepy instead.

"What of this dragon's heart you told Bleda about?" Rüdeger prodded. "That is a wondrous thing. How did you come by it?"

I found I was too sleepy to reply. I had never even spoken the name Siegfried to Rüdeger. I closed my eyes and slept where I was, my head on Rüdeger's knee.

When I woke the next midday, I had a terrific hangover. I realized the ascent through the heavens was not something one could take every other day, even with the best of guides. Still I knew that somehow, through the night and ritual, my outlook had changed. I felt myself no longer a separate entity. I felt myself connected to everything in the world and personally felt the effects of good or of disaster brewing leagues and leagues away. I could feel it even so far away as Siegfried was.

chapter 25

THAT TIME I SPENT AS Bleda's adopted daughter—it was nearly a year and a half—I look back on now as perhaps the happiest of my life. It was idyllic, to be mistress of my own tower, to be courted by folk from hither and yon. Often all they wanted was just someone to listen to them, to take their griefs and sorrows seriously. So I did, drumming and reading blade bones and runing. Although I sometimes amazed even myself with the magic of these things, they were merely secondary. This was for the entertainment of my mind.

For my body, there was the hunt. I hunted alone or, as I learned their tongue, with the Huns, who made splendid companions. I was constantly challenged to keep up with them. I conferred with the shamans, who really were very skilled in their knowledge of herbs and remedies, magic and showmanship, as well as more spiritual things.

And then there was Rüdeger. When I grew able to negotiate the Hunnish world on my own, he became simply my best companion. Although he never moved in permanently, he sometimes stayed with me at the tower for weeks on end. He liked to cook, he liked to clean, and heaven knows, the tower often needed it. And we talked. About everything under the sun. Talk was like water flowing downstream with him. There was naturally such an attractive, earthy Vanir cast to his way of thinking that it couldn't help but rub off on me. And one day I told him about a dream I'd had.

"I dreamed my bearskin—that ratty old thing—I dreamed it had a new white lining. I didn't see much of it, just a little. But it was enough to make me think it might be of feathers. White feathers, of an egret? Or ...?"

"Or a swan?"

"Yes, perhaps it was a swan."

"You know how the shaman makes his costume."

"How?"

"Through dreams, he is guided to it. He is told what feathers, what skins he must gather. He is often even told where to hunt for the creatures he sees, how to take them, what parts to use."

"I didn't dream any of that."

"Well, perhaps it will come to you."

"And is this all the costume that's come to you, Rüdeger? Still this wool and the linen coif? After all these years?"

He nodded. "After all these years. And when I dream, it is only of spinning."

That doesn't surprise me, I said to myself, watching his hands twist yet another long thread between sky and the earthy spindle below. *When you do nothing else all day.* But I smiled and said nothing aloud. He did spin more yarn than any one soul could use, and I was often the beneficiary of his labors, though what I should do with skein upon skein was not always clear—I who had never set up a loom in my warrior life, now living among people who made felt instead.

And then, one day in spring, Rüdeger came to me from the Hunnish city with more than just another finished skein. "Bleda Khan has received a request from a foreign embassy to confer with you."

"Well, this is not the first time I've done so. If Bleda doesn't mind exporting his power—and since he's given you the message, I suppose he doesn't in this case—then I don't mind, either."

"It's from Burgundy this time, and I—"

I turned quickly to some arrows I was feathering in the good sunlight so Rüdeger might not catch any change in my coloring. In my confusion, I missed a sentence or two that he said. I let the arrow fall to my lap and fingered the ring I wore on my left hand instead.

"Will you go to Burgundy, then?" His tone told me he was repeating himself.

"No. No, I won't go to Burgundy." The ferocity of my statement surprised even me, and I was expecting something of it.

"Well, then, will you receive the Burgundians if they come here?"

"It surprises me that Bleda would have anything to do with these Burgundians."

"Does it, Brynhild?"

"It does indeed, considering where they sit, right on his southern border. And how they refused to be conquered when the Huns overran their eastern homeland but fled instead to this new land and, even now, refuse him tribute."

"I didn't think of that. Well, perhaps as refugees they have so little, it isn't worth asking for tribute."

"I've heard differently."

"Brynhild? What have you heard?"

"What I want to know is, have they offered him any tribute?"

"I didn't think to ask."

That Rüdeger! Sometimes he was so slow to grasp essentials.

"Shall I go back and ask?"

"Yes, Rüdeger. Perhaps you'd better. And tell Bleda I advise caution with these Burgundians."

"Is it really your powers that tell you this, or … or something else I can't quite put my finger on?"

Rüdeger was also at times able to be very astute. "Or perhaps," he mused, "Bleda Khan means for this envoy to come. Perhaps so he—or you—can learn something of the Burgundians' plans. It is, after all, to be only a group of women who come."

"Only women, you say?"

"That's what I'm told. A princess of Burgundy come to consult you because of your fame and because you are a woman. Come to consult you about some disturbing dreams she's been having. Her escorts are to leave her at the border, and their place be taken over by Huns.

Perhaps," and he caught my eye with more astuteness than I was comfortable with, "you might be able to lead her conversation incidentally to other matters."

"Yes. Perhaps I might."

So, in the end, I let her come. I should have learned to trust my instincts instead.

She came on one of those rare May days of absolute perfection when the whole world seemed a-song. All last year's dead and brown was suddenly overwhelmed with a new vigorous green it seemed impossible anything could ever kill again. Swallows swooped back and forth with daubs of moss and mud and last year's fennel stalks to make their houses under the eaves of my tower once more. Anywhere there was shade, woodruff was sweetly blooming, the tiny white specks on foliage like shooting stars. We Germans liked to add this greenery to our mead or wine for an invigorating tonic. Everywhere, its woodsy scent was similarly at once intoxicating and invigorating.

Gudrun, they called her. She was just like the day, that princess of Burgundy, virtually overflowing with life and sap and good spirits. She was so different from other young women I was used to—more recently Huns, but in the past, those chosen to ride to Valhalla. She absolutely luxuriated in her femininity. It was all her dour Hunnish escorts could do, I'm sure, to keep from raping the whole entourage. Had I the equipment, I would have done as much myself, for spite. But the Huns must certainly have had Bleda's diplomatic purpose drummed into them, for they were as stoic as stones, and the princess and her maids took liberties like field poppies all over them.

She was pert and petite, with movements that ran through her body like a playful breeze through grass. How would it be, I wondered, to be so small? To have a body that did not demand fighting for room for itself at every move? Her blond hair had not the first dinginess of age. Thick and straight, it forever swept her face like a new-made broom of straw. Her journey to my tower had offered her the opportunity to pick a crown of pale blue harebells, forget-me-nots, sprays of apple blossom, wild crow's bill, and blood-red sweet William, all of which sat upon her hair as if it had grown there. Her cheeks exploded into delicious bloom at the slightest provocation. Her long lashes kissed frequently over clear blue eyes, just the color of her harebells, and her features were all of such an evenness and beauty that they seemed familiar. I'd have been intimidated if I didn't have to spend so much effort suppressing annoyance in her presence. What such a girl could have in her mind to travel so far to consult a seeress about was difficult to imagine.

She leapt out of her gilded cart like an exquisite jewel popping from its setting in a necklace and swung straight towards me. She carried a small casket of regal gifts and was flanked by two of her maids bearing less costly but more bulky items. I didn't bother to look closely at these things, not only because there was no luxury she could offer that I did not already own, or could have owned had I so desired. But I also wanted to avoid the nagging temptation to scrutinize these items closely, comparing them to the ring on my finger. I did not want to betray an eye that could not help wondering if they were the sort of things that might have once belonged to a dragon hoard, a hoard won by Siegfried and taken from him by what treachery I longed to discover.

I waved Gudrun and her two maids into the tower, glad for once that it had Rüdeger's neat hand upon it, and that he had thought to arrange my wealth to best effect, more like a shrine and less like a bridal chamber than I had first proposed.

Then I consciously dallied at the door and spoke to the Huns, lounging and playing at knucklebones for disastrously high stakes on the backs of their ponies while they waited the next phase of their duties. It seemed to me a good thing to show this girl my mastery over the dark mysteries of Hunnishness, if nothing else.

"Has Bleda Khan carried out a recent small skirmish? Have there been executions near the Hun's city?"

"No," they replied to both questions. Their black eyes followed mine up to the sky, and they shrugged. I hadn't seen a sight like this

for many months, perhaps not even since I'd come to the tower—two dark Odin birds circling in the patch of blue above my head.

"Bleda Khan feasts in peace today, honored shamaness," the Huns assured me.

So I mimicked their shrug with what nonchalance I could muster and entered the tower after the Princess of Burgundy.

chapter 26

SHE WAS A GIRL MEANT for sunshine. Bringing her into the tower was like dumping a shovelful of dirt on a flower bed. I lit a single saucer of oil and set it where it would not serve her features over mine. Then I said, "You have dreamed, princess?"

"Yes, I have."

Good. She had not expected me to know even so much. "Dreams often forecast only the weather."

"This one was different," she insisted.

"Tell me your dream."

She looked from one of her maids to the other, but in the gloom their faces told her little. "It was about a hawk," she said.

"A hawk. That usually signifies a bridegroom of some sort."

"Yes, that's what everyone in Burgundy said as well."

"But you have journeyed from Burgundy and come to my tower."

"Yes."

"Go on."

"I dreamed I had a hawk on my wrist, a fair hawk, a powerful hawk, feathered with feathers of gold."

"It is *your* bridegroom, then, and a king's son, because of the gold. Maidens often dream of their bridegrooms, and what should be more natural than that you, a king's daughter, should be wedded to a king's

son?" Still, gold need not speak only of a king's son, I thought to myself, and stole another glance towards the gifts Gudrun and her maids had set on my side table, thinking of gold and dragon's hoard.

I saw at once that she was not a stupid girl. Indeed, I saw that her maiden frivolity, even to the crown on her head, was a defense wielded—with very careful, keen intelligence—as well as I carried a shield. But intelligence put to such a use could be spellbinding. The reality of self could too easily be overcome by such a false front, especially when more and more intelligence put into the illusion could render the girl herself more enthralled than anyone else.

Gudrun followed my eyes to the gifts and seemed to read my thoughts as well as I did hers—or should have been reading hers. She certainly was no innocent now. Neither of us spoke, and yet in the pause the name Siegfried seemed to be fairly shouted between us.

This cannot be, I thought, and something similar must have passed through Gudrun's mind as well, for she quickly covered it with girlish prattle. "I dreamed that nothing in this world was as dear to me as my hawk, and all my wealth I would cast aside rather than him."

So much for girlish superlatives and her skill in wielding them. She looked at both of her companions for confirmation of this skill, and I said, "I think perhaps I need to confer with you alone."

When the maids were gone, she blurted out, "How did you know?"

"How did I know what?"

"That what I have to say couldn't be said in their presence, yet I didn't know how to dismiss them without hurting their feelings?"

I shrugged my best shrug of deep wisdom.

"You see, that about the hawk was only one of my dreams, the dream I could tell everyone in Burgundy."

"It is a common dream," I agreed.

"The other dream, the one that brought me here, has been weighing on my mind for so long." She leaned forward with great earnestness, clasping her knees. "But I could tell no one. No one could share my fears, and so I must confront *you*."

"*Confront*, you say?"

"Yes. That's what I mean."

"Go on."

"In this dream, this other dream, we went out into the forest, a great number of us from the palace. And you were there too, Brynhild."

"I?"

"I dreamed of you, Brynhild, and your name, and even how you look, your hair and brynie just so, though I never heard your name before or ever saw you, I swear by sweetest Frigga."

"Go on."

"So we were there in the woods, and we saw a great hart. He was more wonderful than any deer any of us had ever seen, and his hair was all golden."

"Like the feathers of the hawk."

"Yes, even so."

"Go on."

"And we would fain take this hart, although none of us had weapons. Only I, I alone, was able to get him. I called to him, and he came to the sound of my voice as tame as any lamb. I put my arms around that dear, golden neck, and he seemed better to me than anything else in the world. And all my wealth I would cast aside rather than him."

"Just like the hawk."

"Yes, even so. But then you, *you*, cruel Brynhild, you came with your bow and arrows. You came and you shot and slew my deer, even at my very knees. And such grief was that to me, that I could scarcely bear it." She buried her face in her hands.

"Is there more?" I prodded after a moment.

"Well, yes. Then I dreamed that you gave me a wolf-cub, hoping that would take the place of my wonderful hart. But I cared not at all for the wolf-cub, and the wolf-cub besprinkled me with the blood of my own brethren. Nothing could recompense me for the loss of that deer, nothing. So as soon as I heard of your name—that there really was a Brynhild—and of your fame, I knew I must come here and beg of you to unstring your bow. I know not why you should harbor me such ill will. I pray you, ask what you will of me, but do not cause me this hurt I foresaw in my dream. The dream alone has nearly burst my heart with grief. If it should become reality—" And here words failed her.

Then I spoke the name that before had been nameless. "Siegfried," I said.

She looked up and paled perceptibly.

"Siegfried is with you in Burgundy, isn't he?"

"Yes, there is a hero in Burgundy called Siegfried. He … he has sworn fealty to my brother, the King."

"He stays of his own free will, then?"

"Yes … yes, he does."

What could mean her hesitation? I puzzled for a second, then said, "And Siegfried seems to be the hawk and hart in your dreams."

"Is that how you interpret it?"

"Is that how *you* interpret it?"

"Yes."

"Has he indeed been made your bridegroom?"

"No," she answered. "No, of course not." It was clear from the toss of her maiden-loose hair that she was not a bride.

"Is it likely to happen?" I asked.

"I … I … If it's the will of heaven."

"You're not betrothed, then?"

"No."

"But you would like to be?"

"It's not a maiden's place—"

"You're in love with him in any case, aren't you?"

"Why do you attack me so harshly?"

"I don't attack you."

"I've done nothing."

"You came to me, didn't you? Asking counsel, in what amounts to an affair of the heart?"

"Yes."

"And you love him, don't you?"

"Yes."

"And he? Does he love you?"

"I … I cannot say."

"You cannot say?"

"A maiden is not permitted to say in such cases—"

"But she can hazard her guesses."

"Siegfried daren't be too forward."

"Daren't he?"

"I am my brother's sister, after all, and he is a man of no land or people."

"Has Siegfried given you any cause to believe he returns your love?"

"Yes, yes, I think he has." She almost shouted in defiance, and the hot bloom was back in her cheeks.

"Very well," I said and felt myself withdraw from the fray. "Very well."

"Please swear to me you won't kill him."

"Why should I want to kill your—your lover?" In spite of my withdrawal, my voice sounded very dangerous, even to my own ears.

"I can't imagine why."

"Go home."

"I pray you, Brynhild—"

"Go home in peace."

"You are so great, and I am—"

"Go home, I say! What do I want with Siegfried? My power is in my loneliness, don't you see?"

"I … I guess."

"And don't you worry about Siegfried. Siegfried can take care of himself."

"I know that. That's why I love—"

I didn't let her finish. "Has he told you?"

"What?"

"How his skin was spelled by the warm worm's blood?"

Gudrun worked her hands up and down the skin of her own arms, and her eyes grew large with wonder. "No."

"It has. He lives a charmed life. No weapon can harm him. Least of all, one of mine."

"No weapon?"

"Save in one spot alone. But this is a great secret."

"Tell me."

I liked having this power. It was like a strong drink I should never have tasted.

"You must never tell a soul," I told her, "not even Siegfried, that you know." It was some compensation for the loss of what I had hoped would be my life.

"For Siegfried's sake, I swear I'll tell no one."

"There is a spot on his back where the spell did not take, where the blood did not touch. It is a small spot, no bigger than a linden leaf, right in the center of his back."

"How do you know this?"

"I know."

"How do you know this? I'm certain no one in court has seen him shirtless. He even wrestles in a vest."

"Trust me, I know." I stood up and took complete control of the lamp, swinging it away from her as I turned my back to her instead. "What you might do, if you wish to preserve him …"

"Anything!"

"You might work some shirts for him, shirts with fine needlework on them, such as I'm sure your hands can do."

She took the compliment with a blush and a glance at her hands, but no denial.

"Work into this pattern the shape of a linden leaf right in the spot where he is vulnerable, right here …," I showed her on my own back, "… between the shoulder blades."

"A linden leaf?"

"So you and anyone else might better see that spot, to protect it from harm."

She looked hard at the spot I rubbed on my own back with my thumb, memorizing it. "Yes, yes. I'll do that. On every shirt."

"It might help the magic, too, if you—if you weep a few of your precious tears onto that spot before you stitch over it."

"Yes, I will."

"Good."

"Thank you. Brynhild, many thanks. You'll never know how helpful you've been to my poor heart."

"I'm glad."

"They all scoffed at me, asking how could a seeress so far away provide comfort those at home could not? But I knew you could help, and you alone."

"Then our business is complete."

She clasped my hands, almost spilling the hot oil. When I set down the lamp, she kissed my hands and thanked me several times more. Then she took the priceless necklace off her breast and pressed it on me as yet another gift.

"You know, I have a brother," she said, "my brother Gunther, the King of all Burgundy. He is as yet unmarried. I wish you could meet him—he could meet you. He is a dreamy sort of fellow and very particular about a wife. None seems to be good enough for him, but you, you I think just might—"

"Haven't I said?" I broke in sharply. "I am Brynhild, a warriormaid and seeress, not beholden to Odin or to any man. I do not marry."

"Yes, of course. That's what you said. That's as it should be. But I am certainly beholden to you, and I shall sing your praises throughout Burgundy!"

PART IV

Gudrun's Wending

chapter 27

TOLD THE SEERESS BRYNHILD that Siegfried stayed in the kingdom of Burgundy of his own free will. But that wasn't quite the truth.

Brynhild has no concern for appearances, but I can't help feeling her interior holds more self-confidence than mine.

Siegfried had, in fact, come to Burgundy of his own free will, and I remembered well that day …

"Lady, come at once," my maidens called, urging me to join them on the parapet. "There is one coming outside the gates who is like one of the Gods."

And so indeed did he appear, all golden in the setting sunlight with weapons—and shoulders—fit for the Gods, astride a huge grey-white stallion that could only be descended from Odin's Sleipnir himself.

"I think it's Siegfried," exclaimed one of my maids with a thrill.

And so it was.

Siegfried had been to Worms before, of course. The very name of that city we Burgundians held came from his exploit against the worm, the great dragon whose hoard he stole. But I had been very young at the time and had thought him a quiet, somber sort of older man. I'd grown up quite a bit in the intervening two or three years. Some of my maids had always been in love with him, but now, as we watched from the parapet it was my turn to be smitten in a very serious way and for the first time in my life. Siegfried, that God-man on a divine horse, had that effect on everyone.

After the first greetings in the courtyard were over, the men had gone out of sight into the hall. I went to my mother's room to seek her council and comfort in regard to my new and confusing feelings for this man.

Mother kept her room apart, herself apart in it, and only her children and one or two trusted maids were ever allowed to visit her there on the top floor of the castle. Much as I loved her, it always made my flesh creep a little to visit her. Being in Mother's room was like being in the belly of a live creature. I imagined I could even hear it breathing through the skins interspersed with grey-green bunches of herbs that hung everywhere from the ceiling to cure. The breath moved like spirit through the smoke that hung there on all but the warmest of summer days from a poorly drafted fire in a hearth built of lumps of basalt. Three-legged pots stood on the floor near the hearth, each with its bone-handled spoon carved with strange blood-rubbed runes. There was an old quern there too, with a bone handle that looked ominously human. Compared to such implements, the bed, a pile of skins in a forgotten corner, was an afterthought. Truly, I had never seen her retire there. Rarely did she move from the three-legged stool on which she sat and presided over her realm, at whose feet we oft gathered. And it was certain her realm was not bounded by the shelves of bottles and potions that ringed the walls. Indeed, looking closely, I could see she had trouble confining her great height and strength to one little stool. Somehow, I knew she could see through those walls she never left.

I asked my mother what a maid should do when such confusion in the face of a warrior overcomes her. She only laughed and stroked my hair. She liked to do this as if I were her favorite doll with raw flax for hair.

"Don't fool with that one," she crooned comfortingly. "That one wears the curse of Odin on him."

"How can one so fair be cursed?" I cried, and took little comfort.

"Such feelings pass," she said, laughing again gently. I wept on her lap all the time that beautiful stranger met with my brothers down in the hall.

But soon enough, my brothers came to her room to seek her council, as I had, about this God-man Siegfried. "He's come for the hoard," said my brother Gunther.

"All of it?" asked my mother.

"All of it. And he seems to be in some kind of great hurry, keeps looking off down the Rhine as if he hasn't a moment to lose to get back with that hoard to … to wherever he's come from."

When it came to my feelings on the matter of Siegfried, my mother had casually discounted any real concern. With my brothers, she changed her tune when it came to *their* feelings.

My brothers—the eldest, Gunther, reigning as King and heir of Giuki, my dead father—and Guttorm, younger than me by a year, and a great tease. My half-brother Hogni was not a part of our blond-haired trio, evident by his name and his dark features and stature. As dark, short, and compact as a Roman, he was. His build and looks, and perhaps even his brooding nature, he must have gotten from *his* father, who was murdered when Hogni himself was but an infant. Murdered, they say, by Helgi Halfdansson the Dane. Neither able to protect his mother or take revenge for his father's death, Hogni seemed forever fated to brood about everything.

My mother—*our* mother, I should say—came as a widow to my father, who himself was newly widowed and bereft of all his children from that earlier marriage by the incursions of the Huns. If tall tales could be believed, my mother was once a maid of Odin. Whether or not it was true, she had always seemed to me to be quite capable of taking care of herself, and the rest of us as well. For though he was nominally King, Gunther had more the soul of a minstrel and would rather pluck at his harp than rule. He consulted with Mother on everything, as he had come to consult her about Siegfried and the hoard.

With her three sons standing before her, I could see in her eyes just how fiercely she loved them, loved all of us with a love she'd go against heaven for. Her face was now a net of lines, but I could still see she had once been beautiful, with delicate features. As she sat here in her room by her hearth, she wore a simple white coif. But sometimes she let me comb out her hair, and I knew that, too, must have been glorious. It was mostly grey now, going to silver, but I could still tell the wonderful rust color it had been. Too bad she hadn't passed that down to any of us.

Mother laid her hand thoughtfully, almost fretfully, on her chin and said, "Well, he cannot have it."

"I know, Mother," said Gunther.

"Even though you and he won it from the Romans."

"It was *he*, mostly," Gunther admitted.

"You didn't steal it from the Romans!" I insisted. "Siegfried killed a dragon for it."

"Hush, child." Mother stroked my hair.

"But everyone knows it was a dragon's hoard."

Mother sighed. "Perhaps, Hogni, you should tell her."

So Hogni, always the pragmatist, told me. "Certain tribes allied to the Romans have a special formation they muster into battle."

"Like the boar's head wedge All-Father teaches our men when he loves them?" I tried to sound knowledgeable about such things.

"Yes, only in this formation, their front line is chained together, one man to his neighbor, so none of them will break and shame the others by proving himself a coward. They call this formation a dragon."

"Are you trying to tell me it was only such a formation that Siegfried defeated?" I protested. "Romans? Mere men?"

"Believe me, sister," Hogni said. "It is no small matter to defeat even such a dragon."

"I don't believe it. He is a greater hero than that. The greatest in the world."

Hogni went on despite my protest. "It happened that there was a half a legion of Romans and their federati escorting south to Rome the taxes of all of Gaul, gathered for five full years and carried in score upon score of plodding carts. We Burgundians were desperate, having just been driven from our ancestral homes to the east by the Huns. We had joined with our new neighbor, Goar the Alan, in proclaiming Jovinus of Moguntiacum as emperor of the Germanies against the usurper Romans. But this had been in form mostly, a way of proving ourselves good neighbors, and the Alans did nothing to make good the claim in diverting Roman taxes to us or to themselves. We Burgundians decided this caravan must not go to Rome. It must be plundered, even if we did it alone. The Romans met us near a mountain that stands sentinel on Rhine's valley. That mountain now bears the name Drachenfels, "dragon crag," because it was here we chose to meet them. And it was here, when they understood our intent, that their front line deployed itself in just such a dragon formation."

"But the dragon even had a name," I insisted.

"Fafnir?"

"Yes, Fafnir."

"Some say the name of this federate people was Fafnir. I'm not certain, but I am certain that Siegfried broke this front line single-handedly by forcing them over a cliff so that one man dragged all his companions after him."

"That's true," Gunther said. "And what's more, at the bottom of the cliff Siegfried cut out all their hearts and sewed them up into a bag after having—so they say, although I never saw it—roasted them and eaten some of the still-warm heart."

"In any case," continued Hogni, "I remember how he returned from this fray black from head to toe with dried blood and—where we Burgundians had hoped only to cull a cart or two trailing at the end of the caravan—thanks to Siegfried, the legion all fled or was destroyed and left all the loot to form the basis of our present kingdom."

Gunther put an arm around my shoulder. "If it's any comfort to you, sister, I for one shall continue to sing songs of this exploit as if the enemy were a dragon, and since you were not there and were only very young, you may believe as you wish."

"I won't be coddled with tales of fancy," I insisted, shrugging off his arm. "But if what you say is true, Siegfried, as the hero of the day, is entitled to nine out of every ten carts."

"Which brings us to the present problem," Gunther said, looking to our mother, who turned away and looked into the fire instead.

Guttorm piped up. "One in ten carts of that haul was enough to make our family rich enough."

"Yes, but Siegfried is a man alone," said Hogni. I could see he protested rather too much in this vein because as only a stepson of Burgundy his attachments were restricted at best, and he had to work to maintain them. "Siegfried is as unattached as the wind—no family or retainers, no tribe depends on him."

"He did leave it with us," Gunther agreed, "without a care in the world, without a backward glance."

"As if touched by some curse of All-Father," our mother murmured, saying no more as she gazed steadily into the fire.

"He is unattached now," I agreed, "but he may not always be so." I blushed with the anticipation this thought brought.

"But we—we have set ourselves up here in Worms with many obligations," Hogni said.

Mother mused, "We have made ourselves obliged to send back to Rome as tribute over the next few years all that Siegfried and your father stole from them, in order to be allowed to stay in our place here by the Rhine."

"True, Mother."

"We could deal honestly with him—"

"You must deal honestly with a man like Siegfried!" I exclaimed.

Mother continued, ignoring me. "We could return his portion to him—"

"Not quite all of it, Mother," Hogni said. "We've already begun to whittle away at that."

"Exactly." The firelight had turned my mother's face to bronze. "We could give him what is left of the hoard. He may be in such a hurry to get where he is going that he may not miss a cart or two."

"But then how are we to pay next year's tribute when it falls due in the spring?" reasoned Hogni.

"That's the problem," Gunther agreed.

"There is only one thing to be done." Mother rose.

"I knew you'd think of something, Mother."

"You must convince him to stay."

"Stay? How can we do that?"

"He is frantic to get where he is going," piped Guttorm.

"And where is that?" Mother asked.

"He will not say."

"Well, you must make him forget it."

"How are we to do that?" Gunther repeated.

"By making Burgundy so attractive, he will lose all desire to go elsewhere."

My brothers exchanged glances.

"Must I spell it out for you? Feasting, drinking. Give him gifts. The best of everything Burgundy has to offer. Give him wenches, too, if that is his pleasure." Mother ignored my whimper of protest here.

"It will break us!" Gunther cried.

"It will break us if he leaves us," Mother said with calm rationality, "taking his claim with him."

"But will such inducements work?"

"They will work for tonight. You must make them work for tonight. In the morning, we shall see what we shall see."

"He seems ready to ride off even tonight, even in the dark and with a storm coming on."

"Well, he will not. Not without his hoard. Not for one night at least. You must see to it. Clearly a reasonable man can see that a hoard such as that cannot be gathered and loaded all in the dark. And in the morning," Mother repeated, "we shall see what we shall see."

"Mother," Hogni objected, "I don't think anything we can do or say will sway him." Hogni was always the last holdout in pessimism.

"But perhaps something I have …" Mother's shadow danced along one of her long shelves of mysterious vials and juglets.

"Magic, Mother?"

"We'll wait and see."

chapter 28

THAT NIGHT, A STORM OF such ferociousness as I have never before seen blew in. It was easy to believe that it was Thor himself pounding on the roof with his giant-killing hammer. I hadn't been willing to believe it when Mother said Siegfried bore a curse, but during the night, I wasn't so sure. I began to wonder even why she and my brothers let him under our roof, hoard or no hoard—or why, once he was here, they were so bound and determined to keep him.

So I wished and prayed for the storm to stop as I burrowed under the furs and feather tick. Still, such thoughts did not deter me from my newfound love. If anything, the thought of a divine curse made the object of my affection all that more attractive because of the hint of danger, of the forbidden.

The storm kept me awake much of the night, eyes clenched and fur over my head. My brothers assured us that when they returned down to the hall they would do all the entertaining of Siegfried they could, but I never heard it. Their guest, it seemed, was not in a mood to share in much entertainment. The only thing I did hear over the storm was Mother in the room next door.

Now, whatever folks may say about Mother having once been a Valkyrie, as long as I've known her she's taken her power in a different form. As long as I've known her, she's had a reputation as a wisewoman and something of a magician as well. "Wisdom and a bit of magic—that is where a woman must look for power," she always told me. "Once she has her hands full of children, she can't count on force of arms or even the goodness of men's souls anymore."

All that night I could hear the rise and fall of the chant of her runes in counter rhythm to the rise and fall of the storm. It certainly countered as far as I could hear any partying down in the hall. She had stayed up all night like this while casting spells before, leaving the house smelling of strange fumigants in the morning. But I never remembered her working with such intensity before; it wasn't just a storm she was fighting.

At one point, I started out of my fitful sleep and listened. Mother wasn't alone. She usually shooed her maids out when she magicked. I had two of them squeezed in with me and my maids that night, in rugs on the floor. But this person in Mother's chamber was no maid.

"You're mixing thistledown in a thimble, Thora." It was a man's voice. A stranger's.

I was confused. My mother's name wasn't Thora. Everyone I knew called her Ute, Queen Ute of Burgundy. But she answered to this strange appellation all the same. "What are you doing here?" She didn't sound pleased to see him, this strange man in the women's apartments. I knew this was no lover. Since my father's death, I'd often wished one for her.

The storm rose, their voices fell, and I heard nothing but murmurs, which might just as well have been sheets of hail drumming the eaves.

Then Mother raised her voice again. "Why should I believe you?" I'd never heard such anger in her voice, and I wondered if I shouldn't get up and call the aid of arms to her. "Why should I trust you for one moment? After all you've done to me and mine?"

"Because—" the stranger said, and spoke in a weird sort of verse that sent a shiver down my spine.

> "Because Word-Changer has a care …
> To see that Siegfried doesn't slip back to the scene …
> Of his trysting in ten days too …

Nor yet in ten years either."

Their voices dropped once more but continued swirling around each other for a long time. I heard only snatches of strange, incomprehensible words:

> "Blend in the bowl the might of earth's bowels …
> And … sky and sea … with the life-sap of your son …"

Then at last, I heard a man's heavy tread in the corridor. The visitor was leaving.

As quickly as I could, I made my way across the over-crowded floor of my room, lifted the deerskin we had for a door, and squinted down the dark corridor. It was a man, all right. Very tall, wearing a broad-rimmed hat and carrying a staff, although he swung it carelessly as he walked, so he obviously didn't depend on it. At the top of the stairs heading down to the hall he paused for a moment, and the next instant he was gone, simply disappeared. The twisted handrail—a thick oak branch with only the bark stripped, once white, now grimy with use and age—appeared suddenly through his solid form as if he had turned into thin air.

His cloak, I remember, was the angry black of the night, swirled with flecks of white as if with snow. Had he been outside, his sudden disappearance would have been a little easier to explain, as he would have vanished against the stormy night sky, just like that.

I crept back to the warmth of my bed, and the next thing I knew, Mother was at my side, gently stirring me awake. It must have been fairly close to morning, although it was still dark, and the storm hadn't let up one wit. The cock was crowing rather crossly and half-heartedly at the whole prospect from his shelter on the porch under the low eaves.

"Siegfried? Is he gone?" I asked, preparing to have a broken heart.

"No, not yet. But he's threatening to."

"In this storm?"

"I want you to get up, get dressed in your very best—the pink silk should do nicely, with the ermine edging."

I did as she bade me. My hair she fixed herself in two long plaits and bound them in red yarn where they hit my waist.

"Lovely," she said when we were done. "Now, I want you to go down and take this to him."

"Him? You mean Siegfried?" My heart began to make its presence known uncomfortably.

"To Siegfried." She thrust a large bowl of wrought gold into my hands, our finest, from the dragon's hoard. I could see that new runes had been cut it its side and reddened with blood. It was warm to my touch.

"Mother, what is this?"

"A morning posset."

"But what's in it?"

"Curdled milk as in any posset. Mostly."

"And what else?"

"Never you mind."

"Mother, you're trying to poison him."

"Hush, no! I'm not trying to poison him. Not now. Only later, as a last resort."

"I'll have nothing to do with this if it'll hurt him in any way." I tried to shove the bowl back to her.

"It will not hurt him."

"I'll drink it myself rather than poison such a man as Siegfried."

"Gudrun, don't!"

But I had already taken a good swallow. I remember a faint taste of lavender, and then nothing at all—until Mother brought me back.

"This is the antidote," she said, waving a very small glass vial at me threateningly. "This is all the mixture there is in the world, and if I have to keep using it on you, there won't be any left for your lover Siegfried. Now, you see, you're not dead, no worse for wear, so you may go downstairs and do as I bid you. Gudrun, I am your mother. I would never do anything to jeopardize you. You know that."

She pinched my cheeks firmly to bring some bloom to their wintertime pallor. And then I went downstairs.

Siegfried hadn't gone, not yet. But he was dressed for the weather and had saddled his own horse outside.

"So, I'm going," he was shouting at my three cringing brothers as he paced back and forth in a fury before them. His fury was magnificent to see. "I'm going with this one pathetic sack of goods you've scraped together of all the wealth that was mine. I'm going and, with this wealth, such as it is, I will gather together an army. And with this army, I will return. By my life, I will return, army or no, and I will burn Worms down around your thievish heads. Then I will see if there isn't wealth forthcoming. By my life, I will do this!"

My brothers said nothing of any consequence, although Gunther promised him two wagonfuls if he would only wait out the storm so they could get to the storehouses where it was kept. "Only a madman would go out in a blizzard like this," he reasoned.

Well, Siegfried seemed to be that very madman. But I plucked up my courage as I held out the bowl and walked directly to him. "Please, sir, if you must go, I pray you might at least not insult our hospitality by refusing to warm your insides with this posset before you do."

I smiled my prettiest smile, and Siegfried grunted. He took the bowl, examined and recognized it. He said, "Well, I shall finish this off, the better to carry this golden bowl with me to add to my small gain here." And he downed the whole posset without coming up for air.

That was the last we ever heard from Siegfried about the burning of Worms. We never heard another word about his riding off, nor about his pilfered hoard. He sat down with my brothers to more soured milk and bread and cheese, seeming content to comment on the wonderful ferocity of the storm. Later that day, Mother had me put powdered snake heart on his meat. "It will turn his heart," she said.

From that day, he was a fixture in our hall, as if he had forgotten any other home or any other business. He rode that magnificent horse into battle with my brothers, hunted with them, swilled the mead, and told the tales around the hearth when their labors were done. Within a year they had cut their wrists and exchanged blood, swearing blood brotherhood, my two brothers and Siegfried. Hogni stayed apart from the romance of this, brooding as usual. And then it was becoming common talk that it would be only natural if Gunther should give me to this favorite companion of his.

chapter 29

AS I LYING WHEN I told Brynhild the seeress that I thought Siegfried loved me? No, I don't think so. At least, I was willing to read interest in his every move.

There was, for example, the time when Siegfried and my brothers went out to fight the Danes of Helgi Halfdansson and the Saxons, who had long ago been conquered and made Danish allies under their King Luideger. To exact revenge of Helgi was always a driving force in our hall, for Helgi it was, our Mother never failed to remind us, who had murdered Hogni's father. Still, the distance to the Saxon battlefield was much further than one would normally take for spring campaigning, and Helgi was an incomparably fierce foe. We couldn't rest easily in Worms while the best of our men were gone.

And then, one day, a lone horseman on a white stallion was spied from the parapet. It was Siegfried, safe but riding alone. I had to hear the way of it at once, and as my mother wouldn't leave her room even for this, I stood for her in the high seat when he was brought into the hall.

"Rest easy, lady," were his first words to me. "I come as but a messenger to inform you that your three brothers are all well. They come with the main body of Burgundians and should be here by evening."

I gave a few quick orders to see that everything would be in readiness for their arrival, then I turned back to Siegfried, blushing at the calm and steady eyes with which he met mine. He seemed to suffer no confusion in my presence.

"I had the feeling there was something I should find or see along the Rhine," he explained, "so I took that route instead, while your brothers and the others preferred to ride further out of the Hunnish territory."

"Did you see what you had meant to see?"

"I did not."

He had wanted to ride on ahead, I told myself, as his miraculous beast would allow him to, and vague unnamed things in Hunnish territory were nothing. I let myself believe this in the interest of comforting my heart. "So tell me, Lord Siegfried," I said. "How did the battle go? How was the victory won?"

"King Luideger is dead, and perhaps a hundred of his men. The Saxons took heavy casualties while we Burgundians sustained no more than forty wounded among us all."

"Ah, and who was the brave hero to whose sword we owe the death of the Saxon King?"

"Lady, it was I, your humble servant, but only because your brothers had weakened him first."

"I guessed as much. But you abuse yourself, Lord Siegfried, to give credit elsewhere. I can see with a seeress's eyes that you had more to do with it than you will confess, and such humility does not become a hero such as you are."

Siegfried made no apology for his humility, and this hurt me. I knew the Siegfried I'd known before the magic posset would not have done so, and I pressed him further. "So, is Helgi dead? Is my mother avenged?"

"The Dane contrived to escape our onslaught."

Again, the steady, passionless look of his eyes disquieted me. The Siegfried of former times would not have let Helgi escape, of that I was certain. But, "Such is Fate," I said, managing a shrug. "This is indeed good news you bring me, Lord Siegfried. Such a messenger deserves a reward so he may bring many more such messages to cheer a lady's heart in the future. But you are too exalted to accept a messenger's fee."

He bowed stiffly. "Were I lord of thirty lands, I would be honored to receive a gift from your hands, Lady Gudrun."

A man wouldn't say such things unless he had an interest in a lady, would he? Otherwise such groveling would be too distasteful. So, since I was in the high seat that morning, I sent the treasurer to bring as much as he could carry from the storerooms where the hoard was kept. And as the treasurer brought it in and laid it at Siegfried's feet, I saw some life come to Siegfried's eyes as they looked upon the gold, *his* gold, as if they caught fire from the gleam of it. I saw the struggle there was to quench that fire of memory, the result being that he refused the gift and divided it up amongst my maids who were standing beside me in the room. The squeals of delight from the maids as they got the amount of a dowry apiece put an end to our interview.

Later that night, as she was helping to pass the victory mead, one of my maids told me how Siegfried had eyed the necklace he'd given her keenly and then, when she passed, tried to break it from her, calling her and all Burgundians thieves. "What can this mean, lady?" the girl asked, anxiously fingering the necklace like stolen goods.

"I see you still have it."

"Yes. Your brother the King quickly plied Lord Siegfried with a golden bowl of curdled milk, and that seemed to calm him at once. He never looked at me again."

We did have to keep slipping him the lavender-tasting posset from time to time, whenever it was clear he was just about to remember something he had forgotten. We never dared to use the antidote, and that disquieted me. Then I began to have the dreams I went to the seeress to have interpreted.

I was much comforted by my visit to Brynhild, more so when I had stitched a shirt or two for Siegfried with the linden leaf motif on the back.

Not long after that we were married. But still there was the posset, still there could be no antidote. And I could never escape the feeling that, along with his memory, we had also erased a part of his soul. He was as strong as ever, as fearless, and yet …

I even went to consult with an old woman in Worms who had been taken as a slave to Rome where she served many years as something we don't know here in Germany, called a harlot. The Romans like blonds, but when her hair turned grey and her teeth fell out they granted her freedom and sent her back to Germany. She was full of secrets of the trade which she delighted to impart to me for a piece or two of the dragon's hoard, for when the Romans freed her, they neglected to give her the wherewithal to live that freedom. Thanks to her, nothing lacked in our bed-closet, mine and Siegfried's.

And yet, I still couldn't forget the fire in him as he had paced there before the hall door, ready to go out in that storm to—to where? I had to admit, for all that old woman's advice and for all possets, he never displayed that same fire again.

Now, I had told my brother Gunther all about this woman Brynhild when I returned, of course. But honestly, I wasn't the one to suggest it. He came up with it himself one night as he sat idly plucking at his harp, going to the next tune before he'd finished the first and seeming dissatisfied with them all.

"What do you say, brothers?" he said, finally giving up on a love ditty as a bad job. "It seems to me that I myself should marry and set about the business of giving Burgundy an heir before my sister beats me to it."

I blushed happily, intertwined my fingers with Siegfried's, and looked to see what his reaction to this might be. He was as passive as if Gunther had spoken of the doorpost at the other end of the hall.

"So, help yourself," Hogni said. "It seems to me there has been no lack of offers around here, princes with their comely daughters to pawn off, each one more accomplished and beautiful than the last—at least to hear their fathers speak."

"But it seems to me," said Gunther, taking a series of chords down the scale, "that there is no woman in the world that would suit me more than this Brynhild."

"Brother," I said, "Haven't I told you she'll hear nothing of marriage?"

"So you have. That makes her all the more tantalizing to me."

Gunther broke at once into an impromptu song, the heroic burden of which was "The Wooing of Unwilling Brynhild," at which everyone laughed. But it seems that he was quite serious and got more serious in the next days.

At last Siegfried said, "Well, if you're to win this recalcitrant maid, Gunther, my friend, it seems I had better go with you."

"You?" scoffed Hogni. "A man does better to woo alone."

"Yes," conceded Siegfried, "but I know the way to this Brynhild."

"If Gudrun can find it," suggested Guttorm, "it cannot be too difficult a way."

"Yes, but I know … I know Brynhild."

"You do?" asked Gunther in surprise. "Why have you never mentioned this before?"

"Because … because … I forget …," said Siegfried in confusion, putting his hand suddenly to his head, which had become the sign to me that I needed my mother to brew more posset.

"Brynhild is the name of this famous woman?" my mother asked when all of us children passed the plan by her.

"Yes," Gunther replied. "You don't approve?"

"It's not that, son. Whatever makes you happy. It's just that …" She was suddenly thoughtful, almost sad. I guess I had failed to give her this detail of a name when I'd given her my version of my pilgrimage to consult the seeress. To my brother in want of a wife, this woman needed a name. To my mother, it was enough to call her "the seeress." At least at the time it seemed so.

"You know this Brynhild?" Hogni pressed.

"Mother, did you ride with her?" asked Guttorm.

"The Brynhild I knew should be old enough to be a grandmother, as I am," Mother said, "and yet—"

"And yet what, Mother?"

"And yet … who knows? With magic …?"

"Should I not go woo her?" Gunther, for all his heroic noises, would have done anything Mother told him.

"Go, my son. I can think of no one I'd rather have for a daughter-in-law if she is the same. You have my blessing to try for this Brynhild. If she is the same Brynhild I knew, I also know you will not win her unless it is fated to be."

Very shortly, they did set off on this wooing, all four of them, to the dangers of the Hunnish lands and, it began to seem to me, the even greater dangers of this Brynhild.

As he set off, I thought I saw in my husband's eyes something of the fire I had not seen since that early stormy morning, just before I handed him the posset of forgetfulness.

PART V

The Curse of Odin

chapter 30

THERE WAS A TALE BEING bantered about by every minstrel with two strings under his fingers that I spent my time up in my tower pining for Siegfried and working up his deeds in tapestry after tapestry, using the finest threads of gold and crimson. Such tale-mongers never saw the mouse's nest I made of any needlework I ever set my hand to. Perhaps they confused me with Rüdeger, who could certainly sew a fine seam if he set his mind to it. Mostly, however, he still preferred the Norns' work, spinning.

It was true, however, that I was sewing on *that* day. I was trying yet again to repair my brynie. The laces were forever breaking, and the leather would soon turn to yellow powder in my hands if I didn't replace it. There I was, enjoying the sun on the parapet of my tower, breaking laces and swearing a blue streak when I looked up at a flap of wings. My first thought was that it must be Odin's bird, come to cackle at my attempts to maintain the status of a warriormaiden after all these years. I usually gave him little enough to disparage, even if it incurred his wrath for me to say so.

But this bird wasn't a raven, it was a hawk. The princess of Burgundy's dream was immediately called to my mind. A beautiful little harrier, mostly white, but with markings of gold—she was clearly a manned bird, as betrayed by the dangling jesses and small bells on her feet that rang as she walked up and down on the edge of the stone parapet. Piercing the air with a shriek and eying me with brows that tended to scowl with disapproval, she seemed upset that I was not a hare or some other sort of useful prey.

"There she is!" came a voice from the edge of the woods below.

So, there was the man to whose leather fist those jesses belonged. The bird shrieked a welcome down at him. But I also knew that voice. My heart raced as if I had been a hunted hare indeed. I dropped the brynie, probably breaking another lace or two in the process, but I didn't care. I leapt to the southern parapet whence the voice came. Yes, that was the horse Grani I'd driven into the Schlei. The stiff, erect figure astride him I knew so well, the curly golden hair that went into frenzies when it was wet that I had longed to touch until it permeated every dream—

"Siegfried!" I yelled, but the noise caught in my throat.

I noted that was the hair, yes, but cut in the Burgundian style—a short, effeminate fringe in front and long in back, a style that did not become the Siegfried I knew at all. Before I could unstrangle a clearer sound from my throat, I saw that, though he rode far in front as Grani would always carry him, he did not ride alone. Three, four, more, retainers accompanied him. The fact that we were not alone made me cautious. *Before I make a fool of myself,* I thought sensibly, *let me consider how long it has been—no word, not a sound from him while I was abandoned. Nearly two years now, two years.* Yes, caution was called for, if not outright hostility.

"Is this it?" I heard one of the other men ask. "This is the bower of the bride?"

Siegfried turned in the saddle to answer this with what seemed but a lighthearted jest, and it was then that I saw the needlework on the vest that he wore. It was figured with convulsions of vegetation, acorns, blooms, and leaves from a dozen plants and all the seasons combined. But plain, even at this distance, was the centerpiece, the heart-shaped lime green of a linden leaf.

I reached for my bow, fitted an arrow, and drew. I would have let fly, too, had a contingent of Huns not appeared at that moment and surrounded these trespassers.

"We mean no harm!" I heard one of the other men try to explain to the Huns, but the Huns were not so easily convinced.

"Take them to Bleda Khan," barked the commander of the Huns, and though Siegfried and his companions did not understand the words, they had no choice but to comply.

Just before the group of horsemen—Germans surrounded by Huns like the pale pith of a reed by tough brown bark—disappeared into the woods, Siegfried turned and whistled his hawk to him. She flew off at once, piercing the air with her call. As he raised his gauntleted fist to receive her, he saw me for the first time.

He didn't wave. Indeed, he didn't seem to recognize me at all. There was something in his eyes, however, that seemed to say he was struggling with the feeling that he ought to recognize me.

Two days later, I was practicing shooting—taking leaves off a linden at fifty paces—when Rüdeger rode up.

"And who is that deadly arrow for?" he asked.

"No one," I said. "No one you know."

"Try me," he said.

I said nothing, recollected concentration, and let the arrow fly. It flew true, singing, exulting as it went, and we watched it and what was left of the leaf and the branch it had been on drop to the earth like a dead weight.

"Bleda Khan is holding a band of Burgundians captive."

"Oh?" I said nonchalantly.

"He sent me to tell you."

"How can it concern me?"

"He said you might want to know."

"I want to know why he hasn't impaled them yet. On stakes over ant hills."

"Is that what the seeress recommends?"

I let another arrow fly, and we watched it hit its mark.

"They are spies," I said as I lowered the bow from sight.

"That's not what they say. They say they come in peace."

"It's the job of spies to lie."

"More than peace. They say they've come on a bride-seeking mission."

"I'm sure Bleda could spare them a slave girl or two. He needn't give them any Hunnish blood."

"Actually, it's you they've come to court."

I laughed out loud, and a moment later, Rüdeger joined me. I loved the sound fading away in the woods. "I can't marry all of Burgundy."

"Just one of them, of course."

"Which one?" I was suddenly sober.

"I don't know their names. But the one preeminent among them. Their king."

That could only mean one among them, the only one my eyes had even focused on. I said his name to Rüdeger for the first time. "Siegfried."

"Yes, it seems to me they did call one of their number by that name."

"Siegfried's become King of Burgundy in all this time?"

"You know this man?"

"Siegfried is—was …"

Rüdeger came up in the tower then. I meant to tell him very little, but once I started talking, it ended up being quite a lot. Perhaps too much.

Rüdeger's little smile fissured its way between the boulders of his face as I talked and found myself desperately brushing tears from my eyes. "It's a good thing, then," he said, "that Bleda Khan hasn't impaled them on ant hills yet."

"But Rüdeger, don't you see? All is not well here. Why did it take him almost two years to return instead of just the ten days he promised?"

"I imagine it takes a while to win a kingdom."

"Two years! And now he comes with all these other men. Who are these men?"

"No doubt he has won friends and vassals."

"And the treasure, the treasure that was supposed to replace the power I must surely lose when I lose my maidenhead. I see no glimmer of treasure."

"He can't very well cart that treasure here under the Huns' noses, I don't suppose. Surely he knows Bleda would want a sizable cut."

"I do see your point there."

"No doubt that's what took him so long—securing the hoard and his position before he could come for you."

"Oh, Rüdeger, I'd love to believe you."

"You're the one with the seer gifts, however."

"And I get confused. What I want so desperately to see battles with what caution tells me I must see, until I don't know which is which. What does Bleda say to all of this?"

"Well, Bleda Khan would be very loath to lose the most powerful of his shamans, particularly to Burgundy, with whom he has but an uneasy peace at best. But he also knows that you are so powerful, he cannot bid you. If you tell him to impale these fellows, he'll be only too glad to oblige. But they conjured him in your name, and he dares do nothing, neither kill them nor hold you here against your will."

"Ah, but Rüdeger, I still sense a trick."

"You have great powers of discernment."

"It *is* a trick! Odin is out there, somewhere, plotting all this to my ruin. And yet—"

"And yet?"

"Siegfried is the greatest man that ever lived. He knows absolutely no fear. He is strong, stronger than I am."

"And that, no other man can claim." Rüdeger was wistful.

"Odin had to let a generation pass in his creation till he, even a God, could come up with a man like Siegfried. And I …"

"You love him."

"What is it that little Burgundian princess said? 'I dreamed that nothing in this world was as dear to me as my hawk, and all my wealth I would cast aside rather than him.'"

"It sounds like love to me."

"But is it love?"

"What I have seen of the disease."

"Or just a terror of facing Odin and all the rest of this life alone?

Growing so tired—and, yes, afraid—of having to do everything. Of being alone," I repeated.

"Brynhild, you are not alone." I think Rüdeger touched my hand, but I didn't feel it.

"Yet he wears that vest, that vest I told *her* to make him. She is making his clothes. What else is she doing, eh?"

"If your wisdom teaches you to suspect a trick, perhaps you should play a trick yourself."

"What's that you say, Rüdeger?"

"Put him to the test. Some great, impossible test …"

"Yes, yes," I repeated with sudden hope and excitement. "A test. A test that only Siegfried could pass."

"And that would test both his resolve and his faithfulness."

"Rüdeger, you are brilliant." And I hugged him till his coif slipped off to one side.

"Tell Bleda not to kill them," I said. "Not yet. Tell them the man who wins me must pass through certain trials I set for him. Only a man who has slain a dragon can survive these trials. And, having passed them once, he will treasure more deeply what he has won. Even Siegfried will think twice before he wanders off to try to win another beauty, eh?"

"And if he doesn't pass?"

"If he doesn't pass—well, Bleda has my blessing to do with them as he pleases. Nay, my command is that if he doesn't do away with them in the longest, most tortuous way possible, all the curses of Brynhild will be on his head and on his family forever."

"I will ride to tell him at once."

"And Rüdeger?"

His eyes brightened at the sound of his name on my tongue. "Yes, Brynhild?"

"There is something I want you to fetch for me."

"Anything."

"Some magic from the Father Shaman. I'll need a lot."

CHAPTER 31

"HAT IS THIS, SOME KIND of joke?"

I looked down off the parapet at the man with dull blond hair. Though tall and dressed in fine silks with a chain of royalty adorning his breast, he was but a pathetic figure. The first thing he had done when nearing the tower was to sit down on a stone, unsling a harp from his back, and begin to play. His repertoire, though I didn't let him get very far through it, was all about maidens in springtime and was just as sappy as the birches are in that season. My first thought was of Aed and that unfortunate incident, and I wondered what sort of cruel message Siegfried was trying to send me with this. But it turned out not to be Siegfried's message at all.

"Mistress, I am Gunther, King of Burgundy, and I have come to woo you for my wife."

"*You?*" I laughed out loud. I couldn't help it, and I enjoyed the sound of it echoing off the tower under my feet and losing its way in the forest beyond, beyond the copse where the Burgundians had hung their shields in the branches, intending to stay for a while. "You are the best Burgundy can field? By the Gods—no, I know no Gods who would not be insulted to have their names brought into such a farce. And the same goes for swearing by my life. By the dust on the bottom of my boot, off with you, and let's have no more of your caterwauling."

"Lady, if you'll but hear my suit—"

"Off, I say. You abuse me and my patience." I sent a few arrows sailing after him, for I had my bow at the ready. But I shot wild, just to scare him off. I was saving the good shots for the heart-shaped leaf of a linden.

"Mistress, you oblige me to use rougher means," Gunther shouted back, panting, from out of bow range.

"Do your damnedest," I shouted back. "Or didn't they warn you? I've held fifty Hunnish warriors at bay. I'm Brynhild, warriormaid. No one's daughter, no one's sister, and certainly no one's *wife*."

It wasn't long before Gunther came out of the shelter of the encircling trees again. He was on horseback now, both he and his horse under a crust of ceremonial armor. The rose of Burgundy fluttered from a banner on the end of his lance. He paced the horse towards me with proud and studied elegance. I'd show him this was no costume mummery and let off a few more arrows. Had I been in desperation, I would have gone for the unprotected limbs of the horse. But I've always thought it was a shame for good beasts to die for the follies of their masters. I went for the man instead.

Gunther's armor, though decorative, was also functional. The few darts I aimed at the more unprotected portions, he managed to catch on his shield with a modicum of skill. The horse kept clopping towards me. It was time to let fly the magic.

Now, Bleda's shamans had control of, among other things, a black powder, the secret of which they had brought with them from their home in the far east. This powder was highly explosive and needed but a spark to go up with a cloud of smoke, a noise like thunder and a terrific smell of sulfur. I'd first seen a demonstration of its power when Father Shaman had made his ascent to heaven. With it he had created the thunder and lightning of the second heaven. It was also possible to pack this powder into tight, hollow tubes of a colored fabric they have that is something like parchment or birchbark. They like to use these "firecrackers," as they call them, for great celebrations. A clever magician can mix substances with the powder so it will fire with different colors and shoot up in the air a hundred feet with a noise like the howling of trolls, exploding with ribbons or sprays of sparks like any geyser in my Iceland. It was really a wonder to see, and the Huns loved its display, for they were accustomed to it. But it was terrifying to the unsuspecting.

Now, I had none of this parchment wrapping the Huns preferred, but I had stiff leather and reeds and the barks of certain trees. And I had made a thousand of these tubes, a pile beside me to light and throw over the battlement, and many others littering the field before my tower with them. I had only to set the tip of a hemp-wrapped arrow alight and shoot it to any of a hundred spots I had marked in my mind's eye, and the black powder would do its magic.

And so it did. I'd even set strings of these tubes joined by specially treated lengths of Rüdeger's good yarn so that the explosions ran along the ground, one right after another, like the movement of an underground giant—*boom, boom, boom*—just like that. Their impact was so great that it even sent bits of stone flying in what could be a dangerous shower. The effect was so gratifying that I set off two charges just for the fun of it. But that first was all that was needed. Gunther's horse screamed and reared with fright, then bolted, leaving the King of Burgundy to endure the billows of smoke and wild whistles and pops alone on foot. He scrambled after his mount as fast as he could, and the dust cleared on an empty field. Then there was nothing for a while but bird song and the low muttering of Burgundians among themselves, trying to make up their minds whether to leave in defeat or what tactic to try next.

I'd almost decided I'd made nine hundred and ninety-eight tubes of magic black powder too many and would be reduced to using them just for sport as the Huns did. But then the warrior and his mount appeared again, just where I had seen them vanish.

At least, the warrior was the same, but this was a new horse. *Just as I thought.* That first horse was not going to let himself be ridden again in a hurry by anyone. And now I saw that this replacement was not just any horse. It was Grani. *Ah, shrewd thinking, Siegfried.* If any horse could make its way through my field of magic fire, it must be Grani. *Shrewd, but not quite shrewd enough. Have you forgotten,*

Siegfried? And if you've forgotten this, what else has slipped your mind? Grani will carry no one but you. Even I could only ride when you held the reins and I clung to your waist behind. Remember?

Yes, I could see Siegfried now, walking at Grani's flank, encouraging him to carry the other man, "Come on, boy, go on. Carry the good King for me, for my sake. Go on, boy."

I set off one charge to advise Grani of the wisdom of his balking at this burden, and then all was quiet on the field yet again. I was about to leave the parapet and call it a day when the mood in the opposing camp suddenly seemed to change. The wind was right for me to even be able to overhear some of their words.

"I've no wish to inherit your throne just yet, brother," said a very young voice, just changing.

"This has been a fool's errand from the start," a dark and deep voice cautioned. "Keep such things to your ballads, Gunther."

Then Siegfried's name: "Siegfried, impossible! She'll see right through this fraud."

"Well, if she does, she'll have to understand that everything I do is undertaken in your name, my King." That was Siegfried's voice, certainly.

And then, suddenly, there was Grani and a rider again. The rider urged Grani forward, and Grani obeyed, holding his head proudly and setting one heavy hoof in front of the other, slowly, deliberately. I set off a charge right under those feet. Grani's head tossed with displeasure, but the rider kept him under firm control, and the horse stepped forward again without losing stride. I set the charges as fast as I could, one after another, until the field was like the steam of our Iceland before me. Still the horse and rider kept coming. As the last of my magic smoke parted about them at the foot of the tower, I understood the ruse. Only Siegfried had faced Iceland and not flinched at its terrors. Only Siegfried was a hero who could pass through fire. As he knew no fear in coming to me the first time, so he knew no fear now. Yes, see how he stretched that armor to the breaking point. See how he'd had to set Grani's stirrups lower. That was Siegfried down there, wearing the King of Burgundy's rose-crested helmet and straining the buckles of his armor with the violent compression of his body.

I had a pot of boiling oil ready for this point in the game, a pile of stones to drop, and a whole row of iron-headed spears that at this range could pierce armor. But I didn't use them. I sat where I was on the parapet, heard my suitor dismount, and set his shoulder to my tower door. That tower door had withstood a whole contingent of Huns who'd had failed to take it, but the old wood splintered like glass before Siegfried. I heard the rest of the Burgundians give a cheer as they stepped into the open, out of cover of the cool forest. I heard his boots on the stairs. I remembered the sound of those boots from another time, a time of stars and warmth. The very shadows on the stone wall behind him came back to my mind.

I heard his voice. "Madam, I have won you for Burgundy." He gave a stiff little bow of the head. I dared to look at him when he was bowed for the first time.

"So you have, Siegfried. But you knew *you* would be welcome any time." My heart raced, and my breath came with a sudden great urgency towards him.

Then I met his eyes, and my heart grew chill. Those were not Siegfried's eyes glinting at me through the slits in the visor he was still refusing to take off. They were blue, yes, but not as blue. There was no fire there. And why did he not remove his helmet?

I looked away in sudden confusion. I should perhaps have taken him on there in one-to-one combat, both fully armed as we were then. Perhaps I would have lost then, and that would have been the best thing. But perhaps I wouldn't have lost. This wasn't the Siegfried I had known.

"Allow me to go down and get my things together," I said.

"Of course," he said. He preceded me down, mounted Grani, and was gone.

I packed in a daze, slowly but sparsely, for I could think of nothing I needed.

When I came out, they were all waiting for me, all the lords of Burgundy. Only the King was still afoot, dressed again in the armor and clothes Siegfried had been wearing a moment before, but with the helmet off and held gallantly under one arm.

"Lady, will you do me the pleasure of allowing me to lift you to ride behind me on my saddle?" said Gunther the King.

This was not the King's horse. They'd found him another, perhaps the one they'd held in reserve for me all along. His own horse was skittish behind the rest. This was a smaller, daintier mare. We would have to ride together until his own calmed down.

"This is not the horse that won me," I said scornfully. "And you are not the man. The horse who won me is a divine steed, son of Sleipnir, that I helped his master to win from Odin. There is the horse, there is the man."

I pointed straight at Siegfried on his Grani and saw a look pass between him and the King. What was that I saw pass over Siegfried's eyes? Some sudden life, as if some sudden memory were dragging itself out from the bottom of a bog. Well, let them sort it out for themselves.

"That's the only horse of all the horses here that I will deign to ride," I said of Grani. "And if I can't have that one," as no one was in a rush to put me there, "then I'll ride my own."

I went to fetch my favorite, the taller of the two Hunnish ponies I kept hobbled in a meadow nearby, threw on the saddle and my few belongings, and rode it quickly past the waiting Burgundians.

"Lady, Burgundy is this direction, to the south," one of them called after me.

"So go southward if you wish. But I am riding east, to the encampment of the Huns."

It was Grani's hooves that thundered after me, Siegfried who caught my reins and pulled me up.

"Lady, I undertook this challenge in good faith, that if we should breach your tower, you should marry me."

It was Gunther, panting after us, whose words I heard. But it was the battle going on in Siegfried's eyes that had my attention.

"And I say you displayed poor faith. You sent another after me, you sent this one, and he is the one who won me. Do you dare gainsay me?"

"Of … of course, lady, on my life." Gunther was a terrible liar.

"Do you dare swear to this in ordeal before Bleda, King of the Huns?"

The King of Burgundy was somewhat taken aback, but he said, "Why, yes, yes … of course."

"Gunther!" hissed a younger Burgundian at his king. "Enough!"

But the King silenced this and any other dissent.

"Then you will tell this—this *man* of yours to let go my reins, and you will ride east with me, not south."

"Let go, Siegfried," said the King.

Siegfried had already done so, and I didn't wait a moment to spur my pony forward.

Chapter 32

HE RIDE TO BLEDA'S TENT city seemed endless. All the way, the Burgundians discussed what they should do about me. One of them persisted that they should quit while they were ahead, that no one could hope to enter the camp of the Huns a second time and then be released unharmed. This one seemed to be the youngest and therefore had the privilege of giving voice to cowardice without much shame. The King sometimes agreed with this point of view, but it was Siegfried who kept asking, "What honor is there in retreat? There is no honor if we leave now," and by this, as by the repetitive refrain of a song, the King was mostly swayed. Several times I got the impression that Siegfried had no real thought of his own. He merely spoke what the King wanted to hear. They were like one mind in two bodies.

There was a third option vented. This was given by the small, dark, fierce one who kept saying they should take the advantage they had won while they were ahead. "She's out of her tower and alone. We could surround her and carry her off to Burgundy by force—at once."

"There is no honor in such action either," said Siegfried, and the King concurred, as if to his own mind.

But it disquieted me that they could speak of such things in my hearing, as if they thought of me as a Hun who didn't know their tongue, as a child or an idiot. Or worse, as just a woman who could be discussed in her presence with impunity, waiting for their good will to know what was to become of her next. I chose my path with care, seeking to ride on defensible terrain as much as possible and not let myself get cornered anywhere. If the terrain were with me, I was quite sure I could hold my own against these Burgundians as I had once against ten times as many Huns. Against these Burgundians, I'd hold my own, but not when Siegfried was added to their number.

By all means, I tried to keep the rest of the Burgundians between me and that hot-headed, dark one. I rejoiced when Siegfried's voice kept being raised on the side of honor—whatever his stranger's brain might consider to be honor these days. And, as soon as I felt I was close enough, I set my pony at a gallop towards the safety of the Hunnish enclave.

It was a warm day, and where my legs met the skin of my mount they were wet with our combined sweat. When we arrived, the froth from his mouth and nostrils was flying back and wetting my knees. I shouted to the Hunnish guard, some of whom I'd hunted with and knew well, to watch for the Burgundians on my tail and to deal with them as they thought best. I would take my place in Father Shaman's yurt, sending Rüdeger as go-between until I should hear Bleda's word on the matter.

But soon I realized Bleda, and indeed all the Huns, were much occupied with other business.

My pony had to pick his way carefully through the throngs in the encampment. And what throngs there were! Men, women, children pressed into the already too narrow passages between their tents, waving flowers and full-leafed branches and singing. Girls in groups of five, six, or sometimes seven, unfurled bolts of white felt over their heads and danced in formation under them—their feet in soft, dyed-leather boots making dainty steps—accompanying their dances with songs in their thin, high, nasally voices. It was difficult to pick the burden of a song out of such voices, especially for one such as myself for whom Hunnish tones were still foreign. But soon enough I understood; Attila had arrived.

I did not see the great leader of men until that evening. The Hunnish shamans had, for the most part, abandoned their tent, which they had occupied for many hours before with attention to the sacrifices and chants that would make this a state occasion. But Rüdeger and I were not required until the formalities of supper began. There was plenty of time to give him all the details of my predicament.

Because of the heat of the season, these formalities began a little later than the ninth hour of the day, when they were usually scheduled. We waited until the first breath of cool was already moving through the camp like a healer among the fevered. And then, in our degrees, we stepped over the threshold of Bleda's high tent. Each, including the Latin priests, poured a libation of mare's milk to sanctify the proceedings.

I took my place in the high tent between Rüdeger and the unhappy Christian priests in the second rank, behind the Hunnish shamans, both Bleda's and Attila's—for Attila had come heavily accompanied. Half of the throng outside belonged to him. Bleda's queens were entertaining Attila's in another tent, so I was the only woman present. But I was used to that.

Because of the heat, the sides of the tent were propped open to let the night in and to let many more men participate in the festivities than would otherwise be allowed. Through the open flaps, as the night progressed it became difficult to tell the sky's stars from the pine torches of the onlooking multitude as one faded into the other. As there was no fire needed, the two kings took the place of that sacred focal point on couches, Roman-style in the center of the tent. Indeed, Roman booty sat at the center as well.

To Bleda's right were seated those he most wished to honor on this occasion, mostly visiting Huns of Attila's elite bodyguard. To the left were the less honored—tonight, local Huns and confederate Germanic chieftains, among them the Burgundians. My ire raised impotently at this sight. I felt it was indeed unfortunate that my foes hadn't been executed yet, and their position in the tent, although to the left, made it a more distant possibility by the moment.

But the reception was going on without consideration of my concerns. There were more formalities, that of Bleda greeting his brother

and then each guest in turn with a sip of mare's milk and a prayer for his health, which the guest returned. An army of cupbearers saw to it that the rite did not lose momentum. And then the food was brought in, platters of meat and curds from horse, sheep, and goat indiscriminately mixed, and cakes of flat bread to wrap it in. The platters were set on low tables convenient to the height of people sitting on the ground. It was a bit more awkward for the kings to eat from their couches, but their purposes were dictated more by ceremony than by their bellies. Each king made it a point to help himself from every low table in turn around the tent, taking no more from one than from the next, lest there be offense. Among the tableware and crockery were many fabulous pieces of gold and silver, all booty. But the kings themselves drank from plain olive-wood goblets and ate off wooden trenchers. They also distinguished themselves from the rest, not by the wealth of their costumes, but by their simplicity.

Attila was shorter than his brother by almost a head, but broader, thick in the chest like a bull. I saw none of the humor in his eyes I had come to appreciate in Bleda. What was a twinkle when Bleda smiled gleamed like iron in the sharp squint of Attila, and Attila never smiled. *Perhaps*, I thought, *these were only differences caused by the one being host and the other guest.* Still, I couldn't help but remember my own prophecy to my patron before I even realized he had a brother. And every time I looked toward the guest king, the feeling that had prompted that prophecy returned, sending a shiver down my spine.

When all had eaten as much as they could, the tables were cleared, and the entertainment began in the space suddenly available. The first diversion, contrary to custom, was provided by Attila.

"Older brother," the King began with fine Hunnish formality, "I have come today in part to hand over to you some fugitives fled from your tents to the Romans. I have convinced the Romans to return them, so I return them to you."

"How did you convince the Romans?" Bleda asked.

"Need you ask? I simply promised not to invade them. For this promise, they also gave me several thousand pounds of gold as tribute."

"Do I get part of the gold as well?" Bleda smiled congenially.

"I made the treaty, not you."

"Of course, younger brother."

The appellation did not sit well with Attila. "I bring you these hostages," he said, "only because I don't want them. I've already taken the liberty of impaling those I thought deserved it, but these, I'm not so sure. Some use might be found …"

With a wave of a short-fingered and ringless hand, Attila called up a clanking of chains outside the tent, and presently the fugitives entered. Mostly, they were women and children.

"I take it the men were impaled," Bleda commented. "Ugly women, sickly children. And skimmed the cream for yourself."

Attila shrugged without committal.

But there was also, nearly last among the fugitives, a small, dark midget—hunchbacked and clubfooted—whose face was black and noseless even by Hunnish standards, who lisped through a harelip. The sight of such a creature burdened by chains set the tent a-roar with laughter.

"Zercon!" Bleda exclaimed through his laughter. "Zercon, you rascal! Run away from me, will you? How shall I punish such a deed?"

"Oh, master," squealed the thing, groveling on the floor. This and his strange sort of speech set on more laughter. His speech was a curious mixture of Hunnish, Gothic, Latin, and some other sounds which nobody could identify, but which might have been the tongue of the wild people of the Libyan desert where he had been found, if they were not the sounds of beasts living in the same spot. Still, the gist of it seemed to be: "Oh, master, don't be angry. I am punished enough by having tried to escape on legs like these. How could I have hoped for it?"

These words delighted Bleda. He had the midget loosed from the chains and, while the rest of the prisoners were led away as more fitting for his wives to deal with than his own dignity, the Khan caused Zercon to climb up at the foot of his couch where the strange being sat gratefully rubbing his swollen ankles.

"But tell me, Zercon," said the King to his fool, "why did you try to escape? Haven't I always treated you well?"

"You have master, but for one thing."

"And what might that be?"

Now the chirps and squeaks and gestures which answered this question were incoherent, but their meaning was plain. Bleda had never given this creature a wife. The obscenity of his expression delighted the tent to no end. Even the Burgundians took pleasure in it.

"Well, I shall remedy this at once, Zercon." And Bleda called to a retainer: "Fetch that woman Ione, will you?"

To Zercon, and the merriment of all, he continued, "You will like her, Zercon."

"Is she beautiful?"

"Indeed. And she has been, until this day, a servant to my wife."

"A servant to the queen, master! This is honor!"

"Honor indeed. So let's hear no more of you trying to run away on those crooked legs of yours."

The woman was ushered in, and Bleda made short work of the ceremony: "Ione, I give you to this fool here to be his wife."

"Master, you jest," the woman laughed with merriment, but merriment strained.

She was indeed a comely woman, a slave of Greek origin, with a fine, willowy figure and thick dark hair in braids that she could sit on. She saw that this was no jest. "No, master. Don't give me to this creature. I—I cannot bear to look on him."

Her horror as Zercon rolled off the couch and towards her made the tent all the merrier, and nothing could have been more comical than the contrast between his ugliness and her beauty.

"Woman," Bleda teased, "for what you must do, there needs be no lights for looking."

The tent roared, and then Ione let out with such a string of abuse at them all, including both kings, that I feared for her life.

But Bleda only smiled in return, smiled in particular at Zercon, who was cringing at his side from the volley. "Ah, Zercon. Did I forget to mention that she has been dismissed from my wife's service?"

Ione said fierce things about Bleda's wives. Had anyone else dared to say such things, the tension in the tent would have been palpable until Bleda avenged his wives. But because the words came from this woman in her distress, where there might have been tension in the tent, there was only merriment.

"Perhaps you did, master," said the cringing fool in all four languages at once.

"Well, she has been."

"For what infringement, master, pray?"

"For her shrewishness." Bleda had to say this twice to be heard over the woman's continuing abuse, but when it was heard, it was appreciated.

"Master, don't marry me to a shrew."

"It is too late," Bleda said, wiping tears of laughter from his eyes. "The deed is already done. Now, off with you, you two, and make like husband and wife or Zercon, I shall have you whipped. And Ione, treat him well and in a humble, wifely fashion, or I'll permanently spoil your fabled beauty by cutting off your ears."

Ione turned in a fury of humiliation to escape out of the tent, and Zercon hobbled after. At the threshold, he tripped and fell.

"Ione," Bleda called. "Come and pick up your husband. Can't you see he's come a long way and has difficulty walking? Ione, as you value your ears."

She did. And the incongruous sight of the tall, beautiful woman carrying the small, ugly, squirming man like a baby kept the tent out of breath for several long minutes.

"Now, brother," said Bleda, turning to Attila. "Aren't you sorry you didn't keep that fool for the delight he can bring?"

"I cannot stand the sight of such mutation," Attila replied.

Attila was on his feet and had been, if any of us had noticed, since the prisoners had been brought in, and was pacing back and forth as if to walk off a bad meal. "Such weakness," he snapped. "Such frivolity! I return him to you, brother, because such an aberration seems to suit the decay you've fallen into around here."

Attila was in earnest, and the tent fell suddenly sober to hear him as if it had been dropped off a mountainside.

"Look at you, brother, look at you! Is this a Hunnish way to live, idling with dwarves and pretty slave women? Brother, you have not moved your encampment in nearly five years. What Hun lives like this, in his own filth, like Germans? Like Romans, in their town cages. It is unhealthy, it makes you weak. Look at this!" He gave a sudden vicious swipe at his couch.

"I sought to honor you, brother, by offering you a couch."

"A couch! A couch with fleas! A true Hun never sits still long enough to collect fleas."

"Well, where would you have me go?" asked Bleda, suddenly almost stupid.

"Where? Where? Have you reached the end of the world?"

"No …"

"No? Then a true Hun keeps moving. A true Hun follows the horizon until he reaches it. Your men grow soft, brother. Your subjects cheat you, hide their foodstuffs from you under their dung piles, under your very nose, and you do not punish them."

Bleda shrugged. "I figured we had enough."

"Enough! The true Hun follows the horizon!"

"But we have reached the Rhine."

"The Rhine? The Rhine? What is the Rhine? Have we not rivers in our homeland that make the Rhine seem like a stream a child can jump? What of the Danube? The Volga? We cross these daily, use them as highways, not boundaries. What is beyond the Rhine? Haven't you a Hun's curiosity to find out? A Hun's ambition? Burgundy! You could have Burgundy conquered this year before the leaves turn."

Attila's hand waved over my suitors as if it were a broom, sweeping them from the face of the earth. They couldn't understand what was being said, but smiled and nodded at the attention. The rest of the tent, those who could understand, had begun to seethe like a pot set over leaping flames.

"The Franks!" Attila cried. "The Gauls! Rome! Even the name of Rome should not daunt a true Hun. If you were to come at Rome, brother, from the west, and I from the east, we would have them trapped in pincers. By this time next year—"

"Brother, brother!" Bleda had begun to laugh again as if his brother, too, were some sort of entertaining freak. "Brother, you speak in the company of many people."

"I keep no secrets from my men," Attila said. "They know I will never lead them where I will not go myself. They are party to all my counsels. They at least know I will never lead them into effeminate torpor."

There were loud cheers from the right. Bleda nodded, smiling, to these men. "And I would never keep any Hun from my counsels, either," he said. "But let's not talk of such things by night."

"You are a disgrace," Attila said in a quiet, dangerous voice, leaning far over his supper couch till he was flat nose to flat nose with Bleda.

"Such talk craves the sobriety of daylight, when men sit upon their horses." This brought cheers from the left, but they were not as fervent as those from the right. "Now, now, let me offer you all, honored guests, dearest kinsmen, the pleasures nighttime affords for the labors of the day."

Bleda rose, forcing his brother to take an undignified stance over the couches to keep his eyes trained on his head. Bleda clapped his hands smartly, and a train of fair slave girls was brought in, one for each man present and more, so none could say he'd gotten the dregs. Now there were cheers from all sides.

After a pause, Attila flung himself away from the couches. "Very well," he said. I think only Bleda, Rüdeger, and I were listening now, all others in the tent having found distraction. "Very well, we shall see what tomorrow brings."

"Good, younger brother, good," said Bleda. "Have you a liking for anything you see here?"

"Not I."

"Are you certain? I must surely allow you first pick."

"Well, then … yes."

"Name her."

Attila turned suddenly from the bevy of girls before the couches, who giggled or wept according to their experience, and looked me straight in the eye. My eyes dropped in spite of themselves. "I could do with some German flesh tonight."

"I do have a German girl or two among the—"

"Not there. Here."

"That one?"

Attila's eyes narrowed to slits as if to crush me between the lids. "Yes."

Rüdeger's hand found mine and pressed it protectively.

"But, brother, don't you see she is among my shamans?"

"You keep altogether too many shamans."

"How is it possible to have too many in one's train who know the many paths to the spirit world?"

"If you are too much in the spirit world, this present world is lost to you."

"This is one thing you cannot ask of me," Bleda reiterated.

Attila fixed me with one long, last look. I noticed that his collar was that of a wolf cub pelt with the head still on, slung over his shoulder. For some reason I remembered the strange dream of the princess of Burgundy, how she would be given away to a wolf cub. Rüdeger pressed my hand.

"You're right," Attila said, turning away. "I will not raid your bushel of shamans."

Bleda seemed to suddenly think that he had countered his brother once too often that night, and that this might be dangerous. "It's a curious thing about that shamaness," he said, conciliatorily.

"What's that?" said Attila, hardly listening.

I heard Bleda begin to tell a good portion of my story, including the differences with the Burgundians I was asking him to mediate.

"Outwitted the Burgundians, has she?" Attila asked with refired interest. "Sworn to give herself only to a man who can defeat her—and that man's not of the Burgundians?"

"What, brother? Would you take her on?"

"No, no, not I," said Attila, calling himself to sudden discipline. To enter such a fray would be beneath his dignity. "But I think this is sport you and I should not miss. You certainly not, since you have been called upon to arbitrate between them. I say we should all see this trial—tomorrow."

"I meant to have horse racing and wrestling between our Huns for our amusement tomorrow."

"There will be time for both. This contest between the cream of Burgundy and a shamaness is not something I would miss. I'd give up any number of horse races to see it."

"Very well. Very well, brother, yes. It should prove good sport." And Bleda sent for the Burgundians and a translator to come so he could explain the plan.

Rüdeger pressed my hand.

The Burgundians were somewhat annoyed to be distracted from the bedfellows they were choosing for the night. Siegfried, I had noticed, had taken a buxom Briton, and even Gunther, for all his romantic lays, was at least toying with the idea of taking one or the other of two Celtic sisters. The Burgundians found this a very hospitable custom among their enemy, who they otherwise considered only half-human.

The Burgundians' annoyance grew less, however, when they understood what Bleda had planned.

"Brynhild?" I heard Siegfried say. There was a jerk in his voice, like one suddenly jerked awake.

"Yes," said Bleda. "You know who I mean."

The Khan gestured in my direction. Siegfried turned, and his eyes met mine. They were *his* eyes, I could tell, not those of that stranger who'd peered at me before.

"Brynhild!" he said again, and the joy in his voice infected my heart with equal joy. He was coming towards me; he would climb over every shaman between us if need be.

But there was the King of Burgundy, pressing a drink on him. It was not a bowl of the banquet's last mare's milk, but something else, something he carried in an aurochs horn strapped across his chest.

"What? A drink now?" Siegfried growled. "Now, when I see my beloved for the first time in … in …"

The memory of that time failed him. The drink was pressed on him in that vacuum, and suddenly, my Siegfried was gone again.

"He is anxious for the trial to begin," King Gunther apologized to King Bleda as he accepted the challenge. They would contest for my maidenhood on the morrow, would I part of it or no.

Then all the Burgundians went back to their selection of bed partners. In the meantime, Siegfried's Briton had been claimed by someone else. But nothing to loathe, Siegfried chose another—a small dark girl, pretty enough but with a limp. He took her by the hand, laughed loudly at something she said—though what language they conversed in, I could not say—and left the yurt without a backward glance.

chapter 33

"EWARE YOUR BROTHER ATILLA—OH, Bleda Khan—and all his schemes."

I announced this in my best shamanic voice, standing there in my complete armor in the center of the space cordoned off with a rope and dangling horse tails in preface to the tournament. My words were stifled in the heat of that high summer morning and the dust raised on the Hun-beaten plain. Attila always flattered himself by saying nothing would ever grow again where his horses' hooves had trod.

For his part, Bleda smiled at my words over the dusty throng, shrill with anticipation. His people were fur-capped even in the heat; the sweat burnished their faces and loosed a stink from the skins they wore. I could tell he heard me, but he did not call off the contest. The only effect my words had was to cause a number of the Huns to scramble to change their bets. The fact that I dared to say this in the presence of the steely eyes of Attila himself made some readjustment of the odds in my favor.

My opponent strode into the dusty field opposite me. He wore the gilded armor and helmet of the King of Burgundy, but I couldn't see his face. The swell of his figure straining at the laces made me suspicious, and a quick glance over the unhelmeted Burgundian faces standing behind him confirmed those suspicions. The King of

Burgundy was not standing and watching among his retainers. But neither was Siegfried. It was Siegfried I would fight for my freedom, then. The sun had risen above the mounded tents, and I was already sweating beneath the weight of my armor.

The first contest was the spear throw. I was to throw first, as I had won the toss of a Roman solidus.

Siegfried took his stance at twenty paces, setting the great shield with the rose of Burgundy firmly before him. I threw.

The iron point bit into the center of the rose with a satisfactorily heavy thud. "It's pierced right through the shield!" the audience told me and each other, and again scrambled to rearrange their bets. But Siegfried had stood his ground. *He's like a wall*, I thought.

And now that wall took his step-step-skip to throw, and I braced myself. I missed a breath or two as the wind was knocked from me. My shield cracked along the grain from the blow and fell from my hands in two pieces. But I stood my ground, and we had to go a second round.

My shaft was embedded so deeply in the Burgundian rose that the end had to be hacked off, and I had to be handed a new shield, one larger than the usual small Hunnish round shield, but still I would have preferred a more solid, German one. At this point, I hadn't that option.

I threw again, aiming for the former embedded point where I knew the wood would be weakened. I sent the point in so deeply, it drew blood from the holder's hand and, right through the center of Burgundy's rose, the shield broke in two. The pieces dangled limply from the nails of a brass boss, the only thing they still had in common.

But my opponent's next blow knocked me off my feet, and I lost the round.

I went to Rüdeger in the side lines, removed my helmet and mopped my face with the cloth he offered as the next trial was announced. Through the sting of sweat, I saw that removing his helmet was not a luxury that Burgundy's champion could take. But he was binding his bleeding hand in a bit of torn linen. Was this indeed Siegfried? The dragon's blood should have spared him this injury if it was. But perhaps the disease that was affecting his brain had some effect on his body as well. Rüdeger gave me an excuse to look away, offering me a swallow of water and one of encouraging mare's milk. Then I reentered the field.

The stone came almost to my knees. I tested its weight with closed eyes, then heaved it to my shoulder in two moves. It weighed about as much as a man. *I have picked up such from a battlefield many a time,* was my thought. *Riding at a full gallop, and I have brought him to my saddle. I was trained for this,* I thought, and threw.

A Hun came out and dropped a square of red felt, one where I stood, one where the stone fell. I could tell by the ahs and the scramble for bets that it was a good throw, but Siegfried equaled it.

My next throw was even better; I pressed it with the Valkyrie song from my lungs. Siegfried's fell a hand's breadth short. After two trials, we stood even.

I drank again and wiped mare's milk mixed with sweat from my face. My opponent didn't remove his helmet.

And now was the final determining long jump. I jumped well, better than I have in my life, about twelve ells in full armor. No one else in the audience could meet that, and their noises proved it. But my opponent's legs reached further and stayed up longer.

"Burgundy wins," Bleda declared. Then suddenly leaping to his horse—the less said about the rout the better—he announced, "Races now! My best horse against yours, brother."

Bleda urged his pony through the general chaos that had erupted when Siegfried won and bets were claimed, denied, bargained for. He rode up to us where we stood, right where our jumps had landed us, almost side by side. "I am sorry to lose such a fine shamaness," Bleda said, "but this was the deal, and you were defeated, Brynhild, fair and square."

With a sudden movement, I grabbed my opponent's wounded hand, tightly so that for a moment pain would confuse him, and then I reached up and whipped the helmet off. "But look, my lord—look, Bleda Khan. This is not the King of Burgundy. Look, this is the man who's won me, not that Gunther. Look! There's been deceit again. This man I will go with, but not Burgundy's Gunther. Look!"

And Bleda looked. Now I suppose for Huns, we Germans look as much alike as their many faces look to us. But Bleda looked and saw some difference he could recognize in Siegfried's face, blotchy with heat and exhaustion as it was.

Bleda grew thoughtful. "Yes, I see," he said. "This is not Burgundy's king. Hey, fellow, what's the meaning of this ruse?"

Now, Siegfried had no knowledge of Hunnish, but he knew he was discovered. As he stood there in confusion and I in triumph, Bleda's pony suddenly reared as if it had gone mad. Siegfried thought at first that this must be part of his punishment, but, being afraid of nothing, he stood his ground when he might have reached up for the bridle and calmed the beast. For this was no attack, but some sort of sudden terror such as never hits a well-trained animal for no reason.

Now, I cannot say for certain and can only say what I saw. But what I saw, through the plunging millstones of the horse's feet, was a Hun, fleeing fast in the opposite direction. It was no Hun that I knew—it was one of Attila's men. And in his hand was what seemed to be a red-hot poker.

The horse leapt and flailed, and I was thrown back in spite of myself. Bleda kept his seat well, as any man can who's all but born on horseback. But the pony was not to be calmed. And then the accident—if accident it was—compounded itself. A second Hun I didn't know chose that instant to run and clear the field of our spent spears. Instead of scurrying quickly out of harm's way, he approached the frenzied circuit of the bucking horse. So it happened that when Bleda at last was thrown, a spear had pierced him through the chest. The butt vibrated in the dusty air.

Such was the death of my protector, Bleda, the King of the Huns. When his body reached the ground on its impalement, it was already still, and in the heat the flies had already found the wound.

Where there had been the confusion of holiday before, more deadly chaos now reigned, pandemonium, riot. Others, apparently, had also seen what I had seen, perhaps with even clearer perspective, for there were instant shouts of "Murder! Treachery! Fratricide!" It did not take long for more blood to be pouring—Hun against Hun in horrendous civil war.

"Come, lady. Let me lead you to safety. This is no place for us."

I looked up and there was my opponent, safe behind his helmet once more.

At that moment, Attila happened to ride by. His mount was a huge black stallion of Germanic stock with blood-red trappings. "To horse! To horse!" he was calling, and his horn blowers following in his wake were doing what they could to echo that call with a sound that would carry further. It was impossible to tell whether the call to horse was in order to escape or to get better advantage in battle.

Not caring which, I caught hold of the bridle made of red-dyed, braided horsehide and said, "Attila! Your righteous judgement, O Attila Khan."

"Who is it who asks judgement at a time like this? You, shamaness?" He raised his sword above his head. "I wonder if I should cut you down where you stand. You gave unfavorable judgement against me earlier today, I recall."

"My lord, I did only as was my calling."

"Do you still seek Bleda's good, shamaness? Should I kill you or take you as booty?" He lowered his sword and squinted his eyes at me, though no smile followed that squint. "Last night I wanted German flesh, and I was denied. Today, it seems, I am over-occupied fighting my own kindred and must be refused again."

"German flesh shall be the death of you, Attila. A German—and a woman." Those words came from my seeress source—I knew it, and I put it in such tones that he, too, could tell it was so.

Attila threw back his head and laughed, but he never smiled. "Is this prophecy, shamaness? Ha! A German woman! Ha! I am Attila, by the burning sun I follow across the world. A German woman! If I brought you into my camp, what would be the outcome of that, I wonder?" Under his helmet he still wore his sheepskin cap, and under that were his thin dark eyes, cutting like knives.

"I would do for you as I did for Bleda."

"Bleda is dead. I've no wish to join him."

"But I warned him by speaking the truth. I can do the same for you."

"Such warning I do not need. *To horse, men! Fight! For Attila!*"

But still I held to the bridle until his horse foamed at the mouth and the braided hide burned my hands.

"I only beg you to look on the face of my opponent, see that he is not the King of Burgundy, that I was defeated today under false pretenses."

I tore the helmet off of Burgundy, and Attila gave him a glance. "All Germans look alike to me," he said.

I looked. It was Gunther.

"But they have changed costume again! They have cheated. Bleda Khan saw, he confirmed!"

"Bleda is dead," shouted Attila, rearing his horse and wrenching it free of my weakened hands.

"*But look, look!*" I cried, the burning in my hands having reminded me. "Don't you remember, Attila Khan, how I wounded my opponent in the spear throw. Look at this left hand, my lord." I caught Gunther's hand and thrust it toward the man on the prancing black steed. "Has this hand held a shield against a spear throw of mine today? Look! Unscathed as a baby."

But Attila had stopped giving me any notice. "*Bleda is dead!*" he shouted the war cry. "*Dead! Long live Attila!*

"Come on, Burgundy," said the new Khan of all the Huns. "Get the women and children out of the way. Bring them to safety. This is no place for women and children today!"

chapter 34

EVERYTHING IN THE BURGUNDIAN CAPITOL of Worms was as it should be, from the fledgling storks trying out their wings and gangly orange legs on the rooftops, to the profusion of late summer rebloom on the roses. It was hard to believe that Burgundians were refugees and had lived in this place not even as long as Gunther had been alive. But of course, they had the Roman complex of foundations to build upon, as the Romans had the earlier Celtic Borbetomagus. Between the Roman Civitas Vangionum and the Burgundian Worms had come the onslaught of Genseric and his Vandals. This tribe had since moved on westward, taking their share of the Roman Empire in Spain. They stayed only so long to fluff the pillow as it were, softening the harsh lines of Roman settlement. When Giuki, Gunther's father, had led the remnants of his people here, the place was practically abandoned. Yet, thanks to sturdy Roman construction, there was hardly a roof that needed replacing, and they could turn their attention at once to the garnishes of life.

A spar of the rolling Hessian hill land thrust westward here towards the forest-covered Palatinate Mountains. Dark as the mountains were, they were not impenetrable: Caesar's clear valley wound through them west to Gaul and the present Frankish lands. Skirting Odin Wood and its mountains, ran the road linking the Rhine to that other vital artery, the Danube. And binding the whole north to south was the shimmering ribbon of the Rhine. So there were three regions lending their wealth to the folk here, three layers to prosperity: the wood and game of the forested mountains, the golden fertility of the plowed hills, and the bounty of fish and traffic of the river.

Worms was situated on three Hessian hills on the west bank, above the high-water mark of the seasonal floods. The citified population that Gunther ruled spread over all three hills. It pressed particularly against the vast cherry orchards that skirted the southwestern flank, which in spring presented a lacy white underskirt to the settlement and into the fields beyond.

The highest of the three hills, the central one, separated from its neighbors by a pair of low Rhine-wending brooks, claimed royal prerogative. Here was the great three-aisled, clerestoried peristyle that had served as the Romans' forum and market for the goods that met at this crossroads from all four directions. The Burgundians still traded here. On a mound dead-center stood the round pillar by which the Romans had begun the subjugation of the countryside to the grid of their miles. Here were the ruins of the temple. The old statues of classical Gods and Goddesses, marked by Vandals' runes and moss, were missing hands and faces. They were comfortable now like old uncles and aunties, this one with her mossy birthmark, that one with his limp, without which the old homestead would not seem like home. They did not seem to mind this hard, cold stone house, though German Gods will usually refuse to inhabit temples that are not made of holy, warm wood. Many had in fact been redubbed for the Germanic Gods they most resembled – Rosmerta, Epona, Tyr, Freyr—and received their appropriate sacrifices in their appropriate seasons. But sheltered in a side room of the sanctuary was also Christian worship. Gunther, no less than Bleda, was required to tolerate it. Rüdeger had been right. Christians were everywhere these days. Though they preached continence, they seemed to multiply like maggots on a dung heap.

Gunther's palace itself was the old Roman citadel, drafty and smelling of damp stone in winter but pleasant enough in late summer: Romans built better for the warm seasons. Its stones—like all the stones in forum, temples, and streets in between—were white. Where had the Romans found all this white stone? Why had they bothered? These stones were now mortared with the softening growths of woodruff and thyme, which scented the place and, in their proper times, grew softer still with bloom. There were strange, large, brilliant-blue birds left behind by the Romans, called peafowl. The Germans named them a word that echoed the wail of their cry, "Pfau!" They were quite tame and could be eaten, but the meat wasn't much, nothing compared to a fat duck, say, or a big-breasted goose. But alive, the cocks especially, were truly wonders—with tails like great iridescent fans bespeckled with eyes like the eyes of a God. Spring in Worms was always dampened by their mournful, love-sick cries.

And everywhere, everywhere were these roses planted by the Romans and then—without their armies of slaves put to no other task than keeping the bushes pruned—they grew wild, reverting to the pale pink and single ring of petals of their original stock and cloying the air. I doubt the Burgundians had the rose for their emblem before they came to Worms, but it was certainly appropriate now. The men liked to say as a motto, "Manly beauty, but beware my thorn."

In my opinion, someone had pruned the men of their thorns. They even worked roses into my bridal crown.

Worms was as it should be, and so was the wedding. Usually sowing season presses, or the weather's just right for haying, a widower's children need a mother right away, or alliances call for immediate oaths over mead between groom and father-in-law, which is all that is technically required to prevent bastards.

Burgundy's lord, however, had time and leisure where others did not. He had a great desire that I have no longing in the future for what I'd missed, although his desire was little consolation to me. He also had an inordinate passion for the ceremonies of love, thinking thereby to capture the reality of it, much as he thought plucking on his harp and singing tales of heroes could capture heroics and adventure for himself.

When I say all was as it should be, I mean on the groom's side, of course. There was no bearing of the dowry gifts—armor, bedding, and a forward-looking cradle—on a flowered cart a day or two before the event. There was no distaff thrust out in front over the oxen's heads, the taller the better, to encourage the groom about his business. But what he could of tradition and propriety, Gunther manufactured from his side.

It was the waxing of the moon, so our love might wax as well. Odin's day, Wednesday, was avoided so that through no further honor to my former divine lord would I be tempted to leave the new mortal lord Fate had condemned me to. Friday was the day chosen, of course, the day sacred to Freya, the Goddess of love.

When he came to fetch me to the temple to perform the libations, Gunther was greeted at my door by a man wearing my dresses. This was to confuse the malevolent spirits who might follow us if this precaution were not taken. It certainly could not have confused Gunther, who had ordered the masquerade in the first place, although he pretended to be greatly surprised and commented on the ugliness of the bride. I should have been flattered by the care for my welfare, but it was Siegfried who volunteered for the part, and the sight of him simpering behind his beard and trying to flirt with Gunther—playing *me* when he should know me better—that was agony. I couldn't get away from that sight fast enough, but this too had its repercussions. The company took this as unmaidenly eagerness on my part and teased about it.

The procession was led by blowers of cow-horns followed by little girls strewing rose petals. Always those roses! Banners and garlands of greenery were draped under arches and on walls, spiraled up the Roman pillars of the town and caught at the corners with spears and lances festooned with ribbons red and white, the Burgundians' rosy colors. Clouds of doves were loosed into the pink dawn light of the square, a sacrifice to fair Frigga. Personally, I was struck mostly by the birds' ridiculously tiny heads.

Then, after we had been marked with the sign of Thor's hammer on our foreheads, when we rose from kneeling in the temple, I was annoyed to find Gunther treading on my dress. I looked to him for some pathetic apology equal to such clumsiness, but received instead a shout of triumph. It was traditional among Burgundians that if a groom managed to tread on his bride's dress, he would have the upper hand in their marriage. The bride could counteract this by contriving to step on her groom's toe at some point before getting her skirt pinned to the floor. But this I had failed to accomplish.

It was the same sort of imagery practiced earlier in the day when my hair was being arranged to receive the heirloom bridal crown of Burgundy, wound round sprigs of rosemary for perpetual remembrance. Gudrun, my sister-in-law, undertook all such matronly duties. Although I was told I had a mother-in-law they reverentially called Queen Ute, I never saw her. She kept, I was told, strictly to her rooms. More importantly to me than Gudrun's status as my sister-in-law was that she was Siegfried's pregnant wife.

"Now, Heidele, that's bad luck," Gudrun had scolded the maid for trying the bridal crown on her own head. "Now you'll never wear one of your own."

"I wish I'd known that," I said to them. "I'd have found some bride's crown to snatch before this day."

The girls had tittered, misunderstanding my words, for they couldn't believe I really meant what they'd heard me say. Of course I did, but then I couldn't remember when in my life I'd ever see a crown lying around asking to be tried on. And if I'd ever known these little facts of matrimonial etiquette, I'd forgotten them. Bridal behavior was something that never occurred to us in Valhalla. This ignorance had the effect that when we left the temple, the Burgundians had the added excitation of knowing that not only was their King marrying a Valkyrie, but that he had demonstrated his virility and dominance over me, even if it were only in such a clumsy way.

The way back to the palace was the same as the procession there, with songs added. This time, however, we were waylaid by onlookers. Siegfried at the helm, in men's clothing now, stole their monarch's hat—a green thing made foppish by roses and the long feather of one of the peacocks—and made off with it. They led him on a merry chase, and finally he good-naturedly bought it back from them, not with blows as I would have done, but with a flagon of mead all round.

Then there were the tilts, not man to man and horse to horse, such as I might have enjoyed, but each man riding separately against a rose-wound wreath suspended from an old Roman arch. Strung among the roses were pearls and glinting ornaments of gold. It was these dead, sterile things the warriors were weighing themselves against.

I was obliged to watch it all from under a white rose-covered bower. This shielded me from the sun, not to be halted in its plummet to the southwest. It also kept me from any participation in the contest, for which the wasting muscles in my arms longed. But it could not shield me from the plain wedding-day symbolism of wreath and lance. Or from Gunther's equally plain good humor when he was obliged to let Siegfried carry the day.

A light evening rain, sounding like the gossip of matrons on the canopy of leaves, put an end to the outdoor portion of the festivities.

"What good luck!" exclaimed Gudrun as we scrambled for shelter.

"Good luck?" I repeated in astonishment.

"Of course. It's good luck for a bride to be rained on. Each drop promises a well-favored child. I was married on a day as dry as a bone, and there must be a dozen drops on your bosom already."

"By my life, I'll not have a dozen children," I snapped. "I'd die first." Then I gestured to her swelling belly. "And so much for your dry bone."

Gudrun laughed merrily, working hard to take everything I said in the best possible light. That was hard work indeed.

chapter 35

HE WEATHER SENT THE PARTY indoors, but this did not mean that the relief of having it end. A bride must not take her crown off until midnight and, of course, everyone must hover around to make certain she doesn't fail. And should there be any other attempt, either on her part or on the part of anyone present to disrupt the solemnities, a pair of swords is thrust in the wooden rafters above her head to hang there throughout the evening, close at hand in case the groom and his best man should have need of them.

I could reach up and help myself handily to these weapons, I thought. One for me, one for Siegfried. We could still hack our way out of Burgundy's hall to freedom. But every time I sent a look in the direction of him who they called Fafnirsbane, it was enough to tell me he would take the groom's part instead. So I sat helpless under those blades, my hands in my lap, feeling the pressure of both crown and swords, and watched the festivities pass.

Two full kegs of mead were dispensed that evening to keep the party running inside the hall alone, dispensed in flagons that dripped down the elbows. The drink stuck there, gathering grime. There were other, more delicate, liquids too. Wine in the style of the Romans was an art not lost in Worms. There was kirsch from cherries and cordials fermented from any other fruit available. A pear, for instance, had been caught in a delicate glass bottle while still hardly more than a blossom, allowed to grow there, then picked when ripe, covered with aqua vitae, and set in the sun for a month or two. The sight of a full-grown golden pear within the greenish glass at the bottom of a narrow neck it could not possibly have passed through was more wonderful than either the taste or the rather too-subtle effect.

Then there was board after board of all the appropriate foods. The bridal soup to begin with—rich with barley, leeks, lentils, and gizzards—floating with stodgy herbed dumplings and marrow balls. The soup was important—a bride needs plenty of liquid, I was told, and certainly must get only a little of it from the kegs. So there were fruit soups as well. One of dried cherries with soured cream, and (of course, this was Burgundy) one of rose hips well-chilled in spring water, sprinkled with slivered spiced nuts.

There followed thirty-two geese, some stuffed with plums, some with sage and rosemary; four swine, their fat turned to crackling and served by the side; venison; and a wild boar with an apple in his mouth. There were two calves, roasted whole, and a peacock, his feathers preserved and arranged behind him as if still strutting. *Now what*, I wondered, *is the symbolism of this dish?* There were fish, dried or pickled, tarts of apple and hazelnut. There were terrines and pickles of cabbage, beet, and carrot. There were six kinds of cheeses from the soft summer kind thick with ewe's milk, to the hard, sharp variety from goats. There was blood pudding and head cheese, white wurst and red—all served with quantities of dill and the eye-stinging horseradish, which I have heard the Gauls call "German mustard."

One whole storehouse door had been taken off its hinges and set between benches to bear the burden of bread alone. There were bread braids, breads twisted into pretzels with poppy seed or salt, bread stuffed with soft cheese, and bread stuffed with plum preserve or liberally sown with dried bilberries. In the center of this board was a tower fully three feet high made of egg puffs individually stuffed with cream and drizzled all over the outside with honey. Just beneath this masterpiece was one simple loaf wrapped in a new linen cloth. This was handed to me to hold: "You must break this up in the first soup you make for Gunther," instructed Gudrun. "That will lead to marital harmony."

"I'm not likely to make him any soup at all," I replied, and after that we both looked out at the crowd with smiles just a little wider than was necessary.

I was instructed to feed scraps to the household cats with great ceremony, cats being sacred to Frigga and protectors of hearth and home. The only time Gunther took a helping from the board was when he was assisting a guest to fill a substantial blue-and-red-checked kerchief or two with the rest of the leftovers to take home. He drank liberally, however, and I was glad to see that. Grooming and hosting at once was a thirsty business. When I saw his horn dry, I was careful to see it full again quickly.

But the most important factor in his thirst was his occupation with the music. Gunther had lined up more than an evening's worth of the best Burgundy had to offer, and I could tell that when all else failed, it was with music that he hoped to make me a willing bride. It is always the case that we think what impassions us must likewise impassion others.

Some of the music was at least loud. Horns blared, threatening the old Roman rafters of the hall. Then a chorus began tunes that everybody knew—rowdy songs, bawdy songs. Then viols and harps wound their way about a rhythm thunked out on an upended bench, and folk rose to dance, men to one side, women to the other, under wreaths of ivy and roses. These performances brought an involuntary smile to my lips. But they were not to Gunther's taste.

He would let them go on as long as he could, nervously taking long draughts and shifting heavily first forward and then back in the high seat next to me. And when he could bear it no longer, he would get to his feet and announce the next number. He himself provided the next number when necessary. He did it more than a few times that night, favoring everyone with long, meandering, chaste tales of honor, love, and little action—full of intricate turns of phrase and artful alliteration sure to impress those who might be impressed by such things. Myself, I tended to drift in and out of attention, finding the song so little progressed when I returned that I couldn't tell how long I'd been gone. Silently, I cursed the heat of the room and what wine I had taken, Coming to my senses, I had a maid fill Gunther's horn to the rim and thrust it in his hand when he'd return from passing all that dry air over his throat. To myself, I murmured a rune of alertness.

Mercifully, midnight came at last. I had only to be blindfolded and, in a game, catch the girl who was fated to marry next. I don't remember who it was. It seemed, in fact, that I caught two. They fairly threw themselves at me in their eagerness to join my fate. Then we were led to the royal chamber by a circuitous way, round the hall and the outbuildings in a sashay step through the night drizzle to which a thumping on pans, kettles, and shields kept time.

Gunther managed, straining embarrassingly, to carry me over the threshold to avoid the evil spirits lurking there. But tradition said nothing of the evil he carried within me. There I saw that the chamber had appropriately been hung with finery and roses, the door was closed behind us, and I could take off the crown at last. Although not half as heavy as a helmet and cuirass, the weight seemed ten times more oppressive.

And then I was alone with my husband.

The center of the room, indeed, practically its only piece of furniture, was the bedstead, a massive piece enclosed in dark slabs of walnut, walnut that was heavily carved with the intertwining limbs of fruit trees and flowers. Gunther stood across this bedstead from me, his features pale and sickly in the wave of torchlight. For some purpose I couldn't fathom, he adjusted the torch in its bracket to throw its light across the brocade and rose-strewn slab that peeked out between the wide-flung doors of the closet bed. The coverlet was carefully embroidered on each corner with the protecting hammer of Thor. Perhaps he was checking to make certain the appropriate pieces of bread were still under a corner of the bed to ensure that our children had good teeth. Perhaps he was looking for Frigga's beast, the live cock or prickly hedgehog, that tradition warned would be hidden in the sheets or elsewhere—but that seemed not to be the custom in Burgundy.

I only hoped he didn't discover what things I had untraditionally placed there as well.

When he was done, the light did seem more dangerously mesmerizing. By it, he took off his boots. The sour smell of his feet filled the room.

"Well." The joy in Gunther's smile was strained with nervousness.

And then, while approaching me he tripped over the only other piece of furniture in the room, a cradle. The cradle was not a usual furnishing in his room, that was clear. It was another traditional thing for a wedding. That he tripped over it seemed proper to me.

I turned as he tried to recover himself, loving every bit of cruelty I could muster. "I was happier in my tower," I said.

I turned to where I knew Gram was, on the top of my few bundled possessions. I could not wear it as a bride, but I could see its hilt dancing in the torchlight. One leap, and I could have it. But I didn't need it, not quite yet.

There was a sudden crash outside the door, and a voice I knew as Siegfried's gave a battle cry.

"Siegfried!" I exclaimed and thought, *He's come to rescue me from this fate, rescue me so I don't have to do it myself.*

A torrent of other crashes followed. *But the door is not locked*, I thought, and I guess a crease of worry pressed my face, because Gunther said, "Don't be afraid, Brynhild, my wife, my love. It is an old marriage custom we have here called *poltering*. The folk have saved up broken crockery for months. They're beating pans, showering us with dried peas, and even breaking new pots against our door. It's meant to scare the evil spirits away. Eh, listened to that! Siegfried's brought along his whip to give it a good cracking. Don't be scared. They'll soon get bored and go to bed. It won't last long."

One evil spirit it didn't frighten in any case. That was the one that had been fluttering with me ever since the day Bleda died, and it came now and wrapped itself firmly about my heart. "I'm not scared," I snapped. But how disquieting to have the hoped-for sounds of battle turn out to be only the sounds of rowdy domesticity, clashing pots, and breaking crockery. And Siegfried in the forefront, cracking his whip the loudest and yelling, "Evil, depart!" A whip? The Siegfried I knew would never consider using a whip on Grani or anything else.

Gunther used the time to carefully but reverently move the cradle out of the way and rid himself of royal chain and belt, everything but trousers. Then he laid back on the bed to wait out the exorcism. *By my life, what a pale, weak chest*, I thought, *and belly already paunching to hold up his harp*. It looks like a tub of curds and whey, the hair so fine and colorless as to seem nonexistent. For my part, I paced, never more than a leap from Gram, muttering runes for alertness under my breath.

chapter 36

CTUALLY, THE FIRST NIGHT WAS EASY. Before the *poltering* was over and in spite of it, a steady deep resonance from within the room told me the drink and the exertions of the day had gotten the better of my groom. That and the fact that I'd carefully filled his pillow with a mix of catnip, nightshade, lavender, and hops. I didn't know the complete secret of sleep thorn yet, but these at least I knew were part of its ingredients.

As soon as I was certain of my success, carefully avoiding any contaminated bedding, I set my own bed up in a far corner and allowed myself to go to sleep. I slept long and well, and was up early in the morning, fully refreshed, while Gunther still snored on.

I went out to the butts and spent the day target shooting, missing no more than my usual best. At taking down hanging wreaths, I did every bit as well as Siegfried had done the day before when he won the wedding tournament.

The next night was somewhat harder. We had to leave a quiet supper of leftovers and enter our room to even greater quiet. There was sharp anticipation in this quiet. Had I been in his shoes, I personally wouldn't have said a word on the matter, but Gunther being Gunther must have told someone about the previous night's failure. It is true that my herbal mixture is never known to work so well the second night as when fresh. I had held out some hope for it to have some effect, however, as I was unable to renew my supplies. But somebody—surely Gunther would never have thought of it—had seen through my cunning, and all traces of the herbs had been removed. The bedding had been made fresh without even a lingering fragrance.

I saw what had happened, and Gunther saw that I saw.

"Nice supper, wasn't it?" he said, working deliberately on his boots.

"Rather too much savory in that soup."

"Yes?" Was that a wrinkle of worry in the uprise of his voice?

"They put more in it tonight, though there was quite enough yesterday."

"Indeed. We should put you in charge of the soup, my love, I suppose."

And then it hit me. Savory is a love potion. So there were two of us in the castle playing with herbs and spells. I had not been cautious enough. Having seen this, I saw instantly that Gunther had rubbed some sort of ointment on himself as well, probably something with marjoram, thyme, wormwood. This was a well-known recipe. Perhaps there was some southwood, too, since Worms had such good trade connections to the south where this plant, also called maid's ruin, is grown.

Well, I wasn't going to let it be the ruin of me. I scratched a finger along his forearm, wiped it on a cloth, and chortled to let him know that I knew and was not daunted.

He changed the subject. "I've written you a song," he said, reaching for his harp. "I meant to play it for you first when we were alone last night." He tuned and repeated, "I meant to, but ..."

But what, he didn't say. He began to sing instead. It was like any other song I'd ever heard him sing, except the names and places had been changed. Burgundy was "once upon a time, far, far away," the handsome prince was named Gunther, and I, it was obvious, was meant to be the princess expected to live happily ever after. I stopped it right there. "No song, Gunther."

"But I've written it just for you, my beautiful, brave, and heroic Brynhild, my—"

"Look, Gunther. I know you didn't win me except by ruse. You know it. I have sworn before Odin and heaven and, more importantly, by my life as well—I will not be bedded by any man who cannot best me. Clearly, Gunther, you are not that man."

"But we are man and wife." There really was sorrow and hurt in that voice.

"I have gone through the actions for you because Attila made things a little difficult any other way. But still we are not married, not yet. And I mean to do everything in my power to see that things remain so. You know you're not my equal physically. We've tangled before. You know it. Siegfried is the only man who will ever bed me."

"But— but Siegfried is already married."

"Yes, and to be a papa and all. But I suspect some magic has been worked on him. That is not the Siegfried I knew."

"You knew him?"

"Yes, and this is his ring, his promise made to me before he knew your sister."

"This is real?"

"You recognize it, perhaps? From a hoard Siegfried won by slaying the worm that gave its name to this city of yours?"

Gunther had taken my hand to look at the ring. He had a good long look at it, then dropped my hand. "He was promised to you?"

"Yes, under oaths that would blacken heaven. And you, or somebody here in Burgundy, has made him break it. There is a curse on this house because of it."

Gunther paused, considered, then struggled mightily forward with the difficult dialogue. "If you'd only let me sing my song, it would perhaps tell you about the hoard and answer all your questions and—"

"Well?"

After another long pause of consideration, Gunther told me a tale without music, but one that did indeed belong in minstrel's tales. He spoke of how Siegfried had sworn fealty to him and sworn blood-brotherhood as well—"Yes, under his own free will!"—and that these oaths were more forceful than any promise of love. "Surely you can see that life as the wife of a man who has Siegfried as his vassal must equal and, in many ways, best life as a mere wife of Siegfried," he concluded.

"No, I don't see that. I will never see that, and you and yours will never make me see that. You—and Attila—made life with my Hunnish protectors impossible for me. I have learned by cruel experience that life for a single woman in this world, even if she has all the skills of a warriormaid, is not easy. So I've come here to Burgundy and married you—pretended to marry you—in order to regain for myself something you've taken from me. I've no intention of ever being your wife in anything but name alone, and you are certainly not the man to force me. I also intend to stay around in Burgundy as long as I must. I intend to break this spell you've cast on Siegfried and, by my life, to help him regain every scrap of what is rightfully his."

"I notice you do not call on any God to sanctify your plans for the future."

"And what God should I call on" I asked, "but my own strength and that alone?"

Gunther nodded and was silent. I think there may have been tears in his eyes, but these made me more scornful than ever.

"So, if you'll kindly give me a coverlet or two," I said, taking the initiative again, "I'll make my bed in the corner like I did last night, and we can keep up the pretense for your people if you'd like. Although I'd prefer it if you'd arrange for separate accommodations, it can certainly wait 'til morning. And perhaps it needn't come to that at all. I'm willing to confess that your power as King of the Burgundians wouldn't be worth a mess of rotten rose hips if your failure were commonly known. I do need the pretense as a shield before me for a while at least, until I have accomplished what I came to Worms to do. So, if you'll give me a coverlet or two—"

"I'll sleep in the corner," Gunther said. "You may have the bedstead."

I thanked him, but not very profusely. If he was going to be gallant, he was welcome to what he asked for.

"Before you go," he said, holding a large flat bowl of soured milk out to me, "please take the evening libation with me."

I took the bowl but smelled, as I moved it to my lips, the telltale scent of lavender. So I spilled most of it out and took but the smallest sip. Then I scrambled up into the closet of the bed, making certain the doors were latched behind me. It wasn't much of a latch, merely the carved wooden tendril of a rose that swung from the door on one side to latch over the pistils of a rose on the other, but it would have to do.

That, and a certain wakefulness I called down upon myself by the recitation of a rune.

The next thing I remember was being awakened in the bedstead by a growling, grunting noise, as if the bearskin had come to life again beside me. There was almost total darkness, but I could see enough to tell that the latch on the bed-closet had been forced from the outside, probably by the simple use of a dagger blade, as that's all it would have taken.

This thing beside me was not just beside me, it was all over—like some cheeky but ignorant dog—on my breasts, between my legs, snuffling and prodding. For one moment, a wave beginning in my navel and swelling outward urged me to give in to these proddings. A quick curse against the heat of the savory in the evening's soup and whatever else had been with the lavender in the libation, helped me fight off first the feeling and then its provoker.

My primary struggles were met by the sudden prick of a dagger at my throat and Gunther's voice saying, "Just lie still and do as I say, and you won't get hurt."

The unaccustomed ferocity in that voice took me by surprise, but it was not like I'd never had a knife to my throat before. Granted, it was only with the earnestness of the training fields of Valhalla, but we had been taught certain moves to make. I took one deep breath to calm myself, another to repeat a rune of concentration, one more to let my assailant relax a little and think he had me won, and then I struck.

His groin was vulnerable with erection, and, in a moment, I was the one with the dagger.

I was taken by surprise again by the swiftness and violence of Gunther's counterattack. I lost the dagger in this one, but at least he was not the one to recover it. This made the fight fair once more, for I soon realized that this was not the normal Gunther I was fighting. Someone must have given him a drink not unlike that Odin gives to his berserks. That knee to the groin should have incapacitated a normal man—and certainly a normal Gunther—much, much longer than it did. The same went for many another well-aimed blow I landed on him. There wasn't much skill in his fighting, only a fearsome wildness and the inability to feel pain.

We tumbled out of the bedstead and onto the floor. At first, I tossed him like straw onto the threshing floor, but the battle grew a little less equal every moment as the wildness of his blows began to tell on me—I had no immunity to them as he had to mine. When his blows did not land quite right, the simple force of their madness was enough to knock me back into the wooden knots of carved roses with bruising effect. I took one particularly bad blow to the back of my head. It may even have made me black out for a moment, though it was difficult to tell in the dark, fighting more by sound and smell than sight.

But as I lay prone from this blow and Gunther pulled his flailing limbs together to launch yet another attack, my head found lucidity—and my hand at the same moment, a weapon. By the feel, I knew it was leather. At first, I thought it was a boot, but as I took it up I found it was a belt. I got a pair of good blows, heavy brass buckle first, at the figure growling and lumbering at me. Even a berserk had to back off and think about blows like that, and while he did, I quickly circled, knocked him face-first to the ground, and pinned both arms behind him. The arms I quickly lashed together with the belt in a berserk-proof knot. With Gunther thus handicapped, it was easy enough to keep knocking him back down every time he struggled to his knees, as long as it took for me to find a rush lamp on the wooden ledge inside the bedstead and to strike a flint to it.

By this light, I did proper job of binding him. It was necessary first to stop those inhuman bellows, which I did with a fistful of linen. Then I trussed him like a pig for market, leg to leg and legs to hands, using every ropelike thing I could find in the room, even tearing the red silk bridal hangings into strips when I had to. Last of all, I used my own bridal girdle, tablet-woven as it was with golden thread throughout, to finish off what turned out to be quite a pretty package in the end, with the golden tassels hanging down in front.

Then I hoisted Gunther up and hung him like that from the sturdiest hook I could find in the wall.

"Now we can get some sleep," I told the eyes blinking berserk fury at me over the bandaged mouth. "And you tell whoever it is providing you with your potions that next time this happens, you will not get off so easily. Next time, I will shave off that puny beard of yours and cover you in pitch, all of this before I cut off your manhood so I can remain Queen of Burgundy without all this fuss."

Then I picked up the rush light and carried it into the bedstead with me, ignoring the rhythmic thumps the bundle was managing to make as his fury swung him into the wall behind him and back out again. Just before I blew out the light, it happened to fall on a glint of metal, and I discovered Gunther's dagger among the tousle of bedclothes. I chuckled, scrambled around until I found the scabbard, and then I climaxed myself a couple of good times before I blew out the light and pulled the broken closet doors to.

When I had taken all the refreshing sleep I needed, I awoke, luxuriated in the bed, and then got up. The bumping on the wall had stopped long ago. Gunther was still a bundle on the wall. I luxuriated getting dressed as well, luxuriating in the body that was still strong, still mine. I made certain Gunther's blinking eyes saw every luxuriation.

"Still mine," I said to him with a nod.

Then I left without another word and went out to the butts to train.

Nobody else was training that day. It was as if they were avoiding the place. I saw no one until, along about noon, a lone figure approached. I knew the stride. It was Siegfried.

My heart raced with the anticipation of some change, some great and joyous triumph. He was coming to me, and we would ride off together instantly. But the minute I could see the whites of his eyes, I could tell the spell was not broken. I turned from him and forced the flush from my cheeks. I refitted the arrow I'd drawn and let it fly. It went true.

"Good shot," Siegfried said as he approached.

"Thank you," I replied shortly.

"I've brought you a little something to eat."

"Thank you," I said.

"They told me to, in the kitchen, in the palace. They are concerned for you."

"Do you always do everything they tell you?"

Siegfried didn't reply but spread the contents of a large kerchief out on the ground in the shade of a linden. The pale seed tags of the tree were beginning to fall, spiraling earthward and sticking fruit down in the grass below. Siegfried partook of everything as if to assure me that it was all safe to eat, but this only made me more cautious. I knew I didn't want the same spell on me as he had on him. Still, I was famished from the night's exertions and from a morning of exercise as well. Despite my victory in the bedroom, I was by no means out of danger, that was clear. I had to keep my strength up. So I ate carefully, cracking my own nuts and choosing early apples that showed no sign of the prick of a poison thorn.

As we brushed away the crumbs, Siegfried spoke for the first time since his arrival. He spoke quietly. "You shouldn't have done that to King Gunther. You shouldn't have shamed him like that."

"Some witch should not have set a berserk at me then."

"He is your liege lord, promised to love and obey."

"To Hel with love and obey. To Hel with Gunther."

Siegfried said nothing but looked down at the grass between his knees and toyed with the seed tags in deep sadness for a while. Then he got up, gathered the kerchief and walked back to the castle.

My bow and quiver were right where I'd left them in the grass by my side. I saw the embroidered linden leaf on the back of his shirt quite plainly as he strode off. It would have been an easy shot. I even stroked the smooth yew of my bow for a moment, considering it. But I didn't take it.

chapter 37

HAT EVENING THE ENTIRE CASTLE hall lingered after supper as if loath to go to bed, though what the attraction was, I couldn't tell. Gunther, always quick to entertain with a song, was still wearing bruises from his night spent hanging on the wall and was not in the mood. Other attempts at levity, storytelling, or games were even less skillful and fell flat. I was quite certain I had not been drugged, so I felt no shame, only common sense that the rest of Burgundy seemed to have lost, when I yawned and said, "I think I'll retire now. Good night."

A chorus of, "Good night, Queen Brynhild," followed me out of the hall.

I was given only enough time to undress, climb in bed, and pull the closet doors to, when I knew I was not alone in the room. A pair of boots dropped to the floor, the rush light went out, and then the closet doors were thrown open.

"Gunther," I said. "Remember, I warned you. I warned you what would happen if you tried this again."

There was no reply but a firm grasp about my waist. So I lifted the weight off my chest and threw it as I'd thrown the stone in Bleda's camp. I heard a crash and knew that at least the little cradle was broken into kindling.

But that was just the beginning of the fracas. There commenced a tumult of crashing crockery and splitting wood, such as no wedding night has had before or since. Surely, they must have heard us on all Worms' three hills, but no one made a peep to interfere.

I knew the door was open. I could have staggered out whenever I wanted, made that escape, or called for help. More than a few times, when I felt myself being bested, my mind flitted longingly over such options. But these were no options. Everyone on Worms' three hills wanted me bested that night, and I knew it. The odds were more in my favor within these narrow walls than they were without. Here, where I could toss my single opponent from one wall to the other, I did so—

And he did the same to me. From that first throw, I could feel how well matched we were. If anything, he had the edge of skill. What potion can grant that? I had little time to wonder. Certainly, his was the advantage of weight. But I was quicker, and since I'd started out naked, my sweat was soon making me a very difficult thing to hold. "Like quicksilver," I runed my body. "Think like quicksilver."

And it worked, to a point. To a point. But this thing that renewed his grasp again and again, this was not Gunther. This wasn't even Gunther as berserk. This was something—something very different. Something—something more like me. Something that in its aggression and power felt right in response to my own. The match, when it linked like the interlaced fingers of one pair of hands, was complement of such flattery, that I knew I might be swayed. But I resisted—to save my life.

My attacker was in no way deterred. I could see his shadow quickly picking out the largest splinter left of the cradle, one of the rockers, and then coming at me, wielding it as a club. By my life, he was fast! I only just had time to swing the bed-closet door as a shield to protect myself from the blow. I kept swinging with all my might and soon had him pressed helpless between wall and closet door. I jiggled the press a few times to make certain the knots of the roses left their impression. I had him then.

But only for the length of two panted breaths. I realized that the room had been effectively cleaned of handy ropes. Even the bridal hangings were gone. Reaching for my girdle, which was the only rope I knew where it was, was a stretch and, making that stretch loosened up my weight on the door enough to let him explode out and escape. As I was knocked back by the violence of his explosion, my hand grazed Gram. The sword was closer to hand than my girdle, yet I had not reached for it, and as my opponent tossed me roughly to the floor, it was too late for that. Yet he did not reach for the sword, either.

What a strange, wild struggle this was, where total conquest was the goal, yet death, even serious injury, could not be tolerated! Killing an opponent was easy. Overcoming physically yet preserving the physical in good enough condition for a different physicality to come—that was a very fine line to walk.

Every time he got me to a point where my death was the next step, my opponent would stop and pant a breath or two as if having stopped the runaway of a cart downhill. The man having accomplished this feat was obliged next to expend as much or more energy to overcome an uphill stretch. And yet the momentum of one violence also swings into the next. Where the one began and the other ended was not always easy to mark. Perhaps it did not exist at all. At exactly what point did seeking to control my movements, to pin my shoulders and hips helplessly become a ride seeking to join their movements to his? More than once the vise grip of my legs trying to pin and throw him suddenly found itself moving with quite another urgency. I always managed to catch it there, catch him where aggression turned to lust, and turn it back to antagonism.

But when has love not been an antagonism? And union not an attempt to obliterate what is separate in another?

I knew blood was flowing, from me in several places and from him—from his hands at least, when once I managed to catch them under Gram's scabbard and press down with my full weight until the fingers swelled, then burst with blood. I got a good grip on the shirt and would have made a most telling restraint had not the fabric—which was too fine and dainty by far, chosen with a woman's mind—torn and let him escape once more. Now it was naked flesh to naked flesh, and I had lost my handicap, if indeed handicap it was, to be unencumbered by clothes. For, all too often, a certain pressure on my breasts held me down longer than it should have.

Now it was my opponent's turn to get me pressed between the bed-closet door and the wall. I had one hand loose, one hand that groped across the liberated muscles of that back, looking for a hold, and which then suddenly felt a smooth, heart-shaped patch of skin in the midst of shoulders like blades of sandstone.

"Siegfried," I said out loud—what truth I suppose I must have guessed at all along.

There was silence and, for a moment, only the pressure from the other side of the door. His very breathing was now distinguishable to me from any other breath on earth.

"Siegfried," I said again, almost pleading.

A quick hand, the fingers bloody from the fray, came up from beneath the door and caught me under the pubic bone. I jerked, braving the knots of the roses to resist the onslaught, but there was not much place against the wall for me to resist it to. I came back to it, resisted again, and then the slip from attraction to resistance became a reflex I couldn't control. I rode it until the spasm came, and I greeted it with a cry kept as quiet as possible.

Then the pressure of the door was gone, and he carried me to the closet. There he threw me face down and himself crosswise on top of me. He worked breast and clitoris as any other winning wrestler works arm and leg, until I'd climaxed twice more.

"In ..." I gasped, managing only one word per breath, one word per spasm. "Siegfried ... I ... want ... you ... please ..."

I groped for his swollen manhood, seeking to cram it on myself as one does the lid on a pot of custard ere it comes to the boil. And with movements so swift and rough, I knew he was as anxious for it as I was, Siegfried tossed me over and complied.

All three hills must have heard my scream, half of satisfaction, yes, but also half of agony as the wound he made cut deep. Even so must the warrior feel whose jugular has been severed, even so must the blood sacrifice held over the sacred cauldron feel the knife in the hands of a skilled priestess, even so did I feel as each joint throb of heart and womb pressed the maiden strength from my deepest vein. Not only strength but even that strange bloom I'd taken for granted, like breath, like only so much being alive. My youth—it, too, seemed to fade from me to the dull ache of exposed mortality. Odin's curse—it was fulfilled.

And I wept as I had not done since my frustrations as a powerless child.

"Brynhild, Brynhild," Siegfried's voice came, crooning, comforting. And I knew that whatever had possessed him before had left him with the burst of his seed, like poison matter from an inflamed boil. "Brynhild!"

This was the Siegfried who'd left me two years ago. At last. And I could no longer fight off even so weak a thing as tears. I wept at the reunion.

Side by side we lay in the tousle of the bed, piecing together what it was that had become of us, sometimes no more than one word at a time.

"Am I …?"

"In Worms, my love."

"And … and married?"

"Married, Siegfried. But alas, not to me."

"What's her name?"

"Gudrun."

"Ah, Gudrun. But how?"

"A trick. A drugged drink."

"A drink …" Siegfried struggled to get his mind around it. "I knew it was a drink."

I reached out of the bed and retrieved a bowl from the floor. Of course, it had been knocked over in the battle, but enough of the thick soured milk still coated the inside to leave no doubt. "This?" I asked.

Siegfried sniffed cautiously. "Yes," he said.

"Don't touch it," I warned, and tossed the bowl from me. "They left it here so it would be the thing you'd reach for to quench your thirst after … after your exertions. You must be careful, very careful."

"So must you, my love."

"I know. Only plain water, preferably only what we've drawn ourselves."

"She must be a powerful witch indeed."

"Who's that?"

"Their mother. The Queen Mother."

"You think it's she?"

"I'm certain of it. Her name is Ute."

"She keeps a pretty close seclusion in her rooms, doesn't she?"

"I'd never seen her, either, but she does have a reputation for spells. And it's said she, too, was a shieldmaid once."

"Poor woman!"

"How can you sympathize with her, after what she's done to you—to us?"

"If it's true she was a shieldmaid, who knows what she's endured? She has my sympathy."

"Oh, my love! What I've done to you?" He stroked me most tenderly from breast to thigh, as if afraid of doing more damage.

"It's all right."

"No, it's not all right."

"You speak truly, love. I'm afraid I shall never recover from this." We tried to giggle a little, then I continued: "I don't blame you. It was a curse set on me for all time by All-Father."

"All-Father!" Siegfried spat. "He is nothing but a doughty old man!"

"Old man or no, there is power in his curses. And I got on the wrong side of them."

"So, it seems, did I."

"At least we're on the same side of them together."

"There are consolations, I suppose." He kissed my hair lightly, then stayed, breathing the smell of my sweat and my sex with pleasure.

"But now, Siegfried, now that the curse is accomplished, now I need you more than I ever did before. Without you now, I am nothing."

"Not nothing. You're still the most beautiful woman in the world."

"But no longer the strongest. And beauty without strength must fade."

"You know," Siegfried said, beginning to chuckle. "You know, I remember now. When I had you conquered and bound, I was supposed to go out and fetch Gunther to finish the job. He's out there right now, I'm sure, pacing the hall, waiting ..."

"Let him wait." I joined his chuckles. "Poor Gunther!"

"Poor Gunther? First it was poor mother witch, now it's poor Gunther!"

"Poor Gunther. A cuckold before he's even a husband."

"Very well, but what are we to do about this now? He has the treasure."

"Does he?"

"I certainly don't know where it is."

"I still have the ring here."

"Ring?"

"The ring from the hoard. You gave it to me, remember?"

"Oh, yes, of course. But that's all we have of it."

"Why don't you take the ring now?"

"I want you to have it, Brynhild."

"But if you have it, and know what it is, it might be a way to force Gunther into revealing the rest."

"That's an idea."

"In any case, Gunther will deal with you more as an equal than he will with me. In the meantime, I have begun to spy a chink of light in the person of that dark man, the half-brother, Hogni. I will work on that chink—if you take the ring."

"All right, I'll take it," he said and cupped my hand with his in a caress. "I can see the outline of some plan here, if not the specifics yet. King Gunther! You are his wife."

"Not anymore, my love."

"There isn't a soul in Burgundy who doesn't think you are. It will be a hard bond to break from here in their midst."

"Siegfried, you've already done it. Quite handsomely."

"And I am Gudrun's husband."

"Soon to be the father of her child."

"This is a pretty kettle of fish! What are we to do?"

"I don't know, except that the treasure must be first."

"I don't know," Siegfried echoed. "But at the moment all I want to do is to set another pair of horns on Burgundy's head."

So we loved. We loved and discussed, and discussed and loved, and never did call for Gunther that night.

When we could not escape the glare of daylight any longer, Siegfried left me. And I … I got dressed, went out to the butts, and picked up my bow.

I couldn't even bend it to string it anymore.

chapter 38

I SAT UNDER THE LINDEN near the butts in the shade where Siegfried and I had shared a luncheon but no communication. Now that I was certain the spell was broken, that there would at last be communion, he did not come. My useless bow was just a stick and some dried hart sinew in my hands.

By all received wisdom, I should have been happy. I loved and was loved. But time seemed to have ended for me. There was no future in the present of my love.

I'm not certain how long I sat there. Long enough for the sun to shift from one side of the lime leaves to the other. I could almost see through their delicate veins now with the back lighting. The laborers at harvest in Burgundy's vineyards had eaten their midday meal and were now back at work, their timeless songs drifting over donkeys' backs laden with baskets of deep red grapes and the neat rows of abundant vines.

The cold nose of a curious dog woke me from my reverie. The nose pushed my hand up to her ears, and I fondled them, still half mindless. She was a cross of Celtic wolfhound, like all the young lords favored, a huge dog, standing well over my head while I was sitting. This one—with the black guard hairs, dangling teats from a recent litter, and tiny ears—I knew to be Hogni's.

And here came the master, striding up after his dog with a bow and a quiver full of arrows for an afternoon's practice.

"That's odd," said this eldest of the Burgundian brothers as he approached.

"What's odd?"

"Why, my queen, that my dog should be friendly to you." Was it my imagination, or was there a hint of sarcasm when he said those words, "my queen"? "Lady's never liked you before. Always I've had to hold her back while she growled deep in her throat. At a threat."

Now that he mentioned it, yes, I did remember such behavior on the part of his dog. But I had chalked it up only to the fact that I was a stranger in Worms. The master, who should know, seemed to credit his dog with a superhuman judge of character.

"If I didn't know better, my queen," he continued, still with that hint of sarcasm, "I'd be tempted to say you were changed in the night to someone new."

I said nothing but refused the hound's further demands for attention.

"Is that a Hunnish bow you have there?" Hogni persisted in his demands.

I nodded.

"May I?"

I handed it to him. He strung it easily, and I flinched.

"They are wonders, aren't they?" He tested the string with pleasure, taking a stance not unlike a God. "The Gods, they say, have pigeon shoots."

"That's in spring," I reminded him.

"Yes, when we mortals emulate them. I wonder if they don't use bows like these."

I smiled in spite of myself, bemused that mortals should try to fathom the ways of the Gods.

"May I?"

I nodded. Hogni fitted an arrow to the string and let it fly. It overshot the target.

"It takes some getting used to," he apologized. Instead of trying again, he sat down next to me, yet at such a distance that his dog had room to come between us where she sat, her tongue hanging out as she panted with the pleasure of human company. All I saw of Hogni was his finger with the dirty nail, running up and down the pieced-horn edge of my bow.

"You know, I lived among the Huns for a time. As a child."

"Did you?"

"I was very young. My mother sought refuge there after we left Saxony."

"Saxony?" I repeated. But I didn't pursue the topic. I don't think I wanted to know.

"Very young. Before she married the King of Burgundy, her second marriage." I had never heard this man say so many words before. Perhaps he hadn't heard himself say so much aloud.

"I'll bet she doesn't even imagine I remember," he continued. "But I do. In fact, it looms large in my memory. It was watching Huns at practice—horsed, with such bows—that I first felt a firming in my heart, a pulling away from the *we* of Mother and I to just *I*. *Me* as a male. It gave me my first idea of what manhood must be, what I would be as a man. Perhaps it is because this image was Hunnish that I feel so out of—"

He stopped himself here, as if he had said more than he wanted to.

I looked around the panting chest of the dog and into the face of this man I'd managed to ignore quite well until now. He was a dark and brooding sort, this elder brother-in-law of mine, his black hair conforming ill to the Burgundian fashion of bangs. His eyes were dark and seemed never satisfied with anything they saw. But his thin lips were pressed thinner still to silence that dissatisfaction beneath the black moustache that he never seemed able to decide whether to let grow or shave off. What must it be like to have a mother marry again? Certainly, it happens all the time, but in this case it had left a mark. To have the affections that had once been one's whole world suddenly transferred to another, three others in fact—all fair and well-favored to one's own grim darkness. Hogni, I knew, was termed Lord of Troneck, but I understood that this was a fiefdom of little account, given to him as a sop by his usurping younger brother. This younger brother took the title of King, but one look was enough to tell that he was but half the man Hogni was. At least, one look in those black eyes was enough to tell that the man behind the eyes thought so.

I looked away from the danger in those eyes.

"I'd blush, too, lady, if I were you," Hogni said. I had to let the meaning of the words sink in before I was aware that it was me he was addressing again, and not his dog. His voice was suddenly very quiet, but contained great violence. "Gunther may not mind the slight to our honor performed last night, but I do."

So this was a fosterling who took on the causes of his accepted house with more ferocity than the true-born sons. Such is often the case, I've found. He had to work to be allowed to have such causes, after all, and the momentum grows steadier over the years.

"I don't know what you mean," I said. I turned away, for I could feel the unusual weakness of a blush again.

"Don't you?" Tension rose in palpable waves from the back bent forward under his brass-ringed brynie, until the dog got up and moved off, sensitive cur that she was.

"Gunther's a damned fool." Hogni suddenly threw the bow down in my direction and got to his feet.

"Siegfried deserves me!" My voice exploded after him. "Siegfried deserves everything he can take from you thieves! You have robbed him of his rightly won hoard as well as his memory and—yes—his promised bride."

Hogni didn't turn, but I could see the swelling of his short, thick torso under the mane of black hair. It swelled to fill every crevice of brass the brynie gave him.

"Why should anything he's done give him these things?" Hogni said. "I was at Drachenfels, same as he was. I killed my share of Romans that day. For all that, I was young, and it was the first action I'd ever seen. Just because I didn't kill the first line, that doesn't make my actions any less valiant. Where does Siegfried get these things—bride treasure, that sword Balmung? He is an orphan, the fosterling of dwarves. If valor and deeds count, I am his equal, as I am your husband's superior.

And if birth counts, if Gunther is any measure, then in this I surpass Siegfried. I demand only what is mine. I demand only justice."

The black mane flew as he turned suddenly, lunged to his wool-wrapped knees before me and violently grabbed my shoulders. "I shall have what is my due!" he said. "Or, if I cannot have it, no one shall have it."

And then he was up and gone, whipping the dried grasses he passed with his common bow and calling up his dog to keep his fury company.

Was it the sudden loosing of my maidenhead that made possibilities where before there had been none? The lust in those black eyes, like some sort of chained monster! Was it a lust for all things he had been denied, watched on while others enjoyed, and he, faithfully, was obliged to rejoice in their enjoyment? Or was the compulsion I had felt, that I could only ever be happy with one man, part of Odin's curse? Was Siegfried just an illusion created by the God and there, in the Lord of Troneck, was a man whose dark passion was best suited to mine?

Choices had been made and could not be made again.

chapter 39

AFTER THAT, I WAS REALLY at a loss. I had no idea what to do with my time that did not include weapons training of some sort. For the first time in my life, the activity was denied me.

For a number of days, I wandered around in a haze of tedium that tended towards depression. By night, I was obliged to give Gunther his rights, but only once. I suppose my performance so paled in comparison to the promise held out to him by his romantic songs, that he gave it up. Or perhaps Siegfried had already managed to speak to him, laid on him some threat Burgundy's King knew the killer of Fafnir the Worm would be only too happy to carry out. In any case, I was spared.

The treasure itself did not seem so immediately forthcoming. Because we were now obliged to move in different spheres, my glimpses of Siegfried were rare enough, and then our words were curtailed to but rigid formalities. This was, however, enough to tell me that his mind was still his own, and that a good portion of it was always thinking of me. Somehow, soon, he would find a way to bend Burgundy's will to our own.

By default, I found myself drawn into the circle of Gudrun and her blushing, giggling maids. Because of their mistress' condition, the entire group was under specific bans. We might not leave the house on a clear night without covering our heads, lest the child get star rickets. We might not pass through any gate lest the child get gate rickets. Crossing our legs while prayers were offered would make the child have rickets of the hips. We might under no circumstance pass by a graveyard or watch the slaughter of animals, which was rather difficult that time of year when every yard had its stuck pig and wildly fluttering fowl.

Any serious activity thus curtailed meant there was that much more room for the frivolous. Certainly, I took no pleasure or interest in their light-minded gossip, their concern with things and dress and outward appearance, their feigned modesty and studied helplessness, their tournaments where the lance was no more than a needle and the blood drawn only a bit of red-dyed silken thread.

The favorite subject of every tapestry was, in order to flatter the princess, the exploits of Siegfried. As I couldn't hope to match their skill at turning flesh and blood into linen and wool, and as I resented this turning of life—my life—into a thing of past tense, there was no pleasure for me sitting at their elbows. There in the solarium, the sun glancing through the half-opened windows took on a steeper and steeper angle every day.

It was perhaps the very last day of the year that could be called warm. Gudrun, with her usual what-can-possibly-be-wrong-with-the-world-for-a-princess-of-Worms and love-me-because-I-am-so-cheerful bubble, invited me to take advantage of the weather and join her early in the morning in a trek down to the Rhine to bathe. I complied, first because I had little choice, and second because the palace of Worms was growing claustrophobic with the same faces, the same round of formalized, stifling inaction.

We took a roundabout way, gathering herbs as we went, trying by the tyranny of Gudrun's tradition to gather the "proper bunch," as it was known, of healing herbs. Nature, so they say, blesses such bunches at this time of year with her kindest and most generous mood. In the meadows and borders of the cornfields we found milfoil, vermouth, and arnica beside the more common savory and thyme—but nowhere near the seventy-two varieties it was said one must have for perfect benediction. I wasn't sure I even knew seventy-two herbs either by name or virtue.

At last we came to the beach. The beach down to the Rhine here was smooth, battered at high flood by boulders and branches, in winter by ice, so only grass and straggly bushes impeded our progress. But here also the fishermen found it convenient to set up their shops, and these we did have to bypass for the sake of Gudrun's pregnancy, to avoid both the sight and smell of any gutting.

Just at the foot of the royal hill the water was caught, slow-moving, in a bit of an inlet, shallow and protected from the main force of the river. Across the river, a row of silent poplars stood sentry, beginning to blush gold for joy at the changing play of their light in the early autumn stream. Here on the near side, behind a screen of low-hanging willows, we shed our clothes.

Gudrun was naked first. Her swelling belly was a source of pride, and she emphasized it as she let herself into the water, clinging to ropes of willow and squealing childish exclamations over how cold the water was. I looked the other way, my back already shivering with disgust at her trumped-up femininity before I ever touched the water. I entered quickly, upstream from her and without either willows or preliminaries.

My glide sent a wake of water over the swollen belly of Burgundy's princess, and she scowled, suddenly not nearly so cheerful.

"We have customs here in Burgundy," she said.

"Yes," I snapped. "I am all too familiar with your customs. I feel like I've been in a dungeon these last weeks because of your customs."

"It is customary in Burgundy for women of lower station to bathe downstream from those of us of higher station."

"And what makes you of higher station?" It annoyed me that all reverence for my skills, oracular as well as of the battlefield, had gone. "I'm married to your brother. I am a queen, while you, your brothers tossed you off on a landless vassal. I'd say I have precedence."

"Siegfried is not without property. Siegfried is lord of a great hoard."

"Oh, is he now? You confess it? And just where might this hoard be?"

I looked at her keenly. My device to get some confession from her had worked. She bit her lip and turned away to wash her hair, saying no more. Her hair was of such a pure blond that even wetting couldn't darken it. She stood so the tips of it, crossing her belly, met the surface of the water like the graceful, drifting branches of the willows. My hatred immobilized me momentarily, then I swam out further, into the place where the current turned from cloying to swift stream. My limbs loved the tug at them. Swimming, my body felt strong and whole again, defiant. I loved it.

Then I felt crippled by hatred again. Gudrun was calling me. I had to stop swimming and tread water to hear her.

"Brynhild," she repeated her charge. "You shouldn't swim out so far. It's dangerous."

"To Hel with danger." Perhaps I wouldn't have spoken so harshly but that the freedom of my limbs had freed my tongue as well. And I was tired of the court's constraints.

"It's not ladylike," she insisted. She herself couldn't swim a stroke.

"What do I care for ladylike when ladylike makes you a toy with a childish mind?"

"I am thinking of my brother's honor. If any fisherman or other of our subjects should come by and see their queen thus, naked and … and *swimming* …"

"To Hel with your brother's honor."

She was fuming now and probably would have let me swim on in peace, but I had to push it. "And what do you know of ladylike, anyway?"

"I beg your pardon."

"What kind of lady is it that wins and holds her man with spells and potions? What kind of lady is *that*, I'd like to know?"

Now the roses of her cheeks blanched out like whey being strained from cheese.

"How do you know that?" she hissed.

I shrugged, smiled, and dove off, swimming under water as long as my lungs could take it—and they loved the pained gasp of air at the end.

When I had finally had enough and pulled myself dripping and prune-wrinkled from the water, Gudrun was sitting on the bank, dressed, her hair drying in perfect sheaves in the sun. Her eyes, dark with grey anger, followed me as I flung myself in the sun on the bank to dry.

"At least I am not an adulteress." Her voice was quiet, but venomous.

I laughed. "Whatever do you mean?"

"I mean, Siegfried had your maidenhood."

"I don't deny it."

"You don't?"

"Because your brother is such a weakling, he could never manage to take it."

"So who's married to the better man now?"

"Ah, but who has the better man's love?"

Her eyes bristled with fury. "It isn't true. Siegfried loves *me*. He did this out of love for *me*, so my brother wouldn't be shamed."

"Did he now?"

"He did, he did. By ever-sweet Freya, it is true. He told me. We laughed at you when he told me, when he came to my bed and told me. We laughed. He showed this ring, he gave it to me and laughed at you—you a common whore. Yes, now that you are no longer one of Odin's, you can be called by that name and live in fear of it like the rest of womankind. Whore!" She flung the word once more, scrambled to her feet, and was off towards the castle without me.

I dressed slowly and eventually followed her. I tried not to let her words have their desired effect. If I could ignore the words, that would be the whole victory there. But I wasn't used to fighting with words, or to defending myself against them. Gudrun was right about one thing. That single word "whore" could now take its toll, whereas before, as a maid I could have laughed at it in total immunity.

And then there had been the ring, *his* ring with the snake grasping its own tail and the ruby eyes, *my* ring on her hand. Of that there was no mistake. How could she have had it, or known about our night together, if Siegfried hadn't told her? Told her, laughing, in bed together …

Whore! It had its effect. What other reason was there for the dragging out of our escape from this enslavement here in Burgundy but that Siegfried, even without the drug, was in on their little joke?

Whore!

By the time I had reached the castle, the word was like poison in every limb. I went straight to bed with a lethargy like death. The thought of putting food into that body nauseated me. Dehydration and starvation seemed as fast and painless a way to go as any. Even lifting a hand or getting up to relieve myself was more effort than I ever wished to expend again.

It seemed I slept, but I know that even sleep was a state of vigor I could not attain. It seemed that Gunther, then others of the household appeared, peering under the edge of the glazing on my vision. They tried to get me to eat, to speak of what ailed me, anything. It even seemed to me that once I saw Thora, my old comrade-in-arms Thora. She called me by name. But then I knew I must be delirious, so I shut my eyes and mind against it.

It was days, perhaps a week before I heard a voice I might respond to.

"Brynhild."

It was Siegfried, but by then, response was almost a lost art to me.

"Brynhild."

I turned from the closet wall and felt the pressure of his hand on mine. And then his lips.

"What … what are you doing?" My lips cracked with a lack of water when I spoke.

"Creeping into bed next to you. Do you mind? If you are going to die, I want to die beside you."

It was difficult for me to understand what these words might mean. The effect was more physical than rational as I felt warmth begin to work its way into my limbs, not from my heart outward, but from where his arm banded my waist, from where his leg touched mine.

Then he said other words. "Courage, my love. I have put Gunther in a vise from which he cannot escape. In three-days' time, he must either produce the treasure that is owed to me—to us—or he must face me in the butts, to let force of arms demonstrate to all Burgundy who has the right in this matter. He will not face shame before his subjects. He must give in. And then—then we will be free. I know what has stricken you. Gudrun confessed all to me, even how she stole the ring from my finger where her jealousy found it. You must let her suffer these pangs, not you. For you are the one who owns the love of Siegfried, and I don't care who knows it now, or what trials Gunther must face to regain his honor, if such a thing is possible any longer."

My brain moved slowly over these words for a time, having forgotten the knack of making sense of one word after another. "What is that you're chewing?" was the next thing I managed to say.

"This? Why just a bit of chervil. I've been told it makes the pangs of hunger and thirst a little easier to bear."

"Who told you that? That witch the Burgundians keep hidden away? Didn't I warn you to be careful of her?"

"You did. But you also told me you loved me, and you wouldn't be doing this to yourself if this were true."

"Does it work?"

"What?"

"The chervil?"

"Oh, yes, mightily."

"Give me some."

He pressed a feathery leaf in my face. I hadn't the strength to chew it and had to gag it out. Siegfried held me up firmly till the gagging passed. Then he bent over me and kissed a wad he had chewed into my mouth. That I could keep down.

I knew he lied. Chervil does nothing for hunger pangs. It is the greatest stimulant for a weak appetite and a weaker will. Where would he have learned that, save from a wise woman, a witch? Nevertheless, I let him lie, and so let myself be saved.

PART VI

The Secret of the Leaf

Chapter 40

"OTHER!" I CRIED, BURSTING WITHOUT ceremony into her room. "Mother, Siegfried is still in that room with that—that *whore*! It's three days now. Mother, I won't stand for it."

"You will stand for it, Gudrun," she declared. I had rarely known her so fierce.

My mother stood tall and cool in the midst of the room, commanding over my brothers who were also present. The room was dark—Mother always kept her room dark—but there was a pall over everything as well that let me know I had interrupted something. I didn't like it when I was left out of things, as if they considered me too childish when here I was, going to have a child of my own, and nearly two years older than Guttorm, in any case.

"That 'whore,' as you are pleased to call her," Mother continued, "is as dear to me as any of you. She is my firstborn, one might say, my child before any of you came along, before I ever thought I would have another. By my life, I will not let her die if I can help it."

"But where …?" I tried to ask.

Mother did not seem inclined to tell the story now, and I knew well enough it would never do to press her. She did say, "Siegfried, it seems, was the only one who could bring her 'round, so Siegfried it must be. She is sitting up now and taking some broth. This is good. She will recover now."

"Siegfried told me she even let him comb her hair," Hogni said, though what Hogni had to do with anything, I didn't know.

"That is good." Mother smiled thinly.

"But what else is he doing?" brooded Gunther.

"In this crisis," Mother insisted, "it doesn't matter. Believe me, I have known the depression that comes when shield-maidenhood ends. All-Father is most cruel in his fury. May you all be shielded from such wrath."

"May it be so," we piously repeated, although the chance that any of us would ever be chosen by Odin as she had been was out of Fate's mind.

"Meanwhile, Gunther," Mother continued, "there are more important things for you to worry about than being done out of a wife. You have taken care of the treasure?"

"Yes."

"Siegfried's treasure?" I asked.

"Yes. It took the greater part of these last three nights, having only Hogni and two slaves to help me," Gunther said, "but it is hidden."

"Hidden?" I echoed. "Where?"

"They dropped it all into the Rhine," Guttorm said, showing off his superior knowledge of things.

"You've drowned it?"

"Yes, but you needn't ask where," Gunther said. "Guttorm knows so much, but the precise location he doesn't know, nor will we tell him until our deathbeds. Hogni and I alone know, and the slaves. But the slaves we killed when the work was done, and drowned them in the same spot."

"You killed people for this treasure?"

"They were only slaves," said Hogni in his cool, dark way. "And even cutting their tongues out would not have kept them from leading others to the place."

Gunther added, "Now only Hogni and I know where the dragon's hoard is. We can haul up bits of it as needed, but we have sworn deadly oaths to one another by our swords, that they might fail in our hands if we divulge. Neither of us will disclose this secret until the other is dead and we ourselves lie on our deathbeds."

Things seemed to be rapidly falling out of all control. These were hardly the brothers I remembered. "But the treasure was Siegfried's," I said. *And mine as his wife, and my child's.* This thought should have given my words more power, but they fell limp with impotency.

"This is good," Mother said to her two eldest sons. "Still, if you do not take even more immediate action, I fear you—we all—shall be done out of a kingdom. Tomorrow is the day Siegfried expects satisfaction."

"And the only satisfaction he can take is at the bottom of the Rhine," Hogni said.

Gunther admitted, "Ever since he spent that first night with my wife, he has refused the drink. He knows it all—Brynhild is in with him on this. His threats of exposure are now such that I could not survive."

"The duel he calls for tomorrow will be nothing less than a battle for the kingship of Burgundy," Hogni prognosticated.

"Perhaps not quite so serious a thing," Mother said.

"Mother, you know it will be so," Gunther said, "and all the berserk potions in the world could not make me win in such a match."

Mother nodded. "Siegfried is clearly God-blessed by some magic I do not understand. Well, now that he seems to have brought Brynhild around, he has served his purpose."

I laughed nervously. "Mother, what on earth are you saying?"

Mother did not meet my eyes, but looked on my brothers instead. "Hogni, you are the only one who has not sworn blood brotherhood with him. It must be you. Otherwise we will bring the curse of fratricide down upon this house."

"I shall undertake this with pleasure," Hogni said.

"Whatever are you talking about?" I still could not believe the direction their words seemed to be heading.

"But it's still not going to be easy," Guttorm spoke up, "even for

Hogni." They listened to him, whereas they continued to ignore me and my growing terror.

"No, it's not." Mother nodded. "As I said, he is God-blessed."

"And I know something more of that God-blessing," Guttorm continued. "It is not just that he seems to have eyes in the back of his head and the strength of a field full of bulls. It is more."

"Tell us, son."

"One day while he was helping me learn to throw an ax, the ax slipped out of my hand. By All-Father, it was an accident, but it hit him in the leg. He wasn't even wearing any trousers that day, just a smock. It hit him blade first, and with all my strength, such as it is. On any other man, it would have cut off that leg. But I swear as I stand here, it didn't even draw blood. Not one drop."

"What did Siegfried say?"

"Nothing. He just laughed about it and said, 'This must be my lucky day.'"

"God-blessed," Gunther muttered, and the others shook their heads in wonder.

"But I know what that is!" I exclaimed.

"You? He has told you?"

"No. No, I imagine he forgot about it, like everything else, with the drink." I spoke on, glad at last to have their attention, to know something they did not. "But Brynhild told me."

"Brynhild?"

"Yes, when she was living with the Huns, and I went to consult with her about my dreams. She said he had bathed in dragon's blood, and no point or blade on earth could injure him."

"We are done for," muttered Gunther with his usual ineffective dramatics.

"Dragon's blood? Or human blood," mused Hogni darkly. "Roman blood."

"Whatever it was, he bathed in it all over. Except for one spot. One spot where a linden leaf fell and stuck between his shoulder blades. I know the place well," I said, blushing with pleasure. "I can feel it, even in the dark. And I have marked it. On every garment I sew for him,

I have stitched the figure of a linden leaf over the very spot, so I can always keep him safe there, don't you see? Brynhild told me I should."

"Thank you, Gudrun."

I basked in the beam of my mother's rare smile. She turned all too quickly to Hogni.

"Yes, thank you, sister," he said. "Thank you very much."

"Brynhild told her. Can we trust Brynhild?" asked Gunther, very much in doubt about the faithfulness of his own wife.

"Perhaps. Perhaps not," Hogni admitted. "But it is something."

"You'll keep that spot safe, too, now won't you?" I asked. "Now that you know the secret. Now that I'm going to have his baby."

"Oh, I certainly will, sister," Hogni assured, nodding gravely.

I frowned at him suspiciously. Hogni can tell a lie as easily as heaven's truth. I've never been able to tell the difference.

That was the last thing I remember anyone saying before they patted me on the head and sent me out of the room. I didn't put up too much fuss. The pregnancy sent me early and gratefully to bed most nights. Still, I fought the sleepiness long enough to make a circuit past my brother Gunther's room where I knocked on the door and tried the handle. The door was locked from the inside.

"Siegfried?" I called softly. "Husband? It's me, Gudrun. Come to bed with me tonight, won't you?"

An impatient bark told me he would not. I think perhaps there was a giggle behind the bark as well. *Her* giggle.

"Siegfried, I want to warn you. Please come and let me tell you. They are plotting—and I told them. Maybe I shouldn't have. Should I have told them? Siegfried?" I didn't dare speak any louder or more urgently than that, lest my brothers overhear.

Only a growl and more giggles answered me. In the light of the single torch halfway down the hall, the grain of the wood on the door seemed to become an ogre's face, with long fangs, grinning hungrily at me. The child inside me turned and kicked, as if struggling to escape from an evil. For his sake, I hurried off to my room alone.

It was the next morning, while we were all making preparations to go down to the butts to watch the contest of honor between the King my brother and my husband, that riders came breathless into the keep, announcing, "Helgi! Helgi Halfdansson! Helgi's ships are rowing into Burgundy through the Huns' lands to the north. Our defense—oh, King!"

Now, I am as afraid of Helgi as the next person. His name has been a terror to me since I was a child, and I often thought of my mother, widowed by him and subjected to other horrors she wouldn't even talk about, until just imagining them could bring tears to my eyes. I thought it was very brave the way my brothers were instantly armed and ready to ride off at the head of Burgundy's finest, leaving the chill of an autumn wind to blow unchallenged through the tournament ground.

Siegfried, too, was drawn by the call from that horrible woman's side and joined them in the ride to the north. He was wearing that lovely crimson shirt I made for him, that suited him perhaps best of all. I remember seeing the linden leaf on it as the last thing before distance blurred the colors. It made my heart beat very proudly that he wore my handiwork, and the fact that I had done all I could in his defense made me not so frightened anymore. I prayed to both Freya and Frigga of the hearthstone to protect that dear spot for me.

But I did think there were some odd things about the whole matter. First, it was odd that the marauder Helgi should be here in Burgundy, so far from home just as the seasons were changing, just as he should be heading back to the island fastness of Denmark with his booty for the winter.

The second thing concerned the messengers. I mean, I knew both of them and I also knew that they had been in the hall just the night before. Perhaps I wouldn't have noticed them if I hadn't been sitting in the hall alone myself that night, missing Siegfried terribly. Siegfried who wouldn't know who had been in the hall and who had not. Even if these men had been sent out to guard Burgundy's borders immediately after I retired last night, they couldn't have covered much distance between that time and the time we all saw them come back to yell their warning of Helgi's approach.

In fact, they couldn't have ridden much beyond the outskirts of Worms itself.

chapter 41

AND THAT NIGHT I DREAMED a dream. It was more real than any I'd ever had, more real even than the dreams I'd had about the hawk and the stag. Mother says that can happen when you're with child.

I saw our men marching out towards the north, just as I'd seen them that morning. And then, suddenly, there was no Helgi. I guess new messengers must have come, saying Helgi had been driven back by the Huns or something. My dream didn't show me for certain. Anyway I, for one, felt very relieved.

Siegfried said, "Well, then, brother, you and I must go back and have our trial, for I am anxious to be about my business."

Gunther said, "Certainly, brother, I will give you satisfaction. But at the moment, aren't we still friends? It seems a shame to waste such a cool, brisk day full of promise, the grain fields ripe and coming down, and we out here with our weapons and all. What do you say we turn to the mountains for a hunt?"

The rest of the party were amenable, and Siegfried, though impatient, stemmed that feeling with graciousness when promised there would certainly be a trial on the morrow. So they turned westward to the mountains, their forests a comfortable patchwork of warm reds, yellows, and oranges as the season turned.

My dream was suddenly awhirl with the superstitions that usually precede a hunt. Usually they are undertaken half in jest, the comment often being made that, truly, the skill of the man has more to do with his success, don't we all know? But now in my dream, they seemed so vital that my heart raced to a panic that they were not being considered.

"Let's hope we all have good luck," the men called as they fanned out to each take a separate neck of the woods.

"No, don't say good luck!" my dream-weighted tongue shouted. "Never say good luck to a hunter. You must say 'Break your neck and your leg as well,' to keep the game from being frightened by your words."

I wanted to advise them, "Count the arrows in your quivers, men! There must be an uneven number, or you will fail. And you must have a woman jump over your bows, or they will not shoot straight. Here I am. Oh, Siegfried, my husband! Brothers! I'm here. I'm here, here, my skirts lifted up, ready to jump, no matter how high you hold them for me!"

But my cries fell on the deaf ears of the night, and my attempts to jump were just so much thrashing between the sheets.

Now my vision followed my husband Siegfried, and saw how the game fairly leaped out of the thickets and onto his spears. Boar and buck, hare and partridge, he took more than his fair share of them all, and left the terrain empty for the others in the party. How proud I was to be the wife of such a man! Siegfried was about to return, having now as much as he and his men could carry among them, when suddenly there was a muffled roaring in a fern-covered bank ahead, and out rumbled a large boar bear, charging at full speed. Was it just the blur of a dream, or did I hear the sound of my brothers' laughter in the woods behind the bear?

With marvelous quickness, even for the quickness of dreams, Siegfried leapt directly into the path of the charge and threw the beast with his bare hands. Then, with dream-quickness, he tied the creature up as ever my brother Gunther was trussed when Brynhild hung him on the wall. Siegfried tied the bear to his saddle alive, and began to walk Grani back to the place appointed to rendezvous after the hunt.

There, in a wooded meadow, the cooks had set up shop to receive the game. What were so many cooks doing along on an expedition of war? I wondered, but then chalked it up to the irrationality of the dream. As yet their knives and plucking fingers were unemployed, but they had a wealth of pots and kettles to hand, as much as ever dream provided of culinary confusion, and as never a party of war would require.

Into this hurly-burly, Siegfried, from behind a copse, loosed the bear, now mad with fury, and had a good laugh with his men—and me, watching on as the dreamer of this escapade—while cooks and kettles went flying in all directions, and one pot, a three-legged copper thing, got fast on the bear's head.

And then Siegfried arrived on the scene to save the day, dealing with the bear a second time in an hour. He dispatched the creature with a kitchen knife, as if it'd been no more than a docile milk cow, and so added the bruin to his overwhelming bag for the day.

"Bears mean much to Brynhild," I heard my husband say. "I claim the skin for her."

The cooks set their outdoor kitchen to rights and soon had haunches and steaks a-roasting to please any gathering of lords. I saw Gunther go among them, praising the work but carrying with him a large pouch of salt, which he sprinkled far too liberally on every piece destined for Siegfried.

"By my life," said my husband when, by the folding of time in on itself that the dream gave, he had sated his hunger for a while, "I have such a thirst! Gunther, my brother, have we no drink to wash down such rich food?"

"Alas, good brother," replied Gunther. "Wine was forgotten when we set out in haste expecting battle this morning. When our plans suddenly changed, I sent some men back for a keg or two to lighten our afternoon, but either the fools dawdle, or they have lost their way."

"Or they have drunk it all themselves," suggested Siegfried.

"There is a pleasant clear brook not far from here," spoke up Hogni then. "I passed it on my own rather fruitless hunt."

"Water it shall be then," said Siegfried in good spirits. "Who will race me then to this brook?"

"I will," said Hogni. "I admit to a thirst myself. But you must allow me a handicap. Everyone here knows, Siegfried, that in an even contest, you are unbeatable."

"Very well. I shall save my winning to the trial tomorrow. Today I shall run carrying my shield and spear—and wearing my helmet."

"That sounds fair enough," said Guttorm.

And so, at a count from Gunther, the race was on.

Even burdened by his gear, Siegfried easily outdistanced Hogni's short legs. When my husband reached the bank, he stood panting there beneath the canopy of changing leaves, which still seemed nowhere near death. Their autumn colors were so much more vibrant than green had been.

Siegfried's golden head seemed to lead the colors like a general. "Onward," shouted his hair.

And the trees shouted "Glory!" in the colors of a bronze and golden army.

"Glory!" echoed back the little stream.

So Siegfried waited for my brother to catch up with him and then gallantly bade Hogni to drink first. Hogni did so, flopping belly down over the edge of the stream. Then he got up and offered to hold Siegfried's shield and armor while my husband took his turn.

My husband laid his great length down in the impression left by Hogni in the grass and pressed out another foot's length beyond it. *So lay yourself down in my bed*, I sang to my husband through the haze of the dream. *So kiss love from me as you kiss water from the taut surface of the stream.*

But then I was shamed by the intimacy, because I saw that Hogni was shadowing at the edge of my dream. I knew he was there, but whenever I tried to set him in focus, he was somewhere else, just at the edge. So I looked back toward my husband. Suddenly, instead of love, horror filled my gaze. For I saw how the linden leaf I'd stitched so lovingly on his shirt stood out like a bull's-eye in the butts. And there, at the edge of my vision, I saw the point of Siegfried's own spear raised in Hogni's hand.

I tried to call out a warning, but I choked on it, the way one does in dreams. Then I saw a swirl of just a few images: Siegfried struck—Siegfried rising up and staring in disbelief at the face of treachery—Siegfried throwing helmet, stones, handfuls of fallen leaves, and whatever else was nearby with deadly accuracy at my brother—before Siegfried, the hero, fell headlong and moved no more.

I knew it was the wrong season for the linden to be blooming but still, in my dream, its spent pollen rained down upon Siegfried where he lay face down in the flower-dotted grass. The yellow powder quickly turned brown in the sun, and the life-humming bees turned to death-eating flies. Ravens circled overhead.

I saw Siegfried's body loaded on his own shield, his legs dangling off it from the knees and requiring six men to bear him. These images braided and swirled in and out of my nightmare, letting me first know that it was a dream and then, with that knowledge, extract myself from its horrors.

I lay panting in the dark, holding my heart as if it would break. And then I felt the baby kick, strong enough to wake me, as it could now do. And I knew that this son of Siegfried's was strong and well.

"Siegfried, come and put your hand here and feel the baby," I called out.

But there was no answer, so I knew I was still alone, for all that the dark did not feel unpeopled. It seemed my brothers had been there. Helping a drunken Siegfried to bed. But now there was nothing breathing in the room but me. I quickly murmured a prayer to Night, riding over us with her black horse dripping its sweat as dew, prayed to her against bad dreams and night haunts. Then I turned over, found a way that was comfortable to lie with my awkward belly and leg supported on a firm roll of cushion, and went to sleep.

This was my dream. It was a true dream. And in the morning light, I found it was not a cushion I rested on. It was Siegfried's body, dead from a wound through the linden leaf I myself had stitched and of which only a few, too few, shared the secret. My unborn son and I sat up, covered in Siegfried's gore.

"It was Helgi," one brother told me.

"We were set upon by thieves," said another.

"Not Helgi at all, but the Huns," said the third.

One brother after the other came to view my grief and revise one another's stories. In each pair of eyes in turn I saw my gory presence reflected. "Siegfried would never have turned his back on enemies such as these," I said.

My brothers muttered this and that and told my maids to take charge of me and to clean me, which I allowed them to do with no more resistance than if I were a rag doll.

I was conscious of nothing until, at one point, the most fearsome scream echoed off the walls of the castle, as if all the spirits of the long-dead Romans had come back to haunt, and those of the Celts before them.

"Brynhild, Brynhild," whispered my maids one to another, lifting their heads from me like a herd of does suddenly startled and alert in the woods.

The moment of consciousness brought to me by that scream—another woman screaming for my husband where I could not even weep—suddenly brought the images of my surroundings to me with the force of a blow. I saw the mound of bloodied bedclothes as if we were drowning in it. I saw one maid taking away a basin of water turned to blood from sponging me off to dump from the window, and another maid bringing fresh water to start all over again. From this blow my head reeled, and I was mercifully sent into unconsciousness again.

PART VII

Death Pyre

chapter 42

HEY BUILT HIS PYRE ON the white flags of the agora before the old Roman temple. They used linden wood.

"Put extra wood on it," I told Gunther. "I intend to join him on it."

Well, my husband tried to dissuade me, but he was as ineffectual in this as in so many things. "What will people think, Brynhild?" he said.

"If they think any other thoughts than that you are a pathetic, fratricidal excuse for a king, as you are for a husband," I told him, "they're a pack of fools and don't deserve any better. In death, Siegfried shall win the trial as he would have in life."

"What will the people think?" was all the further he could imagine to say.

The Burgundians sought to cover up their crime by providing richly for the cremation. They strewed the pyre heavily with rosemary, as well as anyone who came in contact with the corpse. The clean, grassy scent on my hands reminded me that they'd done the same to my wedding crown when I'd been married. Marriage and funeral seemed part of one whole, and very much the same.

The little hut set on top of the pyre was richly hung with the best local furs and foreign fabrics they had gathered from their crossroads market. In their midst, on brocade cushions, Siegfried was laid as if but asleep, the great well in his back unseen. The best mead and wine were left in jugs for him, the choicest cuts of the sacrifice. The knapsack containing the smoked dragon's heart went where his hand, if it were to move again, could easily grasp it.

About him were arranged his favorite weapons, and in his hands I replaced Gram, which I had won from him so long ago. What use was it to me? I couldn't swing it anymore; I could hardly lift it. As I did so, I saw on the little finger of his right hand the ring, the serpent ring holding its own tail with no beginning and no end, glaring at me with ruby eyes. At this sight, I let out yet another long wail, which was the only way I could keep my heart from breaking before the fire could reach it. Then I had no hesitation to move quickly, to fold that hand over Odin's curse of runes on the blade of Gram, for I was not going to see another sunrise to need such a thing as a sword.

Then Gunther brought forward Siegfried's favorite dog, a cross between a Roman mastiff and a grey Celtic wolfhound, and slew it, setting the body up afterwards quite lifelike as if guarding his master's feet.

Then it was Grani's turn. But the horse was, if anything, more skittish than ever, since he smelled his master's blood. They hadn't been able to load the body on the beast's back to bring my lover home, and now, as they tried to lead Grani out, he thrashed out as if to take vengeance himself on those from whom it was due.

"I'll do it," I told them to keep Hogni from fitting an arrow to his bow and dispatching the horse in that unholy way.

"There, boy—there, boy," I murmured.

Grani's eye was still wild and offended, but his nickered softly in reply. I approached carefully, talking to him all the while, and then he allowed me, almost with gratitude, to put my arm about his great grey neck and slowly, slowly lead him through the crowd to the agora.

All the while I spoke to him: "Grani, boy, I am leading you back to Odin, back whence you came. Yes, you are going with Siegfried, your master—and mine. You will be with Siegfried there. He's going back too. Back to Odin whose creation he was, just like you. Goodbye. Do you remember how we first found you? Siegfried and I together. How you swam to him across the stream and knew your master at once.

Almost as I knew him when I first saw him, Grani. Almost as I knew him. Knew there was none like him, nor ever would be, not in my lifetime. Well, he's gone now, Grani. You know that, don't you? You know it, I know it. So no other terror can come to us greater than that. Compared to this loss, even death—death itself—is less than the sting of a fly."

So I brought him to the pyre. Someone handed me a knife, and I made short work of it, Grani sinking out of my hands almost gratefully. They added the horseflesh to the mound.

And then it was my turn.

"Do you want me to …?" I looked and saw that it was Hogni speaking, dark Hogni who had relieved my hand of the knife and was offering to do the same for me as I had done for the horse.

"No," I said. "I'll wait for the flame."

So they brought the torches sputtering stars into the rising evening wind and stuck them into the foot of the pyre.

I was glad. Glad to see the red plague overcome the linden, and the linden bloom to new life like a tree in the last blaze before winter. Like a field with poppies the year after a battle, fertilized by the red blood of the slain. I was glad I was wearing my red silk with the richest brooches, glad I would come to my bridegroom that way, as I had always meant to—glad of the maiden way I was still wearing my hair, long and unbound, so it covered my body clear to my knees with gold. Crowning it, I wore my raven-feathered helm, and I was glad the leather of my brynie had endured for one more lacing up.

I was glad of the new little life I was carrying under my heart, his child whose presence, a token of our love, I could hardly wait to announce to Siegfried when we met.

And I was glad the wind was blowing up a storm, glad the fire would be fiercely hot when first it touched me, so it would not have to touch me long. And then the storm would come and spatter the pyre with coolness and mingle our ashes into a fertile mud.

The flames were already too hot to bear from where I stood. I should step back, but I knew I must step forward, into the heart as Siegfried had had to do to reach me in Iceland. Into the heart, I remembered from the lesson of the wife of the fallen King of Saxony so many, many years ago. What was it Thora had said to me then? "To have a love worth dying for," I think it was. I could almost hear those words of hers now in her own voice.

Against the gathering storm, I saw grey smoke rising. Grey, the spirit of Grani already carrying his master to glory. I had heard the talk around me when folk thought I was too full of grief to listen. I heard them say that there was no use for a pyre; Odin had not sanctioned it; it was the Burgundians' way of covering up their evil deeds; there was no glory for a man pierced from behind. But I thought differently. Even if Odin were not accepting of the sacrifice, somewhere, some other divinity was. Perhaps it was only the divinity of Siegfried's own soul, but it was there. This I had thought, and now I knew it was so as I saw Grani's powerful gray limbs leap off the earth, free of the mortal coil, bearing his master on his back. I knew it must be Siegfried there, though the face was obscured by smoke, for Grani would never carry another. Even me he would only take if Siegfried allowed it. So I must leap up at once and be swept into his arms, or be forever left behind.

I stepped forward and then I saw that, burned already to the bone in the heart of the flames, Siegfried's hands were empty. Somehow, someone had stolen Gram while I was occupied with Grani, perhaps. The same hands that had despoiled Siegfried of life now offered this final indignity. I looked away from the flames in anger, determined on revenge.

It was then that, off to the left, even as I had seen it at the pyre of the Saxon, I saw the broad-rimmed hat with a single eye peering out at me from under it, the sturdy staff and the swirl of storm-grey cloak. It was Odin.

Or it was not. It was only his statue there in the court of the temple brought to life by the palpable waves of heat rising off the pyre between us.

I took another step. The wind whipped my skirt before me, and then I felt its silk begin to melt off my legs. But it *was*. It was Odin, in the flesh. The pair of soaring ravens, caught off balance in the power of the wind and tossed here and there like chaff at the threshing, should

have confirmed it. He was laughing at me. *So, yes, old One-Eyed, you have won after all!* I wanted to shout at him over the roar of the flames, but at that same moment, the statue of Frigga came to life over to the right. Frigga, Odin's wife—Aesir only by adoption, by abduction some would say, but Vanir in her soul, with whom he had constant enmity. Frigga, over whom Odin would never dominate, try as he might, for she was a Goddess in her own right.

And now it seemed that Frigga took on the alabaster features of my old companion-in-arms Thora, kindly smiling on me. Thora, as she had come so long ago when I stumbled alone from the winter woods after two weeks' trial.

"Come this way," I heard her call, holding out her arms. "It is enough to have known such a love, and then to live on with the divine power to make new life of his death knocking under your ribs. This way, Brynhild. My child."

I took another step, this one veering to the right, turning my back on Odin, the fire now to my side. But at that moment, my dress and loose hair exploded into flames about me.

Thora's strong arms caught me. Perhaps her arms were not quite strong enough to pick a man in full armor off the battlefield at full gallop anymore, but they were quite strong enough to sweep me from the pyre and roll the fire out against the cool flags of the agora.

Then she called her maids, and they bore me off to a high cool room where there were healing herbs for my burns.

To the rest of the Burgundians, I suppose it did seem that the fire consumed me and that I joined my love in death, that at last they were rid of me and the embarrassment I caused.

But they were not.

And neither was Odin. With an angry sweep of his cloak, the God called his birds to him and vanished from the agora into the night that was now so crowded with pain.

"We shall live to fight him another day," Thora said, among many other crooning things. And I knew she was right. Even through the pain, I realized that as long as the One-Eyed blinked at me, kept his ravens circling over me, it was the greater victory to keep on living. To live and fight 'til not only the curse of my life but the curser himself was destroyed.

Watch for Book III, coming soon!

Suggested Further Reading

This is a historical novel based on the saga that comes in several medieval versions: the Old Norse *Poetic Edda*, *The Völsunga Saga*, and *The Nibelungenlied.* All are available in affordable Penguin translations.

The verses preceding the beginning of this book are from *The Nibelungenlied*, those in Chapter 9 are from *The Völsunga Saga*, and those in Chapter 20 are from *Burnt Njal.* All are in the public domain. Those in Chapter 24 are from *Shamanism: Archaic Techniques of Ecstasy* by Mircea Eliade, Princeton University Press, 2004. Permission has been written for. All other verses are written by me.

The answer to the question, "Isn't there an opera where the fat lady sings?" is … yes, there are four very long ones by Richard Wagner. The interested reader might watch the operas: *Das Rheingold*, *Die Walküre*, *Siegfried*, and *Götterdämmerung.*

The thirteenth-century *Danish History* by Saxo Grammaticus served as a source for many details.

On bogs and the bodies found in them:

- *Through Nature to Eternity: The bog bodies of northwest Europe* by Wijnand van der Sanden
- *The Bog Man and the Archaeology of People* by Don Brothwell

On other aspects of Norse life and religion:

- *The Religion of the Northmen* by Rudolph Keyser

- *Myth and Religion of the North: The Religion of Ancient Scandinavia* by E. O. G. Turville-Petre
- *Norse Mythology: A Guide to the Gods, Heroes, Rituals, and Beliefs* by John Lindow
- *The Lost Beliefs of Northern Europe* by Hilda Ellis Davidson
- *The Well of Remembrance: Rediscovering the Earth Wisdom Myths of Northern Europe* by Ralph Metzner
- *A History of Old Norse Poetry and Poetics* by Margaret Clunies Ross
- *The Skalds, a Selection of Their Poems* by Lee Milton Hollander

And for the Huns:

- *The Huns* by E. A. Thompson

about the author

Ann Chamberlin believes that the purpose of storytelling—as of all true art as well as all true religion—is to support positions in exact opposition to the views prevailing in a culture's powerhouses, whatever those views happen to be. Nowhere is this more crucial than in the retelling of history. As Milan Kundera tells us, people in the powerhouses are not so interested in who will control the future as in who controls the airbrushes in the labs where the past's photos are retouched.

Born and raised in Salt Lake City, Ann Chamberlin also spent big blocks of time as a child in Europe, where her father was visiting professor of mathematics. After flitting from school to school and major to major—including theater, history, and English—she finally majored in Archaeology of the Middle East at the University of Utah. She spent a summer in Israel excavating the biblical city of Be'er Sheva, traveling throughout the Holy Land and living in the old city of Jerusalem for a month. She reads Hebrew, Arabic, Egyptian hieroglyphs, and ancient Akkadian, as well as French and German. She has traveled across all of North Africa, Turkey, Syria, and Jordan. She has two sons and twelve chickens and lives in an old farmhouse on nearly two acres near Salt Lake City.

Ann is the author of twenty books, mostly historical novels. Three of them were on the Turkish bestselling list. She is the author of many plays, which have been produced across the country from Seattle to New York and in Bogota, Colombia. To find out more about Ann and her books, please visit her web site at

http://www.annchamberlin.com

www.ingramcontent.com/pod-product-compliance
Lightning Source LLC
Chambersburg PA
CBHW020935310726
48980CB00007B/783/J
* 9 7 8 1 9 5 1 9 3 7 8 9 8 *